WAVE OF DREAMS

A SECONDARY WORLD FANTASY

UNEXPECTED HEROES
BOOK 3

MARTY C. LEE

Bookaholics Press

As M. Cate Lee

Book design and publication by Bookaholics Press LLC, Provo Utah
Edited by Carole Malone
Front cover design by Brenda Camp Walter
Back cover and chapter heading illustrations by Naomi Rasmussen
Map by Michelle Allan and Naomi Rasmussen
Author photograph by Melissa C. Baxter

ISBN-13: 978-1-950230-08-2 (epub)
ISBN-13: 978-1-950230-09-9 (mobi)
ISBN-13: 978-1-950230-10-5 (paperback)
ISBN-13: 978-1-950230-11-2 (large print)
ISBN-13: 978-1-950230-28-0 (hardback)
ISBN-13: 978-1-950230-62-4 (audio)

Published by Bookaholics Press LLC
Provo, Utah bookaholicspress@gmail.com

Contact the author at MCLeeBooks.com

For Tad, my best friend,
and Ruth, who saw this one coming.

CONTENTS

Map of Kaiatan

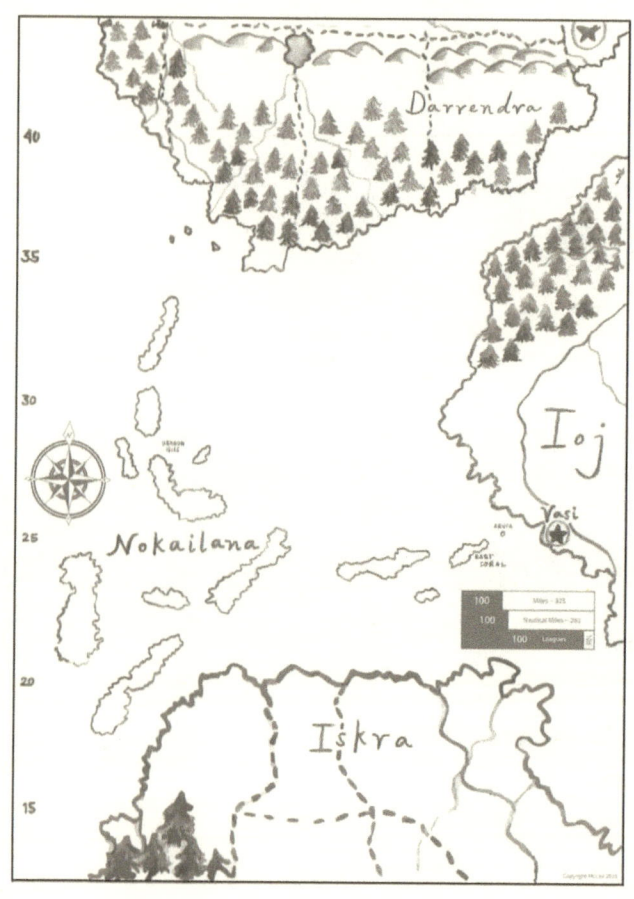

1. PARTY

(EAST CORAL ISLAND, NOKAILANA)

Makanavailea's favorite number is six, so a Nokai child becomes an adult on their six-thousandth day. The occasion is marked by a large party.

Everything You Ever Wanted to Know about the Nokailana Islands but Were Too Lazy to Ask

The only thing she wanted was a nice party and a chance to see her friends. Was that too much to ask?

Niamolenulanami bounced on her webbed toes and looked east. Her bleary eyes picked out white wings on the horizon where the lavender ocean met the apricot sky. Either a bird close by or a much larger flyer at a greater distance.

"East is Ahjin's island. He's coming, he's coming!" Nia cheered. She couldn't possibly have her party without her best friend.

"I'm not sure Alupa is actually Ahjin's," Kalalamoanani said. "Doesn't it belong to the gods?"

"Pffft." Nia waved her hand. She didn't bother to correct her near-sister's mispronunciation, but the gods had created Arupa for Ahjin, to provide neutral territory while he served them. That made it his even more than his original country of Ioj, eastern land of the winged people.

"Is everything ready for your party?" Kala asked.

Nia sighed. "Almost. For the six-thousandth time, I'll finish before Ludik and Zefra get here."

The spring weather was clear and safe, so they would have left Iskra only three days ago to make it on time. They had the farthest distance to travel, so it wasn't surprising they were last to arrive. At least Ludik's apprenticeship meant he didn't have to come from the far north this time.

"The lights?" Kala asked. "The hammocks? The food? The music? What about the suits?"

"Mom is collecting the suits right now. Why don't you help her?" Nia looked east and bounced again while Kala flounced away. She had been anticipating this party for months, and now she could hardly wait. Besides finally seeing her friends again, her mom had been hinting that her gift for Nia would be a big surprise.

After a few minutes, Nia sat cross-legged on the worn dock, leaned her elbow on her knee, and propped her chin on her fist to speculate again on Mom's present. It might be a pretty new dress, but since Mom was a seamstress, that wasn't much of a surprise. Could it be something for her house? A trip to visit friends? A new bottle of perfume?

The waves sparkled in the morning light. Bird song drifted on the cool breeze, and colorful fish swam in the clear, lavender water. Back and forth in the sparkle. Nia's eyelids drooped. Back and forth...

She fell backward and hit a pair of legs.

White feathers tickled her nose, and an amused voice said, "You're lucky I got here in time to save you."

Nia looked up and blinked in the sunlight, batting his wings out of her face. "Well met, Ahjin. It's about time. You neglected me all winter."

"You know the gods have been keeping me busy." Ahjin dragged her to her feet and into a warm hug. "Leaving long enough for Ludik's wedding made them anxious to cram everything into my head at once. And I left Arupa at dawn. Halfway on the ship, halfway by wing."

"Busy is boring." Nia yawned in his ear. "I've been awake since dawn, too." She pressed the traditional Nokai kisses to her best friend's cheeks.

Ahjin grinned. "You're taking this very seriously. I didn't know you ever woke that early." His wings twitched with a hidden laugh.

She sniffed and stepped back. Ahjin wasn't nearly as funny as he thought he was. He did look nice, though, with black trousers tucked into black ankle boots, and white wings folded against his blue-embroidered jacket over a pale green shirt. A silver star hung on a chain around his neck. He would look older than his seventeen years, except his white hair had been wind-combed into its usual mess of wild curls during the flight from his ship.

"I want the best party ever," Nia said. "You're just in time to help me finish everything before Ludik and Zefra arrive."

Ahjin spread his four-fathom wings and crouched. "What do you need?"

"We've made adjustments for you landlubbers. I'll drag the atolla as close to the surface as possible, if you'll set up hammocks in the trees." She pointed to the best grove left on the beach after the disasters of last fall.

"Right away." Ahjin winked and sprang into the air, turning somersaults on his way to the trees. He waved at the Nokai who pointed and cheered. He was so beautiful in the air, it was a shame his new job with the gods had ruined his plans to be an aerobat.

Nia dove off the dock. The warm water flowed over her gills as she swam down to the nets all sixteen of her siblings had helped fill yesterday. As she tugged one end of the long net upward, the atolla jellyfish blinked their alarm sequence. She fastened the net around a large boulder at the far end of the beach, then tied the other end to the dock until the row of flashing lights stretched under the water along the edge of the small island.

Perfect. Zefra and Ludik would be very impressed when they arrived. Ahjin had seen the lights before, though never so close to the surface.

Ahjin swooped down and landed beside her, already without boots or jacket. "Hammocks are up. What's next?"

"We're putting the food on the island instead of underwater, but the fishermen need help gutting their catch."

Ahjin wrinkled his nose. "I'll gut fish if you don't make me eat them raw."

"Would I torture you like that?"

"Yes." Ahjin folded his arms.

"Look!" Nia pointed south toward a white-sailed ship flying a lavender-and-bronze Rikatsu flag. "I thought they would never arrive."

"It might have taken Ludik longer than he expected to join Zefra from his apprenticeship," Ahjin suggested. "Or perhaps the wind was against them."

Nia sniffed. "If they don't hurry, we'll run out of time."

Ahjin laughed. "Since when have the Nokai not had time to party?"

"Never. If you let me know when the others arrive, I'll spare you from the fish. I need to talk to the musicians and get the suits from Mom."

Ahjin narrowed his eyes. "Suits? We can't stay on land?"

Nia widened her eyes at him. "And miss out on the water? Don't worry, Mom made a suit to accommodate your wings."

Ahjin winced. "What color?"

Nia pressed her lips together to contain her giggle. "It's a surprise."

She'd picked something he'd like, but it was fun to watch him squirm. Unlike his boring tastes, her own suit today complemented her lavender hair with a cascade of purple flowers and violet ferns and was perfect for a celebration.

Ahjin narrowed his eyes. "I don't like surprises."

"Nonsense. You just don't like being on the receiving end." Nia ran across the soft sand before he could respond. When she dared a glance over her shoulder, Ahjin was flying through his familiar aerobatic sequence.

And speaking of surprises, what *did* Mom have for her?

Nia finished her errands just in time to run back when Ahjin circled above the dock. She skidded to a halt and dropped her basket as Ahjin landed and a tall Darrendrakar jumped over the rail of the Iskrin ship to the dock without waiting for a boarding plank.

"Well met, Ludik. Did Nemerra come with you?" She tugged on his sleeve until he bent for her to kiss his cheek. Due to Darrendra's odd customs, the eighteen-year-old jaguar shifter was already married.

Ludik grinned. "My wife couldn't come. I'll tell you about it later." His brown skin was darker than the most tanned Nokai, but his gold hair could fit in if he let it grow longer than a half thumb-length. His knee-length tunic was as wildly colorful as anything the Nokai wore, although in geometric patterns instead of ones from nature, and the small gold hoop in his left ear gleamed in the sunlight.

The plank lowered from the ship to the dock, and the last of her guests joined them with frequent glances at the flashing lights under-water along the shore.

"Well met, Zefra." Nia bowed casually and got a formal Iskrin bow in return.

"Bright day, Nia." Zefra's stark white skin was covered from neck to ankle in a tan robe, with an equally drab scarf concealing her hair. Only the fifteen-year-old girl's yellow-and-turquoise embroidered belt had any color.

Most of the southern desert-dwellers had depressing views on wearing colors. Nia intended to make Zefra more fun.

"Good news. I borrowed ocean suits so everybody can swim." She ignored Zefra's wide-eyed stare at Nia's own knee-length, curve-hugging suit.

"Kamea is about the same size as you, and she had a full-length one in your clan's colors." Nia handed a pile of thick, spongy cloth to Zefra, who stared dubiously at the turquoise flowers on a yellow background.

"Nobody's as tall as you, Ludik, but it's warm enough to wear short trousers." The stack she gave Ludik was printed with vivid green and purple birds.

"Bright day, Nia. What about me?"

Nia turned and saw Zefra's older brother walking down the plank. He was a few inches taller than his sister, with the same tilted, deep brown eyes and white skin, but a wide smile and blacksmith's muscles. Last summer, he had flirted with her. Now that she was an adult, possibilities for courting were endless.

"Izo! I didn't know you were coming, but we can find a suit for you, too."

"I wanted my visit to be a surprise," Izo said. "I hope 'tis a welcome one."

Nia bowed again. "Very welcome." She straightened and threw him a flirtatious smile.

Izo grinned at her. "I would not mind an introduction to Nokai customs."

Ahjin snorted. Nia kicked his ankle and kissed Izo on both cheeks. Izo returned the gesture.

Nia glanced at the Iskrins' knee-high boots. "The sand is warm today. Why not go barefoot?"

Zefra looked at her feet. "You want me to remove my shoes?"

"Do not be a cold ember, Zefra." Izo leaned over and untied his boots. "When in the islands, do as the islanders do." He pulled off his boots, yanked his sister's laces, and ran from the dock.

When Zebra tried to chase him, she tripped on her laces and landed in the sand. After a few deep breaths, she removed her boots and stood with dignity. "Where should I leave these, Nia?"

Nia grinned. "Right here." She led everyone to the hammocks, and the visitors took turns changing into their ocean suits behind blankets hung for privacy. Nia's extensive family left the ocean and waited with her, still dripping.

Ahjin went first. His suit fit well, fastening under his wings like a backward vest, but navy was so boring. Since his bare arms and legs showed the lightning scars he hated, the color was a worthwhile sacrifice to reduce attention.

Ludik's trousers reached his knees, but the shirt ended a hand above his waist. The blackened tip of a walrus tusk dangled on a leather cord around his neck. It hadn't shown under his tunic, and Nia wondered at his choice of jewelry. Nemerra had nearly died during their last misadventure in Darrendra. Why would he wear a reminder of it?

Zefra crept out, shoulders hunched in her skintight suit. Her black eyebrows furrowed below the braided crown of bright red hair that warned of her gift from the desert god.

Izo changed in half the time as his sister and emerged in lavender trousers printed with orange shrimp. He dangled his shirt in one hand and ran his other through his wavy black hair. "Sorry, Nia, but my shoulders do not fit. Do you have a bigger shirt?"

Nia examined his bare shoulders with appreciation. Swinging a blacksmith's hammer did wonders for his muscles. All his muscles...

"What shirt?" she asked dreamily.

Kala and the other island girls giggled. Izo and Zefra both blushed.

Nia made herself stop admiring Izo. "No one will mind if you go without. My family wants to meet all of you. This is my mom, Aolanikalia, and—"

Ahjin tapped her shoulder. "It took me a month to remember everyone's full names, and you know Zefra will die trying. Can we skip to the short names? And no offense to your wonderful family, but perhaps we might save some introductions for later?"

Nia wrinkled her nose. "If you insist."

Most of her family laughed and walked away. Kala dug in her heels and stayed, gaping at Izo.

"This is my mom, Aolani," Nia said, "and my younger sister, Olina, and my little brother, Kaliya. Kala is my near-sister. Later, I'll introduce you to my fathers and other parents and far-siblings."

"More than one father? Other parents?" Izo wrinkled his forehead.

"They're the dads of her brother and sister," Ahjin said. "The family gets really complicated after that. I'll explain later, if you want."

Izo's eyes got big. "Three husbands?" he mouthed at Zefra.

She held up her hand, fingers forming a circle.

Izo gulped and turned back to Nia. "Where is your father?"

Nia hid a frown. "My dad, Alaneokawakani, died before I was born."

Her mom made an odd noise but waved off Nia's concerned look.

"At least you had two... step-fathers," Izo said.

"I am glad of that." Nia smiled despite the old unhappiness nagging her. Her fathers did love her, but with seventeen kids in the family, time was a limited resource. They paid more attention to their own children, understandably, but that left her alone. She would have liked to have her own dad in her childhood home.

Mom hugged her, probably not fooled by her smile. "Should we prepare the food?"

Nia frowned. "*After* I finish the introductions. Family, Zefra and Izo are siblings. If you see a big black kitty wandering around, that's Ludik." She sidestepped his grab and laughed. "And you already know Ahjin. And now we can eat."

Kala twirled her persimmon hair around her finger and smiled at Izo. "The girls need strong muscles to carry the full baskets."

Izo cast a wide-eyed glance at Nia.

Nia blew him a kiss. "They won't hurt you."

Kala and Kamea took his hands, and Izo turned as scarlet as a snapper.

"If you help us with the bread, dear," Nia's mom said to Zefra, "Nia and Ahjin can pick fruit."

She leaned to kiss Zefra's cheek, and the Iskrin flinched, then bowed and followed Olina and Aolani, still hunching in her clinging suit.

"We go this way." Nia dragged Ahjin inland, toward the orchards.

Nia had invited the whole island, so everyone who wished Nia a joyful six-thousandth day was finishing their own chores or working on a party task. There was no shortage of cute boys, and most of them took advantage of her new adult status to exchange cheek kisses and ask when she could go for a swim.

Nia flirted with all of them. So many boys, so little time. Her cheeks hurt from grinning when they arrived at the orchard. She handed Ahjin two woven baskets and placed her own at the bottom of a tree. "You pick the high ones."

Ahjin crossed his arms, baskets dangling from one hand. "Why are you acting like that?"

"Like what?" Nia said. "And pick while you talk."

Ahjin flapped his wings and jumped to a branch. "Why are you kissing all those boys?"

"Because they offered!"

"Do you kiss everyone who asks?" He threw the fruit into the basket.

"I won't kiss a pirate, if that's what you mean." Nia picked several fruits. "But there's nothing wrong with our island boys, and I like Izo."

Ahjin climbed to a higher branch. "Why don't you settle on *one* of them?"

Nia stared up at him. "Are you jealous? There are plenty of girls who'd like to kiss you. If you want attention, just smile. You'd have girls lining up for fathoms. I can find you one tonight."

Ahjin dropped an orange on her head. "I can find my own girl, thanks. We're talking about how you're having a hard time finding someone."

Nia rubbed her head. "Stop that. It isn't hard to find a nice boy. Look how many are available." She waved at a young fisherman in the distance. "Come help me cut these."

"What boy do you want?" Ahjin flew down and put his basket next to hers.

"What difference does it make? Almost any of them will do. Love is like fruit." Nia cut and pitted two mangoes and put half of each together. "See, they fit."

"Perhaps you're not a mango." Ahjin peeled two oranges and pried them in half. He put different halves together and showed Nia the gaps where they didn't fit. "Perhaps you're an orange."

"Are you saying I'm lumpy?" Nia threw a mango pit at him.

Ahjin ducked. "I'm saying you're unique." He tugged her hair and handed her an orange-half. "I like your uniqueness. You deserve someone right for you, not just any boy who's available."

Nia laughed. "In that case, I'd better try all the oranges to see which one is best!"

Ahjin threw his hands in the air. Since he peeled oranges silently while she chopped mangoes, she considered the argument won.

As they carried the baskets to the party area, everyone else streamed in. The mats were soon full of platters and baskets of delicious-smelling food while her guests sniffed appreciatively.

"Thank you for coming," Nia shouted above the crowd's chattering. "Welcome to my six-thousandth-day party. Let's eat!"

Everyone attacked the food like a shiver of sharks. Nia filled a plate and greeted everyone, accepting congratulations and yummy kisses.

Izo eventually disentangled himself from Kala and the girls who eyed his impressive muscles. Nia hooked her arm through his elbow. He was such a kind, handsome, and *interested* boy.

Yes, indeed, chasing boys would be as easy as picking oranges, and a lot more fun.

2. SURPRISES
(EAST CORAL ISLAND)

Enjoy yourself. It's later than you think.
Nokai Proverb

Nia's party was going well. When her happy guests' stomachs bulged with food, the other islanders waved and wandered home. At last, only her family and visitors remained.

"Why don't you take your friends on a quick tour?" Mom asked.

"That's a great idea." Nia beckoned the others. "Most of the islands are covered with gardens, so the food is on the beach, musicians are on the fishing boats, and you've seen your hammocks. The fishing grounds are mostly northwest." She click-whistled for Ya'eel. "The dock is for visitors, and the fishermen and women usually beach their boats on the sand. Can everyone swim? If not, Ya'eel can help you." She looked at the two Iskrins.

Ya'eel breached behind her, squealing a welcome.

Zefra's eyes widened as the dolphin splashed back into the water.

"Our migration route includes a yearly stay by the ocean," Izo said.

Zefra nodded, lip caught between her teeth.

"I thought we could see the roads," Nia said.

Since her friends couldn't breathe underwater, they couldn't enter her house or the festival area, but the roads were beautiful. Since the Nokai didn't need them for travel, they used them only for navigation and enjoyment.

"Oh, that's a great idea," Ahjin said.

"Don't trip on the atolla net." Nia swam over the flashing lights and ducked underwater, pointing to different sights.

The coral reef was a lively backdrop to the houses under the surface. The sun shimmered in ripples on the bottom of the lagoon. Schools of colorful fish chased each other. The scraping of beakfish feeding on coral algae was loud enough to cover the chatter of Nia's friends. The explosive cracks of thunder-shrimp were even louder.

Once she could see all the roads together, she looked for her friends' reactions. Zefra's mouth hung open, and Izo whistled. Ya'eel swam circles around the two, making sure their clumsy paddling kept their heads above water.

From here, the roads formed a colorful picture of fish jumping through waves and coral. There on the fin of Blue Damselfish Road was her own tiny house with its domed roof and a glowing jar of plankton-light in its sun-feeding station. She pointed to her house, then to herself. She had lived alone for a couple of years, since her singing started making enough money to support her. Though she hadn't been quite an adult when she moved out, she was close enough to all her large family to be safe. But it was easier to live alone than to see her siblings' dads come to visit their children and remember that she didn't have one.

The usual festival area was at the end of the path, near the deeper ocean. After other interesting sights, including one of the many dolphin pods, they returned to the surface.

"And that's the village," Nia said. "Time for music and dancing."

"Oh, no," Ahjin groaned, looking eastward.

Nia followed his gaze. Another boat was sailing into the harbor. The large flag on the mast displayed the emblems of all five gods above a small banner with Ahjin's seven wind curls.

Nia shoved at her dripping braids. "What's wrong?"

"It's Lyell." Ahjin pointed to a black-and-gray-streaked head next to a small black puppy held on the railing.

"I didn't know they were here," Nia squealed. She hadn't seen the Wolf since their disastrous trip to Darrendra last fall. The border guard had escorted them to search for a murderer, and it had cost him dearly.

"He came out a couple of weeks ago," Ahjin said, "when the winter storms calmed enough. But they aren't supposed to be *here*. Since he's my new Chief of Staff, he's supposed to keep Arupa under control while I'm here."

"Don't be a sand crab." Nia said as he watched the ship. "They can come to my party."

"Oh, no!" Ahjin lunged for the shore. "She fell, and I can't swim fast enough."

Nia turned quickly.

The black puppy was gone, and Lyell dangled half over the railing, reaching toward the waves. "Nia," he bellowed, "help Tala!"

The rest of Lyell's family had died in the murderer's fire. If Tala died, he would drown in sorrow.

Nia swore and dove underwater with Ya'eel as Ahjin ran along the beach. Behind them, the others yelled for help, and more splashes echoed from other Nokai. The dolphin reached the ship first, and when Nia arrived a moment later, he was pushing their target toward the surface. The puppy slid off his head, and Nia grabbed her.

"Good job, Ya'eel. Hang on, Tala." She stroked for the surface, emerging as Ahjin arrived.

"Stay up there, Lyell," Ahjin shouted. "We got her."

Nia's family stopped swimming and tread water.

"Is she breathing?" Ahjin whispered.

Nia shook the puppy upside-down. A small stream of water leaked from Tala's mouth, and then the black pup took a breath.

"She's fine," Ahjin called up. "We'll meet you at the dock."

The ship moved on, and Nia's family headed back. Tala barked and tried to dive.

Nia pulled her back to the surface. "Wolves can't breathe water."

Tala barked her puppy-squeak and tried to dive again.

"Let me help. I can swim without arms." Ahjin swept his wings along the water, holding out both hands until Nia handed over the wolf pup.

Nia led them back to the dock, which bounced above them as the ship was tied up. Nia pulled herself up, then took Tala. Ahjin was still climbing out when Lyell rushed down the gangplank. The Wolf's tunic was as colorful as Ludik's, except for a bit of brown trim, and he was only a few years older despite his gray-streaked hair. His belt held two long knives but no sword.

"Tala," he shouted.

Nia held out the soaking wolf pup. "Here she is, Lyell."

Tala licked Nia's nose and barked before jumping at her father. His light brown eyes, naturally lined with black, were suspiciously bright.

Nia kissed the shapeshifter's cheeks. "You're welcome, but why are you here?"

"Visiting friends and keeping an eye on His Holiness."

Ahjin shook water from his curls. "I told you not to call me that here."

Lyell shrugged. "When is the Mouth of the Gods off-duty?"

"At my party." Nia said. "Don't make my friend unhappy."

The other Darrendrakar shuffled off the gangplank, eyes lowered. The young man was a little taller than Ahjin, sturdy, and brown. Medium brown skin, red-brown hair, and dark seal-brown eyes. His tunic was as colorful as the other Darrendrakar's, but in a pattern halfway to the No-kai style.

"Well met," Nia said. When he didn't respond, she glanced at Lyell.

"Kaito is part of the Pinniped tithe." The Wolf nudged the young man off the dock.

As a consequence for the murders last fall, Darravani had sentenced all the Pinnipeds to send a percentage of their people to help the other races. Some of them came to Arupa to help Ahjin, while others spread across the world for other projects.

Nia rubbed her hands with glee. The Nokai would get a net full of variety today. The novelty of Ahjin's wings had worn off in prior visits, and East Coral Island traded with the Iskrins, but Nia didn't remember a single Darrendrakar coming before. Thanks to Lyell's surprises, her family could meet three different kindreds of shapeshifters instead of just Ludik.

Everyone trekked to the beach for more introductions. Nia sent her uncle Enaki for a suit while Tala rolled in the sand until her fur stuck out. Zefra returned to her regular clothes, but everyone else let the spring sunshine dry their ocean suits.

When Enaki returned, Nia sent Lyell to change. The Wolf strolled out with a grin, turning to show the too-short fish-covered suit. "Do I look finny in this?"

Nia's family looked at each other in confusion, but Nia laughed, glad to see Lyell's sense of humor had survived Tala's accident.

"Music is this way, everyone." Nia cuddled Tala as she walked. "I hired the musicians with the most knowledge of foreign music. Several of them know some Iojif and Iskrin music. I'm afraid only one of them knows even a few Darrendran songs." Nia winked at Ludik. "You're so far away and don't welcome us to your parties." She squinted at Kaito. "After being separated for millennia, I suspect your music is very different from the rest of Darrendra. None of the musicians mentioned Pinniped anything."

Kaito shrugged.

"You can hear something new, then," Nia said.

They arrived at the new clearing, created by tidal waves wiping out an orchard. The musicians on the boats tuned their instruments, attracting laughing, toe-tapping Nokai from all directions.

Lyell snatched Tala from Nia's arms as a handsome islander with palm-green hair swung her into the dance. She watched through gaps in the crowd to make sure all her friends found partners.

Ludik danced with a young girl even shorter than Nia. His eyes crinkled at the corners as he watched the bouncing child.

Izo danced in a circle with two young women at once, then three and four. Red crept down his bare chest, but he kept dancing. Nia smiled and waved, happy he was enjoying himself.

Zefra moved stiffly as she tried to copy her partner's wild moves, as if she hurt. Nia chuckled. Only Zefra's dignity was injured. Practicing fun would be good for her.

Kaito shuffled his feet awkwardly but swung his pretty, violet-headed partner in competent twirls.

At first, Ahjin's scars got stares from those who hadn't seen him since he was wounded rescuing the gods. His first partner was a toddling child who shrieked in delight as Ahjin alternated between steps on the ground and swoops through the air. When a blushing young woman replaced the child, Ahjin tucked his wings and stayed on his feet.

Even Lyell and Tala were swept up by a plump matron with a baby on her hip. The two of them danced pleasantly in the middle of laughing children.

Now that her friends were having fun, Nia abandoned herself to dancing. Her green-haired partner was replaced by a taller boy with sky-orange hair and then a stout old grandfather with graying indigo curls and the best moves she'd ever seen.

Now *this* was a party!

After flirting her way through most of the Nokai crowd, Nia moved to her friends.

When Ludik danced with her, he laughed outright and swung her off her feet as if she were still a child. At the end of the music, he dropped her on the ground by Lyell and threw himself under a tree to rest.

Lyell gave her a hand up and twitched his head toward Kaito. Nia drew both of them into a circle dance with Tala and Zefra.

Then it was Izo's turn. The music slowed, and she pulled him closer, wrapping her arms around him. "Isn't this fun?"

"I have never attended such a lively party." Izo slid one arm around her waist. "Or met such a delightful girl."

"Woman," Nia corrected, fluttering her eyelashes. "I'm grown now."

"Grown, indeed," Izo murmured, leaning down.

Nia lifted her face toward him until she felt his warm breath on her cheek. Just a little closer...

The music ended, and the crowd applauded.

Izo straightened with a sigh.

Ahjin tapped Izo on the shoulder. "My turn."

Without waiting for a response, he grabbed Nia's hands. As the musicians started a new, bouncy tune, he swung her skillfully through the crowd.

"I had no idea you dance so well," Nia said.

"You haven't watched, then," Ahjin said, frowning. "I'm not quite as popular as Izo, though."

Nia squinted at him. "Are you unhappy about the girls or the dancing? Or are you jealous of Izo?"

"None of the above. Are you happy about the boys or the dancing or Izo?"

Nia giggled. "Oh, all of it."

Ahjin frowned. "Do you plan to work your way through every boy here?"

"Don't be silly," Nia said. "I don't need *all* of them."

Ahjin raised one eyebrow. "How many do you need?"

"I haven't decided yet."

Ahjin danced in silence. When he finally spoke, he sounded sad. "Does Izo know you're playing with him?"

Nia laughed. "He knows we're having fun."

"Does he know he's only a temporary suitor," Ahjin clarified, "with no chance at a serious relationship with you?"

"Serious relationship?" Nia coughed. "Why would he want that?"

Ahjin raised his eyebrow again. "He's Iskrin, not Nokai. Have you seen the way he looks at you?"

"Grimy sea turtles, of course." Nia smiled. "I like the way he looks at me."

Ahjin sighed. "You're not stupid, but you underestimate the difference in cultural expectations. Despite variations in courtship flexibility and length, most societies aim for monogamous marriage."

"Not the Nokai," Nia said. "Your cultures have divorce as an escape; we only have death. I have ten parents, and only two have married. Nobody else wants to take the chance of being stuck in a bad relationship. I might never marry. Certainly not now! I'm too young."

"So am I," Ahjin said. "But Izo is a little older, and I'm sure he's thought about it."

Nia frowned. "I wouldn't marry Izo, anyway. I want children — eventually — and the races can't interbreed."

"Perhaps Izo isn't worried about children," Ahjin said, "but I suspect he cares about fidelity."

Nia peeked through the crowd. The handsome Iskrin was talking to a pretty Nokai girl, but he watched Nia.

Her heart fluttered, and she smiled at him before she turned back to Ahjin. "That's not fair. *You've* been flirting with all the girls."

"I've been friendly," Ahjin said. "*They've* been flirting. And I've been careful not to give the impression I'm seeking a relationship."

"Don't you want a sweetheart?" Nia asked. "Why not?"

Ahjin swung Nia away from careening dancers. "We were talking about you and Izo."

Nia pouted. "I'll think about it. Now can we enjoy the dance?"

Ahjin twirled her silently until he handed her to her next partner.

Nia tried to enjoy herself, but Ahjin's words kept slipping into her mind. Her prior glee at endless partners and flirting opportunities soured. When two handsome Nokai gave her flowers at the same time, she noticed Izo's frown. Why couldn't Ahjin keep his mouth shut?

When the musicians played the last song, Nia was almost relieved to end the dancing. She gave farewells with the customary cheek kisses. A few young men kissed her cheek closer to her mouth than traditional, but she merely smiled. After the last of them left, she turned to her friends.

"What would you like to do now?" she asked.

"It's time for gifts," Mom said.

Nia bounced on her toes. She'd waited long enough for Mom's surprise.

"Ours are with our bags." Zefra stomped toward their hammocks, and Nia's friends followed.

Nia grabbed Ahjin's elbow. "Is she angry at me?"

"I suspect she's frustrated you're flirting with so many boys besides her brother." Ahjin tugged her braids and followed the others.

Mom sat gracefully on a mat and fidgeted with something in her lap. Zefra and the others returned almost soon enough to keep Nia from exploding with excitement.

Nia dropped to the ground. "Who's first? Mom?"

Mom fidgeted. "I — I think I'll wait."

Ahjin settled next to her as the others chose mats. Kaito handed him a package tied with lavender ribbon and gave a small envelope to Lyell.

"I will go first." Zefra shoved a lumpy bag at Nia. "Here."

As Nia opened the bag, Zefra twitched until she sat on her hands. Inside was a pair of semi-familiar boots.

"Are these my old desert boots?" Nia asked. "I like the new decorations."

She had hated the boots from her second day in the desert, even before they wore bloody blisters on her feet. But someone had softened the plain leather and decorated them to be Nokai-colorful.

"Nemerra helped me," Zefra said. "They should not rub your feet now."

"Thank you. I wished for boots in Darrendra." Mostly to protect her feet from hot ash, cold air, and sharp teeth.

Lyell gave her the envelope, which had pretty yellow flowers painted on the outside and spiky bumps distorting the thick paper from the inside. "I hope you have somewhere to plant these." He rubbed Tala's ears. "They say 'thank you' for last fall."

"You're welcome," Nia said. "And thank you for the flowers."

She blinked back tears at his mourning stripes — one narrow, dark brown stripe sewn around his neckline for his wife, and four along the hem for his children.

Ludik, grinning widely, handed her a palm-sized wooden box. It was beautifully worked and polished, with a lid inlaid with a shining cat eye made of nacre and silver.

Nia narrowed her eyes suspiciously, then laughed before she could help herself. "This is revenge for my wedding present, isn't it?"

Ludik smirked. "Maybe, but open it."

Inside, the box was divided into six little compartments, padded but empty.

"I don't understand," Nia said.

"It's to hold your perfumes," Ludik said.

"Oh." Nia frowned. Last fall, she and Zefra had turned Izo's first gift of perfume into a fiery missile to save Nemerra. She turned to Izo hopefully.

"Sorry, Nia." Izo handed her a small, fabric-wrapped bundle. "I brought something else this time. Zefra did not like having her hairpins warped into lockpicks, so I made her lockpicks for her hair."

He plucked a pin from Zefra's crown of braids and showed Nia how it divided into a pick. "I also made a knife." He grabbed another hairpin, despite Zefra swatting at him, and pulled a finger-length, needle-sharp knife from the sheath. "I made you the same for your lovely hair."

Inside the package, Nia found another set of special hairpins, with metal heads faceted so the copper and steel glittered in the sun.

"They're beautiful," she cooed.

Izo beamed.

"Perhaps you don't need my gift, then." Ahjin gave her the ribbon-tied package.

Inside were gorgeous hair combs decorated with flowers made from dozens of tiny, painted seashells.

"Don't tell me you made these yourself?" Nia asked.

Ahjin laughed. "I have no such talent, but now that the gods are paying me, I can shop in Arupa's market. I've researched dyes, too, and I think I can duplicate Makana's colors."

Nia grabbed her braids. The Nokai goddess, Makanavailea, had fabulous rainbow hair. "Oh, yes! I'd love that. It will make up for cutting off the burned part."

Lyell jerked.

"I'm sorry," Nia babbled. "I didn't mean to mention it."

"Never mind," Lyell said. "It is just bad memories."

Nia glanced at Tala and blinked hard. She had lost a few inches of hair in the forest fire, but Lyell had lost almost everything. She glanced at Kaito, who knelt silently with empty hands, then turned to her mom.

"Your turn, Mom. What's the big surprise?" Nia teased.

"First, I have to tell you something. I said your dad died when you were little." Mom rolled the tube in the lap. "That might not be true."

Nia gasped and sat up straight. "You lied? Why? What happened to him?"

"No! Not exactly." Mom took a breath. "I don't know. He went on an expedition and never returned. But he left a map of his plans, and now that you are an adult with allies, maybe you can discover his fate." She removed the protective leaves and unrolled a scroll.

Nia leaned forward to see. "Where did he go?" Excitement and confusion tangled in her heart like a writhing octopus.

Mom put her finger on the middle of the map. "To the Dragon Isles."

Nia choked. "But they are cursed!"

3. CURSED
(EAST CORAL ISLAND)

As recompense, the Seals will send one tenth of their people for five generations to help other kindreds or countries, including workers to His Holiness. If they fail, they will die.

Darravani's decree after the Death of Kairri, first year of His Holiness, Ahjin the Great

Ahjin frowned at Nia. "Your father went to the Dragon Isles north of Nokailana? They are loosely claimed by Makana, but the water is too cold for you Nokai, so she ignores them."

"Because they're cursed!" Nia hopped up, lavender braids flying above her eye-blinding ocean suit.

Like all Nokai, she could hide in a flower bed or a school of colorful fish. It had taken Ahjin weeks after they met to convince her he preferred quieter colors.

"How?" Zefra asked.

"I don't know. Nobody comes back." Nia sat again, tugging her braids across the gills on her golden neck. "Never mind. Mom, why didn't you tell me?"

"What could you do?" Her mother smoothed the map. "Alaneo heard the Dragon Isles had some rare herb to make our fortune. I begged him not to go, but he didn't believe in the curse. He took one of his brothers, two cousins, and a crew of sailors." Aolani sighed. "But they never returned."

Ahjin had almost lost his own parents last year when the tornadoes spawned by the gods' capture had ripped through his city. Though Nia's loss was old, his heart ached for her.

"Why did no one follow them?" Zefra asked.

"Everyone else believes in the curse," Aolani said. "I wanted to search, but I found out I was pregnant with Nia. Before she was old enough for me to leave, I met Manuai and then Zeva. With three babies, I couldn't follow Alaneo."

She stroked Nia's hair. "I'm sorry, dear. When you were a child, it was simpler to let you think he died. I'm sure he's dead, or he would have come home." Her lip quivered, and she blinked rapidly.

Nia flung her arms in the air. "Why would Dad be so stupid as to go to the squid-sucking cursed Dragon Isles? No stupid trade goods were worth his life!"

"He wanted to build a secure foundation for any children we might have," her mother said.

Nia burst into tears. "I wanted *him*."

"And I never got the chance to tell him about you," Aolani said.

Ahjin put his arm around Nia in a pitiful attempt at comfort. She leaned into his shoulder and dripped tears down his sleeve.

"Why are you telling her this now?" he asked Aolani. "What good does it do?"

Aolani flicked a glance at Ahjin. "Until last year, I had lost hope. But now, with the aid of your friends, Nia, maybe you can discover what happened to him? We could—" She swallowed. "We could hold a proper funeral."

Zefra held out her hand. "May I see your map, please?"

Aolani spread it on the sand, and Izo and Ludik held the corners for Nia and Zefra.

Zefra put one finger on East Coral Island. "Here we are, and these are the Dragon Isles?"

She hovered her other hand halfway between Nokailana and Darrendra. The islands were indistinct blobs, lightly sketched with many question marks.

Ludik looked at Ahjin. "Why are they called Dragon Isles? Are dragons real? Do the gods know about the curse?"

"I didn't know I should ask," Ahjin said, "but none of the gods have mentioned dragons, the Isles, or a curse."

Last year, they had fought several monsters they hadn't known existed, allies of the newly returned fifth god. Ahjin served all the gods now, but it wasn't fair to expect him to know everything. The gods had dumped so many tasks on him, he hadn't had time to ask anything extra.

Nia smiled through her tears. "I guess we'll find out, then."

"Zefra, you're our map expert," Ludik said. "Do you see anything else useful?"

"I do not know yet." Zefra turned to Nia's mother. "Do you know his exact route? How long did he expect his expedition to take?"

"He planned to start on the east side," Aolani said. "But without good maps of the shore, he didn't know where to land. And he had no idea where to find the herb. He planned to return in six months."

Zefra measured the map distance with her thumb. "It will take us two weeks to reach the southern end. Twice that or more to circle the islands, longer if we land and explore. Two weeks back again." She looked at Nia and Aolani. "Unless we find answers immediately on the southern isle, it would take at least two months. Can you supply such a trip?"

Nia pulled free of Ahjin's hug, hope creeping across her face.

Ahjin tried not to wince. If none of the crew had returned, her father was certainly dead.

Tears ran from Aolani's teal eyes. "I've saved for sixteen years. I can provide a ship, food, and water. However, I don't know if any sailors will go. The curse is widely believed."

Lyell cleared his throat. "Would it help if the Mouth of the Gods asked the sailors to go?"

Ahjin's wings sagged. He hated using his rank to influence others' choices.

Aolani wiped her face and sat straighter. "It might."

Nia squeezed her webbed hands together and watched Ahjin with pleading green eyes.

Ahjin's wings sagged even farther, and he fidgeted with the silver star around his neck. "I don't believe in curses, but I'll request their service."

He would do it for Nia, even though it made his feathers itch.

Nia squealed and threw her arms around his neck. He turned his head to smile at her just as she leaned in to kiss his cheek. Their lips met briefly before they both jumped back. He looked away, face hot. While she had kissed his cheek many times, this was the first time she had missed her target. It felt odd.

"Would it narrow the search if we knew more about the herb?" Izo asked.

"I only know a little," Aolani said. "Pakai grows in marshy shade as a shrub with five yellow petals and ragged teardrop leaves. It kills mosquito larvae and repels insects. Alaneo thought it would be valuable at home and for traders carrying perishable goods and cloth."

"We can watch for shady wetlands," Zefra said.

"How many of you will go with Nia?" Aolani asked.

"I will," Zefra said.

Izo winked at Nia. "I will, too."

"Ahjin?" Nia pled.

Ahjin pushed aside his lingering embarrassment to brush a tear from her cheek. "I can't. I have to return to Arupa."

"He can stay until you leave," Lyell said.

Ahjin glared, but the Wolf ignored him.

"What about you, Ludik?" Nia asked.

Ludik smiled. "Now is a good time to tell you Nemerra is expecting."

Nia clapped her hands. "How wonderful!"

"Expecting what?" Ahjin asked.

Nia smacked his shoulder. "A baby, birdbrain. Ludik, do you want a girl or a boy?"

Ahjin rubbed his shoulder, feeling stupid.

Ludik pursed his lips. "Our kindred usually have multiple births. My older brother and sister were littermates. I had two brothers with me in my litter."

Aolani blinked. "We have two sets of twins in our family. But three babies? How will you even feed them?"

Lyell smoothed his daughter's fur. "My wife and I had five babies. At once."

Ahjin glanced at the brown mourning stripes on Lyell's tunic. Their deaths still felt like Ahjin's fault. Asking for rain to extinguish the fire had been his first big attempt in his new job to get the gods to cooperate, and he had been too slow. Even now, despite their agreement to let him mediate, their distrust of each other remained.

"Mom, how long will it take to gather supplies?" Nia asked.

"I'm already working on it," Aolani said. "We'll be ready within a day or two, if Ahjin can recruit a crew."

Ahjin grimaced. "Should I start now?"

Nia glanced at the lowering sun. "No, it's late. Besides, you're still my guests. We should celebrate today and prepare for the journey tomorrow. If you agree, Mom?"

"I do." Aolani smiled. "You're something to celebrate. I love you, dear."

"I love you, too, Mom."

Ahjin smothered his sigh of relief. "What's next, Nia?"

"Supper with the family and star-watching."

"Oh, good, a meal," Ludik said. "I worked up an appetite while dancing."

"You always have an appetite," Nia teased.

Ludik shrugged and jumped to his feet. "Which way to the food?"

"I'm hungry, too," Ahjin said.

Izo nodded.

Nia giggled. "Boys."

Aolani smoothed Nia's hair and headed for the beach. "The other parents made supper."

Nia's family cheered as they walked out of the trees. "Joyful six-thousand, Nia!"

Nia waved and blew kisses. "Thank you all. Let's eat!"

Happy chaos descended on the food until everyone had a full plate or two.

Ahjin sat against a handy tree and let his wings relax. He balanced his plate on his knees and shoved at his piled food to keep it from sliding off the edges. Perhaps he had taken too much, but Nokai food was almost always delicious. Nia had even accommodated what she called his "squeamish sensibilities" with a bowl of cooked fish among the many raw delicacies.

Someone sat on his foot, and his plate jerked, dumping one of his precious cooked fish into the sand.

"Hey," he protested, curving a hand around his plate.

"Sorry." Nia scooted back until she barely touched him. "I thought you might like company."

"Of course." Ahjin took a bite. "Thank you for the cooked fish."

"Of course." Her usual beaming smile seemed dimmer, and her thick eyelashes trembled from time to time.

He shifted his plate and leaned one knee toward her shoulder. "I'm sorry about your dad. I'll talk to the sailors early in the morning. I wish I could go with you, but I have... things to do."

"You don't sound excited. What... things... do you have to do?" Nia leaned her elbow on his knee and picked at her raw fish.

She normally loved disgusting raw fish.

"The same old stuff." Ahjin shrugged. "The gods have a never-ending list of religious books for me to read, ceremonies to learn, worship to conduct, petitioners to hear, blah blah blah."

The gods were never satisfied, and he never got enough time to fly. Lyell was supposed to help him but was making things worse.

Nia flicked his knee. "Behave."

"Sorry, Nia. You know I hate people telling me what to do."

"Yes, but you've been doing it for months now. It's what you signed up for."

"Not really." Ahjin stuffed the last of the fish in his mouth. "I agreed to help the gods, not deal with petty politics. And Irajahan will hate me forever, so he won't even listen."

Nia snorted. "You can do it, and someone needs to keep an eye on him. Don't tell me you care what he thinks."

"He hated me even before I became Mouth. But I would like to know if my extra bargain to free his priests even helped anyone." He didn't mention the loss of his flying. "Anyway, you wouldn't recognize Arupa right now. Things have changed a lot since autumn."

Nia touched the combs she had jammed into her hair next to Izo's hairpins. "You mentioned the market. What else is new?"

"Lots of visitors," Ahjin said. "Some are petitioners to the gods. Some come to shop at the market, which is turning into a place to find rare and valuable items. A lot of the visitors come to gawk at me or try to bribe me with gifts." He rubbed one of the lightning scars on his hands. "You'd think I'd be old news by now. And then Lyell arrived with a shipload of people."

"How long has he been there?" Nia asked.

"Only a week. He spent all winter recruiting workers in Darrendra. Most that came are Seals, but he found a few others."

"Does Tala always stay in her wolf shape?"

Ahjin shrugged. "She likes it, and Lyell thinks she can protect herself better that way." He refused to look again at the brown mourning stripes.

"How is he as your Chief of Staff?"

"Chief of everything, really." Ahjin rolled his eyes. "I get up in the morning, and he tells me what to do all day long."

"Oh, I bet you love that," Nia said.

"He's trying to help." Ahjin scraped his plate clean and laid it aside. "At least he decided what to do with the Pinniped tithe."

"What *are* you doing with the Seals?" Nia glanced at Kaito sitting in the darkness.

Ahjin ticked them off on his fingers. "Gardeners, fishers, merchants, temple-cleaners, guides, messengers. No guards, of course. We choose the guards from the other Darrendrakar or the Iskrins, with a few Iojif for aerial views, and Nokai in the ocean." Some of the Seals weren't allowed to fight against other Darrendrakar, even in self-defense.

"And what does Kaito do?"

"I don't know," Ahjin admitted. "Lyell spends a lot of time talking to him, but I don't know why. And Kaito doesn't talk to me at all. Honestly, I don't know if he *can* talk."

Nia sighed and leaned her head on his knee. "What will we do?"

"Come here." Ahjin pulled on her elbow until she scooted back, then wrapped his arm around her. "In the morning, we'll talk to the sailors, and then you can go find your dad."

Nia laid her head on his shoulders. When damp spots soaked into his shirt again, Ahjin pretended he didn't feel them.

Ahjin woke in twilight, grabbing the edges of his swaying hammock. A tiny, wet tongue licked his cheek.

"Stop, Tala," Ahjin mumbled, closing his eyes again. "Sleep."

"It's time to rise, Your Holiness." Lyell's voice didn't hide his amusement.

"No." Ahjin pushed away Tala and turned over. "Leave me alone."

"Tip him out. Yes, I mean it."

Tala's warm body disappeared. Before Ahjin processed Lyell's words, his hammock turned upside-down. He fell, almost landing on his head.

Lyell stood above him, his pup in his arms. Behind Ahjin was Kaito, frowning, hands on the hammock.

Ahjin took a deep breath. "I don't. Think that. Was necessary."

Kaito let go of the hammock and cast a distressed look at Lyell.

Lyell nudged Ahjin with his boot. "Get up, Your Holiness. You promised Nia to recruit sailors today."

Ahjin shoved his curls from his eyes and stumbled to his feet. "They're Nokai! They won't even be awake yet."

"True," Lyell said, "but you need to get ready."

Ahjin narrowed his eyes. "I plan to eat breakfast."

Lyell cleared his throat. "To formally appeal to the Nokai as the Mouth of the Gods, you need to look the part."

Ahjin grinned. "Can't. I left my uniform on Arupa. Kassian's pendant will have to do."

He flicked the silver star around his neck, glad his horribly clashing regalia was at home. The gods had argued about what it should look like and which part should represent whom, and the result left *him* suffering.

Lyell motioned to Kaito. "I plan better."

The Pinniped pulled a satchel from behind a tree. The emblems of all five gods were burned into the leather.

"No," Ahjin groaned. "Five different colors are so garish."

"You needn't wear all of it today," Lyell said. "Makana's sash is enough. And a clean shirt and combed hair."

As he named each item, Kaito pulled them from the satchel. The shirt, a brilliant violet, would barely coordinate with the lavender sash, but Ahjin never wore such bright colors if he had a choice.

He held it up with two fingers. "What is this?"

"Makana made suggestions about your wardrobe." Lyell grinned. "When in Nokailana, dress as the Nokai. We did keep to a single color for your tastes."

Ahjin examined the purple waves and multi-colored dolphins embroidered on the sash. If that was a single color, his wings were palm leaves. The goddess could drown her suggestions in the ocean. He shoved the pile at Kaito and turned to Lyell, who held up one hand and tilted his head.

Ahjin looked over and down. Kaito knelt on the ground, eyes screwed shut, hands trembling around the clothing and comb.

Kaito's first experience with the gods had been traumatic, and Ahjin was partly to blame, though he had been trying to help. His request for Darravani to have mercy had only partially worked, and Kaito hadn't been around Ahjin long enough to trust him.

Ahjin held a deep breath and counted warm air currents. When he reached twenty, he exhaled and gently took the bundle from the Seal.

"Thank you, Kaito. I can dress myself. Will you please find me breakfast?"

Kaito stumbled to his feet and jogged through the trees.

By the time Ahjin dressed and untangled his curls, Kaito was back with fruit and bread.

Ahjin jealously watched his still-sleeping friends while he ate. "I'm ready, Lyell."

The Wolf led the way to the beach, where sleepy fishermen and women stumbled in to prepare their ships.

"Good to see you, Nokai of the East Coral Clan," he said in trade tongue. "If you direct your attention to the Mouth of the Gods, we will distract you from your work as little as possible."

The crowd glanced at Ahjin but paid most of their attention to their torn nets.

Ahjin twitched the sash straighter and pushed a curl out of his eye. "Well met, sailors," he said in Noki. The gift of languages was one of the few pleasant consequences of his job. "I need to hire a crew of brave and trustworthy souls for a two-month expedition."

A flock of hands rose.

"My friend, Nia, is going to the Dragon Isles."

All the hands fell. The sailors turned back to their nets.

Ahjin slapped his diplomatic face over his disappointment. "You will be well paid."

No response. Time for a different wind.

"How many of you have lost family at the Dragon Isles?"

A few hands raised partway before dropping again.

"Don't you want to know what happened to them? We'll search for your families as well as Nia's. You may stay in the ship; others will take the risk of landing. Besides being paid for your efforts, we'll share any trade profits we find."

Silence, but some of the hands slowed.

"They're cursed," someone muttered. "Nobody comes back."

Ahjin inhaled. "I don't believe in curses. Or dragons. As Mouth of the Gods, I tell you Makana approves of the brave and the curious. Who will join this adventure?"

Several people flicked their gaze from his scars to his sash and back again.

A young man with palm-green hair lowered his net. "I'll go." Under the others' stares, he hunched his shoulders and dragged his net to his boat.

After a moment, a stout, middle-aged woman volunteered. That triggered a trickle of others.

Ahjin left Lyell to make arrangements and stalked back to bed, ripping off the sash as he went.

First the gods had ruined his plans to fly with his family, and now he couldn't even go with Nia.

No, the touch of the gods was no blessing.

4. HEALER
(EAST CORAL ISLAND)

You can outdistance what runs after you, but not what runs inside you.
Darrendran Proverb

Ludik woke late in the morning, smiling. Today he would return to Nemerra.

Around him, people streamed toward the wharf, their arms piled with barrels, baskets, and packages. The other hammocks were empty, even Nia's.

Ludik put on his boots and grabbed his healer's kit. He didn't even know where to go in this chaos for the morning meal. Someone laid a hand on his shoulder, and he whirled.

"Fair winds," Ahjin said. "I thought you'd sleep all day."

"What is going on?" Ludik asked.

"They're loading for Nia's trip. Breakfast is this way."

Baskets of fruit and fish waited on the beach, and Ahjin grabbed an apple while Ludik filled a bowl.

"You're my excuse for a break," Ahjin said. "I've been awake a long time, and Nia is remarkably industrious today. And when she isn't nagging me, Lyell is."

Ludik tried to count the Nokai but lost track. "How did Nia persuade everyone?"

Ahjin buried his apple core in the sand. "Aolani is calling all her favors due."

Ludik finally saw their friends in the horde of Nokai. He waved, and Nia and the others delivered their loads and abandoned the line.

Nia grabbed a mango. "What took you so long?"

"I overslept," Ludik said.

Nia rolled her eyes. "*Why* did you oversleep?"

"I stayed up too late."

Nia punched his shoulder.

"I miss Nemerra," Ludik admitted. "It's the first time since our wedding that we've been separated. Last night, for every star I saw, I thought of something I love about Nemerra."

He smiled and touched the marriage ring in his ear. The stars were as bright as her shining eyes, and the moon was almost as radiant as her love.

Nia sighed happily. "What happened then?"

Ludik shrugged. "I ran out of stars."

"That's so sweet."

Zefra frowned. "There are thousands of stars, Ludik. You could not actually — Ow, Nia."

Nia frowned at her. "Don't spoil the romance, Zefra."

"I think 'tis romantic, too, Nia," Izo said. "We should walk on the beach and discuss it."

Nia beamed at him. "That's a great idea, after we finish loading."

She led him back to the line, and Zefra followed, muttering.

Ahjin raised an eyebrow. "I should help. Are you joining us?"

"No," Ludik said. "I came for Nia's party and to study tropical diseases."

"So, how do you like your apprenticeship?" Ahjin asked.

"I'm still not entirely convinced I should be a healer," Ludik said. "Hunting is better."

"I thought you decided that last fall," Ahjin said. "You're good at healing."

Ludik shrugged. Faced with Nemerra's possible death, being a better healer had sounded like a good idea. Reality was more disappointing.

"Okechuku says he is pleased with my abilities, but I haven't even learned enough Iskrin to read the books without someone translating them. Okechuku keeps sending me on visits like this to try to get me caught up to the other apprentices, who have been studying since they were children. I will never be good enough."

"You can do it." Ahjin rubbed a faded scar on his face. "*I* know you can."

"I don't think I even like it," Ludik grumbled. "But if I finish my lessons today, I can leave tonight. Nemerra is very pregnant, and I'd like to get back soon. If I don't see you later, keep well."

Ahjin's eyes widened. "How pregnant? You haven't been married long."

Ludik's face grew hot. "Long enough. A Felid pregnancy lasts seven months, and we've been married almost six."

"Well." Ahjin cleared his throat. "Congratulations again. Give my affection to Nemerra, and let us know when your babies are born. If I don't see you before you leave, good flight." He clapped Ludik on the shoulder.

Ludik picked up his kit. "Which way to the healers?"

"Through that grove, then right. They have a hut in the shade." Ahjin shook out his wings, then shoved his hands in his pockets and strolled toward the ship.

Despite Ahjin's scanty directions, Ludik spotted the lone building as he exited the trees. It was bigger than the word "hut" implied, but Ahjin came from a large city with elaborate public buildings. Ludik's home village had one-story homes, and community meetings were held outdoors. He had spent the last five months in Iskra, which was mostly migratory tents.

The windows were open squares, covered by woven shades or exposed to the spring air. Two women and a boy read in the closest room. Ludik debated knocking on the door or merely calling through the window, but the boy looked up and caught him staring.

The boy jumped to his feet and babbled a stream of Noki at the old woman, then dashed through the building and flung open the door. He gushed at Ludik, reaching toward his skin.

"Kama!" the old woman barked. "Don't touch strangers, and use a language he understands!"

The young woman, barely more than a girl, grabbed the boy. "Sorry, sorry," she said in awkward trade tongue. She scolded the boy under her breath until he bowed his head.

"He is young." The old woman's trade tongue was only lightly accented. "And now he will get the other healers." When the boy didn't move, she tapped him. "Right now!"

The boy ran through the trees, yelling, while the young woman laid mats in a large circle and filled a pitcher with water.

The old woman beckoned Ludik. "Well met. Come in, come in. I am Lelei. You are Ludik, sent here by Okechuku, yes?"

"I suppose that is not difficult to guess." Ludik settled on a mat with his healing kit beside him. "Thank you for teaching me."

"It benefits all," Lelei said. "Okechuku's letter said you will teach us to prepare a salve in exchange for our lessons, yes?"

"Yes." Ludik pulled out a jar of his ointment. "It is a traditional Darrendran recipe."

He handed it to the old woman, who unscrewed the lid and smelled the salve. In his first visit to Iskra, Ludik had used it to heal Ahjin's shredded muscles from the giant scorpion attack. Now, as Okechuku's apprentice, he spent most of his time between lessons teaching others to make it.

A man skidded noisily to a halt at the threshold and smoothed his sunflower-bright hair. Behind him, other men and women jogged toward the building, barefoot and rainbow-haired.

Lelei returned the jar. "Come in."

When every mat was full and the youngsters had found spots in the corner, Lelei introduced everyone by their short names. Ludik immediately forgot their names anyway, mentally tagging them by hair color and age.

"We will discuss tropical diseases and treatments," Lelei said, "and then Ludik will teach us to make his healing ointment. Are you ready?"

Ludik pulled a stack of Iojif paper from his kit and held the writing stick above it. "Ready."

The Nokai healers threw information at him as fast as he could write and sometimes faster.

By midday, Ludik's fingers had cramped. While he clarified a few notes, the boy and young woman set up a small feast outside.

"Come eat," Lelei said. "Rest your mind and refresh your body."

Ludik helped the old woman to her feet. Once outside, the smell of hot fish and sweet pineapple instantly woke his appetite, and he gobbled as fast as politeness allowed. The boy ate even faster, and Ludik was only halfway finished by the time the boy's plate was empty.

He scooted next to Ludik and stared at him. "My name is Kama, and this is my sister. How long have you been a healer?"

"Only apprentice," Ludik mumbled through his fish. He didn't mention he wasn't sure he wanted to be a healer. The other students ate, drank, and dreamed of healing, sacrificing everything in their quest. Ludik still wanted to go hunting and spend time with his wife.

"But you're famous," Kama protested. He pointed toward the walrus tusk fragment hanging around Ludik's neck. "Did that come from your adventure with the gods?"

His sister tweaked the boy's ear as Ludik quickly swallowed his mouthful.

"It is fine; I do not mind the questions." Ludik put his plate on the ground. "The tusk came after my friends and I stopped a feud in Darrendra. It reminds me of the dangers of hate." He looked at the older healers. "Did any of the Pinniped tithe come here?"

"Not here," Lelei said, "but some work on the next island to repair the damage from the tidal waves last year."

Ludik nodded. "They will make their way around. They have generations to pay for their crimes."

He made a fist around the blackened tusk. Nemerra's wounds were healed, but his heart still ached. And poor Lyell was unlikely to feel safe before Tala was grown.

"I don't care about the Seals," Kama said. "I heard Nia's stories about how you saved them all. How could you do that as just an apprentice?"

"I was not even an apprentice then," Ludik explained, "only a hunter. But my identical brother and I sometimes switched places. I learned some of his healing lessons while he practiced his archery. We thought we fooled our elders, but they knew all along. Remember, your elders are wiser than you."

He stared until the boy nodded. The healers smothered smiles.

Though Ludik didn't mind answering questions, he didn't like remembering how badly things had gone wrong.

"I did not even know I could heal with more than my ointments and teas until Shri Okechuku told me. We were lucky the Iskrin healers could fix the mistakes I made with my friend's wings. And later, it was only the grace of the gods that saved us."

The boy sighed. "It must have been so exciting to rescue the gods."

Before he could stop himself, Ludik roared in the boy's face.

Kama scrambled backward into his sister, eyes and mouth wide. The other healers shot to their feet.

Ludik shut his eyes and held his breath. His heart cramped and stuttered. When a trembling hand patted his shoulder, he put his hand over the old woman's and looked at the boy.

"I watched my friends die, one by one. I was the last and could not save them. As I fell dying, I was sure we had even failed to protect Darravani, and the world would be destroyed. It was not—" He took another breath. "Exciting."

"I'm sorry," Kama whispered.

"It is never exciting watching people die," Ludik muttered.

His sister filled a cup. The water trembled as she held it toward Ludik.

He drained it in one gulp and put it gently on the ground. "Now, I believe it is time to make a salve. Do you have the herbs?"

"We are ready." Lelei led the way to an outdoor stove and a long table.

The healers spread around the table as Ludik approved each herb and explained how finely to chop them and how to enhance their natural properties with magic, if they had any. Every time he corrected someone's technique, they flinched, no matter how softly he spoke.

Thanks to Okechuku's training, Ludik could tell with a touch if the Nokai healers added magic to their herbs. Lelei was strong, and a younger man with turquoise hair wasn't bad, but most of the others had no more than a trace of power. Yellow-hair had none at all, though his physical skills were impeccable.

"Now you must make a choice," Ludik said. "This salve works with herbal properties alone, and only two of you have much power. Do you want to use the unenhanced herbs also, or make only a stronger batch?"

"What would you do?" Yellow-hair asked.

"My brother makes it with no power at all," Ludik said.

"Then let us all contribute," said a middle-aged woman with rosy hair. "But will you tell us who can make the stronger salve?"

Ludik nodded at Lelei and Turquoise-hair while he lifted the kettle onto the stove. "You two. Now we simmer the herbs in the oil."

The Nokai healers watched the pot and Ludik as if either might explode. By the time they strained the oil and added honey and beeswax, Ludik was exhausted by the attention.

"Well done, all of you," he said as they poured the last of the salve into small jars.

"You're a fine teacher." Lelei gestured toward the hut. "Now let us test you as a student."

They spent the rest of the day reviewing the morning's information, until the written words swam in his view and he forgot trade tongue.

Lelei freed him long after the sun set. Kama escorted him onto the Iskrin ship where his belongings had been loaded.

"I am sorry I scared you, Kama." Ludik reached for a Darrendran arm clasp.

The boy made a face, then ducked in for a hug instead. "Sorry I made you sad," he murmured before scampering off the ship.

Ludik found a spot in the shade of the cabin and fell asleep while the captain waited for the tide.

~~~~

When the rising sun woke Ludik, he didn't see land in any direction. The Tukiko camp had moved to the coast during his trip, but Iskra was three days away.

Nemerra would be waiting. She was his heart, his reason for being. The past six months had been the best of his life. She was kind, loving and intelligent, and wonderful in every way. Though her pregnancy meant she wasn't as slender as before, her smile was as warm and her skin glowed, and her russet hair and honey-brown eyes were even more beautiful. His apprenticeship was his job, but his life was Nemerra. And soon, he would be back with her.

A coo broke his daydreams. In the shade of the sail, a small cage held something with gray feathers and bright eyes.

A small cabin boy tugged on Ludik's elbow, offering a plate of fish and flatbread. "'Tis a beautiful morning, yes? Are you hungry?"

"Yes, thank you." Ludik braced his legs against the sway of the ship. "What is in the cage? Are those for eggs or just meat?"

The boy gasped. "They are messenger birds. Captain lets our clan know when we are coming. It gives an advantage in the market, if we can time the announcement of the goods." The cabin boy nodded sagely. "I will be the best merchant captain in the fleet when I get big."

Ludik looked down at the tiny boy and grinned. The boy was too busy surveying his imaginary future to notice.

"Will you announce our arrival?" Ludik asked.

"Oh, certainly," the boy said. "We loaded fresh Nokai fruit. This early in spring, it will sell like water in the dry season."

"Would he mind if I sent a message of my own?"

The boy shrugged. "You could ask." He took the empty plate and scampered away.

The captain had no objection, so Ludik squeezed tiny words on a scrap of parchment. At least Darrendran symbols were more compact than Iskrit runes and much more than Iojo or Noki characters.

"Coming home. Lessons and party good. Nia searching for father, lost years ago on expedition for pakai."

Ludik took the note to the captain, then looked for a task to distract himself for three days.

～～～～

A return message unexpectedly arrived on a bird the next morning. The captain read it and cursed, then handed it to Ludik.

While the captain shouted orders to turn the ship around, Ludik read the note, written in trade tongue and necessarily short.

So few words to crush his heart.

5. LOADING
(EAST CORAL ISLAND)

The smallest Iskrin clan is the Hotaru, known mostly for their legendary map-makers.
Iskrin Culture and History, vol. 2

*Z*efra followed Nia and Izo inland, curling her toes away from the scratchy sand. Despite her friendship with Nia, Zefra did not like her brother making a fool of himself over someone who had no intention to marry. Did he not realize butterflies never settled? Izo was hardworking and faithful and deserved a wife to match him. At nineteen, he was still plenty young enough to keep looking.

They reached the heap of supplies from Nia's mother, now a third the height it had been this morning. Zefra leaned her map against a tree, grabbed the nearest basket, and headed for the ship.

This quest was important for Nia to find her father, but also for Zefra. Almost a year ago, Kassian had asked her to help him find a new home. Ludik's wedding — and the search for a murderer — had delayed her, and then winter had limited her search to Iskra and to the maps of legends Lyell had given her. She needed to look around the world, and the unclaimed Dragon Isles were the best possibility. If she found land for Kassian, her reputation would keep her steadily employed for the rest of her life.

Nia's expedition was Zefra's best chance before Kassian gave up on her and hired someone else. The opportunity to spend more time with her friends was a welcome bonus. She had missed them over the winter. Even Ludik had been too busy in another district to visit.

At the ship, Ahjin looked at the tag on her basket and showed her where to put it.

"Why are you doing manual labor?" Zefra asked. "Is there not something better for you to do?"

Ahjin raised an eyebrow. "Lyell thinks so. He has a stack of paperwork for me." He shuddered.

Zefra pursed her lips. Paperwork was more fun than manual labor, though all worthwhile jobs were honorable. "Will Ludik help us prepare for the trip, too?"

"I just talked to him, and he has something else to do." Ahjin raised his voice as Nia and Izo finally ambled on board, laughing together. "Ludik will leave for Iskra tonight. We might not see him before then, so he asked me to give his farewells."

Nia smiled. "He's welcome to stay longer, but Nemerra will be excited for him to return." She put her crate on the deck and turned for the next one.

"What is all this?" Zefra asked. Nia had the same gift of languages as Ahjin, given to her at birth by her goddess, Makanavailea, but Zefra spoke only Iskrit and trade tongue, not the Noki on the labels.

Nia pointed at each container. "Fruits, vegetables, dried fish, rice, chickens for eggs, salt, sugar cane, flour, and a little fresh bread. Fishing nets, coal, pots, rowing boat, tarps, compass, flint & tinder, and all the barrels around the edge hold water."

"I can handle our fire needs," Zefra said.

Izo chuckled. "We should call you Flint, dear sister."

"Only if I call you Tinder." Zefra snapped her fingers and held the flame under his nose.

He laughed and leaned backward to avoid the fire.

Zefra absorbed the flame and turned back to Nia. "That is enough variety. Did you get the right quantities? Where are the hammocks and weapons?"

The corner of Ahjin's mouth quirked, but he said nothing.

Nia exhaled. "Why don't you ask Mom your questions?"

Zefra nodded. "An excellent idea. Where is she now?"

"In the clearing where we danced. Do you know the way?"

"I put it on my map of the isle." Zefra left the ship and retrieved her staff, then headed inland, following her map.

Nia's mother sat in the dance clearing, surrounded by scribbled lists on sturdy leaves.

Zefra sat beside her and stared at the foreign script flowing in unrestrained curves, so different from the structured Iskrit runes.

"May I help you, Aolanikalia?" she asked. "What task is next in priority?"

Nia's mother smiled and shuffled the lists. "You may call me Aolani." Her trade tongue was adequate, with a musical accent. "Are the supplies loaded? If we are ready today, you can leave on the morning tide."

"When I walked by, the pile was much smaller," Zefra assured her. "But I have questions about the supplies."

Aolani put down the lists. "Go ahead."

"How did you determine how much food to take," Zefra said, "as opposed to what to restock? How did you know how many sailors would agree to go?"

Aolani smiled again. "Enaki has used my ship since I bought it a few years ago, so I know the minimum number required to crew it and the maximum that will fit. I picked a number between, guessed how much food you need to get to the islands, then added a bit more. If I stocked too little, you can fish more." She paused. "I believe Ahjin persuaded more to go than I expected. I doubt I overstocked."

'Twas not a precise method, but it would be undiplomatic for Zefra to say so. "We should gather more now, then, before your helpers go home."

Aolani patted her hand. "It will be fine."

Zefra inhaled. "If you are sure. Or we could ask the captain his opinion."

"She will be fishing until you leave," Aolani said. "This is my responsibility. It will be fine."

"It is good practice to take a little extra," Zefra said, "in case of unexpected difficulties."

Aolani's eyes crinkled. "There is more food in the ocean than in the desert. I'm sure you'll find more if you run low."

Zefra gave up. "Will the sailors take their own weapons?"

Aolani blinked. "I'm sure some of them will. Will you take your staff?"

"Yes," Zefra said. "And my sword, and knife, and bow. I did not bring my armor, though."

She frowned. Even though she had come for a party, she should have been more prepared. Now she would have to face cursed islands without her lacquered leather vest.

Aolani's mouth dropped open. "You brought all that with you? What did you think would happen here?"

Zefra shrugged. "Before Ludik's wedding, we hunted a murderer."

"I don't think weapons will help against a curse," Aolani said gently, returning to her pile of lists.

"They might," Zefra muttered in Iskrit, before switching back to trade tongue. "What are your plans for the unexpected, then?"

"Like what?"

"I do not know. That is why it is called the unexpected."

Aolani laughed. "We will see what happens and deal with it then. It will be fine."

Zefra already hated that expression, as well as the island lassitude. Nia was her friend despite her careless attitude, not because of it.

"Why do you want to go on this expedition?" Aolani said. "You don't seem to be enjoying yourself."

"To help Nia and to search for land for Kassian," Zefra said. "His brothers and sisters, the other gods, have divided most of the known world among them. While changing the divisions is theoretically possible, finding something unclaimed would cause less contention. I searched our Iskrin maps, including ones so old they tell of legends, but did not find anything suitable. Iskra is a vast continent, and starting without a plan would be futile. But Ahjin says Makana does not care about the Dragon Isles. They might work for Kassian."

Aolani smiled. "You must be excited at the prospect." She divided her notes into two piles.

"What is left on your lists?" Zefra asked. "May I help?"

Aolani tapped the leaves together and slid them under her leg. "Why don't you go help Nia?"

No one wanted her help.

Zefra rose and bowed, then walked toward the dock, using her staff to knock offending leaves from her path. When she passed the heap of supplies, 'twas the same size it had been on her way inward. No one was carrying supplies anymore. No one was in sight.

The ship was empty, supplies half put away and half stacked in random piles, and hammocks sprawled in a tangled mess. Why was no one working?

Zefra pulled the first hammock until it separated from the heap. 'Twas unwieldy to fold it alone, but she persisted until she made a tidy square. She worked her way through the jumble, growing more frustrated with each one she folded alone. When she reached for the next-to-last hammock, the rope burst into flame.

Zefra dropped it and inhaled, reaching for serenity, then stuck her hand in the fire and absorbed it. The deck was only charred, but the rope was ash. She tossed the ruined hammock overboard and marched off the ship.

She found Nia and Izo on the beach, using baskets to pack sand into shapes and flirting madly.

"Well met, Zefra." Nia tapped the damp sand from a basket and cheered when it held its shape. "Do you want a basket?"

"Where is everyone?" Zefra asked. "There are still supplies to be loaded."

"The villagers will come back tomorrow," Nia said, "after they finish their own work and get some rest."

"They cannot just stop," Zefra said.

Nia laughed. "Why not? They don't need to work *all* day."

"What about the supplies?"

"They won't leave," Nia said.

"What if someone takes them?" Zefra asked.

Nia gaped at her. "Crusty crab shells, why would anyone take them?"

Izo cleared his throat. Zefra felt her face grow hot. She should not have insulted her hosts. Of course the Nokai were too honest to steal.

She bowed. "I apol—"

"If they want some fruit," Nia continued, "it is easier to pick it from a tree than undo a crate and annoy Mom."

Zefra straightened and stared at Nia, then at Izo, who raised his eyebrows and shrugged.

"Your mother does not seem to have a system to be sure the preparations are complete," Zefra said. "I tried to help, but she thought I would be of more use helping you."

"Don't worry," Nia said. "We'll finish tonight. Or maybe tomorrow, before we leave."

"But—"

"Why don't you find my brother and sister and ask them lots of questions about Nokailana?" Nia tapped the sand from the basket again. "They've never met an Iskrin. It will be a novel experience for them."

"Go ahead." Izo smiled. "I will keep Nia company." He packed sand in the empty basket while Nia smoothed the edges of a half-finished sculpture.

Zefra sighed. "I will return." She followed her map to a couple of likely spots. She did not find Nia's siblings, but she did find Ahjin reading a stack of papers in a tree.

"If you are not busy, Ahjin, would you translate for me?" Zefra asked.

"I'd be happy to." Ahjin spread his wings and glided to the earth.

They meandered along the island shore until they found a group of children running and giggling in a game.

"Bright day," Zefra said. "I'm looking for Aolani's children."

Ahjin repeated it in Noki.

A violet-haired girl dodged a little boy and shouted. Ahjin translated, "Olina, Kaliya, you have a visitor."

Two children left the game and slid to a stop in front of Zefra.

When they spoke, Ahjin translated.

"Your skin is so white," the boy said. "Are you sick?"

His sister elbowed him. "She's Iskrin, silly. They all look like that."

The boy nodded. "I understand. White skin and red hair means Iskrin. And the brown-skinned ones are Pinneys."

Zefra smiled. "Not quite. Do you want to exchange questions? Ahjin will translate for us."

The girl bounced on her toes, like Nia always did. "We can ask you anything?"

"Anything," Zefra promised. "But first, tell me your names." She settled cross-legged on the sand and waited for the children and Ahjin to sit.

"I'm Olina," the coral-haired girl said. She looked about the same age as Zefra's next-youngest sister.

She rattled off her age in days. Zefra pulled out her slate to do the arithmetic and nodded. Yes, twelve years old, a little older than Risa.

"What is your full name?" she asked.

"Olinamalulani." Nia's little sister pronounced each syllable separately.

Ahjin grinned but did not repeat it. Zefra carefully said the name.

Olina grinned. "Most strangers can't say our names well."

"The Iskrin consider names important," Zefra said. "I wish I had a book that told the meanings, though. Nia told me the Nokai do not teach that."

"Oh, I know mine," Olina said. "We choose our names for pretty sounds, but Mom knows more meanings than most Nokai." She rattled through an explanation of how her name came from her father's.

Zefra turned to Nia's brother, whose uncombed, lime-green hair had leaves stuck in it. "And you?"

"He was named after his dad, too." Olina nudged him.

The ten-year-old boy was named Kaliyakaomoana, and Zefra made notes of the name meanings for him and his father.

"Now, to answer your questions," Zefra said. "First, most Iskrins have black hair."

The children wrinkled their noses like they had drunk vinegar. "How boring," Olina said. "Enaki has brown hair. That's why he only has one child. Nobody else wanted to take the risk of ugly children."

Zefra blinked. While she knew different cultures had different standards for marriage and relationships, she had never heard of hair color being one of them.

She jumped into her next question.

~~~~

Ahjin ran out of time at the same time the children ran out of questions. Zefra still had more, but they would have to wait.

The children ran back to play, and Ahjin flew slowly toward Lyell, who stood at a distance with another stack of papers. Zefra headed to the shore. Perhaps Nia had rested enough to work again.

Nia and Izo were still on the beach, lying on their backs and naming cloud-pictures. Their abandoned sand sculpture had half-collapsed.

"Your siblings are going to dinner now," Zefra said. "Olina wants to know if you will join them."

Nia yawned. "I'll stay here now and visit Mom tonight. I want to ask her questions about Dad in private."

"I enjoyed meeting your family," Zefra said.

"They like you, too." Nia pointed to the sky and whispered to Izo.

Zefra poked the crumbled sculpture with her staff. "Why does your mother know the meanings of names when the other Nokai do not care?"

Nia shrugged. "Mom has a few quirks. You should like it, since it satisfies your endless curiosity."

"Do you not wonder anything?" Zefra asked. "What about your father?"

"I wonder why you don't know how to rest." Nia draped one wrist across her eyes. "I do wonder about Dad, but once I talk to Mom, we can't find any more answers until we get there."

Izo covered his mouth, but his eyes still smiled.

Zefra stabbed the broken sculpture, then shuttered her inner eyelids and spoke calmly. "I thought this quest was important to you. How can I rest when your plans are inadequate?"

"Thank you," Nia said, "but this is my expedition, and it will be fine."

"You are just like your mother," Zefra said.

Nia beamed. "Thank you."

"Neither of you take things seriously."

Nia frowned. "And why should we? Life is not serious. Relax and have some fun."

Izo brushed sand off his legs. Although his Nokai pants were longer than Lyell's, they were as snug. He should have changed back into his modest Iskrin robe by now, as Zefra had. Nokailana was corrupting him.

"Relax, Zefra." He bit into a slice of mango.

Yes, definitely corrupted.

"It will be *fine*, Zefra." Nia turned back to Izo.

Zefra patted her belt pouch. She had brought her little travel slate to make notes. Tomorrow, things would be done right.

6. DUTY
(EAST CORAL ISLAND)

Come see the Machols' Magnificent Aerobats! Winged wonders! Daring dives! Fantastic flying! One day only!
Advertising poster for Aerial Festival

Ahjin woke on departure day to faint sunlight outlining the palm leaves above his hammock. He turned his head and found Lyell and Kaito hovering.

"Good to see you, Ahjin," Lyell said.

Tala caught a small lizard by the tail with her clumsy puppy paws and barked. The lizard squirmed, and the tail broke off. Tala sniffed the twitching tail while the lizard ran for his life.

Ahjin checked for the satchel but saw only a stack of paperwork in Lyell's hands and a covered basket in Kaito's. He sat up in the hammock. "What are you doing, Lyell?"

Zefra and Izo rolled over in their hammocks, but neither opened their eyes.

"We brought your morning meal." Lyell removed the lid of the basket, which held fresh fruit, hot bread, and steamed rice.

Ahjin's stomach growled. He peeled half a mango with his belt knife before slicing the flesh. Juice dripped down his chin with every sweet bite.

Lyell tapped the papers until the edges matched exactly. "After you eat, we can go through the merchant applications and the harvest tally. I have the latest housing plans, and there are still new arrivals who need work assignments. When you finish, you can catch up on your religious texts." He held the papers toward Ahjin.

Ahjin stuffed rice into his mouth. The gods bossed him around and now Lyell thought he could, too. Lyell was supposed to work for *him*.

He swallowed his mouthful. "Religious observances first, Lyell. The gods don't wait." He kept eating while Lyell pursed his lips and cradled his papers.

"Very well," Lyell finally said, "your prayers may come first."

Zefra jumped up and shook wrinkles from her robe. "Bright day, everyone." She pulled a comb from her belt pouch and unbraided her hair.

Izo yawned and slowly rolled from his hammock. He sat cross-legged on the ground and laid his hands on his knees for prayers. His bare shoulders gleamed white in the dappled sunlight. After Zefra combed her hair, she joined her brother.

Ahjin settled beside the Iskrins. Sunrise was a great time to pray to Resef the Omnificent. He laid out a rune message to the Iskrin god of fire explaining Nia's trip, then closed his eyes. His actual prayers took only a few minutes, but Lyell wouldn't dare interrupt him until he appeared finished, and Ahjin could think while Zefra and Izo meditated.

That reminded him, he needed to ask if news had been spread of the Iskrins' physical need for sunlight. Though it didn't matter to those at home, traders and diplomats should be aware when they visited other lands.

Zefra stirred, and Ahjin opened his eyes. His runes were barely changed; no messages from Resef today and only a simple "yes" on the Dragon Isles. He dropped the runes back into the bag.

"Are those obsidian?" Izo asked. "Ohh, are those the ones Resef made for you?" He reached out a finger, then snatched it back.

"Yes." Ahjin tossed the bag to Izo. "Here, see."

"Be careful!" Izo peered inside the bag with an amusing mix of fascination and panic.

"They're rock," Ahjin said. "They'll survive."

"How long did it take you to learn to read them?" Izo asked.

"No time at all," Ahjin said drily. "Just like Darravani's flower code and all the languages, the dictionary was installed directly into my head."

Izo winced and returned the runes. "Somehow, that does not sound fun."

"No," Ahjin agreed. "But if you'd like breakfast, Nia would say it's ripe for the picking." He winked at Kaito, who stared solemnly back. Some people had no sense of humor. Ahjin offered the siblings the last of his bread. "The fruit trees are back there."

Zefra nodded. "'Tis on my map." She braided her hair as she walked away. "Come, Izo."

Her brother snatched the bread and followed.

Lyell hurried back. "And now for the paperwork."

"No," Ahjin said. "Four other gods still need attention. Why don't you and Kaito take Tala for breakfast or a swim. I'll find you when I'm ready."

Lyell frowned, but he separated Tala from another lizard and motioned Kaito to follow him.

When they left, Ahjin sighed. Though the Wolf did a lot for Ahjin as his chief of staff, the bossy pest was driving him crazy. But that problem would have to wait. Ahjin really did have to check with the other gods.

With so many island flowers around, this was a good time to talk to Darravani the Omnifarious. He wandered along the island, finding a suitable assortment, then laid the blossoms in a pattern of basic greeting and inquiry for the Darrendran earth goddess. He dropped the final flower into position beside an upside-down note explaining about Nia's quest and waited. After a minute, the plants that indicated greetings rerooted themselves. The inquiry flowers sank into the ground, and a single red carnation sprouted. "Yes" for the Dragon Isles.

Kassian the Omnipresent was simple. Ahjin gave a mental twist to the note, and the paper vanished. Alas, he could only send small objects like notes, and only to Kassian. If Ahjin could send anything anywhere, that would really increase his ability for pranks. He'd mentioned the possibility to Kassian, though not the reason, and had been repeatedly denied.

His note reappeared with an addition at the bottom. "Zefra's search is approved. If you help her, we might find a resolution earlier. Whenever you have an answer, let me know. Kassian."

Ahjin didn't blame him for his hopes. Until he found land to host them, Kassian couldn't gather people for himself, and the eldest god was tired of being lonely. That was, after all, why he had returned last year. At least he no longer fought the world for his perceived rights.

Three gods down, and good news for his friends going on the trip.

Ugh. Until Ahjin got to the beach, that only left Irajahan the Omnipotent, All-Powerful God of Air. Though he was technically Ahjin's own god, patron of Ioj, Ahjin had liked it better when he could believe the gods were myths designed to maintain the power of the priests.

Even his telepathy was no blessing, since he could only use it with others with the same ability. That limited him to Irajahan, who held a grudge against Ahjin, and his priests, who mostly shared their god's antipathy. Fair enough; Ahjin hated Irajahan, too, for ruining his life.

Ahjin walked toward the beach. "Oh, Irajahan, My Lord Omnipotent, how are you this morning?"

Silence echoed inside his head. Some lovely times, Irajahan didn't answer.

"I don't know why you have to bother me so early," Irajahan whined.

And other times weren't so lovely. "I apologize, Almighty. Should I contact you later? We're sending an expedition to the Dragon Isles to see if they're suitable for Kassian. Do you have any advice?"

"Go away. And stay home and mind your own breezes. Kassian can deal with his own problems." Irajahan slammed the connection shut.

Ouch. Ahjin winced, but having the cranky god absent was worth the pain. Sometime, he'd have to talk to Irajahan — again — about Ahjin's required involvement with all the gods, but it could wait.

As Ahjin reached the shore, a black wolf pup bounced through the underbrush, indicating Lyell was nearby, probably hovering with those papers. It was tempting to write every other line upside down or fold the papers into little animals.

But it was time to contact Makanavailea the Omniscient, Goddess of Water. Ahjin sat on the edge of the dock and leaned over to see the ocean. "Hail, Mystical Lady."

Makana's beautiful face appeared on the waves, framed with her rainbow-striped hair. "Good to see you, Ahjin. Did you enjoy Nia's party?"

"I did." The dock shuddered as a line of Nokai headed for Aolani's ship, arms full of more supplies. "It looks like the fun is over, though. Nia

is heading to the Dragon Isles to look for her dad, and she's taking Zefra
to explore the Isles. Since you aren't using them, would you mind relin-
quishing them to Kassian if they're suitable? And do you know anything
about the curse?"

Makana laughed. "There's no such thing as a curse, and Kassian can
have those chilly Isles if he wants them. He'd make a welcome buffer
between me and Darravani's suspicious children. Don't tell her I said
that." She looked behind her. "I have a party of my own, so I'll let you
go." Her face wavered into nothingness.

Ahjin jumped out of the way of the Nokai. He thought the gods had
been getting along better this past year, but apparently there were still
lingering bad feelings. That definitely fell under his job description,
unlike Lyell's nagging list.

When he got back to land, Lyell was waiting.

Ahjin tried to stall. "Where's Tala? You didn't lose her, did you?"

Lyell glared at him. "She's with Zefra. Now, let's review these reports
together." He read the first one aloud and explained everything in
annoying detail.

Ahjin sat against a handy tree, wings spread to the sun, and watched
the Nokai load the ship. At the end of the report, he said, "I can read
them faster myself."

"I want to be sure you understand," Lyell said.

"I'm not stupid." Ahjin jumped to his feet. "Nia needs help, and I
finished the urgent paperwork yesterday. The rest can wait until I get
back to Arupa." He walked away before Lyell could respond.

As soon as Ahjin's feet hit the dock, Zefra told him where to go and
what to bring. When he returned with his ordered parcel, she told him
where to put it.

On his next trip, Nia tilted her head toward Zefra. "She killed the
fun."

Ahjin laughed. "You can find it again." He headed for another box
and ran into Lyell carrying his bag. "Where are you going?"

"Arupa," Lyell said. "The captain will return for you. You will have the
rest of the day to visit with Nia. Kaito will be your personal servant until
you get home."

Ahjin glared at Lyell. "I don't need a servant."

"Your position needs one." Lyell waved his arm, and Kaito headed toward them.

"Oh, no," Ahjin said. "That wind dies as a breeze. Take him with you."

"No." Lyell said. "Kaito, stay with him and do as I taught you. Ahjin, I'll see you tomorrow morning. Don't be late." He dodged the Nokai on the dock and boarded Ahjin's ship with Tala.

Kaito looked at Ahjin.

"It will be a cold wind in midsummer before I need a servant." Ahjin snapped out his wings and flew to the pile of supplies. He made another trip before Kaito caught up, and two more before the pile disappeared.

Before Ahjin could ask Nia what to do next, a Nokai with cardinal-red hair approached.

"Well met, Your Holiness," he said. "I regret I didn't get to know you better earlier."

Ahjin smiled at the Nokai. "You are one of Nia's fathers, aren't you?"

The man kissed Ahjin's cheeks enthusiastically. "Yes, yes, I'm Manuai. I'm so pleased you remember me. We are blessed our lovely Nia's six-thousandth day brought you to us."

Kaito left, returning with fruit juice and cups. Nia's father kept fawning over his good fortune at meeting His Holiness, the Mouth of the Gods, the most important man in the world.

Ahjin tried several times to interrupt, but Manuai blathered without pause. Ahjin raised the filled cup to his lips to hide his grimace. He expected this sort of thing on Arupa, but he thought he'd be safe among Nia's family. Nia certainly didn't care about his position, except as an endless source of amusement. Her mother didn't even seem to notice.

"I have gifts for you," Manuai continued. "Do come see them."

"No need," Ahjin said.

"Nonsense," Manuai said. "You'll love them."

"No."

"Finish your drink and follow me," Manuai wheedled.

Ahjin slipped his hand into his pocket. Once, he'd rifled through Ludik's kit and borrowed a few of the carefully labeled drugs in anticipation of future jokes. Now was no joke, but he did have something appropriate.

He drained his juice and held it out to Kaito for a refill, then dropped a pinch of white powder into the cup. At his first chance, he bumped into Manuai and spilled his juice.

"Oh, how clumsy of me," Ahjin said. "I'm so sorry. Here, take mine instead. I insist. I feel terrible." He pressed his cup into Manuai's hand and smiled sweetly.

"That's kind of you." Manuai returned to his ingratiating babble.

Ahjin motioned to Kaito to refill the man's cup whenever it emptied. It only took a few minutes. First, Manuai blinked. Then he stuttered and dropped the cup. Ahjin grabbed his arm and lowered him to the ground. In moments, Manuai was snoring like a wild boar.

Ahjin grinned. What a bore, indeed! Next time, he should listen when Ahjin said no.

Kaito frowned at him and left with the jug and empty cups.

Ahjin made his escape to the ship where Nia laughed and sang. He found a seat on a handy crate, not far from Zefra, who scowled at her slate as if it were a scorpion.

Nia had a half dozen sailors and Izo hanging on her every word. The young Nokai fisherman with palm green hair who had first volunteered for the trip had found a spot at her side. Nia turned from him to Izo and back with a bright smile. Ahjin watched the nauseating spectacle for half an hour before she noticed him.

"Oh, there you are. This is Malu, who will be first mate, and Inna, our captain."

Inna was the middle-aged woman who had volunteered second. Her creamy blonde hair was tame for a Nokai, only a few shades darker than that of Ahjin's mother.

"Four gods have approved your expedition, and the fifth doesn't matter," Ahjin reported.

"Thank you. Have you changed your mind about coming? I'd love your company while I find Dad." Nia blinked away tears again.

Ahjin glanced at the shore where Kaito sat. "Unfortunately, no."

"We will miss you," Nia said.

Ahjin squared his drooping shoulders. "Did you get everything loaded? All ready to go?"

"Yes," Zefra said without looking up from her slate.

"We'll eat supper here and catch the evening tide," Nia said. "We even have time for a swim. Will you join us?"

"Indeed." Ahjin offered her his arm, and she laughingly let him escort her through her admirers. As they walked to their makeshift changing room, Ahjin lowered his voice. "Do you remember what I said about Izo?"

"Yes, Ahjin."

"Don't forget it," Ahjin said. "He's a good man, and even if you decide you don't want him, you need to be nice."

Nia sniffed. "Yes, Ahjin."

"I'm serious," Ahjin said. "And if you do want him, be even nicer, or you'll scare him away."

She smiled. "I'm very nice. I don't want to hurt him. Relationships should be fun."

Izo still wore his ocean pants, but Ahjin and Zefra changed into their suits and ran for the beach. Kaito shifted, sliding into the waves as a large brown seal.

They swam for hours, until the large, golden moon rose with a mellow glow. The tiny blue and lavender moonlets would be dark tonight. As the sun dropped lower, the delicious aroma of cooking food drifted across the ocean. The crowd dragged themselves from the water and flopped on the sand to eat until their stomachs couldn't hold any more.

"It's time to go," Aolani said. "The winds will change soon."

Everyone followed her to the dock. Ya'eel swam around the wharf, whistling at Nia until she called to him. Besides the captain, Nia, and the two Iskrins, there were about twenty sailors. Their bright hair made as vibrant of a rainbow across the dock as the patterned sail above them.

"Here." Aolani handed Nia an embroidered and beaded bracelet. "This is a copy of the one I made for Alaneo. If you find — maybe you can identify him." Tears slid down her cheeks.

Ahjin ran his thumb along the embroidered birds on the scarf his mother gave him.

Nia tied the bracelet on her wrist and hugged her mother. "We'll be back soon. Pleasant journey, Mom."

Aolani smiled through her tears. "May your journey be pleasant and your companions cheerful, and may the currents shield you from adversity as they carry you to your desire." She kissed Nia on her cheeks, then Izo and Zefra and each sailor. "Pleasant journey, all of you."

The travelers boarded and drew up the anchor. The sails billowed, and the ship swung in a northward arc toward the Dragon Isles.

From the edge of the dock, Ahjin watched the ship disappear, curving his wings around himself to block the chill evening wind. He'd been alone most of the winter, and now he was alone again.

When he finally turned, Kaito was there with a basket of gifts.

Ahjin let his wings sag. "I don't care what they are; I don't want them."

Ahjin's boat returned shortly after, white sail shining in the golden moonlight. He boarded and dropped his bag in his shipboard cabin. He'd be home by morning.

Someone knocked, and when Ahjin opened the door, the captain handed him a sheaf of papers. "Sorry, Your Holiness," he said. "Lyell said to give you these immediately."

"Thank you, Captain." Ahjin shut the door firmly.

He flipped to the end of the pile and found the work assignments. When Lyell's suggestion matched the applicant's request, Ahjin signed it. The others could wait until he talked to the people about their options.

He read through the stack again. Ahjin's personal approval wasn't needed for everything, and if he spent all his time on this, he wouldn't have any left for the important things. Lyell should handle half of these. Perhaps he wouldn't as long as Ahjin looked over his shoulder.

Kassian had suggested Ahjin go with Zefra. Irajahan disapproved, but who cared what he thought? Ahjin grinned. In fact, that might be a good reason to go. Help Kassian, annoy Irajahan, and take a vacation while Lyell learned his job. The longer he thought about the idea, the more appealing it grew. His seventeenth birthday was coming in a couple of weeks, and spending it with friends sounded wonderful.

Ahjin scribbled a note reminding Lyell of his duties. He slid his pack between his wings and snuck out on deck, then flew away. Nia hadn't left long before. He could catch up.

Behind him, a splash echoed across the waves.

7. REUNION
(OCEAN)

Some Nokai claim the Dragon Isles are inhabited by dragon-shifters from Darrendra.

Everything You Ever Wanted to Know about the Nokailana Islands but Were Too Lazy to Ask

Nia basked in the moonlight, talking to Izo. He was so handsome and kind and strong. She patted her sparkly hairpins and laughed at his latest joke. He really was funny. She'd say so even if he didn't have broad shoulders and deep brown eyes.

The sails snapped in the cool wind, and Captain Inna adjusted the tiller. Waves splashed against the side of the ship, and the salt tang of the ocean was sweet in Nia's nose.

This was her third big adventure and the best of all. There were no missing gods, no monsters, and no murderers. She hoped to find her lost dad, but whatever she discovered about him, she had time to explore romance with an attentive young man. It would keep her mind off her worries about Dad. What had happened to him? How had he died? Or if he lived, why hadn't he come back?

Something flapped in the darkness above her.

"Did you hear that flutter?" she asked Izo.

"I only hear the sails," Izo said.

Something thumped on the deck.

The captain called, "Alert!"

Nia shot to her feet as Izo reached for his knife. Fire hissed upward. Nia blinked in the sudden light of the flame in Zefra's hand. Most of the sailors held harpoons, though one had grabbed an oar.

In the middle of the ring of sailors, Ahjin slowly furled his wings, hands outstretched and a sheepish grin on his face. "Hi, Nia. Mind if I come along?"

Nia threw her arms around Ahjin. "Now everything is perfect!"

Zefra dropped her fire into a lamp, which she hung from a hook on the mast. The sailors wandered back to their posts with many backward glances.

"I don't know about perfect." Ahjin leaned over the bulwark. "I thought I heard something."

Nia and Izo leaned with him. Moonlight sparkled on waves turned purple in the darkness.

Ahjin pointed behind the ship where a dark shape surfaced and dipped again. He groaned and banged his head on the wood. "I should have flown faster."

"What is that?" Izo asked.

"Throw him a rope, Izo," Ahjin said. "Nia, please ask the captain to stop or at least slow. Don't come back until I call you. Keep the other ladies away and find something for him to wear."

"Who?" Nia asked.

Izo squinted over the side. "'Tis... a seal?"

"Captain, stop!" Nia ran for the cabins. Somebody must have something for Kaito to wear.

Ahjin finally escorted Kaito to the others, hair dripping salt water on the deck.

"Is there room for us to string our hammocks?" Ahjin asked.

Izo clapped him on the shoulder. "We will make room. The men are portside to satisfy Zefra's tender proprieties."

Malu, the first mate, said, "We'll empty the captain's cabin for the Mouth of the Gods."

"No!" Ahjin shouted. He cleared his throat. "I'm sorry. No, please don't. A hammock with the sailors will be satisfactory."

"But, Your Holiness," Malu started.

Ahjin snapped out his wings. "Enough. Nia, where are the hammocks?"

Nia pointed, and Kaito crept past Ahjin's wings. He came back with two hammocks and strung them next to the others, stretching between the row of hooks on the cabin and the matching row on the bulwark.

"I thought you had to get home," Nia said. "What changed your mind?"

Zefra scratched on her slate. "We will have to adjust rations."

Ahjin sighed. "Thank you, Kaito. Zefra, we can work it out. Nia, can we talk in the morning?"

Zefra put her slate in her belt pouch and blew out the lamp. "In the morning. Warmth to you."

"But, Ahjin," Nia said, "I want to hear your story."

Ahjin climbed in a hammock. "Go to bed, Nia."

Izo slipped her a hug and crawled in his own hammock.

Kaito stood by Ahjin until Nia gave up and left for bed. She swung in her hammock until the golden moon set and she finally fell asleep, only to have nightmares about Dad dying in horrible ways.

༄༄༄༄

Someone jiggled her hammock. Nia groaned and rolled over. The hammock swayed.

"Nia." Something tickled her nose. "Wake up. The morning is half gone." The tickle returned.

Someone should get their stupid feathers out of her face before she plucked them. It wasn't time to wake.

Feathers! Nia shot upright. "Ahjin! I forgot you were here."

Ahjin raised an eyebrow. "Am I so forgettable?"

"No, no." She yawned. "But you should tell me why you changed your mind about coming." She tried to sound as happy as she felt, but another yawn swallowed her smile.

"Hmm." Ahjin looked south. "Let's call it a respite."

Nia rolled her eyes. "Respite it is." Trying to pry information from Ahjin when he didn't want to talk was like looking for pearls in clams.

"Breakfast is ready," Ahjin said. "We're waiting to plan with you."

Nia made a face. "Has Zefra been talking to you?"

"She has a point," Ahjin said.

"No," Nia groaned. "I hate plans. I hate Zefra."

"When you finish waking, you'll realize how foolish that sounds. Be glad Zefra didn't hear you."

Nia tumbled from her hammock, stowed it for the day, and stomped to breakfast. She stuffed chopped, raw fish in her mouth and glared at Ahjin. He ignored her.

Zefra and Izo walked over with the captain.

"Bright day, Nia." Zefra pulled out her slate and sat cross-legged. "The first topic is Alaneo."

"What about Dad?" Nia asked. When Ahjin handed her half his papaya, she ate it slowly, licking every bit of the sweet juice.

"How will we identify him?" Zefra asked.

"He has light pink hair, like a hibiscus flower," Nia said. "If he — is dead, we'll look for a match to this." She held up the bracelet Mom had given her. Tears burned behind her eyelids, but she refused to let them fall.

"If he is alive, why would he have stayed away?" Zefra asked.

Nia popped the last of the fruit in her mouth and shook her head. What if they found him, and he still didn't want to come home? What if he didn't want a daughter? She cleared her throat, then did it again.

"Never mind, Zefra." Ahjin patted Nia on the back. "Some things don't fit in a plan. We'll deal with them when the time comes."

"I reviewed the numbers for food," Zefra said. "I hoped Nia would double-check. We do not want to run short in the middle of the ocean."

Nia rolled her eyes. "I'm sure you didn't make a mistake."

Ahjin tapped her foot with his boot. "I'll help you, Zefra, after we finish here."

"We should have enough," Zefra said, "if we fish every day and can restock fresh fruit for the return trip."

Nia yawned. Why worry about hunger in the middle of an ocean of fish? "It will be fine. Are we finished now?"

Zefra crossed off a line on her slate, pressing so hard it squeaked. "Yes, Nia, that is all for now." She stalked away.

Ahjin shook his head. "So, Nia, what are your plans for today?"

Nia licked the last of the juice from her fingers and wiped her hands on her trousers. She smiled at Izo. "I 'plan' to sing all day, except when I'm sailing. Would you like to join me?"

As a professional singer, she did have to practice, but she loved her job and practice was almost as fun as performing. She'd discovered it kept up spirits on an adventure and was another good way to ignore unpleasant questions.

Izo grinned. "I have an hour before my first sailing lesson."

"I'll fly for a while." Ahjin fastened his jacket and flew straight up. After circling the mast, he slipped into a sequence of rolls, somersaults, dives, and spirals.

Izo watched the aerobatics with wide eyes. "'Tis amazing."

"It is beautiful." Nia removed her hairpins and dropped them into her lap. "Will you sing with me?"

"I do not think I sing well," Izo admitted.

"Then," Nia said, "while I rebraid my hair, tell me how you made these wonderful pins."

With enough encouragement to draw out the details, Izo's story filled the time until his lesson. When Ahjin came to collect him, Izo whispered in Nia's ear, "I enjoyed my time with you, Nia."

She turned in time to catch his kiss on her lips instead of her cheek.

Pink swept over his pale face, but he grinned madly as he left with the captain and Ahjin.

Nia touched her lips and smiled. That was lovely.

She was still grinning when the first mate, Malu, found her. Malu's palm-green hair was wind-blown and splashed with salty water, much like Nia's. No braids could keep the ocean wind from pulling tendrils free.

"Well met, Nia," Malu said. "May I join you?"

"I was about to practice my songs," Nia said.

"I don't know many of the land songs," Malu said. "Do you know any sailor chanteys?"

"Many," Nia assured him. She knew the perfect ditty, with so many verses that she and Malu could entertain the others for half an hour or more. She cleared her throat and threw herself into the rollicking song with enthusiasm.

"I went a-sailing," she bellowed.

"Across the wide sea,

"Alas, I found no one
"To be loved by me."

Nia started the chorus and waved her arms with gusto. Malu joined in with nearly as much volume, although not as tunefully.

"To the north and the south,
"To the east and the west,
"I love a-sailing,
"But ladies are best.
"Oh, I love the ladies,
"And ladies love me.
"Oh, where are the ladies?
"The ladies for me."

Malu wouldn't be bad, if he'd pick a key.

"I looked to the west,
"I searched to the east.
"I found a young lady
"Who cooked me a feast."

They repeated the chorus. This time, sailors joined in, and the song echoed across the entire ship. The third verse went as well as the others.

"I gazed to the north,
"I scanned to the south.
"I found a young lady
"With kissable mouth."

Now, this was fun. They sang the chorus again and started the fourth verse. Ahjin walked toward her with Kaito shuffling after him.

"I stared to the south,
"I watched to the north.
"I found a young lady
"To climb in my berth."

"That's enough, Nia," Ahjin scolded. "You can't see them from here, but Izo and Zefra are as red as Zefra's hair." His ears were red, too.

Nia grinned. A little blush wouldn't hurt them. She led the sailors in the chorus and began the fifth verse.

"I peered to the east,
"I spied to the west.
"I found a young lady
"With generous — ow!"

Ahjin's wing thumped Nia on the back of the head and rocked her forward.

"You mangy seagull," she shouted. "Why did you do that?"

"I asked you to stop," Ahjin said. "Pick a different song."

Nia put her fists on her hips. "You're a tyrant."

He bowed his most formal, learned-in-Iskra bow. "As you like; just stop." He flew to the top of the cabin and perched with his back to her.

Kaito glared at Nia, then stood by the cabin wall.

Malu shuffled his feet. "I'd better go fish." He sidled across the ship.

Nia sighed. She'd been trying to help, but the fun was over. It was just a song, not worth the fuss.

Zefra walked over. "Everyone else on this ship is working. Why do you not do anything useful?"

Nia sniffed. That was hardly fair. "I have a shift in a few hours. Until then, I'm keeping everyone in a good mood. That's useful."

Zefra ran her fingers down the edge of her slate. "Not everyone is in a good mood." She turned the slate over in her hands, then crammed it into her belt pouch. "If you want to be with my brother," she burst out, "you need to be steady. You should not flirt with every man you see."

"I wasn't flirting," Nia said. "Can't I be friendly, either?"

Zefra tightened the scarf around her hair. "Love is about commitment and finding a logical match with the same opinions as you. You should look for compatibility and stability."

Nia laughed. "That's even worse than Ahjin's notions. I'm not looking for commitment, just romance. And I don't want stability; I want excitement. I want my heart to pound. Why shouldn't I let my romances float on a wave of dreams? It's the Nokai way. Besides, Izo and I just started flirting. Who is talking about love?"

"Your mother has loved your father all this time," Zefra said. "You could be more like her."

"Mom had three mates," Nia pointed out with a smile.

"But she did not really want the last two," Zefra said.

Nia wrinkled her forehead. "Why do you say that?"

Zefra counted on her fingers. "Your mother saved your father's map for seventeen years."

"That doesn't prove anything," Nia said.

"She has been collecting resources this entire time so you can rescue your father."

Nia shrugged. "She is a kind woman and a loving mom."

"Your father had pink hair," Zefra continued. "Manuai and Zeva have red and orange, both similar, as if she thought of your father. Even her ship's sail is striped with pink."

"Coincidence," Nia said, but she wondered if Zefra was right and Dad hadn't wanted to stay in a serious relationship.

"Your brother and sister have names that express your mother's desire for him to return."

"They do not," Nia said. "They're named after their dads."

"Olina is 'joyful under heaven's protection,'" Zefra said. "I believe your father had been missing only a few years at that time. Your mother hoped he would return."

"Of course she did," Nia spluttered. "But Manuai means 'happy.'"

Zefra ticked off another finger. "Kaliya means 'sea-faring slayer of the thousand-headed dragon.'"

"Zeva means 'sword,'" Nia protested. "Kaliya's name comes from his."

"By the time your brother was born, your mother had given up hope and wanted only revenge."

"Nonsense," Nia said. "If she gave up hope, why did she send me now?"

Zefra shrugged. "To give you both certainty. Perhaps to return his body."

Nia nibbled on her lip. Mom had seemed happy with Manuai and Zeva. Hadn't she? Had she mourned Alaneo for seventeen years? Was he dead, or had he been hiding for so long?

"I think you're wrong," Nia said, "but if not, it's good we'll find out what happened to Dad."

"Yes," Zefra agreed. "And it would also be good if you did not play with my brother's heart." She stalked off, leaving Nia sputtering like a landed fish.

At the next shift, Nia volunteered to help Ahjin prepare the meal. She sang as they chopped fruits, vegetables, and fish (both raw and cooked), and mixed them with the hot rice Kaito tended.

"Did you measure the rice you used?" Zefra asked.

Nia whacked the knife into a pineapple. Stupid measuring.

"We did," Ahjin said. "And we counted the fruits and vegetables. All is within the limits you planned. And we're ready to serve it now."

With four of them to help, it took only a few trips to serve everyone.

They took the last four bowls for themselves, with Kaito making sure Ahjin got one with cooked fish. Ahjin thanked Kaito politely, then rolled his eyes at Nia.

Nia sat beside Ahjin to eat. They chatted while Zefra struggled to write on parchment as the wind tugged at it.

"What are you doing?" Nia asked. "Do you need help?"

"You could hold the corner for me," Zefra said. "I am tracking our progress on my map."

"You don't have to." Nia put a finger on the corner anyway. "The captain keeps a chart."

Zefra shrugged. "I like maps. But I still worry about bandits. In the desert, raiders hide behind sand dunes and rush caravans. I checked our ship, and few of the sailors have weapons. What will we do if bandits attack?"

Nia laughed. "You're right that another ship might mean trouble. We're too far west for the usual shipping lanes, so company would be suspicious. But there are no dunes out here for bandits to hide behind, so we'd see them from a long distance and could decide what to do."

Zefra looked at Nia dubiously. She rolled the map, made a note on her slate, and finished her food. "I will talk to the captain."

~~~~

That evening, a ship appeared on the southern horizon.

"If we're too far west for merchants," Zefra said, "who is that?"

"What sails and flag is it flying?" Nia asked.

Each country had their own customs for sails. The Nokai used colorful patterned sails and an owner's flag. Aolani's sails were striped pale blue and pink, and her flag showed a loom, needle, and pot of dye.

"White sails," Zefra said. "I cannot see the flag well enough."

Not Nokai, then. Nia squinted in the dim light. She didn't see a border on the sails. Not Darrendran, either. Darrendrakar used flags for the kindreds, but their white sails had to be bordered by a color for the country with which they were approved to trade.

She raised her voice. "Ahjin, is Irajahan hunting you again?"

"I don't think so." He joined her at the bulwark. "Why?"

She pointed toward the sail. "Can you tell if that's an Iojif flag or an Iskrin one?"

Iskrins flew boring white sails under a simple clan flag, often the lavender and bronze of the Rikatsu shipbuilders. Iojif sails were also white, but their merchant flags used more colors and details, like the Nokai.

"No, but it looks pink or lavender. Perhaps with a brown triangle?"

"It must be bronze sails," Nia said, "the Rikatsu symbol."

Ahjin peered at the ship again. "Captain! Stop the ship!"

Sailors scattered to furl the sails. One threw out a sea anchor, a series of small platforms on a rod, to drag against the water. The ship slowed to a crawl.

After a minute, Malu joined them at the rail. "Why are we stopping? Your Holiness."

Ahjin pointed to the Iskrin ship. "Jaguars swim well, but Ludik might appreciate bringing his things with him."

"Look, Zefra." Nia pointed to the tall figure barely visible on deck. "It's Ludik! I said there aren't bandits."

Zefra reached for her slate, and Nia sighed.

8. TRAVEL
(OCEAN)

Though every country has sea-going merchants, many of the world's intercultural traders are Nokai.

Everything You Ever Wanted to Know about the Nokailana Islands but Were Too Lazy to Ask

Ludik watched the Nokai ship grow closer. Salt water stung his nose as badly as his suppressed tears. He crumpled the fateful note in his hands and slung his pack over his shoulder, steadfastly ignoring the new constant shadows following him.

Once Nia's ship stopped, it didn't take long to catch up. The two ships pulled close together, and Ludik jumped from one to the other with the help of his guards.

"I will deliver your letter to your wife," the Iskrin captain promised.

"Thank you, captain." Ludik dropped his pack and turned to his friends as the other ship left.

"What happened?" Ahjin asked. "Why aren't you with Nemerra? Is she all right?"

Nia bit her lip. Ahjin hid his worry a little better under his new diplomatic mask, and Izo and Zefra showed the typical Iskrin bland politeness. The Seal stood behind Ahjin, shoulders hunched.

Ludik tugged on his earring. "She's fine, though a little cranky. She shifted to her leopard form to give more room for the babies until they're born. That is typical of a Felid pregnancy. Can I convince you to take me back to Iskra now?"

"Why didn't you go with the Rikatsu?" Nia asked.

"I sent a note to Nemerra," Ludik explained, "with the captain's trading message. He got this in return." He threw the crumpled note at Ahjin. "I could not convince him to ignore it. 'No one ignores the Shri,' he said, 'for someday their life may depend on them.' And then he lectured me about obeying my *master*. I'm an apprentice, not a slave! When he would no longer take me to Iskra, I tried to swim. They caught me and kept me under guard until we caught up to you. So, will you take me back?"

Ludik tugged on his earring again. If he quit his apprenticeship, they couldn't stop him from going to Nemerra.

Nia stared at him open-mouthed while Ahjin smoothed the note.

"Pakai is petika," Ahjin read. "Need more. Bring map or arrange trade. I watch Nemerra. Okechuku."

He handed the note back to Ludik, who reread the brief message from Nemerra at the bottom. It was gracious of Ahjin to skip her loving words.

"If Nia's father found pakai — petika in Iskrit — they want most of the herb to go to the Tukiko healers," Ludik said.

"Is it that important?" Nia asked. "Dad was only looking for an insecticide."

"I studied petika," Ludik said, "though only in theory. I should have recognized the description, but I have other things on my mind. It's a rare medicine used to treat breathing illnesses, the falling sickness, growths, weak blood, inflammation, and parasites, and it is an effective sedative. Your father could make a profitable trade with the healers."

Ahjin whistled. "Nia, your dad might have a real treasure on his hands."

"Which he now needs to share," Zefra pointed out.

Nia smiled. "We can work it out. Who cares about treasure if I find Dad?"

"So will you take me to Iskra now?" Ludik asked.

"If we don't find my dad—" Nia cleared her throat and tried again. "If we don't find Dad, who else can identify this rare and valuable herb for your healers?"

"Ahjin?" Ludik appealed.

"I'm sorry, I think she's right." Ahjin put a hand on Ludik's shoulder.

"I could swim back." He had done fine before the sailors fished him out.

"How well do you swim?" Nia asked.

"As a jaguar, quite well."

"Can you swim all day and float all night for weeks? Can you fight ocean currents and tides?"

Ludik shook his head. It had seemed like a good idea in his desperation. He hadn't bothered to think of the problems he might face.

"Can you catch and eat fish while you swim?" Zefra sounded more curious than scolding.

Ludik shrugged. "I've never tried, but I don't mind raw fish."

"Can you navigate by the stars?" Ahjin asked. "Do you know the route to Iskra?"

"Could you teach me the route?" Ludik blinked hard. Was there any hope at all?

"Maybe," Nia said. "But if you get lost, Nemerra will never see you again."

Ludik tried to swallow the lump in his throat. It was useless. How long would he be separated from Nemerra?

"Excuse me," Captain Inna said. "May we sail again or do we still need to wait?"

"Set sail," Ahjin said.

The captain headed for the tiller. "Set sail!"

Nia patted Ludik's elbow. "I'm sorry you are delayed, but we're glad to have you here."

"Hmph." Ludik looked at the sails that carried him ever farther from Nemerra. Even their rhythmic flapping sounded like her name. Nem-err-a, Nem-err-a.

"There is room to add another hammock," Izo said.

Ludik plodded after Izo and slung his hammock silently. After the others settled, he lay awake for a long time, matching stars to reasons he missed Nemerra. He had as many of those as reasons to love her.

He spun his marriage ring in an endless circle through his ear. When would he return home? Would he make it for the births? What if something went wrong?

♪♪♪♪

In the morning, the first mate added Ludik to the duty roster.

"Do we have birds on board?" Ludik asked Malu.

"Yes, we have chickens." Malu pointed to the coop, tucked in the shade of the captain's cabin. "There were no eggs this morning, though. Maybe tomorrow."

"I meant messenger birds." Ludik pronounced every word carefully in trade tongue.

"We're not some fancy merchant ship," Malu said. "Why would we have messenger birds?"

"So you can send messages," Ludik said.

Malu laughed. "Next time we're in port, you can send a message."

"When will that be?"

"We're going to uninhabited islands, so... when we get back to Nokai-lana." Malu laughed again.

Ludik walked around the corner of the cabin. When he was out of sight, he punched the wall. No messenger birds. No way to send a message to Nemerra.

It wasn't his turn on duty yet, so to keep his mind off Nemerra, he treated splinters and minor injuries and looked for small tasks.

It didn't make him forget.

Nia's babbled speculations were more distracting, reaching a peak when she thought of the dragons.

"Maybe they're called the Dragon Isles because dragons are real." Nia bounced with excitement in the middle of their group of friends.

Ahjin rolled his eyes. "I already told you, I don't know."

"But it makes perfect sense," Nia argued. "The curse is dragons who eat all trespassers! Oh. What if they ate Dad?"

Zefra covered her eyes with her hands.

Izo patted her on the back and grinned at Nia. "Aren't you worried about them eating *us*?"

"Pfft," Nia said. "We'll be fine."

"If a dragon eats us," Ludik said, "we won't be fine." And how would he ever explain that to Nemerra? He'd rather face the dragon.

"Nonsense," Nia said. "Ahjin's too stubborn to go down a dragon's throat, Ludik would claw him to bits, and Zefra's too hot."

Ahjin grinned at Zefra's indignant frown. "Does this deserve a plan, Nia?"

"How can we plan before we know how big the dragons are or what weaknesses they have?" Nia paused. "We should watch for them, though. I'll tell the captain." She darted off.

Ahjin laughed. Izo joined in, but Zefra shook her head, and the Seal looked worried.

"What do you think, Ludik?" Ahjin asked. "Is your healing magic up to dragon injuries?"

Ludik shrugged. "I can heal you from anything an imaginary dragon can do."

Last fall, Nia had wished to meet Darrendrakar dragon-shifters, but there were none, and no evidence of any other kind of dragon, either.

Nia bounced back and grabbed Izo's arm. "Isn't this exciting?"

"I'm glad this is so entertaining for you," Ludik said. "I can think of something to make this trip better for me."

"Sure, Ludik," Nia said. "What do you need?"

"I want to send a message to Nemerra. I already asked Malu about messenger birds. Do you have any other way?"

Nia shook her head. "I'm sorry. No, Ludik, we don't have any way to send messages, unless you think a note in a bottle would actually work. Ahjin could try to convince the gods to deliver one."

Ahjin shook his head. "Makana can't pass it on in Iskra. Resef and Darravani don't do personal messages. Kassian is flying delicately, staying with Resef without interfering. And Irajahan—"

"No, please," Ludik interrupted. "I don't need an explanation for that one. Never mind." He didn't like the cranky Iojif god any more than Ahjin did.

"I'm sorry," Ahjin said. "I hope the journey goes swiftly and you return to Nemerra before your babies are born. Nia, while we aren't too busy, could I talk to you?"

"Sorry, Ahjin." Nia pulled Izo. "I've got things to do."

After Nia was out of hearing, Ahjin sighed. "It's so hard to talk to that girl sometimes. Remind me why I came on this trip?"

"I don't know," Ludik said. "Why *did* you come? I didn't hear the story."

"Never mind." Ahjin ran his fingers through his wild curls and glanced at the Seal.

What did Kaito know? Ludik looked back at Ahjin, whose wings twitched. "You ran away again, didn't you?" He punched Ahjin's shoulder. "Why did you do that?"

Ahjin glared at him and turned invisible.

Stupid question. If Ludik could have, he would have run away himself. He inhaled deeply. There he was. Ahjin's feather-flecked scent was distinctive. He waited until he heard Ahjin's wings rustle, then pounced with perfect aim, ending with a firm grip on Ahjin's arm.

"Got you! So much for invisibility. Try flying now."

Kaito stepped forward, and Ludik turned to block him from Ahjin. He winked, and the somber Seal backed up with a frown.

Ahjin struggled, but then popped back to visibility. He drew himself to his full height, nearly a foot shorter than Ludik, and brushed off his shirt.

When Ludik let go, Ahjin punched him and shot into the air and straight into aerobatics.

Ludik rubbed his stomach, found another sailor, and asked him about sending messages. That sailor didn't have any ideas, either. Neither did the next five.

At bedtime, Ludik counted stars again, while the sailors furled most of the sails for the night. Each twinkle in the sky was an open wound in his heart.

~~~~

Ludik spent two more days missing Nemerra and sleeping little. As he carried out his duties, every muscle was heavy. It seemed Ahjin's wish for a swift journey was nothing but a useless hope. Ludik would be gone from Nemerra for months. He'd miss the babies' births, and what if Nemerra had problems?

Swift journey. Could he make the ship go faster?

Every night, the sailors furled the sails. Most nights, they threw out a sea anchor as well. Why didn't they travel at night?

Ludik hurried through the rest of his shift, then looked for Nia. She wasn't singing with the sailors or encouraging them in their duties. She wasn't with the captain. She wasn't fishing. No one had seen her.

Ludik resumed his search.

Nia laughed above his head, climbing through the rigging with a green-haired sailor. When she reached for another rope, she missed her grip and fell. The sailor tried to grab her and also fell.

Before Ludik took more than a step, a white blur shot past him.

Ahjin grabbed for both falling bodies. He caught Nia's hand and fell with her, wings frantically beating to slow their fall.

He missed the sailor by inches. Malu bounced off the rigging and crashed to the deck.

Ahjin and Nia smacked down a second later.

"Plague fleas," Ludik cursed. "Zefra!"

Zefra and her brother shot around the corner and jerked to a halt.

"Right." She ran for Ludik's healing kit while Ludik, Kaito, and Izo raced toward the victims.

Ludik scanned all three quickly. Ahjin and Nia were moving, but the sailor was not.

"Take those two." Ludik knelt by Malu and turned him face up. Bruises already flowered across his face. Blood ran from his hand, which had broken bones sticking through the skin. He was breathing, though.

Zefra slid next to Ludik, already opening his kit.

"How are they?" Ludik called over his shoulder.

"Ahjin is just lying here," Izo said, "though his eyes are open."

Nia burst into noisy tears and threw herself on Kaito's shoulder.

"Does anything look broken?" Ludik asked. "Zefra, bandages, ointment, splints." He straightened the sailor's bones and pulled them back under the skin.

"I'm fine," Ahjin mumbled.

Ludik let out the breath he'd been holding and stitched Malu's hand while the sailor was unconscious.

"Zefra, put the splint here." Ludik pointed with one finger while he held everything in place. "Put a dab of the ointment on the split. Don't worry about rubbing it in. Now the bandage."

When she got it halfway wrapped around the sailor's broken hand, he took over. Zefra went to scold Nia, and Ludik closed his eyes to concentrate on his magic. Bones were stronger if they healed slowly, but he gave them a good head start.

He emerged from his partial trance a while later and found the sailor watching him.

Malu's eyes were red, and his mouth was pressed tight, but he didn't speak.

"Fair winds, Malu." Ahjin sat by the sailor. He kept his shoulders hunched and his wings curved around himself. "How do you feel?"

"Mmph," Malu said.

Ahjin nodded sympathetically. "Sounds about right. When our healer gives you a tea, tell him to drink it himself. You've never tasted something so nasty in your life."

Ludik grunted. Nothing was wrong with his teas.

Malu cleared his throat. "Is he a good healer? Will I use my hand again?"

"He's a great healer," Ahjin said, "with magic to make you better. He went all the way across the ocean for an apprenticeship with the best healer there is. I'm sure it will be fine." He glanced at Ludik.

"No worries," Ludik said. "You'll be as good as new in a few weeks."

Ahjin walked away, returning with Nia.

She rubbed a large bump on her head. "I'm so-orry, Malu," she sobbed.

"When will you really grow up?" Ludik asked. "Think about the consequences of your actions."

Nia covered her face with her hands.

"Enough," Ludik said. "It was an accident. Let me look at your head. Ahjin's, too."

Kaito and Izo drew Malu's arms over their shoulders and helped him away.

Ludik examined both of his friends while Zefra cleaned up his supplies. Nia's bump would heal without a concussion. Ahjin merely had bruises and strained wing muscles.

"Since I have you as a captive audience," Ludik said, "I have a question. Can this ship go faster or travel at night?"

Nia sniffled. "Not at night, but you can talk to the captain about going faster in daylight."

Zefra bit her lip and pulled out her slate. "Will that be too fast to fish?"

"We can fish before we sail each morning," Nia said.

Ludik treated the injuries and then hunted down the captain to ask her about going faster.

"I didn't know we were in a hurry," Inna said. "If you wish, we can go faster in the day. Night comes early in springtime, though."

"Why can we not continue after dark?" Ludik asked. "We are out of the regular shipping lanes. Even if we met another ship, the lights on board will warn us. The wind does not stop blowing at night. We have enough crew to divide in three full shifts instead of a short crew at night. We can steer by the stars."

"You're forgetting one important point," Inna said. "We still need to watch for rocks, storms, and other possible dangers."

"So? Where is the problem?"

"We can't see in the dark," Inna said.

Ludik laughed. "I volunteer for the night shift. *I* can see in the moonlight." He paused. "The Iskrins can also, a bit."

"Let me discuss it with the others," the captain said.

"Surely it will be good to shorten our voyage," Ludik said.

"I will talk to the others." That was the captain's last word.

Ludik did not get an answer by nightfall, and once again stayed up late counting stars. Exhaustion finally dragged him into sleep for a few short hours.

⌇⌇⌇⌇

In the morning, Captain Inna gave Ludik a new duty shift to distribute to the sailors.

Ludik worked his way down the list, informing each man and woman of their new assignment. He was almost to the bottom of the list when he noticed an increased number of sailors assigned at night. Could it be? He hurried through the last few, then found his own name at the end. *Ludik, night watch.*

His whoop of triumph drew the attention of the entire ship, but Ludik didn't care. He ran to tell his friends.

"Why the screaming, Ludik?" Nia sat in a corner with Izo, holding his hand.

Ludik's grin hurt his cheeks. "Captain Inna agreed to sail at night."

"How wonderful," Nia said.

Ludik spent the rest of the day in a dizzy haze of joy, anticipating a night shift where they sailed toward the Dragon Isles so he could return to Nemerra sooner.

It was still hours before his watch when he spotted another ship with one Nokai-patterned sail and other plain white sails.

"What do mismatched sails mean?" Ludik asked Nia.

"What do you mean, mismatched?" Nia ran to the bulwark and peered ahead of them. "Some of the Nokai use a variety of colors."

"They're white," Ludik said, "except for the mainsail. And they ran up a plain black flag."

"Crooked shark's tooth," Nia swore. "It's pirates!"

9. PIRATES
(OCEAN)

Better to lose the anchor than the whole ship.
Nokai Proverb

Zefra leaned over the railing to see the pirate ship approaching from the west. Despite the obvious danger, she found herself unimpressed with the merchant vessel. Iskrins took meticulous care of their ships to spare precious timber, but this one was so battered it obviously was not in the hands of its owners. Unfortunately, they could not count on the pirates being as sloppy in a fight as they were with their ship. Even a rusty sword would kill.

"Pirates!" Nia bellowed again. "Throw on more sail!"

The black pirate flag flapped in the breeze, above a mix of Nokai and Iskrin sails. Or perhaps they were Nokai and Iojif sails. White was white.

Fleeing was not an option. The pirate ship was bigger than their small fishing craft, with more sails. Could they fight?

Zefra took the spyglass from Nia and examined the other deck, which was full of men with weapons. Fighting would only end in death.

"I told you there would be bandits," Zefra said. "Are you ready to plan now?"

Nia glared at her and stomped toward the captain at the stern, with everyone following but the sailor on watch.

"Captain Inna," Nia said. "The good news is that it's flying a black flag."

The captain's hunched shoulders relaxed a little. "That's something."

"Why?" Zefra asked.

"The black flag," the captain explained, "means they are out for loot. They'll steal everything not nailed down, but if we don't resist, they won't kill anyone. Pirates who fly a red flag are merciless killers. Whether you resist or not, you won't survive."

"Wouldn't a black flag mean death?" Ahjin asked.

"Red is for blood," Nia said. "They'll paint your decks red with blood."

"Blood does not make good paint." Zefra kept her face straight. "And we need our supplies. We cannot let the pirates take them."

Nia rolled her eyes, and Ahjin covered a grin.

"We will try to outrun the pirates," the captain said, "but if we can't, we have a bigger problem."

"What's that?" Ahjin asked.

The captain cleared her throat. "They take *anything* they want."

Ahjin furrowed his brow.

"And half our sailors are women," the captain finished.

Ahjin turned red, and Ludik clenched his fists.

Zefra felt her own face flame. "Can we win if we fight?"

The captain shrugged. "They have more fighters and weapons. Do any of you have battle magic?"

Zefra shook her head. "I only have fire, and I cannot burn an entire ship fast enough."

"Wood is fuel," Nia said.

"Without something to help it burn faster, and a distraction to keep the pirates from putting it out, it will not work," Zefra restated.

"What if I flew over invisibly and cut down their sails?" Ahjin asked.

"Don't be ridiculous," Nia said. "There are too many lines. By the time you cut enough to help, they'd fill the air with arrows. Invisibility won't help against that."

Ahjin shrugged, then narrowed his eyes at the Seal. "Kaito, were you at Kairri?"

Kaito flinched and looked at his feet.

Ahjin grabbed his shoulders. "We don't have time for guilt, whether or not you deserve it. Were. You. At. Kairri?"

Kaito nodded, turning pale.

Ahjin turned to Zefra. "Are the pirates Nokai?"

The captain flushed an angry red. "That's quite an assumption to make."

"I saw sailors from all four lands," Zefra said.

"I meant no offense." Ahjin raised his hands. "I should have phrased it differently. I was merely clarifying a problem. Kaito can't fight."

"Won't, you mean," Inna said.

"Can't." Ahjin stiffened his chin. "Certain Pinnipeds can't fight other Darrendrakar, even to defend themselves. If he does, he faces death from Darravani. I won't let him fight if there's a chance of Darrendrakar among the pirates."

"I guess we can't fight." Nia tugged on a braid. "We're too outnumbered."

"Can we hide any valuables?" Zefra asked. "Does this ship have any smuggling holes?"

Inna looked to the side and rubbed her nose. "Maybe we could hide a little."

"Can we hide any of the women?" Ludik asked.

"Oh, sure, that's easy," Nia said. "Most of them can jump overboard and hide underwater."

And Zefra would be the only woman left on board, at the mercy of the pirates. She swayed, and Izo put his arm around her. She pulled herself upright and brushed her hands down her robe. "Ahjin, did you bring spare clothes?"

"Yes." Ahjin spun on one heel and ran for his pack.

"Pick out what we *must* not lose," Zefra said. "Izo, have the men take over for any women on shift. Nia, take your map. Can you still swim with two swords?"

"I'll hover under our ship," Nia said. "We can throw a rope overboard for me to grab."

Zefra fumbled with her sash. She shoved her sword at Nia and then elbowed Izo to remove his.

Ahjin returned and handed Zefra a bundle of clothing. He pulled the silver star from his neck and hung it on Nia.

"Do you have anything else that must be hidden, Your Holiness?" the captain asked.

"Nothing else is valuable," Ahjin said. "Zefra, go. We'll work on the rest of it."

Zefra ran to the cabin. She pulled off her robe and put on Ahjin's pants. They were a bit too long, but the extra length tucked into her boots.

She grabbed some cactus needles from her belt pouch and pinned the wing slits closed before she slipped on the much-too-big shirt. Ahjin had powerful chest muscles to support his wings. The shoulder seams landed far down her upper arms, and the sleeves pooled over the long cuffs that fit under Ahjin's bracers.

Zefra looked down at herself. The fine, violet silk draped well across her chest. Years of short desert rations left her scrawny, without Nia's curves, but she still looked like a girl. She removed the shirt and rummaged through the cabin for a long silk scarf. Zefra wrapped it tightly around her chest and put the shirt back on. Better. She wrapped her own dun scarf around her hair, making sure every bit of red was covered.

She took a deep breath and ran back on deck.

The captain ran into the cabin carrying a few valuables and returned minutes later with empty hands.

The ship was as wild as Nia's party, with the men hauling at the sails while the women slid over the stern one or two at a time.

Despite the fishing craft's desperate attempt at speed, the pirate ship grew ever closer.

Ahjin was arguing fiercely with Kaito. The Seal shook his head emphatically. Zefra hurried to help.

"You have to go," Ahjin said to Kaito, probably not for the first time. "I can't have your death on my conscience."

Kaito clutched Ahjin's sleeve and shook his head again.

Ahjin held his breath and looked at the sky.

This would take another tactic.

"Kaito," Zefra said, "we understand you are worried about Ahjin, but you are endangering him."

Kaito's mouth dropped open.

"If Ahjin has to worry about your safety," Zefra said, "then it will distract him from his own. You need to escape so he can think of himself."

Kaito narrowed his eyes. He looked at Ahjin, then nodded. Zefra faced the other direction until a large splash sounded off the ship.

"Thank you." Ahjin eyed Zefra's disguise. "Not bad, but get in the crow's nest, and don't come down, no matter what. Don't even stick your head above the edge." He shook her shoulders. "Do you hear me, Zefra?"

"What about you?" Zefra clutched his arms to keep her teeth from clacking together. "You are too valuable to risk. Why have you not already gone invisible?"

"How can I help if I'm invisible and hiding? No one knows who I am. I look like any Iojif." Ahjin threw Kaito's abandoned pants behind a rowboat and shoved her toward the mast.

"Not quite." Zefra touched a lightning scar on his hand. "If you will not think of yourself, think of the rest of us. You would make a valuable hostage and put the rest of us in danger. Help us by not being a temptation for the pirates."

Ahjin clenched his jaw. "Get up that mast!"

Zefra climbed as fast as she could, without looking down, and slithered into the basket. It was small, meant to hold a standing watchman securely, but she wedged herself into the bottom, glad for once of her slight build.

The mast swayed with the motion of the ship. The basket was woven loosely, so Zefra pressed her face to a crack. Half a stone's throw below, the deck was visible in stripes, and she moved from one crack to another to try to see it all.

The last of the women went overboard. The Nokai men and Ludik took up posts. Their shoulders were tight, and they twitched with every glance north.

Zefra did not see Ahjin. She moved to a different crack and searched another corner of the deck. Still not there.

The crow's nest rocked. Zefra gasped.

"Hush," Ahjin whispered.

She glanced up, careful not to expose herself. No one was visible, but one of the ropes running down the mast was squeezed against the wood. She reached her finger up slowly until she felt a boot sole on the edge of the nest. Ahjin had gone invisible, as only he could. Zefra breathed a silent sigh of relief and pressed her eye back to a crack.

The other ship pulled alongside and furled sails, bringing with it a horrid stench. Grappling hooks flew across the gap and bit into Aolani's ship. The ropes creaked, and the ships banged together, wood squealing in protest. An anchor dropped from the pirate ship.

A line of ferocious warriors surged over the side and spread across the deck with loaded crossbows and drawn knives. They were a mix of races but shared a common distaste for bathing.

Zefra pinched her nose against their stink and tried to breathe quietly through her mouth.

"Give us your treasures!" one of the men roared. Zefra could not tell his race. His skin was so covered with tattoos that the original color could not be seen, even on his shaved head. He wore Nokai ocean pants with a hacked-off Darrendran tunic and a brightly embroidered Iskrin belt. The color combination was almost painful, even with plain Iojif ankle boots.

The other pirates cheered and separated to surround each sailor. They took the harpoons and all the knives, even the tiny quill-sharpeners. Zefra mouthed a prayer of thanks to Resef when they did not search Ludik's boots. At least there would be one knife left on board besides her own and the tiny hairpin blades.

Zefra identified Malu at the tiller by his palm-green hair. The first mate raised his hands. "We're on a rescue mission. We have no treasure or trade goods, only food."

The pirate leader pressed his sword against Malu's neck until drops of blood ran down. "I don't believe you."

Ludik took a step, then froze when a pirate leveled his crossbow at him.

Malu's hands shook. His unbroken hand clenched and unclenched. "I promise."

"If you're lying, you'll be sorry." The pirate looked around the ship. "You'll all be sorry."

Zefra popped her head above the crow's nest and glared at the pirate. An invisible foot pressed on her head until she settled again.

"Search the ship!"

Half the pirates stayed to guard the sailors, and half roamed the ship,

tearing apart planks and opening barrels. They carried most of the food
to their own ship. The chickens squawked like tortured souls as the
pirates dragged them away. The scruffy pirates who searched the
captain's cabin emerged with a small bag of coins.

"Lucky you," the pirate's leader said. "I'm feeling generous today.
We'll leave you the last of the food so you can get home. We'll even let
you keep your fishing gear. You're welcome."

The pirate backed away from Malu, and his friends herded Ludik and
the Nokai into a huddle. "Stay there until we're gone, or we'll shoot you
as full of holes as a fishing net."

The pirates retreated, crossbowmen last. They took the grappling
hooks with them and shoved the ships apart. Their anchor came up, and
their sails expanded in the wind.

Crossbows remained aimed at Aolani's crew.

As soon as the pirate ship was gone, Ludik ran for Malu.

"I'll keep watch," Ahjin called.

An invisible hand helped Zefra wiggle out of the crow's nest and
climb down the first cubit of the mast.

Zefra crept down the rest of the way, making sure to have three
contact points at every moment to compensate for her shaking muscles.
She reached the deck and leaned against the mast.

Chaos reigned again, less frantic but as somber as before. If earlier
was a party, this was a funeral.

Ludik bandaged Malu while the other men stretched over the side,
throwing out ropes for the women and Kaito to climb.

Kaito came first, and when his head and bare shoulders passed the
railing, Zefra turned her head. When she thought it had been long
enough, she peeked back. Kaito was safely dressed and already following
Ahjin.

Nia climbed up next, swords jangling from a rope over her shoulder.
She patted her hairpins and returned Ahjin's star, then walked toward
Zefra.

Of course, she needed to inventory to make new plans. They could
do that while the rest of the women caught up and climbed aboard.

"They took most of the food." Zefra reached for her slate to figure
the new numbers, but her belt pouch was gone. She headed for the
captain's cabin, hoping it was still there along with the belt her little

sisters had embroidered for her. "We will have to take time to fish every day, even if the trip lasts longer. I have not counted the supplies yet, but I know there will not be enough."

Her slate was thrown in the corner with her sash, but her robe was slashed to pieces. She leaned against the wall for a minute before grabbing her slate and belt.

"I think we lost all our weapons, too," Zefra said as she exited the cabin.

She looked up from her slate and realized she was talking to herself. Nia had passed Zefra and gone to talk to Malu and Ludik. That would not help the planning.

A footstep landed behind her, and Ahjin appeared. "I can't see the pirate ship anymore," he said. "Here's your bow and Izo's knives. I'm sorry I couldn't carry your staffs as well."

Zefra blinked back tears. Izo had made her iron-bound staff; he could make her another.

"I have bad news for you, too," Zefra smoothed Ahjin's pants over her hips. "The pirates destroyed my robe. I—"

"It's fine, Zefra," Ahjin said. "You may keep my clothes."

"Thank you." Zefra blushed. What would Mother say if she saw her so immodestly dressed? "We are in more trouble, Ahjin. I do not know if we can still finish this trip."

"Have you talked to Nia yet?"

"I tried. Will you help me inventory while I wait for her to come back?" Zefra asked.

"I'll take port," Ahjin said.

Zefra went starboard. It took far too little time. They had half a barrel of vegetables and one of rice. All the salted fish was gone, and most of the produce, though she found a few runaway fruits behind barrels. When she worked her way back to Ahjin, he had a similarly short list.

"But I have good news," he said. "Look what I found hiding in the oarlocks of the rowboat." He reached behind his back and pulled out her staff and Izo's. "The pirates must have mistaken them for oars in their hurry."

"How did those get there?" Zefra grabbed her staff and ran her hands over the familiar iron bands.

Ahjin shrugged. "The last person I saw there was Kaito, but people were running around a lot."

Zefra swung it in a one-handed defensive arc. "No matter. I'm glad to have it back."

Nia, Ludik, and Malu hurried toward them.

"Ludik, did you save your boot knife?" Zefra asked.

"Yes," Ludik said. "Nobody ever sees it."

"That is a relief." Zefra tucked her staff under her arm.

"We have a problem," Nia said.

"I know," Zefra said. "I told you, we have little food and almost no weapons."

"But—" Nia said.

"I know," Zefra said, "we can fish, and you still want to find your father. I think we are less than halfway to the Dragon Isles. You do still have the map?"

Nia held it up. "But, Zefra—"

Zefra took the map and unrolled it. "Let me see. No, we are a bit past halfway. Will it be better to continue, or to go home, restock, and try again?"

"Zefra," Ludik said.

"Oh, you will not want to delay." Zefra pulled out her slate. "If we ration, mm-hm, and then fish, mmm." She rubbed out numbers and tried again.

"Zefra!" Nia yelled. "The Nokai women swam home."

"That will make rationing easier," Zefra said. "So half the number of people means the rations will last twice as long... Wait. What did you say?"

10.FIGHT

(OCEAN)

When two quarrel, both are to blame.

Iskrin Proverb

"Half our sailors are gone," Nia repeated. "Even the captain abandoned us." Her blood surged like a tidal wave. If it was so shark-fin-important to plan, why wouldn't Zefra listen when she told her what was going on?

"Why did you not stop them?" Zefra asked, as if Nia could have retrieved them with nets.

"Maybe because there were *pirates* above us and if I chased the deserters, I might be seen! Besides, I can't swim with two swords." Nia shoved the swords at Zefra.

"Why did they leave?" Zefra asked. "We had a good plan."

"Plans can't fix everything. They were scared. Curses *and* pirates were too much." Nia wished the other Nokai had a little more faith events would work out. Besides, there was no such thing as a curse.

"There's no curse," Ahjin said.

Nia nodded. "I don't think that matters. They're too far now, and they scattered. We can't round them all up, even if they wanted to come back. More importantly, are we continuing to the Dragon Isles or are we going home?"

"Do we still have enough sailors?" Zefra asked.

Nia smiled. "We won't have much free time, but we can still do it. The ship isn't that big."

"Malu." Ahjin's call echoed impressively, as he had learned from his blustering god, Irajahan. When the first mate reached them, Ahjin said, "You're promoted to captain. Please redo duty shifts with all of us included. Whatever we don't know yet, we'll learn. Tell us what else you need. I'll tell you our route soon."

"I'll have the schedule for you in less than an hour," Malu said. "May I promote a new mate?"

Ahjin nodded, and Malu walked away.

"Zefra," Ahjin said, "please tell everyone about the food."

"We have enough for perhaps a week," Zefra said, "almost all rice. There are a few vegetables, and any fish we catch."

"That's enough to get to the Isles." Nia nearly cheered. They could still look for Dad. And even if Ludik didn't want to go, finding the pakai was important for the healers. He'd feel differently if Nemerra ever needed it.

"But 'tis not enough food to get home again," Zefra said.

"We can restock for the return trip," Nia said. "The Isles are closer. I don't know if we can make it home without more food."

"I thought we knew little about the Dragon Isles," Izo said. "Do we know if there is food there? Or what kind, or when it grows?"

"I'm sure there is," Nia said. "There has to be something, somewhere in the Isles."

"I want to go back," Ludik said. "The Tukiko can send another expedition later. And if you ask the sailors, I think they will vote with me."

"One for and one against," Nia said. "Zefra?"

"I would like to continue, but without assurance of food, I vote to return. It is possible the Isles are uninhabited because there is no food."

"Two against. Izo?" Nia smiled at the handsome Iskrin.

Izo looked at his sister and back to Nia. "I abstain. Any way I vote, I'm in trouble."

Nia frowned at him. "I'm disappointed in your sense of adventure. Still two against and one for. Kaito?"

Kaito bowed his head and stepped behind Ahjin.

"Fine, I'll count your vote with Ahjin. Ahjin?"

Ahjin paused. "Do the sailors get to vote?"

"Not helpful," Nia muttered. "And no, the sailors were hired for a job. They don't get a vote. I'll cast Mom's vote. She owns this ship, and she wants us to keep going. That makes two for and two against. Your turn, Ahjin."

"'Tis cheating," Zefra mumbled, crossing her arms.

Ahjin rubbed his chin. "I'm not sure she'd think that under the circumstances, but if you insist." He flexed his wings for a minute. "The pirate ship headed southeast. I hope our bad luck is over, and we won't see it again. If going on will take us out of its territory, it might be better."

Kaito tugged on Ahjin's sleeve.

Ahjin brushed him off and continued, looking at each person as he mentioned them. "If we go south right now, we might run right into those pirates again. And who knows if Zefra will get the chance to come back to explore for Kassian. The healers need that herb, and if we bring it back this time, Ludik won't get sent out again even closer to the babies' birth. Nia and her mother deserve to know what happened to Alaneo. Izo and I don't mind going along to help you, do we? It is more time to spend with our friends."

He grinned at Izo, who pursed his lips dubiously.

Kaito sighed and hunched his shoulders.

Nia squealed and clapped her hands. "That's a yes. Let me tell Malu!"

She ran to the new captain and babbled a long explanation. When he stared at her blankly, she simplified. "Head north! We go on!"

He folded his arms and glared at her.

Nia glared back. "I told you, we go on."

Malu growled orders to the sailors. He flexed his hands, then gasped and cradled the broken one. "The new roster. The night shift has only the minimum." He shoved a scroll at Nia. "Now get out of my way."

Nia skipped back and found Izo and Zefra polishing and oiling their swords in the lamplight. Ludik worked on his boot knife as carefully, even though it hadn't been dunked in the ocean.

Nia gleefully read the new duty shifts out loud. Ludik watched her until she read his name on the night shift, then turned back to his knife.

"But most shifts start tomorrow," Nia said, "so I'll see you in the morning. Ludik, I'm not tired yet. I'll keep you company for a while."

She kissed Izo's cheek and let most of her friends and sailors make their way to bed. Ludik wedged himself in the crow's nest facing north. Nia skipped off to a good vantage point halfway up the rigging and waved to Ludik.

The setting sun outlined each sail and line on Mom's beautiful ship, shining like hope.

They were going on. After six thousand days without Dad, she would find him. This called for a song. She hummed a hymn of thanks to Makana and then added a celebration tune. By the time she was finally tired enough to climb down, she was full of hope and enthusiasm. Nothing could go wrong now.

<center>~~~~</center>

When Nia rolled from her hammock in the morning, most of the sailors already bustled around in a disgustingly awake mood. Only Ludik still slept, as proper people should.

Ahjin handed her a cup of water and a miserly portion of rice.

She stirred the rice with her spoon, looking for any fish. Any vegetables? Any pepper flakes, even.

"This jus' rice," she mumbled.

Ahjin nodded. "Zefra knows the proper rations to get us to the Isles. We'll see vegetables in our lunch rice, and if we're lucky, we'll catch fish for dinner. Eat your yummy rice and wake up. You're on duty in ten minutes."

Nia groaned. Whose idea was it to have the sun rise so early in the morning?

Ahjin nudged her foot any time she stopped eating. With his annoying help, she was ready by the time the new first mate dragged her away.

She shuffled through her chores for an hour until the morning sun sank into her bones and warmed her mood. By the time the mate asked her to teach Izo the names of each sail and line, she felt like her usual self and bounced around the ship until she found him.

Nia pointed out the mainsail and named its lines until the mate left, then she smiled at Izo. "We have plenty of time for this. Let me show you the back side of the sail."

Izo scratched his head. "Is there something different about the back?"

"Why, yes." Nia pulled him to the sheltered side of the sail, out of sight of the crew. "If you come here and look closely..." She pointed at a line of wood grain in the mast.

Izo leaned closer, and she leaned in with him.

"I do not see anything."

He turned to look at her, and she kissed him.

His lips were warm, and he leaned into her before he pulled away with a gasp. He licked his lips and blinked at her, brown eyes a little dazed.

She smiled and ran one hand up his bare arm.

He turned bright red but smiled and leaned toward her again.

"Excuse me," Ahjin said.

Nia jumped.

Izo leaped away and tripped over his own feet.

"Sailing lessons are that way." Ahjin pointed around the mast.

Izo stood and pointed to a line. "What is that rope, Nia?" Red crawled up his cheeks again.

Nia stuck out her tongue at Ahjin, who shook his head and left. She and Izo went over every line for three sails and practiced four knots. Izo worked solemnly, until Nia couldn't stand it anymore.

"Come here," she whispered, pulling the adorable Iskrin back to the sheltered side of the sail.

"But—" Izo said.

She put a finger across his lips and leaned toward him.

"I thought you wanted to flirt with me," she whispered in his ear.

"I — I do," he stammered. "But this is not usually how a courtship goes."

Nia giggled. "Maybe not in Iskra." She moved her mouth closer to his ear. "But I'm Nokai, and we like kissing when we flirt."

"Ahem," Ahjin said.

When had he shown up again? Nia dropped her head against Izo's chest as he gulped.

"I do hate to keep interrupting," Ahjin said, "but do you suppose you could actually train Izo?"

"I am training Izo." Nia turned to face Ahjin. The moldy seagull had squinty lines at the corners of his eyes. "I'm training him to kiss me."

Izo flamed red again. "I'm sorry, Ahjin. I mean — Ohhh, I will go now." He dashed around the mast and ran for the fishing nets.

"Now see what you did," Nia said. "Mind your own current."

"We've already talked about this." Ahjin patted her shoulder and walked after Izo.

Nia crossed her arms. If Ahjin would leave them alone, Izo wouldn't let a few cultural differences stand in the way of their fun. He said he wanted to learn Nokai culture, and anytime he changed his mind, he could tell her. He was as much of an adult as she was and could choose for himself.

She sighed. And speaking of being adult, maybe she should work for a while to help her quest succeed. Nia walked toward the galley. It was time to prepare the food, and she wanted to make sure her rice had flavor.

Zefra was already at the table, chopping a measly portion of vegetables into a bowl. Ahjin's shirt hung awkwardly on her despite the rolled-up sleeves.

A portly sailor washed the last carrot in a tiny pile.

"I'll go get more vegetables." Nia barely took a step before Zefra grabbed her sleeve.

"This is all for now," Zefra said. "I have nearly finished. Please cook the rice; I have already measured it for you."

"If you're so efficient," Nia said, "maybe you don't need my help."

Zefra set the knife on the table and faced her. A muscle twitched in her jaw. "We all need to help and follow the plan."

Nia slammed her fists on her hips. "Your *plan* is ruining my fun."

"My plan is *saving* your mission." Pink crept up Zefra's neck from her borrowed collar to her ears. "You are not practical."

Nia scowled. "I told you I don't need your help."

"You do not help, and you distract the boys, too." The pink reached Zefra's ears and darkened to rose.

"You're bossy!" Nia shouted.

"You. Are. Lazy." Zefra clipped off each word.

"You are an intruder on my ship."

"You are useless," Zefra hissed. "We do not need you."

"We don't need *you*," Nia shouted, stepping closer to Zefra. If only she had enough height to stare *down* at her instead of up. She dropped into Iskrit and hauled out the meanest insults she knew.

Zefra turned as red as her hair and groped for the knife. "You stay away from my brother!"

"This is Mom's ship, and I'm in charge!" Nia yelled. She leaned forward to whisper, "Your brother likes me better than you."

Zefra waved the knife in Nia's face and flame burst from the hilt to the tip of the blade.

Nia reached behind her and grabbed Zefra's staff from against the wall.

The bulky sailor ducked around Zefra. As soon as he ran out the door, he screamed about fire and knives and girls out of control. If she hadn't been angry at Zefra, Nia would have translated it so they could laugh together.

A loud whistle pierced her ears.

"Both of you, stop right now!" Ahjin rushed through the doorway and stood between the girls.

Izo grabbed a water bucket and ducked under the staff. "Give me the knife, sister." He jiggled the bucket. "Drop it in here."

Nia raised the staff again. Someone pinned her arms to her side while Ahjin wrenched the staff from her hands.

"I said stop. Ludik, take her out."

As she was dragged from the galley, Nia saw Izo throw the bucket of water over the flaming knife. Ludik held her on the deck until Izo dragged out Zefra.

The sailors stood at a distance and watched with nervous faces.

Ahjin stood between them. "What is wrong with you girls? You're *friends*. Why are you doing this?"

"She called me a—" Zefra stopped and blushed.

"She told me to—" Nia looked at Izo and shut her mouth.

Ahjin closed his eyes and drummed his fingers on crossed arms. "Do I need to string you both upside-down from the mast?"

Nia gasped. "You wouldn't dare!"

Ahjin glared at her. "I would. And if you don't behave, I will. You two are banished to opposite sides of the ship until I decide you can be nice.

Izo, keep your sister port after she finishes lunch. Ludik, keep Nia starboard. And don't make me do this again."

Izo led Zefra back to the galley.

Ludik stuffed Nia into a rowboat. He sat on the edge and carved lines into the edge of the boat.

"Is that necessary?" Nia finally asked.

"You tell me." Ludik's voice was mild, but he didn't sheathe his knife. "I thought you would help me go home to Nemerra quickly. Will you?"

"Yes," Nia mumbled, wrapping her arms around herself.

Ludik touched his earring. "You could have fooled me. Is this the way an adult behaves among the Nokai? What kind of leader are you?"

Nia burst into tears. He was right. She had acted nothing like a leader, or even an adult.

Zefra was probably scared after the pirates. She'd been stuck on board, in danger of being discovered, while Nia was safely underwater and out of sight. Even though Zefra's plans were unnecessary, she meant well.

How could Nia repay her with ingratitude and insults? Her insults weren't even true. Zefra wasn't a — never mind, she just wasn't. Nia would be lucky if Izo ever talked to her again after Zefra told him what she'd said.

"I've ruined my friendship with Zefra," Nia wailed to Ludik.

"You could apologize," Ludik said.

Nia flinched. "If she'll ever look at me again." Nevertheless, she had to try. She stifled her sobs and composed an apology. If she was old enough to flirt with the boys, she was old enough to make amends.

11.REVELATION
(OCEAN)

Irajahan's priests are encouraged to marry and pass on their blood, but He is a jealous god and does not tolerate divided loyalty.

Handbook for Winds

As the girls were dragged out of sight in opposite directions, Ahjin still didn't understand what they'd been fighting about, but it was ridiculous. Somehow, he had to calm things again. It wasn't as if they didn't already have enough other problems — too little food, even for their small crew, and all their missions in danger of failure. Fighting among themselves was not helpful.

When Ludik glanced in the bottom of the rowboat and sheathed his knife, Ahjin knew they were halfway back to normal. It wasn't long before Zefra emerged and piled Izo with bowls of rice and vegetables. He delivered food to the sailors while she brought Ahjin his own lunch.

"I'm sorry," she said, face as red as her hair. "I will not let Nia goad me in the future."

"I hope not." Ahjin nodded toward the rowboat. "Be sure you apologize to her, too, and to the captain and sailors."

"Now?"

"If you think you can't apologize properly yet, you can wait."

He blew on the hot rice, savoring the addition of vegetables. Not enough to fill his rumbling belly, but better than nothing. Breakfast had been neither filling nor flavorful.

Zefra nodded, lips pressed together, and took two bowls to the rowboat. She hovered near the boat, then shook her head without looking over the edge, handed both bowls to Ludik, and left.

On her next trip, Malu flinched when she handed him a bowl, and she took a step backward, hiding her hands behind her back. Malu bellowed orders, and the sailors ran to sailing posts and the nets. Zefra picked up a mop and set to work cleaning the deck.

Now that was a good idea.

Ahjin handed his empty bowl to Kaito and walked to Ludik. An untouched bowl sat on the edge of the rowboat. "It's time to let her out."

Ludik groaned. "She stays out of trouble when she's confined."

Ahjin leaned over the edge of the boat. In the bottom, Nia rocked herself, tear tracks on her cheeks and eyelashes matted into wet spikes. "Nia!"

She flinched and bashed her arms into the side of the boat. "Ow. Slimy eels. What do you want?" She wiped her nose on the back of her hand.

Ahjin handed her the rice. "Eat, and come mop half the deck."

"Who died and made you captain?" Nia shoveled rice into her mouth.

Ahjin shrugged. "If that's the way you want it, I'm sure Malu will put you on swabbing duty for the rest of the trip."

Nia swallowed the last of her lunch. "Never mind. Am I allowed out now?"

Ahjin raised an eyebrow at Ludik.

"Yes, I'll keep an eye on her." Ludik grinned. "Does that mean she's taking my turn swabbing?"

"Sure does." Ahjin slapped Ludik on the shoulder and walked off to talk to the captain. It seemed like a good idea to let both girls do a heavier portion of the cleaning for a while. It would give them time to think. If nothing else, it would make them too tired to cause more trouble.

Malu eagerly agreed to the change in duties but insisted someone relay any further messages from either of the girls. "I don't want them coming near me again. For any reason."

If Ahjin didn't know the girls so well, he might feel the same way.

～～～～

It took all afternoon for the girls to scrub and sand the deck to Ahjin's pretended standards. When they finished, he sent Ludik to give Izo another sailing lesson while he took Zefra for hers. Nia agreed to teach Kaito.

Zefra, unsurprisingly, was a quick study. She already knew knots from their last voyage, and most of the names of the sails and lines.

"And stay away from Nia," he reminded her at the end of the lesson.

"How long will it take before you trust me again?" Zefra asked.

"Ask me tomorrow."

Zefra shuffled to a corner and pulled out her slate. She unwrapped her scarf from her hair and draped it to shade her face.

Ahjin went to check on Izo and found him flirting with Nia. Apparently, his anger died sooner than Ahjin's.

"Where is Ludik?" Ahjin asked. "Isn't he supposed to be teaching you?"

"I finished my lesson," Izo said. "Ludik was needed, so I said I would watch Nia for a while." He smiled at Nia, who leaned closer and whispered in his ear. Izo laughed and looked back at Ahjin. "Was there anything else, or are you finished? I promise to keep Nia away from my sister."

"That's all." Ahjin spread his wings in the sunshine and closed his eyes.

It didn't take long for their whispering to make Ahjin sick to his stomach. Why did they have to coo at each other like that? He scooped up his runes and dropped them into his hammock. After fastening his favorite jacket, he sprang into the air. An hour or two of flying would cure his restlessness and nausea.

The spring wind rustled through his feathers as it cradled his wings. Perfect. Warm sun, a cool breeze, and room to move. Ahjin climbed high above the ship and balanced for a moment before he tipped into a dive, wings folded back. The air whistled in his ears as he fell. As the ocean grew larger, the vague lavender mass became individual waves traced with white foam, while violet shadows hinted at the depths below.

The sailors shouted and pointed at him. Someone grabbed for a net.

Ahjin grinned. Time for a show. At the last minute, he spread his wings and shot back into the sky. Once at the top again, he worked through his old aerobatic routine, full of somersaults, rolls, spirals, and tricks designed by Father to amaze audiences. He altered the sequence a little so he could follow the ship.

One routine led to another while the sailors fished and steered and worked. He stayed in the air until the scent of cooked fish reached his nose. Dinner time. He slowly spiraled to the ship.

Kaito met him as soon as he landed. The quiet Seal took Ahjin's jacket and handed him a brush.

"No, thank you." Ahjin pushed away the brush as his stomach grumbled. "I am ready for dinner, though."

Kaito handed him the brush again and unrolled a fresh hair tie.

"We're in the middle of the ocean, Kaito."

Kaito did his usual imitation of a statue until Ahjin gave up, brushed his hair, and tied it neatly at his neck.

"Now may I have dinner?"

Kaito walked away with the jacket and brush and returned with a heaping bowl of rice and fish.

Ahjin took a bite, then weighed the bowl in his hand. "This is twice what I got at lunch. Did we catch that much fish?" He stretched his neck to see what the others were eating. No one else had so much.

Ahjin glared at Kaito and marched to the galley. He poured half his food back in the pot, despite Nia's open-mouthed stare.

"*Don't* give me extra again," he said. "We're all in this together."

Nia sputtered, "But Ahjin, you flew all afternoon, and Kaito—"

Ahjin walked away. He ate quickly, shoved the empty bowl at Kaito, and went to bed.

ᗡᗡᗡᗡ

The next morning, Ahjin was the assigned helmsman. He left Nia asleep, collected two bowls of plain breakfast rice, and traded one to Ludik in exchange for the tiller as soon as his own was empty.

"Do you think we'll make it?" Ahjin asked.

"I don't see why not. We've made good time both day and night."

Ludik shrugged. "All we need is a little good luck to hunt with us." He poured the rice into his mouth without using the spoon.

Ahjin laughed. "Would we recognize good luck if it blew a warm updraft under our wings?" He glanced toward the hammocks and grimaced. "Even good luck can't help when we make our own trouble. I'm bothered by Nia. She didn't used to be like this."

"I think the prospect of romance has mixed unfavorably with her worries for her father."

"Hmm. I hope that's all. If she keeps this up, she'll ruin her friendship with Zefra and drive Izo insane."

"If Nemerra were here, she could talk to her." Ludik sighed. "I wish Nemerra were here. Zefra isn't the only one going insane. Why don't you tell Nia how you feel?"

"I have," Ahjin said. "I've told her several times to be nice to Izo and stop flirting so much. She'll break his heart."

"I'm talking about *your* heart," Ludik said. "A blind bat can tell you love Nia."

Ahjin laughed. "You know bats aren't blind. Of course I love Nia. We've been best friends for a year. I'd do anything for her, but she won't let me help her."

Ludik tugged the hoop in his ear. "Bats aren't blind, but you are. I've known for months that you love Nia. Romantically."

Ahjin laughed again. "You're so in love with Nemerra, you see love everywhere you look."

Ludik patted him on the shoulder. "I do love Nemerra. Trust me, I know what love looks like. Give it some thought. I have chores." He chuckled and walked away.

Ahjin shifted the tiller to compensate for the next wind gust approaching the sail. Ludik believed Ahjin wanted to court Nia. What an idea. Imagine how that would work in real life instead of Ludik's imagination. It would be like courting his sister.

She was his best friend. They spent so much time together, they could almost read each other's minds. Not literally, since Nia didn't suffer with telepathy the way he did, but they predicted each other's actions and feelings. She even laughed at his pranks, as long as he left her hair alone.

As she spent more time with Izo instead of Ahjin, he missed her stories, her songs and jokes, her mere presence at his side. She added excitement and color to Ahjin's life. Everything was an adventure with her. She lightened his mood and brightened his heart. He was a better person around her, more cheerful, generous, and forgiving. When she was gone, he was alone no matter how many people surrounded him.

But courting her? That was ridiculous. Holding her hand. Kissing her.

Like their kiss on the beach. Ahjin chuckled. She had looked so surprised after the accident, as shocked as himself.

His laugh faded as he remembered her soft lips on his. They had felt so odd at the time, but now the memory sent warmth through him.

Lightning shot from the sky and zapped Ahjin. No, not lightning, but a bolt of truth. He did love Nia. Somehow, over the past year, friendship had slid into more. When he told Nia to behave, he thought he'd been defending Izo — and he had been — but he'd also been jealous.

He loved Nia. Ludik was right. He loved her as a man loves a woman, not only as a friend.

He let go of the tiller, then grabbed it again when the ship wavered. How could he have missed seeing it for so long? Was he so used to the habit of friendship that he couldn't see when it changed to attraction and then to love?

Zefra and Nia were both right. Love was partly compatibility, like Zefra said. He didn't mind Nia's peculiarities, and she had adjusted to his idiosyncrasies. They met each other's needs without thinking. If he went along with Nia's fruit analogy, she was the other half of his orange.

But Nia was also right. Love was still nothing without the heart, and she had worked her way into his without him realizing.

Ahjin glanced at the wind in the sails. It hadn't changed. The flutter he felt was only in his heart.

If only he could read Nia's mind, he'd know how she felt about him. His stomach clenched. If she loved him, she wouldn't flirt with Izo. Even among the Nokai, serious relationships were taken one at a time, even if they didn't stay serious for life.

Ahjin squeezed the tiller until his knuckles turned white. Could he build on their compatibility? She'd get bored with Izo, eventually. He could wait. But what if he only imagined possibilities? She'd never fit in his flying world, and he would never truly feel comfortable in her swimming one. Even living on Arupa, in the middle of the messiest combinations of races in the world, they'd have problems.

He dragged his fingers through his wind-blown curls, then laughed. Why worry about problems so far in the future? He was still assuming Nia would accept his love and let him court her. Yes, that was the current problem. First, she had to say yes, and then she had to tell Izo she didn't want him.

He winced. Poor Izo. Here Ahjin had been telling Nia not to break his heart, and now he wanted her to do just that. And Zefra wouldn't be amused, either. Or perhaps she'd appreciate Izo's courtship ending sooner rather than in a later heartbreak. Perhaps Ahjin wouldn't tell her his plans. Anyway, Nia deserved to hear his feelings first. After he talked to her, he could tell the others.

But first, he had to get through his shift. Ahjin checked the sun. He felt like he'd been pondering for hours, but the sun had barely moved. It would be lunchtime before anyone came to relieve him.

It could be worse. He'd use the time to plan what to say to Nia. If he were witty and eloquent, perhaps she'd understand. If he were charming, perhaps she'd return his love.

But he wasn't eloquent or charming, and his pranks were unlikely to make anyone love him. And even before his scars, he had been no more than average in looks, unlike the handsome Iskrin.

<center>~~~~</center>

It was an eternity before Malu relieved him.

Ahjin dashed for the galley, then forced himself to a walk. *Be calm, be charming, be witty.* He collected his food from Kaito and found a seat by Nia and Izo.

"So, Nia, I thought of something today." He tried to swallow the lump in his throat.

"That's nice." Nia smiled vaguely and turned back to Izo.

"I'd like to tell you about it," Ahjin said.

"Sure, Ahjin."

"It's important."

Nia patted his knee. "Later."

Ahjin finished his rice and volunteered to wash the dishes. How could he persuade Nia he loved her if she wouldn't even listen? He dunked the first dishes in warm water, courtesy of Zefra, and swished the soap into bubbles. After washing, he'd have to fill it with fresh water to rinse. Then dry and put away. Nia would have plenty of time to finish her conversation with Izo.

He was halfway through the washing when Irajahan's voice in his head interrupted his thoughts.

"I'm waiting for your prayers. Why are you late?"

"I'm sorry, Omnipotence." Ahjin gagged at the honorific. Appeasing Irajahan was one of the most distasteful parts of his job. "We have no clock on the ship. I can only guess time by the sun."

He put the next dishes into the soapy water. Irajahan had lousy timing; Ahjin wanted to decide how to tell Nia he loved her.

"Of course it's imprecise." Irajahan sniffed. "Resef made it." He paused. "What ship?"

"It doesn't matter. Let me proceed, Almighty." Ahjin recited one of Irajahan's favorite poems of praise while he kept washing. The poem wasn't required, but a standard recital was less nauseating than having to invent his own compliments. Even paperwork was better.

He tried to ignore his worries and the sensation of the god rifling through his mind, concentrating on the poem. "Your wings are mirror bright and her eyes are emerald light."

"What!" Irajahan thundered. "What emeralds? Whose eyes?"

Ahjin sucked in his breath. What had he said? "I — I'm sorry. It was a mistake, My Lord Omnipotent. I apologize. I—"

"You should listen to *me*," Irajahan screamed. "Only to me!"

He never tolerated attention paid to anyone else. Ahjin knew that, so why had he let his mind wander, even for a moment?

He wiped his hands on a towel. "Yes, of course. Let me start again."

"I'm not impressed by second-rate worship. You shouldn't be on that ship against my command. If you won't serve me, I'll destroy you."

Ahjin sucked in his breath. He'd do it, too. He had tried before. "No, please, All-Powerful, have mercy! It won't happen again."

The sudden silence in his mind was deafening. Ahjin abandoned the dishes and ran out on deck. Everyone stared at him as he searched the sky.

Oh, no. "Storm coming! Tie everything down!"

12.STORM
(OCEAN)

When you have no choice, mobilize the spirit of courage.
Darrendran Proverb

Ludik cursed. The sky rapidly darkened, and the wind sped faster than a cheetah. "What did you do, Ahjin?"

Ahjin waved him off as he ran. "Later. Captain, remove the sails!"

Captain Malu gaped at the sky, unmoving.

Ahjin shook him. "That storm is coming for us. Get ready!"

Malu shivered. "Maybe it will miss us."

"It won't, and you've never been in a storm like this."

Ludik recognized Ahjin's grim tone. Every time he turned around, his chances of returning to Nemerra shrank. He ran to help Zefra and Nia throw the hammocks below deck. At least they were cooperating with each other again.

The storm blew closer. The sails flapped, and the circling winds chilled Ludik's skin. Waves rose, rocking the ship and flowing over the deck. The sailors' bare feet splashed in the growing pools as they dashed from sail to sail, pulling them down before the wind tore them to shreds.

Ludik shoved the last bundled hammock at a sailor who stopped working to stare at the massive storm. "Move it. You can be scared later."

Ahjin stayed on deck. "Faster," he cried. "We need two more at the mainmast. Malu! Can we steer the ship at all in the storm?"

Malu shouted over the wind. "Not really, but if we don't point the ship into the waves, we'll capsize. It will take two helmsmen, and I'm useless with this hand."

"I'll do it," Ahjin said.

"Don't be ridiculous," Ludik yelled. "Your wings will snap in this wind. I'll do it. Malu, find me someone to help."

Plague fleas, the ship would not *sink and leave his children as fatherless cubs.* He wouldn't allow it. He braced himself as the ship rolled again.

Malu grabbed a sailor. "Get the sea anchor." He turned to Ahjin. "The wind and waves will still move us, but it might keep us from drifting sideways and rolling under."

Ludik grabbed Nia's arm. "Take Zefra and Izo below and make it safe." When she protested, Ludik pushed them toward the hatch, blinking as the wind blew stinging salt into his eyes. "Save the rest of our supplies, or we will starve even if we don't capsize. Move it."

After all three disappeared down the hatch, Ludik turned back to the chaos above deck.

Besides a tiny storm jib, only one sail still flew, but the wind kept whipping it from the sailors' hands. Ludik lunged for the closest edge and dug in. The gale yanked on the coarse canvas until he feared his fingers would snap. Ahjin and Kaito also grabbed the sail and held on until the sailors could pull it down.

Then the rain hit. The world disappeared behind sheets of water.

Ludik slid on the flooding deck, and the roar of the storm covered the sailors' shouts. Ludik grabbed Malu and shoved him toward the hatch while Kaito helped Ahjin. They reached it blindly and fumbled for the edge.

Ludik handed everyone down, but even his cat balance barely kept him on his feet. It was less a matter of them climbing down the ladder and more of trying not to drown as the water washed them through the hatch. He watched from the top to make sure everyone made it safely, then tossed down his boots.

Izo and some of the sailors caught everyone at the bottom and helped them through the water. More sailors waited to lash their mates into the hammocks restrung on the walls.

Nia waved to Ludik, then wrapped her arms around herself. "I guess it was a good thing half the crew left and the pirates stole our food," she gasped, shivering in her hammock. "We couldn't fit everyone in here while it was full of stores."

Ludik slammed the hatch shut, but water streamed through the edges. He dragged himself across the deck with help from a rope, found the tiller and the other sailor almost by touch, and tied himself to the railing next to him. Even with muscles straining together, they could barely steer.

The sailor leaned toward Ludik. "Keep the bow pointed almost toward the waves. If we get a chance to move, head for the shallowest waves."

Ludik tightened his grip on the slippery tiller and leaned into the turn.

A freezing wave taller than the mast crashed into the deck. The ship rocked so hard to one side that only the rope around his waist held Ludik upright. When the wave passed, the ship whipped to the other side, slamming into the trough with a boom that rattled its timbers.

And then came the next wave.

With crash after crash, waves pounded the helpless ship. It would sink, and Ludik's hopes with it. Never. Going. Home.

Ludik's arms ached from his grip on the tiller. The rope chafed through his tunic, his bare legs turned to ice, and each jolt left new bruises. Beside him, the other helmsman groaned.

Rain poured thicker than a waterfall, and salt spray burned his eyes. The midday sun had disappeared behind the clouds, and the oncoming waves were black against the darkness. The minutes trickled past, each a fight for survival.

By the time Ludik was relieved, he was too cold to shiver. He and his partner staggered to the hatch, then down the ladder into waist-deep water.

Ludik let Kaito shove him into a berth and wrap a net around his hammock until he looked like a spider's prey. The top row of hammocks held personal bags and crates of food against the ceiling, while the row across the middle of the wall was half-filled with Nokai. There were no low hammocks, just water splashing as the boat rocked from side to side.

The dim hold stank of fish. The fragile clay lamps had been packed, and only a single metal lantern banged against the wall with every lurch of the ship.

Between sways, Zefra, barefoot and with Ahjin's clothes plastered to her scrawny body, climbed like a squirrel from hammock to rocking hammock. She wedged herself at Ludik's feet and reached across to touch the helmsman, then closed her eyes.

Within a few minutes, a slow warmth crept up Ludik's legs. He gasped as the heat rose to his neck. He had forgotten what warmth felt like.

Zefra stopped when he started shivering. "Sorry, but I must conserve my energy. Will you be all right now?"

Ludik nodded shakily and rubbed his arms and torso. Now that he knew what it was like on deck, he didn't look forward to his next shift in a few hours.

The helmsman quietly sobbed beside him. Zefra clambered back to her own hammock.

"How does it look up there?" Ahjin's voice choked, and he hugged his stomach.

Ludik shrugged. "Not quite as bad as last year." He reached one foot from his hammock to fend off the wall when it swung too close.

Nia passed him a water jug. "I'm sorry there's nothing to eat."

"How are you all taking this so calmly?" Izo blurted.

"I told you how bad it was when we rescued the gods," Zefra said. "At least there are no earthshakes this time, and the sun is in no danger of exploding."

"I got swept overboard once," Nia said. "I had to swim below the violent waves until the storm ended."

Izo groaned. "My imagination was insufficient." He shifted in his hammock to brace himself against the swaying walls.

Ludik preferred not to dwell on it. "At least Ahjin gave us enough warning to deal with the sails. Did a god warn you or was it your weather sense?"

Ahjin coughed a horrid, gagging hack. "Sorry, this is my fault. Iraja-han is angry at me."

"Why?" Nia asked. "What did you do? No, don't tell me; you didn't do anything. Won't he ever forgive you for being Mouth and ending his conscription of priests?"

Ahjin blushed, his scars branching white across his crimson face. "Tell you later." He paled and retched into a bucket.

Ludik steadied his swinging hammock again. "If I had my kit and a fire, I'd offer you tea. But since you never take it, I'll save myself the trouble."

Ahjin bent over the bucket again. From the sound, he was dragging his toenails through his stomach before rejecting them. He gasped for breath and groaned. "Today, I'd take your poison."

"What, really?" Ludik sat up and clutched the edge of his shaking hammock. The world must be ending if Ahjin was willing to take medicine. "Nia, where is my kit?"

"I will get it," Zefra said. "What should I look for?"

Ludik described the packet and sketched the label's symbol in the air.

She climbed the pitching hammocks again, scrounged near the ceiling, and emerged with a packet she held up for Ludik's approval. After waiting for a temporary calm, she made her way to Ahjin's berth and squirmed in by his feet.

Nia passed a water jug, and Zefra added Ludik's "two pinch" portion to the jug and shook it hard. She held the jug between her hands for a few minutes.

"Here you go." She handed it to Ahjin, then yanked it back while he vomited again.

When he emerged from the bucket, he snatched the jug and downed half of it at once. "How long does this take to work?" he moaned. "Does it make a difference if it's only half-warm?

"It will be warm enough to work," Ludik said. "The time depends. I could predict it better if you took medicine more often." He tapped his fingers together and smiled at Ahjin.

"Not helpful." Ahjin flopped his head back in his hammock and sipped at the jug. "I'll try appeasing Irajahan. Perhaps we've suffered enough to satisfy him."

Nia snorted.

"Hush, girl, I'm praying."

Nia made a silent face of disgust.

Ludik squeezed water from the hem of his tunic. They needed good news. An end to the storm would be best, but even a guess at when it would dissipate would help.

Ahjin finished the jug of tea before he sat up again. "Thanks, Ludik. Your poison is killing the nausea. Unfortunately, Irajahan is... unsympathetic. I suspect the storm will last until he's bored. About the only thing we can do is try to be boring."

Some of the other sailors whimpered.

"Courage, men," Ahjin said. "Be brave. Irajahan is amused by fear. Nia, will you lead a song for us, please? Something to raise our spirits."

Nia cleared her throat and started a comforting rendition of the No-kai lullaby, "Home Again," barely audible over the storm.

Ludik sang with Nia and the sailors until he noticed Ahjin struggling from his hammock. He sat up, but Ahjin waved him down.

Ahjin climbed from hammock to hammock, much less deftly than Zefra. With every lurch of the ship, he clung to the netting until the ship settled, finally making his way to whisper in Ludik's ear.

"I have a message for you, too."

"From Irajahan? What could he have to say to me?"

"You're right," Ahjin said. "I'm sure he's just creating trouble. Never mind." He started to climb back, and Ludik grabbed his arm.

"Wait a minute. Create trouble for me? What did he say?"

Ahjin shrugged. "Irajahan says Nemerra is having difficulties with her pregnancy."

Ludik fought to climb from his lurching hammock, his mind a blur of worry. "What kind of difficulties? Can Okechuku fix it? Are the babies well? Who will take care of her daily needs while I'm gone?"

Ahjin pushed him back. "You can't go anywhere in this storm. Irajahan might be lying to make you feel bad. If it *is* true, she's with the best healers in the world." He pushed Ludik harder. "What good will your drowning do Nemerra?"

No good at all, but if Okechuku couldn't save Nemerra, then his life was not worth living. What good did it do to be a healer if he couldn't help his own wife?

The song ended. Ahjin kept his eyes on Ludik but raised his voice. "Zefra, what does the hourglass say? Is it time to rotate again?"

"Almost," Zefra said. "Who is next?"

"I'll go," Ludik growled. Even the freezing rain was better than lying here helplessly.

"You will not," Ahjin commanded. "You aren't even dry yet."

He kept his hands on Ludik's shoulders while he chose two sailors from the hands that went up, and they waded toward the ladder to the upper deck.

"Nia," Ahjin said, "should we bail out this water?" He tightened the net that held Ludik in the hammock.

Ludik glared at him. Ahjin ignored him and crawled back to his own hammock above the splashing waves of the ship's internal pond.

"Not with an empty hold," Nia said. "The water will act as ballast and steady us a bit. We can empty it after the storm."

"Then we're ready for the next song," Ahjin said.

Two hours later, the sailors were at least pretending to be braver, and Ludik insisted on taking another shift. The storm seemed a little lighter and the waves a little shorter, though the sea and wind were still as cold.

The effort it took to keep the ship turned into the waves was almost enough to keep his mind off Nemerra's health. Assuming Irajahan weren't lying to drive Ludik insane. *Please, let him be as much of a liar as ever.*

When Ludik returned to the hold at the end of his shift, his friends had divided the few remaining fruits. A quarter of a mango in a bowl was lashed in his hammock. He gobbled it in three bites and licked his fingers.

The ship jerked less and less, and the howl outside dulled to a roar and then a mumble. After two more shifts, the ship settled into its usual mild rocking, and Ludik raced on deck followed by everyone else.

Zefra and Malu checked the stars and agreed it was a little after midnight. The storm had lasted half a day.

"We've been blown northwest," Malu said. "I need five volunteers." He ignored anyone who had taken more than one shift during the storm. "We'll start repairs and raise the sails, but we'll stay here until morning. The rest of you go to bed so you can take over in daylight."

"Good night, Ludik." Nia headed for the closest sail, dragging Kaito behind her.

Ludik threw himself to bed in the hold without even the stars to keep him company.

In the warm morning light, Ludik blinked and argued with Nia. Now was his chance to return to Nemerra. Even Okechuku would understand.

"Why can we not head back now? The ship is damaged; it might not last through our original journey."

"Which is another reason it would be better to wait." Nia spoke through gritted teeth. "We need to make some repairs on land, and we're closer to the Dragon Isles than anywhere else. And I already told you, we don't have enough food to go home. We have to land or starve."

"We are still days from the Isles," Ludik argued. And weeks from returning to Iskra, if they did not turn around now.

"Yes, but fewer than to Nokailana, which is the next closest land. Now be quiet and get in the crow's nest before I smack you." She drew herself to her full height.

Despite himself, Ludik snickered. She was chest-high to him at best, and the braids frizzing around her face made her look like a kitten.

She glared, and he raised his hands in surrender.

"Fine, but only because I don't want to drown on the way home."

"Fine." Nia turned on her heel and stomped toward Izo, who waited with hammer and nails.

Ludik climbed the rigging to the crow's nest. Though he spent more time gazing south than the other directions, no one mentioned it.

Between constant repairs, everyone fished as much as possible to supplement the slimmer rations that survived the storm. There were enough tasks to keep his hands occupied, though his heart constantly yearned for Nemerra.

The coal was soaked to uselessness, so the fish was served raw. Ahjin's complaints became the most common seasoning. Ludik had never heard fish insulted so many different ways. Other than Nia's songs, it was the only entertainment.

One evening meal, Nia served the usual raw fish and gave Ahjin a broken plank, despite Kaito's silently frantic attempts to stop her.

"Since you don't like our available fare," she said.

Ahjin held up the plank and grinned. By the end of the night, he caught his own fish and roasted it on the plank Zefra set on fire.

Five days after the storm, the sailor on watch bellowed, "Land!"

Ludik and the others crowded against the bulwark to look for themselves. Slowly, much too slowly, a pale island crept into view. Ludik squinted and still didn't see green, but surely there would be plants farther inland.

Nia cheered. "The Dragon Isles. We're saved!"

They needed to restock their food, but if everyone helped, it shouldn't take too long. Ludik could head back to Nemerra in a few days. Zefra would mark every discovery on her map. Okechuku could send another expedition to collect the pakai, if it indeed grew on the islands.

"Ship ahoy!" the watchman called. "To the north."

"Maybe we can trade with it," Nia said.

Ludik rubbed his chin. "Maybe I can catch a ride home."

After another minute, the watch shouted, "Red flag! It's flying a red flag!"

Deadly pirates.

Ludik's neck tingled. If he shifted, his fur would stand on end. Unless Ahjin convinced the gods to send a miracle, Nemerra would be a widow by nightfall.

13. CROW
(BY DRAGON ISLES)

Wanted: Dead or Alive. "Crow" has black hair, brown eyes, and a prominent nose. Black wings, cut after conviction of multiple murders. Escaped prison with help of accomplice "Lapwing," black hair and tan wings.

Ahjin stretched his wings and battled the urge to fly. Red flag pirates were ruthless. They'd kill everyone.

Nia's damaged ship couldn't outrun the pirates, even to the island tantalizingly within sight. They couldn't fight, either. Half their crew was gone, and the ones left hadn't eaten well in a week.

"Can we hide, Nia? If they think the ship is abandoned, will they leave it alone?"

Nia chewed on her lip. "We look less valuable in our battered state, but the ship is still whole. I think they'd take it anyway."

"Give me the spyglass," Ahjin said. "I'll fly over them. Perhaps I can find out something useful."

Kaito shook his head, but Ahjin ignored him.

Zefra handed Ahjin the spyglass. "While you're gone, we'll pack what we can so we can run."

Ahjin turned invisible and jumped into the pale orange sky. The lovely, clear evening had a mild breeze. Under other circumstances, it would make flying even more of a joy than usual. He soon reached the pirate ship but stayed far enough away that the pirates wouldn't hear his wingbeats or feel the air from them.

The deck was half-covered with crew bristling with weapons. The ship flew twice as many sails as Aolani's ship under a red flag patterned with a stylized dragon with bat wings, continuing in exactly the direction Ahjin wished it to avoid. No, running and fighting were both bad ideas.

The pirate captain sat in a fancy chair on deck. His shiny black hair gleamed in the sun like an Iskrin's, but he didn't have the white skin to go with it. He could pass for a sunburned Nokai, but Ahjin had never seen one with black hair. Could it be dark indigo, instead? Ahjin peered through the spyglass but couldn't tell. If he were a Darrendrakar, he was certainly the palest one Ahjin had ever seen. Ahjin's first guess would have been Iojif, but the captain had no wings.

The sailor who passed on the captain's orders with a high-pitched wail *was* Iojif. He had tan wings and dull black hair and limped with every other step.

Ahjin frowned. Something seemed familiar about that combination.

While he thought, he scanned the ship again. All the races were represented on board. He was too high to hear actual words, but the lilt of different accents drifted in the wind. There were many pirates with the typical rainbow selection of Nokai hair. Several had the un-tanning white skin from Iskra. One was much too dark to be anything but Darrendrakar, though he was much shorter and thinner than Ludik.

There were a handful of Iojif, though none flew. One had a wing that had healed badly from a break. One was missing half a wing. Ahjin squinted to see if others had injuries.

The captain leaned forward to accept a mug, and Ahjin saw lumps on his back under his shirt.

That was enough to bring the missing memory back to his mind. He gasped and turned for his own ship at racing speed. They would need every minute to plan.

He thumped on deck and tossed the spyglass back to Zefra. Everyone gathered close to hear his report.

"They're faster, they're stronger, and they're merciless," Ahjin said. "We have to escape. What options do we have?"

"I can guess how you know they're faster and stronger," Nia said, "but how in the coral reef can you tell they're merciless? Were they torturing captives on deck?"

Ahjin shook his head. "Other than the red flag? I recognized the captain and his first mate."

Ludik tugged his earring. "You know a pirate captain? Why didn't you warn us? Can you convince him to let us go?"

"No, I—" Ahjin took a deep breath. "Let me explain. Late last year, an infamous Iojif escaped from prison with the help of an accomplice. He murdered at least a dozen people. Bounty hunters chased them for months without spotting them. I recognized the two of them on that ship, and I suspect most of their crew were criminals before they became pirates."

"He's that unique, is he?" Nia smiled. "Bright red wings and so on?"

Ahjin shook his head. "Plain black for the captain, and tan for the mate, but I know it's them."

"How?" Zefra asked.

"The mate was nicknamed Lapwing for his distinctive high voice and limp and his coloring — black hair with tan wings."

"I'm unconvinced," Nia said, "but go on."

"They call the murderer the Crow. He had black hair and matching wings."

"Had?" Izo said. "Did he shave his hair? Or dye it?"

"No." Ahjin clenched his fists. "He was declared unredeemable, and his wings were cut off to make it harder for him to catch his victims. With life in prison, that was deemed fair. Now that he's escaped, there's a death sentence on his head."

Nia looked at Ahjin's wings, and her eyes grew shiny.

"Perhaps he changed his ways," Zefra said, "and that is why no one has seen him recently."

"The ship is called Chickadees," Ahjin said.

"Oh, that's so cute," Nia said. "Named after sweet little birds."

Ahjin raised an eyebrow. "Do you know what a group of chickadees is called?"

"A flock?" Ludik suggested.

"Many flocks have specialized names. Chickadees fly in a banditry."

Nia gasped.

Zefra nodded her head. "That is clever of the pirates."

Nia narrowed her eyes. "I don't think it's funny."

Zefra furrowed her brow. "I did not laugh."

Izo covered his mouth.

Ahjin bit the inside of his mouth and practiced his diplomatic mask. Under the circumstances, it shouldn't be so hard not to laugh.

"Enough," he said. "We have to leave. We can take the dinghy to the island."

"Can we swim to the island?" Zefra asked. "If we leave the dinghy, the pirates might think we died in the storm."

"Will they see us swimming?" Ludik asked.

"They can see the ship," Ahjin said, "but are still too distant to see details."

"The Nokai and Kaito won't have any trouble swimming that far," Nia said. "The rest of you should wait until we get a little closer."

"Kaito needs to go south." Ahjin turned to face the Seal. "Swim for Arupa. Tell Lyell what happened and bring rescue for us.

Kaito shook his head vigorously.

"That's an order." Ahjin pointed. "Leave now. We're depending on you to bring help." He held his stance until Kaito's shoulders slumped.

The Seal walked behind the sail. His Nokai pants dropped to the deck, and a loud splash sounded overboard.

"At least he'll be safe," Ahjin said.

"Do you think he will rescue us in time?" Ludik asked.

"Don't be ridiculous. That will take weeks. But he can't defend himself, and it was the only way to get him to leave."

Ahjin wished he could convince Nia to go with Kaito, but he knew better. She'd never agree to that, no matter what lies he told her. His heart pinched. How many times would he risk her life? It was no wonder she didn't love him. All he added to her life was unhappiness.

This was stupid. Escape first, fret later. "Now, are we ready to go?"

Zefra pointed to a small barrel. "That is the last of the food and most of our weapons and personal supplies. It should float on currents to shore. We hoped you could carry my bow again as well as your own."

Malu and the sailors exchanged glances.

"We'll start now," the captain said. "If we spread out the evacuation, we're less likely to be noticed. We'll tie the tiller in place temporarily so the ship will keep drifting toward the islands for you."

"Good idea," Ahjin said.

The Nokai affixed the tiller and grabbed their things, then threw ropes overboard and slipped into the ocean without splashing. The sun dropped lower in the sky.

Izo frowned. "I swim a little, but not well. Zefra does not, either, though she will not admit it."

Zefra smacked his shoulder.

"I'll swim with Zefra," Nia said. "The island is not much more than a mile away. We can do it."

"We can tie a rope to the barrel," Ludik said. "Izo can use it to help him float, and I'll keep an eye on him."

"Let's do it." Ahjin strapped both bows to his pack and buckled it between his wings. He grabbed the staffs and turned invisible again, flying to keep watch while the others made their escape.

The pirate ship sailed closer.

Ludik shifted to panther and splashed overboard. Izo packed Ludik's tunic in the barrel and threw the whole thing into the ocean. He climbed down after it and caught the loop tied around it with one arm. His bare shoulders shone in the setting sun, bright white against the lavender water.

Ludik pushed the barrel, and the two swam toward the island. Izo kicked and flailed his arms noisily, but Ludik's smooth shadow stayed by him.

Ahjin couldn't see the Nokai sailors. They should have been halfway to the island by now. He finally found them, lost and swimming the wrong way.

He pursed his lips to whistle and then choked it back. The pirates would hear him. He waved frantically to Nia and then remembered he was invisible.

Nia and Zefra slipped down the Nokai's escape ropes and swam toward the island. They got a few hundred feet away, and then Nia left Zefra to swim south after the other Nokai. She paused, and her head turned between Zefra and the sailors.

Zefra kept swimming for the island, flailing without much progress.

Ahjin flew lower, not sure how to help, but Nia mouthed something probably impolite and swam after Zefra. Nia easily caught up, moving as sleekly as a dolphin through the water. She motioned to Zefra, who flipped onto her back. Nia grabbed her shirt collar and towed Zefra through the water. Though much slower than Nia's solo swimming, the process was both faster and quieter than Zefra's attempts.

Ahjin's collar would never be the same after Zefra returned it. He allowed himself an invisible grin before flying ahead to check on Ludik and Izo.

Izo's splashing grew worse, but the barrel still held his head above water. Ludik kept pace easily.

Ahjin flew back to Nia and Zefra. They were gaining on the men, though it might take them almost to the island to catch up.

Ahjin spiraled in the air. The pirate ship was close enough now to see details without the spyglass, even in the twilight. Pirates hung from the rigging, shouting and pointing at Aolani's ship, which had stalled in the water. Either the tiller had come untied or the wind had shifted. The pirate ship swung in a big arc, leaving a white trail of froth behind them as they chased the stranded ship. Their red flag spread in the wind, revealing the fiery dragon head.

Ahjin and his crew had gotten off none too soon. Would their ship keep the pirates busy long enough for everyone to escape? The shore offered dubious safety, but at least on land they'd have a chance. If the pirates caught them in the water, they were dead.

He circled between his two groups of friends again and again as they crept closer to the rocks surrounding the island. Ahjin wanted to shout encouragement and tell them how close they were getting, but he couldn't risk being overheard. He couldn't even warn them what the pirates were doing. The only good news was that the failing light turned the swimmers to shadows in the waves, and the pirates hadn't found them.

Unfortunately, he'd been invisible long enough for the inevitable headache to creep up on him. Tonight would be miserable.

The pirates reached Aolani's ship and threw grappling hooks to pull it against their own.

The girls were only a little behind the men now, and the island was just in front of them. Ahjin flew lower and looked for a good landing spot.

The pirates swarmed over Aolani's ship like ants at a picnic, if ants used weapons and nasty language.

There, a break in the rocks. Ahjin flew as low as he dared and popped into visibility, thankful for the near-dark. As soon as he caught Ludik's attention, he pointed to the spot and turned invisible again, taking a moment to breathe through the headache.

Ludik adjusted his course, nudging Izo to follow. Both men made it through the break, but the barrel crunched on the rocks. Izo staggered back through the chest-deep water and bumped the cask over the barrier. As soon as it was in the little cove, he dropped it and collapsed in the water.

Ludik shoved Izo to the rocks and swam back to Nia and Zefra. Nia waved him off, but the panther swam beside them anyway, directing them toward the gap in the rocks. Nia let go of Zefra's collar so they could squeeze through the gap.

Ahjin turned. The ships had separated again, with pirates on both ships. They no longer shouted across the waves to each other, and the silence was alarming. What would they do now? Had they seen them? Would they follow?

Ahjin flew lower and flapped his wings over Nia's head to ruffle her braids.

She waved as she splashed toward the beach. Nia towed the barrel while the others made their way through the water until it was waist-deep, then knee-deep, then only a covering for their feet.

They collapsed on dry ground and lay still, chests heaving.

Ahjin landed by Nia, crouching low and becoming visible again. As his headache slammed between his ears, he grabbed his head and watched the shadows on the ocean, whispering an update to the others.

"The pirates boarded our ship. Now our sails are shifting. The pirate ship is heading north. Ours is following. The Nokai are still swimming the wrong way."

Nia groaned. "They're going home."

Ahjin tried to smile. "At least the pirates didn't burn the ship."

Izo threw his arm over his eyes. Zefra patted her belt pouch, then dropped her hand to the damp sand and closed her eyes. Ludik bared his fangs in a silent growl. His silver eyes reflected the last rays of the sun before it slipped under the horizon and disappeared.

Ahjin shivered. Beside him, Nia shook with cold, and the Iskrins' teeth rattled.

Ahjin crawled to the middle of the group. He wiggled his way to his stomach and spread his wings over Nia and Zefra on one side of him and Izo on the other.

Ludik shook the water from his fur and lay across everyone's legs.

Ahjin groaned at the weight and then sighed as warmth seeped in.

Zefra grabbed a stone and held it for a minute, then gave it to Nia. When she handed the next one to Ahjin, it was warm. He passed it to Izo and toed the next under Ludik's chin. Zefra gave him another, and he tucked it between his arm and his chest.

"We're stranded," Nia murmured.

"No way home," Izo said.

Ludik growled.

"We will plan tomorrow." Zefra's whisper trailed off into a snore.

Ahjin closed his eyes and dreamed of sunshine and home.

14.ISLAND
(DRAGON ISLES)

Better a mouse in the pot than no meat at all.
Iskrin Proverb

Zefra woke, gasping for breath. She shivered in the dark, wet clothes clinging to her skin. When she tried to paddle for dry land, she could not move her arms or legs. She was surrounded. Trapped.

She would drown.

She panicked and struck out with arms and legs.

"Ow!" "Ouch." "What's wrong?" "Hold still." The voices surrounded her.

The weight on her back shifted a little, but she still could not get up.

Something growled, and someone hit her shoulder. "Stop that."

Zefra hit harder. Her legs were suddenly freed, and then the weight on her back disappeared. The blocks to her sides moved, and she shot to her feet.

Zefra was on land, but ominous shadows stood in every direction. She panted and pulled fire to her hand. Only a brief spark flared. She swayed on her feet and raised her fists.

"Zefra." Someone touched her arm.

She swung and tried to call fire again. "Stay away!"

"Zefra, 'tis Izo."

"Izo." Zefra fell to her knees. "Izo, I was drowning."

"'Twas just a dream-scare." Izo knelt beside her and wrapped his arms around her.

"Is it over now?" Nia grouched.

"Go back to sleep, Nia," Ahjin said wearily.

The shadows settled to dark lumps on the ground.

Zefra and Izo shivered together as night changed to blue twilight and the sun slowly rose. Zefra scanned the unfamiliar land. The ocean was only a few cubits away, and the shore was rocky and barren under the pale orange sky.

"At least the sun will warm us." Izo's teeth chattered.

Zefra had been through this before, but he had likely never felt so horrible in his life. She sat cross-legged and patted the ground beside her.

"More than you think. Sit, brother, and I will teach you a trick." She put her hands palm up on her knees.

"Will prayers help?" Izo copied her anyway.

Zefra closed her eyes and tilted her face to the sun. "Oh, Resef, Most Holy Flame," she prayed, letting the sunlight absorb through her skin.

Beside her, Izo gasped. Like her, he covered himself in the desert to prevent dehydration. Despite that, the unrelenting sun provided plenty of light and warmth. Now, they were in a cooler land and had swum in the cold ocean and slept in wet clothes. Fortunately, the short pair of Nokai pants exposed a lot more of his skin to the life-giving sun.

Soon, Izo was smiling again. "Resef is kind to allow our prayers to refresh us so."

"'Tis the sun," Zefra explained. "In the bright desert, our morning meditations give enough energy without even realizing it, but in my first journey with Ahjin, the other two Iskrins and I wilted into hibernation without enough sun, though we still prayed. The sunlight also charges my flame-calling."

Izo gaped at her. "The priests say it is the prayers."

Zefra stood between him and the sun and waited.

After a minute, he shivered in her shadow. "Why does Resef not tell us our prayers have a physical purpose?"

"I imagine he wants us to keep praying."

"You know the truth," Izo protested. "Why do you still pray?"

Zefra laid out wood for a small fire and lit it. "My reasons for praying have not changed."

Izo nudged her shoulder. "I'm lucky you were drained when you tried to burn me this morning."

"Very lucky," Zefra agreed.

The fire's crackle and heat woke the others. Nia swam out and caught a couple of small fish and rolled the barrel past the waterline. Divided five ways, the fish made only mouthfuls, but 'twas better than nothing.

Zefra and Izo left the others warming themselves around the fire and pried open the barrel lid. She reached into the cask, eager for a dry change of clothes, but her hand sank into damp, spongy cloth. The barrel had leaked, and they were in even bigger trouble than before.

She squeezed out most of the water and threw it to the panther. Next were the bags of food. The rice had swelled and stunk of the ocean. The produce was slimy. Nothing was edible. Zefra threw it all in a mushy heap.

The weapons could be saved, if she polished and oiled them before they rusted. Zefra checked to be sure Ahjin still had the bows. Between those and the staffs, at least they were armed.

Zefra turned back to the barrel. Ludik's boots were also soaked. The leather might not survive the salt water. She pulled his knife from the hidden scabbard and put it to dry in the sunlight with the other blades.

The half-empty packs were at the bottom of the barrel, equally soaked. She carried them to the fire and let everyone have their own.

Ludik, back as a man in his dripping tunic, took his pack with a growl and immediately sorted through his medical kit. "Now we know what the curse is," he said. With every pouch of medicine he dumped in a sodden heap, his frown deepened.

"What?" Nia asked.

"Pirates," Ludik said.

Zefra nodded. "Bandits." She had been right all along.

Nia gave her a nasty look.

"Pirates aren't a curse," Ahjin said.

"I think 'tis not a blessing we lost the ship," Izo said.

"At least we got to the Dragon Isles in one piece," Nia said, "where we want to be. We didn't get lost at sea. We escaped the pirates and are alive and uninjured. There's still hope things will work out."

Ludik snarled at her.

Ahjin put his hand over his face. "Enough. If we fight among ourselves, we'll never get home."

"We won't get home anyway." Ludik stomped the pile of ruined herbs into the sand.

"We just need a plan." Zefra reached for her slate. "I can make another."

"NO! No more plans," Nia said. "Your plans haven't worked."

Zefra sniffed. "I disagree. And your lack of plans has not worked, either."

"This is my quest," Nia said. "And we'll do it *my* way. Now that we're here, I'll find Dad. We can look for a way home as we search."

"And how do you suggest we start?" Ludik complained.

"Ahjin can survey from above while the rest of us explore the land," Nia said.

Zefra nodded. Gathering information was always a good start.

"Might as well go now," Ahjin said, "since breakfast is finished."

He flapped his wings for a few seconds, then jumped into the air and vanished.

Zefra covered her eyes until the dust settled. "I will dry our belongings and update my map."

Nia grabbed Izo and headed north. Ludik strolled south, touching the tiny hoop in his ear.

Zefra went through their supplies carefully. She spread out anything that could be saved, carefully weighing them down with small rocks or tethering them to dry grass. The ruined personal belongings went in separate piles. Some items needed special care, like the weapons and Izo's blacksmithing hammer.

Her map would not survive. She spread it gently in a patch of clean sand, with pebbles around the edge. Before they left, she would copy the key details to her slate.

Almost everything of Ahjin's had survived, including the two bows he carried.

She surveyed the results. At least their packs would be light when they left again. They would have plenty of room to add any food they found.

Her stomach growled. Food was a good next step. Zefra grabbed her bow and headed inland.

The island was nearly as bare as the desert, at least in this area. The only grass grew in sparse spikes, and there were no trees as far as she could see. She found no berries, no leafy greens, and no mushrooms she dared try. If there were small animals, they hid well.

Zefra was nearly ready to give up when two birds flew overhead. She quickly nocked an arrow and fired. That bird fell, but she missed the next.

A gust of wind swirled overhead, and Zefra turned to the shore. The whisper of Ahjin's wings left her behind, and everyone else had gathered when she returned with the bird. Ahjin landed and turned visible.

"It's just as ugly to the north," Nia said.

"Nothing south," Ludik reported.

"This island is all like that." Ahjin smoothed a patch of sand to draw a map. "There are five islands in all, three in a row and one on each side, like this. We landed on the small eastern side-island instead of the southern one we were aiming for, which does seem better than this."

"See." Zefra traced the outline of the islands as if they were connected. "This way, they look like a dragon crashed in the water. Head to the south, body, tail, and tiny wings. Thus the Dragon Isles."

She smiled. One mystery solved. Now they just had to find Nia's father and Ludik's herb.

"Oh." Nia pouted. "That's not as much fun as real dragons."

Ludik fingered his burned walrus tusk necklace. "I suggest safe is better than fun."

Nia stuck out her tongue at him. "That's because you're no fun."

"Oh?" Ludik said. "Did you find the pirates fun?"

Nia stuck her nose in the air.

Zefra exchanged a look with Izo. The Nokai had an over-inflated opinion of fun.

Izo turned to Ahjin. "Did you find a way home?"

Ahjin shook his head. "Not yet."

Zefra nodded. Just because Ahjin had found no way to leave did not mean they could not make one.

Nia smiled. "Then we'll have plenty of time to look for Dad."

Zefra rubbed her forehead. Would nothing make Nia be practical?

"Before we continue our search. I suggest we make preparations."
She pulled her slate from her belt pouch and started a list. "We need
more food. Fish will help."

Nia sighed loudly. "Some seaweed is edible. I'll get it."

"I can fish," Izo said.

"There might be rodents," Ludik suggested.

"Your nose will help you." Zefra made a note. "Ahjin, you hunt for
shelter, please. I will cook this bird."

Izo took Nia's hand and walked toward the ocean. Apparently, her
brother was still searching for rain in the dry season. Ludik shifted to
panther and crept through the sparse grass. Ahjin stared after Nia and
Izo with an odd look on his face, then turned to walk inland.

"Are you not flying?" Zefra asked.

Ahjin shook his head. "There might still be pirates out there, and I
don't want to turn invisible again. I'll spare my aching head and save it
for emergencies. We have all day to find shelter." He waved and left.

It took Zefra a long time to gather enough grass to twist into logs for
a fire. While the makeshift logs burned down a bit, she plucked and
gutted the bird, then wrapped it in wet grass and buried it in the ashes.

After a while, the aroma drifted through the air, making Zefra's
mouth water. Ludik was the first to arrive, in jaguar shape with two mice
in his mouth. Nia and Izo came next, with armfuls of seaweed and a
handful of fish. Ahjin returned last and empty-handed, and he cringed at
the sight of Ludik's mice.

"'Tis nearly a feast," Zefra said.

Izo nodded. "Let me add the fish and mice to the fire, and we will be
ready in no time."

"I'm starving," Nia said. "Just hand me one of those fish and don't
bother to cook it."

Ahjin gulped. "I'll try the seaweed, but could I beg you for a bit of
cooked bird or fish?"

Ludik swallowed both mice in one bite, and Ahjin sighed in relief.
Ludik hung his mouth open in a panther grin. He loped away and
returned on two legs a few minutes later, tugging his tunic smooth.

Nia sliced her fish into a nest of seaweed. "The seaweed is fine raw,
too."

Ludik copied her, but Zefra put the other fish in the ashes. When they were cooked a few minutes later, she gave one each to herself, Ahjin, and Izo. Everyone got a single bite of the bird.

The seaweed was clammy and salty but tasted better than Zefra expected. 'Twas no worse than cactus, except for the salt.

"I'm still hungry," Nia complained.

Ahjin's stomach growled.

"This is more than I ever got on my survival trek," Zefra said.

Izo nodded. "There are no fish to catch in the desert, and no seaweed. And we have bows and a hunting cat. We are overflowing with advantages."

"And we have been on short rations for only a week," Zefra continued. "It will be another month before starvation is close. Three months if we find enough fish and seaweed." She glanced at Nia's generous curves. "Perhaps longer."

Ludik twirled the gold hoop in his ear. "We could have been home by now."

Nia grabbed another handful of seaweed and stuffed it in her mouth. "Never mind, this is fine."

"Get down!" Ahjin pushed Nia to the ground and shoveled sand on the fire. As he threw himself on his stomach, he fanned his wings to disperse the smoke.

"What?" Zefra asked, lowering herself despite her confusion.

Ahjin glared and held a finger to his lips. When Zefra nodded to assure him of silence, he slowly craned his neck toward the ocean.

Everyone turned the same direction.

At first, Zefra saw nothing but leagues of ocean and sky. Then Ludik pointed, and Zefra saw a dark shape on the water. The shadow grew larger until she saw the lines of the ship. It could be their rescue! She leaned toward Ahjin to suggest it, and he covered her mouth.

He was ridiculous. What if they wanted to be heard and rescued? She yanked her head away and watched the ship again.

Oh. She recognized those mismatched sails. 'Twas the first pirate ship they had encountered, the one that stole their chickens. She had hoped it would be out of the area by now, on its way to wherever it called home.

Nia dropped her head to the sand. Her silent sigh puffed a hole in the grains below her.

Izo rolled next to Nia and put his arm around her. Ahjin frowned at Nia and then turned his head to glower at the ship.

Ludik glared at the pirate ship. His silver eyes shone with rage. Ahjin put a hand on the Darrendrakar's elbow and squeezed. After a minute, Ludik nodded. He lowered his head a little but kept watching the ship.

They stayed flat on the ground for an hour, until the ship sailed out of sight. When 'twas gone, they returned to their landing site and packed their dry gear to move farther inland. It seemed the most practical course of action.

Before they left the sand, they scoured the rust from their weapons. With no oil to protect the metal, they would have to repeat the process regularly, but at least 'twas a start.

Zefra was still working on her sword when the pirate ship returned. They spent another hour with their faces in the dirt.

Finally, Ahjin dragged them to their feet and made them collect their belongings and walk inland, even with the weapons half-polished.

"We're too exposed here," he said. "I found a valley farther in. It will do for tonight."

Nia babbled protests while Zefra reeled off more logical arguments. Ahjin walked away without a word, until the only thing they could do was follow him to his "valley," a small dip between rocky dunes. At least 'twas warmer, shoulder-to-shoulder in a circle with their backs to the dunes. Zefra leaned against Izo and tried to get comfortable.

"We have a problem," Ahjin said.

Nia laughed.

"Another problem," Ahjin clarified. "If Kaito comes back, the pirates will catch him."

Zefra had forgotten about Kaito. "I thought you only sent him away to protect him."

"I did," Ahjin said. "Do you think that will keep him from coming back for me?"

"If he tells our families we were stranded, they will want to help," Izo said. "How many of them will be on the rescue ship? How many will be captured with Kaito?"

"Or killed." Ludik's voice was grim.

15.STRANDED
(DRAGON ISLES)

Where there is love, there is pain.
Iojif Proverb

"We need to find a way home before Kaito gets here." Ahjin flexed his wings until they hit the dunes surrounding them. He wanted out but couldn't take the chance of pirates spotting him.

"I can swim," Nia said, "if I were ready to give up on finding Dad."

"What about the rest of us?" Ahjin asked.

"I might try swimming anyway." Ludik rubbed his earring and looked south.

"How will you keep from drowning when you fall asleep?" Nia asked. "We already talked about this, remember?"

Ludik crossed his arms and scowled.

"I could fly," Ahjin said, "if there were anywhere to rest on the way. That doesn't help the rest of you. Even if I flew for help, rescue couldn't get past the pirates any better for me than for Kaito."

If Kaito got past the pirates, if he didn't get lost, if he found help. If, if, if. But mentioning the Seal's problems wouldn't get them any closer to home.

"Can we get rid of the pirates?" Zefra asked.

Ahjin raised an eyebrow. "What do you suggest?"

Zefra shrugged at their small group and pitiful collection of weapons. "If the Nokai had stayed with us, it would have been easier."

"What about the gods?" Izo asked.

"Most of the gods won't meddle in our lives," Ahjin said, "and they won't help while we can still help ourselves. And it was Irajahan's meddling that broke our ship."

"When we chased that murderer last fall," Zefra said, "the gods would not help then, either. They always have an excuse."

"I suppose I could try Makana, anyway," Ahjin said. "Her territory is closest, and sometimes she makes exceptions."

"You can't see her in the water until morning." Ludik pointed to the setting sun.

"I'll keep first watch," Nia volunteered.

"I will take last," Zefra said.

Once everyone chose a watch, Ahjin put his arm around Nia and closed his eyes.

~~~~

M orning came too early. Ahjin crawled from the dip and stretched his wings, then wrapped them around himself for warmth. Today was his birthday, and this was not how he had planned to spend it. If he reminded the others, would it cheer them or make them feel worse?

Zefra was already awake and praying with Izo.

Ludik crawled out after Ahjin. "How long do you think it will take Nia to wake?"

Ahjin peeked back in the dip. Nia had fallen over on her side and curled into a ball. Her hairpins had come loose, letting her braids sprawl across the dirt. Despite her disarray, warmth blew through his heart.

"Not long. She's already shivering, and she must be as hungry as the rest of us." His stomach growled in emphasis.

Ludik grinned. "Why don't you go have a chat with Makana while we look for a morning meal?"

"In Zefra's words, it sounds like a plan." Ahjin winked at Ludik and flew toward the ocean.

He should pray to each of the gods, but how could he get a reply with such limited resources? He had no plants to contact Darravani on this barren island, no intact paper to write to Kassian, and he'd somehow lost Resef's runes in the escape from the ship. Irajahan ignored Ahjin when he called.

Ahjin stared into the ocean and called Makana. She did not answer, but he heard a faint echo of music. Makana was most likely busy with a party. It was a common occurrence, and normally, Ahjin enjoyed his low-maintenance duties toward her. It didn't help today, though.

He flew back to the others and discovered breakfast was a pile of mice.

Nia dangled one by its tail and looked dubiously at it.

Ahjin choked. "There aren't enough... mice for everyone. I'll wait until we find something else. Don't worry about me."

Even on his birthday — especially on his birthday — he'd rather go hungry than eat mice. Perhaps not reminding others about the occasion was the better idea. The thought of what they might do to celebrate was horrifying. Besides, the only gift he wanted was Nia's affection, and he had no privacy for *that* discussion.

Ludik grinned. "More for me, then."

Ahjin sat with his back to the others while they ate their disgusting breakfast. "I couldn't contact Makana," he explained. "I think our best idea is to get off this island before we starve."

"If we could get off, we would go home," Ludik said.

"Not necessarily. This island is barren all the way across, but the southern one is bigger and green. We could swim across to find more food."

"We will still be stranded," Izo said. "What good does that do?"

Nia gagged. "Not starving is a good start. Here, someone can have the rest of my mice."

"If we can survive long enough," Ahjin said, "we can find a way home later."

"How far is the swim?" Izo asked.

"A mile or two," Ahjin said. "Perhaps less. You can do it."

"There is no point wasting time," Zefra said. "We can leave now."

Everyone picked up their half-empty packs. Ludik crammed his feet into his water-ruined boots, and they walked west.

The island was mostly bare dirt, decorated with rocks. They walked over small hills and down tiny valleys and found only scattered grass, yellow and dry.

They walked quickly at first, but as the heat rose and their water jugs emptied, their pace slowed.

"I'll be back." Ahjin yanked invisibility over himself and flew off to survey.

The rest of the island was as bad, and when he returned to report, his head ached again. "There's no water from here to the shore. There are no trees, no shade."

Zefra pulled her scarf from her hair. "Nia, cover your gills. 'Tis the best we can do." She tried to tuck her frizzled hair back into a tidy coronet, then gave up.

Nia silently took the scarf and wrapped it around her neck.

The highlight of Ahjin's birthday came when Ludik found a bird's nest with eggs. Only one problem remained.

Ahjin groaned. "Raw eggs, and no water to boil them."

Zefra stared at the three precious ovals and licked her lips. "Ahjin and Nia ate the least this morning. They should have these."

She closed her hands around the eggs and narrowed her eyes. After a few minutes, she handed two to Ahjin and one to Nia.

Ahjin took his and juggled them. They were hot, hotter than the normal warmth of a fresh egg.

Nia cracked hers over her open mouth, and a thick goo leaked onto her tongue.

"Thank you, Zefra." Ahjin cracked his eggs straight down his throat. Half-cooked was infinitely better than raw. His stomach grumbled, but it was the best birthday meal he'd ever had.

"I'll look for more." Ludik stalked ahead of them.

Izo and Zefra spread out to either side.

Even Ludik's sneaky cat ears were too far away to hear. This was his chance. Ahjin fell into step with Nia and switched to his own language for extra privacy. Nia's birth gift from Makana let her speak all languages, but none of the others spoke Iojo.

"I haven't had a chance to talk to you yet."

Nia laughed. "What do you call all the planning we've been doing? We've been talking way too much, if you ask me. My throat hurts from too much talking and not enough water."

"No, that's not what I mean. I wanted to talk to you about courtship."

Nia put her hands on her hips. "Haven't you harped that old tune for long enough? I told you, my flirting is none of your concern."

"No, I mean, yes, I mean—" Ahjin took a deep breath. "I'd like to make it my concern, in a different way. I realized I love you, Nia."

His stomach cramped, and his heart pounded. He had thought this would be easier.

Nia patted his arm. "I love you, too, Ahjin. You're my best friend. I know you think you know better, but I can handle myself."

"I know you can," Ahjin said. "That's not what I mean, either." He grabbed Nia's hand. "I mean, I love you. You're the best thing in my life."

Nia smiled. "I'm not a thing, but I do value our friendship."

Ahjin winced. This conversation wasn't working. "I'd like to court you myself," he blurted.

Nia jerked her hand away. "I don't think so."

Ahjin flinched and stopped walking.

"I do love you," Nia said, stopping beside him, "but not like *that*. Best friends are not flirts."

"I didn't think of it before, either," Ahjin said, "but now I see the truth. I love you. Will you think about it for a while? The idea might grow on you."

Nia shook her head slowly. "I wouldn't want a temporary flirt to ruin our friendship. I value it too highly."

"Isn't that what you're doing to Izo?"

Nia sighed. "I hope not, but we started with a flirting sort of relationship. We aren't the same kind of friends you and I are." She took his hand again. "I don't expect any kind of long-term relationship with him beyond a casual friendship and a connection to Zefra."

Ahead of them, Ludik stood from inspecting the underside of a bush and stared back at their clasped hands. He smiled and walked forward, pointing ahead of them and asking questions of the Iskrins.

"Does he know?" Ahjin said bitterly. Though he appreciated Ludik distracting Izo, it didn't seem to matter. "Never mind. *I'd* prefer to offer you a long-term relationship. Tell me there's some hope."

He tried to smile but couldn't convince his mouth to turn up instead of down.

Nia's eyes grew huge, and she squeezed Ahjin's hand. "Are you suggesting — marriage?"

Ahjin tried to sound casual. "I know how you feel about that. We can decide when we're older. For now, I just want to be with you."

Tears shone in Nia's eyes. "Even if I were interested in a romance with you, I would say no. I want children eventually, and you can't give them to me. I need a Nokai lover for children."

Ahjin's heart pinched at the thought of Nia with an actual lover instead of just a flirt.

"We could adopt," he pleaded. "Can't we work it out somehow? You can think about it as long as you need. There's no hurry."

"I'm sorry." She pulled her hand away. "Don't ask me again. Don't ruin our friendship. Stop thinking of me that way." Her voice shook.

"Are you asking me to stop loving you?"

"Not as a friend, just as a romance. Find someone else." Nia half-smiled, patted his arm, then turned and walked toward the others.

Ahjin pressed his hand to his chest and watched her leave. Her tone had been kind, but she didn't love him. She'd never love him. She couldn't even bear to consider the idea.

Darravani had mended his heart from the lightning last year, but right now, he couldn't tell if it was still working under the pain. He couldn't catch his breath, couldn't move.

She didn't love him. It wasn't her fault; it had to be his. If even his best friend couldn't love him, who could? He was seventeen today, and his life was already over.

After a few minutes, he shuffled his feet and dragged his worthless self after his friends. At least Nia still wanted to be friends, still wanted to be part of his life in some way.

Despite the chasm splitting his heart, it would have to be enough.

He heard Nia telling Zefra, "I don't understand boys."

Ludik glanced behind again at Ahjin but said nothing. When Izo stopped to wait, Ludik pushed him forward. "Just keep walking."

Ahjin silently followed them, wishing he had enough energy to stay invisible all day.

Ahjin tailed the others across the island for the rest of the day, catching up only when they stopped at the strait between the two islands. Even from here, they saw green on the big southern island.

"Ahjin was right," Nia said. "The water's not that wide. Even the rest of you can swim it easily." She didn't look at Ahjin.

"I just got the rust sanded off everything," Zefra complained.

"There's no need to take your packs." Ahjin turned from Nia and took Zefra's bag. "I can carry them across while you swim." He jumped into the air and turned invisible, just in case. "Leave your things in a pile, and I'll come back for them." He flew away before anyone could argue.

The strait was narrow, and the wind was pleasant, and Ahjin made the trip in only a few minutes. Without food, and with half their things ruined, he could manage two packs at a time if he didn't try fancy flying. He took his time finding a safe place, then left both Zefra's bag and his own. By the time he started back across, his friends were in the water.

Ahjin put Izo's pack on his back and held Nia's in his arms for the next trip. It was a mistake. He should have put Nia's on his back, where it wouldn't be a constant reminder of their conversation. His arms ached to hold Nia instead of her pack.

But she didn't love him. What would he do?

He hurried this trip and dumped the bags with relief.

His friends had made it a quarter of the way. Izo and Zefra splashed clumsily, but their heads were above water. Nia and the panther paced them.

One last trip. Ahjin stuffed Ludik's clothes into his bag and flew slowly, watching the progress of the others below. The Iskrins were slower now, but they still swam. They'd be fine.

What about him? Ahjin would even drink one of Ludik's nasty potions, if it might make his heart feel better. He stuffed his love into his broken heart and hoped it would stay there. If he could, he'd tie it shut with one of Nia's ribbons or wrap it in one of Ludik's bandages. This was his worst birthday gift ever.

Ahjin landed on the coast and dropped his invisibility to spare himself more of a headache. He had time to explore while he waited for the others. They needed some kind of shelter, and night would arrive soon. This shore was steeper, leading directly into hills, and might have caves. If they were far enough from the waterline, that would do.

At the third hill, he succeeded. The opening to the cave was narrow and hidden behind a rock. Only a shadow cast by the setting sun showed him the way.

Ahjin poked his head around the rock, trying to see if the cave sheltered predators. The entrance stone blocked most of the sunlight. He'd wait for Zefra's fire to light the way. He listened for breathing or growls but heard nothing. That was promising, though not enough. He marked the entrance with a small cairn and headed back.

Nia was the first to arrive, but she waved at Ahjin and waited for the others.

Ahjin laid Ludik's tunic over a boulder and helped Zefra and Izo out of the ocean.

"Head around the corner." Ahjin pointed the way before giving Nia a hand, which she dropped as quickly as possible. He escorted her after the Iskrins to give Ludik a chance to shift and dress.

"I found a cave," Ahjin explained. "By the rocks. It looked empty but was too dark to see much."

Zefra snapped her fingers and pulled a flame to her hand. "I will go look." She ducked easily through the entrance and disappeared.

Izo followed her, turning sideways to slide through the opening. He came back a minute later, as Ludik joined them. "'Tis unoccupied but has been used in the past. There are bones. Ludik, come see what you can tell us. 'Tis large enough for everyone."

Nia followed Izo. Ludik squeezed in after her.

Ahjin pulled his wings tight and wiggled past the rock, barely making it. He didn't look forward to squeezing past the rock again in the morning. Someone else could fetch the packs.

Zefra stood at the other side of the small cave. She held her flaming hand toward the floor so everyone could navigate around the scattered bones and frayed bits of colorful fabric half-buried in the accumulated sand.

Ludik crouched and traced a body. "These are ribs, spine, leg bones. Oh, there's the skull. It rolled a bit. All of them are showing bite marks." He picked up an arm bone and pointed. "These are from small teeth, like rodents or small scavengers, not from a large predator."

Ahjin gulped. He hoped the poor man died first. Even a pirate didn't deserve death from a thousand nibbles.

"What killed him, then?" Nia asked. "Starvation, dehydration, drowning?"

Ludik shook his head. "He wouldn't have washed in here by accident." He turned over the bone. "These are cuts from a blade. Izo, would you guess a sword?"

Ahjin hid a shudder. How did Ludik handle that so casually?

Izo gingerly took the bone and held it under Zefra's flame. "Either a sword or a hefty knife." He gave the arm back to Ludik and wiped his hand on his pants.

"So he was injured in some kind of fight," Ludik said, "and hid in this cave and died. Maybe the pirates fought among themselves, or else this is one of their victims."

"We can bury him tomorrow," Zefra said, "but we should collect the bones tonight and put them in a corner."

Nia shuddered. "That's a great idea."

"We need Zefra's light," Ahjin said, "but there isn't a lot of room. Nia, why don't you get our stuff while the rest of us clean." He resisted the urge to wipe his own hands on his pants.

Izo grimaced but didn't argue. He slid the large bones toward the chosen corner with his feet while Ludik and Ahjin hunted for small ones. Ludik tallied the bones as they were discovered.

Ahjin shuddered. The task was gruesome, but better than finding a leftover in his bed. And think how Nia would scream if she woke with one tangled in her braids.

Nia dropped her bag and Ahjin's in a corner before going back for the next load.

Ludik swept the tiny foot bones and dropped them in the pile. "Almost there. All we're missing now is the second hand," he said.

Ahjin saw a gleam under a pile of sand. "I found it." He bent to gather them and discovered a beaded, embroidered bracelet under the bones. His heart sank. He gave the bones to Ludik, then turned with the familiar bracelet.

Nia squeezed back in with the last of the packs. "Oh, that's mine," she said. "Did I drop it somehow?"

She pushed up her sleeve. The bracelet from her mother was still tied securely to her wrist.

It was an exact match to the dirty one in Ahjin's hand.

16. COMPANY
(DRAGON ISLES)

The deeper the sorrow, the less tongue it has.
Darrendran Proverb

Nia stared at the two matching bracelets, one on her wrist and the other hanging from Ahjin's hand. How could they match?

Ahjin glanced at the pile of bones in the corner. "I found Alaneo's bracelet on the skeleton."

Nia shook her head. "You're mistaken. That would mean Dad is dead."

He pushed the bracelet toward her again.

Nia gasped for breath as her vision blurred. "No," she moaned. "There must be a mistake! It's the wrong bracelet, or one of your not-funny pranks."

She crossed the cave in three steps and snatched the faded bracelet from him, then untied the bracelet from her wrist and held the two next to each other, turning them to compare every thumb-length. The embroidery was unmistakably Mom's work. The older bracelet had lost a few of its decorative beads, and dirt muted the colors, but the bracelets were otherwise identical.

Ludik wordlessly held out a few strands of faded pink hair.

Alaneo had pink hair. It was true, then. Nia had found her missing dad, but he was dead. A shudder started at Nia's webbed toes and crept through her trembling knees, rising until it burst in her throbbing heart. He'd been dead for so long that nothing was left of him but bones. She would never meet him, never even know what he looked like beyond "pink hair."

It shouldn't make a difference, since she'd been without him her entire life, but somehow, the death of hope still hurt.

"It's not fair." Nia fumbled with numb fingers to put her bracelet back on her wrist, until Ahjin took it from her and retied it. "I just found out I had a chance to meet him, and he's already gone. Someone chopped him to bits. How dare they murder my dad!" She clenched her fists and wailed. "I'll kill them. I'll slice them to chum and throw them to the sharks."

Izo reached for her, but when she sobbed and hit him, he flinched away. Ahjin dodged her fists and put one arm around her, using his free hand to block her punches. When she threw both arms around him, he added his other arm to the embrace.

"I've failed, Ahjin," she sobbed. "Dad is dead."

He patted her back and whispered something in a comforting voice, too quiet for her to hear anything but the tone.

"You have not failed," Zefra said. "Our quest was to discover what happened to him. Your mother thought he died long ago, or he would have come home. Now we have proof, and you can set her mind at ease."

Nia lunged for her. "That's not enough. I want my dad."

Zefra stepped out of range while Ahjin yanked Nia back. She buried her head in his shirt and bawled. His arms tightened around her, but he said nothing.

Nia cursed the stupid pirates, crying for the dad she never had and now never would.

Behind her, the others shuffled through the cave, kicking rocks aside and shuffling packs. Ludik muttered something about "no herbs." Izo carefully patted Nia on the shoulder from a distance.

Nia cried more. When she finally ran out of tears, she hiccuped. Ahjin patted her back. She pulled away and rubbed her eyes.

"So," he started.

Nia shook her head and pressed her lips together. They were not talking about this.

Ahjin pulled the loose hairpins from her braids and handed her the collection. "Your ribbons used to stay in better." His voice was strained, and as he turned away, she saw the gleam of tears in his eyes.

The others stood around them, fidgeting and avoiding her gaze. The blankets lay in two rows, with bags for lumpy pillows.

"Maybe I should use ribbons as well as the hairpins." She walked to the bed by her pack and shoved Izo's gift into a pocket. In the morning, she'd have to fix her hair anyway, and she didn't feel like messing with it now.

Nia threw herself on her hard bed and closed her eyes. Around her, the others lay on their own beds.

Ahjin cleared his throat. "Without a ship, we can't take him back. We'll bury him in the morning, before we leave."

"Thank you," Nia whispered, rolling over with the bracelet in her fist pressed against her heart.

Without the ship, she couldn't even return Dad to Mom. Her quest was a failure, and she was alone. She buried her head under her other arm and cried herself to sleep.

∿∿∿∿

Though the rock at the entrance blocked most of the morning sun, Nia woke when her rumbling belly grew too loud. She dragged herself from bed and packed her belongings, minus her blanket. She cut her blanket in half, then stuffed one part into her bag and handed the other to Ahjin.

"Since we have no coffin," she said.

She and Zefra took their packs outside, then took the men's while Izo searched for a long stick.

Ludik and Ahjin squeezed through the cave entrance a few minutes later, with Nia's ragged blanket cupped between them. They carried their burden of bones to the shore and spread it by the water.

Izo walked up with a crooked branch, half a fathom long. "This is the best I found. Sorry, Nia."

"It will do." Nia coughed through a dry throat.

"Are you ready?" Ahjin asked.

Nia shook her head. "I should look my best, to honor him."

She dug out her hairpins and her ribbons and sat to brush and re-braid her hair. While she worked, the others shook off as much dust as possible and washed their faces in salt water. Ahjin finger-combed his curls and tied them at his neck. Everyone finished before she did, but they didn't ask her to hurry.

When Nia had done her best, she stood by the blanket of bones. She clenched the bracelet and a spare ribbon in her fist and nodded in Ahjin's direction.

"I'm sorry we only have shallow water for his grave," Ahjin murmured. "We can't risk the pirates to find deeper currents." He pulled Kassian's silver star from under his shirt and spread his wings.

Nia pulled herself straight and pressed her lips together.

"Today we gather to bury a missing Nokai," Ahjin said. "He who was lost has now been found. His fate is known, and he shall not be forgotten." He turned to Nia and raised an eyebrow.

Nia took a shuddering breath. "Alaneo did his best for his family, and we love him for it. Dad, we miss you."

Izo took her free hand.

Ludik sang a Darrendrakar funeral song quietly in his deep voice, then Ahjin struggled through the Nokai lullaby, "Home Again." Under different circumstances, Nia would have teased him about his singing. She took a shuddering breath and joined him on the last verse. Her voice croaked, but she owed it to Dad.

Ludik wrapped the bones with a few rocks for weight and tied the blanket with the ribbon Nia gave him. He handed the bundle to Ahjin.

Ahjin held Nia's dad carefully. "Alaneo returns now to the ocean. May it carry him to rest in Makanavailea's arms."

He flew the makeshift coffin straight out from shore until he passed the low-tide line. After glancing once at Nia, he dropped the bones.

As it sank below the waves, tears ran down Nia's cheeks. Now Dad was truly gone.

Zefra held the twisted branch while Izo pounded it into the sand at the high-tide line.

Ahjin returned and carved a notch at the top of the stick, then pried open Nia's fingers and snagged the faded bracelet on the post. "It's the best marker I can manage. Unless you want to take the bracelet home to your mother?"

"It will be fine," Nia whispered. "Pleasant journey, Dad." She wiped the tears from her cheeks and turned inland. "Let's find food and water."

The group trudged in near-silence. The landscape quickly changed from the rocky shore to the same scrubby grass as on the first island, and then to real grass and scattered flowers. The first sight of a tree in the distance sent them all into a stumbling jog. When they heard the burble of running water, they shuffled even faster.

The trees, though unimpressive compared to a Darrendran forest, were green and shady and clustered around a small stream of clear water. Nia tossed off Zefra's scarf and threw herself on the bank. She ducked her whole head underwater, gulping mouthfuls while the cool water poured over her gills and refreshed them. It was a long time before she emerged to wring out her hair.

Ahjin was watching her, but the others were gone.

"They're searching for food," he said. "No one trusts me to recognize edible plants, and I didn't want to leave you alone."

Nia's stomach growled. She ignored his hint at the sorrow she wanted to forget. "Food is a great idea. Want to find berries?"

Ahjin laughed. "I *do* know what berries look like."

"Do you know which ones are poisonous?"

Ahjin groaned and pulled her to her feet. "Who thought it was a good idea to make poisonous berries?"

Nia shook her head. "It's a good thing we don't leave you alone in the wilderness. You'd kill yourself in no time."

"I grew up in one of the biggest cities in the world," Ahjin said. "We had a garden, but it only grew what we planted. And Mother did the cooking."

"And how long have you been studying with Darravani?" Nia asked.

"Less than a year, and most of it has been winter," Ahjin retorted. "And she concentrated on the meanings of plants, not their edibility."

Nia threw her hands in the air and half-smiled. Somehow, Ahjin always made her feel better.

"Fine, you win. Just please don't eat anything until you check with someone who knows what they're doing."

She tied Zefra's scarf into a bag. After some searching, they found a single edible berry bush and picked every ripe or nearly ripe berry. Most of them even ended up in Zefra's scarf instead of in their mouths. Ahjin's frequent teasing was a welcome distraction from her grief, and he didn't even hint at romance between them. Sometimes he came up with crazy ideas, but that one topped them all. At least he had given up on the impossible idea, because she hated hurting his feelings.

They carried their bounty back to the stream and found the others waiting. Izo sorted a pile of spring greens into five portions while Ludik skinned half a dozen rabbits. Zefra had dug a fire pit and laid a small fire with twigs and fallen branches surrounding a flat rock.

"Is it safe to light a fire, do you think?" Zefra held one twig in her hand.

"We're an entire island away from the pirates," Nia said, "and they think we're dead."

Zefra pressed her lips together and rubbed the back of her neck. Nia barely kept herself from sticking out her tongue at the pessimist.

Ahjin stole another berry. "And we've gone up and down a lot of hills."

Ludik juggled his handful of naked rabbits. "And we're surrounded by trees. As long as we keep the fire small, we should be safe."

"And I'm very hungry." Izo pressed his hands to his stomach and licked his lips.

Zefra nodded, and the twig in her hand burst into flames. She touched it to the wood, which caught easily.

Ludik chopped the rabbits into smaller pieces and laid them on the stone in the middle of the fire. "What do we have to eat while we wait?"

"Salad." Izo waved at the green leaves.

"And berries." Ahjin opened Zefra's scarf. "Sorry about the juice stains."

Zefra shrugged. "'Tis the least of my worries."

Nia divided the berries into five uneven piles and gave the three biggest to Ludik, Zefra, and Izo. "We got a little impatient."

Izo looked at her lips, which she guessed were as red-stained as Ahjin's, and smiled. "So I see."

And that was the last comment before everyone dove into their food. Berry salad had never tasted so good.

While they waited for the rabbits to finish cooking, they drank again. When the smell became too tantalizing, Zefra picked the most-done pieces from the stone and handed them around. The salad had been good, but the rabbit was divine. Nia closed her eyes to enjoy it better, licking every bit of juice from her fingers. She opened her eyes and froze mid-lick.

A strange Nokai with midnight blue hair limped toward them, long harpoon in hand. His skin had been dyed to match his hair.

Nia jumped to her feet and yelled, "Pirate!"

Her friends grabbed their weapons and spread out. Zefra dove for her bow, while Nia stole Zefra's staff. No sense letting a good weapon go to waste.

The man stopped and held one hand in front of him. "I mean you no harm."

Ahjin held his unstrung bow like a staff and took a step toward the pirate. "We outnumber you. I suggest you lower your weapon unless you want a hole through your throat."

"Don't be ridiculous," the pirate said. "Put down your weapons and put out that fire. It isn't safe." His gaze lingered on Izo's hammer.

Ahjin raised an eyebrow. "I asked first."

"This is a walking stick." The man looked only seven or ten thousand days older than Nia and her friends, too young to need help walking because of his age, and still hearty enough to be a threat. He wore a pair of trousers so stained the original color couldn't be determined, and a shortened tunic with the sleeves ripped off. A tattered scarf was tied around his neck.

Ludik took a step toward him, knife held low.

"It can be a weapon if you come any closer!" The blue pirate looked around him. "I'm trying to help you. Hurry, before the pirates spot your smoke. I told you, it isn't safe."

Zefra jerked her head toward the stream and kicked an empty water jug to Nia, then stomped out the fire without taking her gaze off the maybe-not-a-pirate. Nia backed up, filled the jug, and emptied it over the smoldering branches. It would have created less smoke to let Zefra absorb the heat, but nobody wanted to tip off the stranger in case they needed a useful surprise later.

"That's better," the blue man said. "I've been watching you. I thought you were pirates, at first, until I saw the way you treat each other. Pirates aren't kind, even to a lady." He took a second look at Zefra. "Ladies."

Nia scoffed. "You're a pirate."

"I'm not a pirate," he said, "though I don't know how to convince you. My name is Kani. And speaking of pirates, could we leave, please?"

"Why should we go anywhere with you?" Ludik asked.

"My home is safer, and I'll answer your questions there. Now, please, let's get out of sight before you draw the attention of the pirates. I'd like to keep them far from here, if you don't mind."

Ahjin raised an eyebrow at Nia. She shrugged. They needed help, and if he ended up being a pirate, they outnumbered him. And they did have advantages he wouldn't suspect.

After a glance at the rest of them, Ahjin lowered his bow. "Very well, we'll go with you long enough to talk. What happens after that depends on how convincing you are."

Ludik's knife vanished from sight.

Zefra handed her bow to Izo. "I must gather my snares."

She ran away and came back a few minutes later, holding three empty snares and a dead rabbit, which she tucked away before taking back her bow.

Ludik smiled his deceptively warm smile and picked up his bag. "Where are you taking us?"

The others gathered their things and spread out behind Ludik.

"My home is that way." Kani pointed north. "The pirates don't go that far inland. Tell me, how did you end up here?" He walked with a severe limp, leaning on his harpoon. That explained the "walking stick."

Nia snorted. "Much the same as you, I imagine. Shipwrecked and trapped by pirates."

Dumb pirates who killed her dad. She swallowed hard and pushed away the thought.

"Hmm," Kani said. "Similar, at any rate. I don't want to talk about it. You're an odd assortment. Are you sure you aren't pirates? I don't think I've ever seen such a mixed crew that wasn't." He asked it casually, but his knuckles whitened on his harpoon.

Ahjin tucked his silver star inside his shirt while Kani watched Ludik. "How can we convince you?"

Kani frowned. "I see the problem." He looked at Zefra and Nia again. "Some pirate crews include women, but I've never seen any so young and... friendly."

Nia laughed. Zefra smoothed her face to diplomatic nothingness and fingered her bow.

Kani sighed. "I suppose I'll have to trust my instincts."

From this close, Nia saw calluses on his bare, webbed feet. He was too scrawny for a proper Nokai, as if he hadn't eaten enough for a year. How did he stay warm in the water without enough insulation?

They walked in relative silence for more than an hour, over more small hills and valleys. Trees grew more frequently inland, but they were mostly small, crooked things.

Eventually, Nia got bored. "Who else is here with you? What do you do all day? How long have you lived here? Don't you like Nokailana? Why don't you go home?"

Kani flinched a little and stared at her with wide amber eyes.

Ahjin elbowed Nia. "I apologize. You don't have to answer her questions."

"Hmm." Kani thought for a minute. "I suppose you should know something about me, if you're to trust me. I'm alone. I've been here a long time. I'd like to go back to Nokailana, but I can't get past the pirates patrolling the waters. And what I do all day is my affair. Is that enough information for you, young curiosity?"

"No, but I can ask more questions later." Nia grinned at him.

Kani laughed.

"Perhaps we can help each other," Ahjin said. "We need to escape soon. We're willing to take you with us, if you help us."

Nia bounced on her toes. Now that she knew Dad was dead, getting home was an excellent idea.

"I told you, there's no way off," Kani repeated.

Ludik rubbed his earring. "I will find a way home."

"Many brains working together think of solutions one cannot," Zefra said.

"If anyone can escape, 'tis this crew," Izo said. "Join while you can."

Kani leaned on his harpoon for a minute. "Maybe I will. You can tell me your ideas. And here we are."

He pointed, but Nia saw nothing but grass and a few scrubby bushes. "Where?"

"You didn't think I'd leave it out in plain sight, did you? Come inside, and let's talk."

17.LAIR

(DRAGON ISLES)

The best Iskrin healers come from the Tukiko clan. The most talented earn the title of Shri. Legends claim they rescue patients from death itself.
Iskrin Culture and History, vol. 3

Ludik followed closely behind Kani. If the blue man intended to betray them, he wouldn't last a minute under Ludik's teeth and claws. And if there was a way to get home, he wanted to hear it first.

As Kani disappeared behind some scraggly bushes, Ludik sped up to keep him in sight as he ducked into a low cave. The floor slanted downward under a ceiling that required a crouch, but after they turned a corner, the cave opened up enough for even Ludik to stand, though his hair grazed the ceiling. The only light was from a makeshift lamp.

"This is nice," Nia said in a dubious tone, brushing a finger across Ahjin's feathers until his wings stopped twitching.

The lair wasn't bad, for a cave, but Ludik didn't think it counted as nice. Kani's bed was a pile of leaves and pine boughs, covered with a patchwork blanket. The dirt-and-stone floor was well-swept but bare. A crate of twigs held a few personal items, and a net slung a stash of food near the ceiling, probably to keep it from mice. Ludik would have left some of it on the floor as bait. He grinned as he imagined Ahjin's reaction to the idea.

"Here's the best part." Kani led them around a corner to a low tunnel, holding the lamp low to show a tiny spring bubbling into the back of the cave. "It's not much, but it keeps me safe. I hide during the day and hunt and salvage at night. I only came out today because I saw your smoke. If you were pirates, I needed to know why you were so far inland. Do you believe I'm not a pirate now?"

Nia nodded enthusiastically. The Iskrins frowned while they nodded, and Ahjin crossed his arms.

Ludik thought they were all too optimistic, but if Kani could help them, they needed to build an alliance.

"As a show of trust," he said, "to show you we are not pirates either, may I try to heal your leg?"

Time would show if Kani was worthy of Ludik's trust, and his healing might as well do some good for someone.

"I don't think you can help it now," Kani said. "It's been this way for years."

Nia smiled at him. "What harm can it do?"

"Very well." Kani rolled up his trousers. A long scar crawled up each leg, cutting them diagonally from ankle to knee in jagged lines.

"Bleached whale bones," Nia swore.

Ludik hissed through his teeth. "Teeth and claws. What happened to you?"

"Pirate." Kani bit off the word.

Ludik touched the scars softly, then pressed harder. Kani winced but said nothing.

Ludik closed his eyes and let his healing magic sink into the old wounds. In some ways, they had healed well. The skin had knit, as had the muscles. But the muscles had healed with crooked connections and would never line up properly. Even if Ludik slashed them open again, there was no guarantee the results would be any better.

He opened his eyes and frowned at Kani. His offer was useless.

"Don't tell me," Kani said. "It's been too long. That's what I expected." He rolled down his trousers and fiddled with his scarf. "I don't think I'll get a better answer, but maybe you could check my gills, too?"

Nia put a hand on her neck. "Your gills?"

"You asked me why I didn't go home. I only told you part of the truth. You should know my shortcomings before we make any plans." Kani untied the scarf and tilted his head.

The gills on his neck were crosshatched with cuts and melted from burns.

Izo and Zefra gasped. Nia gagged and buried her head in Ahjin's sleeve.

Ludik leaned closer and ran a finger above Kani's ruined gills. This time, he didn't even need his magic to know he was still useless. "I doubt I could fix them with this many slashes, but even if I could, the burns have sealed them shut. I am sorry."

Kani nodded and retied his scarf around his neck. "Then let's hear your story, and you can tell me how you think we can escape without me swimming."

"We came looking for pakai," Nia said, "and we jumped ship to avoid the pirates after our crew abandoned us."

Ahjin raised an eyebrow, and she shook her head a tiny bit.

Kani glanced to the side. "Did you find any pakai?"

"We have not had a chance to search." Zefra narrowed her eyes a fraction at Nia. "We are also exploring."

Nia nodded discreetly.

"For Kassian," Zefra finished.

"Is Kassian your employer?" Kani asked.

Ahjin's mouth twitched. "In a way. I'm sure you noticed the upheavals last summer."

Kani's eyes widened. "Between the shaking earth and the typhoons, I nearly died. Let's not mention the tidal waves. Did we change the subject?"

Nia shuddered. "No."

Ludik jumped in with the shortest summary. "The gods were captured by their forgotten older brother, and their battle almost destroyed the world. Now they are at peace, but Kassian needs somewhere to live, and Zefra is helping him look. Now can we plan our escape?"

Kani blinked. "Why do I think there's a lot more to that story? I've never even heard of an older god. And if he's real, how did a young girl end up working for him?"

Ludik snorted. "It was Ahjin's fault."

Ahjin pursed his lips. "Let's save that story for later. Ludik has a good idea. Let's talk about escape plans."

"I've been collecting flotsam and broken branches for years," Kani said. "I hoped to build a raft, but I couldn't manage it alone, and I had no tools besides a few broken pirate weapons." He turned to Izo. "You have a hammer. Since you'll no longer beat me with it, could I persuade you to use it on my raft?"

"You are luckier than you know," Izo said. "I'm a blacksmith. I can probably rework those broken weapons into more tools for you."

Kani exhaled. "Yes, that would work. I already have a sail."

He stood and pulled his blanket from his bed. He handed two corners to Ludik and Nia and held the other end. The triangular sail was made of bits of fabric stitched carefully together. The corners already had holes for the lines, reinforced with close binding stitches.

Ludik ran his fingers along one uneven edge.

"I'm almost finished." Kani cradled it in his arms. "I just salvaged the fabric for the missing section, and it won't take long to sew it in. It's perfect timing. The gods must be on our side."

Ahjin turned his snort into a cough when Nia stepped on his foot.

Izo frowned. "I can make tools, but I know nothing about building boats. Or rafts."

Kani put the sail on his bed. "I can teach you." He clasped his hands together in front of him.

"Won't an open raft be too weak for a trip across the ocean?" Nia asked.

Kani's smile faded. "Do we have a choice?"

"How will we protect ourselves against the pirates?" Ludik asked. "We will not outrun them with one small sail, and we will be too outnumbered to defend ourselves."

"I thought we could avoid them." Kani shrugged. "Just slip by."

"Just slip by?" Zefra repeated.

"The raft will be small." Kani's knuckles turned white. "I hope to be too small to be noticed."

"I want to go home," Ludik said, "but I want to get there alive."

"It will work," Kani insisted, "even if we have to wait for the slow trading season in winter, after the pirates disappear to other harbors."

"Until winter!" Ludik clenched his fists. By winter, Nemerra would think he was dead. His children would be crawling.

Everyone spoke at once, protesting the delay.

"Settle down," Ahjin said. "Let's give this serious thought." He sat on the floor and relaxed his wings behind him.

Ludik crouched and waited. Zefra and Izo sat cross-legged, and Nia tucked her legs to one side and leaned against the wall.

"Now, Kani," Ahjin said, "let's start again. You've been here for a while. What can you tell us about the pirates' habits?"

Kani sank to his bed and dropped his head in his hands. "They come every spring. There are usually only a couple of ships, and they wait to waylay merchant ships traveling alone. After a few good hauls, they go home by fall. I've tracked their patrols, and I can predict them well. They sail by the eastern island about every two days, so if we leave right after a patrol, we can slip through."

"If they always go home before winter," Ludik asked, "do you know where they go?"

Kani shook his head. "No, though I suspect they split up to each country. The pirates that took my ship were a mixed crew."

"You say there are only a couple of ships," Nia said, "but we've already seen at least two, and they stole our ship as well."

"And they have patrolled several times each day since we have been here," Zefra said. "I wrote the times on my slate."

Nia rolled her eyes. "Of course you did."

Ahjin put a hand on her knee, and she said no more.

"That's strange," Kani said. "I've watched them for years. They've never varied before."

Ludik tugged the wedding ring in his ear. Predictability was good; changing an established pattern was not.

"Has anything else changed?" Ahjin asked.

Kani frowned. "Last winter, they stayed here for the first time, maybe because of the tidal waves. Now that the waters are calm again, they'll certainly go home again this fall."

"If you do not know why their patterns changed," Zefra asked, "how can you know when they will return to their old ones?"

"Exactly," Ludik said. "Your plan is too risky."

Kani shook his head. "They've always been the same until last fall." His voice was sad, and he stroked the sail on his bed.

Ahjin nodded. "Under the circumstances, I don't think we can agree to the raft. We don't know if your information is still accurate, and we can't risk being caught again."

"What do we do, then?" Kani asked.

"We survive until we find another plan," Ludik said.

"I can dye your skin for night travel," Kani offered. "Then the pirates won't spot you even if they're out. I could even do your hair."

Nia gasped and covered her hair. "Don't you dare. Ahjin, stop laughing."

Ahjin covered his mouth, but his chuckles leaked through his fingers.

Ludik turned to hide his own grin. Nia might have forgiven Ahjin for dyeing her hair, but she would never forget.

"Nobody sees me if I don't want them to," Ahjin explained to Kani.

"How exactly do you disguise yourself?"

"Perhaps I'll show you sometime," Ahjin said.

Ludik approved of his vagueness. Until they knew Kani was trustworthy, they shouldn't reveal all their secrets. They might need the advantage later.

"I am already dark enough for night work," Ludik said. "What about you, Izo and Zefra?"

"Yes, Zefra." Izo grinned. "Do you want your hair dark again?"

Zefra made a note on her slate. "We will keep that in mind, Kani, but I do not think it will be necessary yet."

"What is next, then?" Izo asked.

"Sleep." Kani stood. "The ladies can share my bed, if they like. When night falls, we can hunt and talk more."

Ludik watched with narrowed eyes to make sure the Nokai didn't mean "share with him," but Kani took the floor closest to the stream.

Nia sat on the bed and slid over by the wall to make room for Zefra. "Sleep well, boys."

Zefra put her boots at the foot of the bed and lay stiffly beside Nia, while Ahjin and Izo spread out by either end of the bed.

Ludik picked a spot close to the door, between his friends and possible danger, and curled up with his head on his pack and his hand near his boot-knife. He closed his eyes and dreamed of Nemerra's russet hair and honey-brown eyes, her loving smile and belly growing with their coming children, her leather-working calluses rough against his skin as they linked hands and leaned together for a kiss.

〰〰〰

When Ludik woke, the trickle of light coming down the entry had slipped into darkness.

Kani was already awake and silently watching the others.

Ludik ignored him and shook Ahjin. "Whose turn is it to wake Nia?"

Ahjin groaned. "Yours, but wake Zefra first so she's at a safe distance. I'll get Izo." He sat, glanced at Kani, then crawled to Izo.

His turn. If he were lucky, this would be the most dangerous part of his day. Ludik leaned above the bed and shook Zefra, then yanked back his hand and inhaled in preparation.

She shot upright and snapped flame into her hand.

Ludik blew it out and hoped Kani hadn't seen it. "Zefra, wake up."

Zefra inhaled. "I'm awake. Do we need a light?"

Kani stirred. "I'll get a lamp."

"If you'll move," Ludik said, "I'll wake Nia."

Zefra jumped off the bed.

And now for the scarier one. Ludik considered the situation, then crouched by the side and leaned over.

"Nia," he half-shouted as he shook her, then lunged backward in time to dodge her fist.

"That was surprisingly easy," Ahjin said. "Fair winds, Nia."

Nia mumbled a nasty curse and stumbled from the bed.

Ludik took her arm and led her outside, where she lay on the ground until the others arrived. One of the smaller moons illuminated the shadowed landscape.

"What's for breakfast? Dinner?" Ahjin squinted.

"I don't have enough for such a crowd," Kani said.

"I still have a rabbit from earlier," Zefra volunteered. "And I can set snares for tomorrow."

"I can shoot in the dark," Ludik said, "if you'll lend me your bow." He wasn't ready to reveal his other form to Kani, supposed friend or not.

Zefra crept back into the cave and emerged with her bow.

Ludik tested it. A much weaker draw than his own, but good enough. He snuck off quietly while Kani insisted they demonstrate their weapons competence.

It didn't take long to find squirrels, and Ludik carried them back triumphantly. Everyone was too busy to notice. Kani dueled with his harpoon against Zefra's staff. He was good, despite his limp, but she was better. Izo cheered her on with enthusiastic whispers, and Nia yawned suggestions.

Zefra whirled her staff and knocked Kani's harpoon from his hands.

"Well done, youngster," he panted.

Zefra bowed, barely breathing hard. "You were a worthy opponent."

Kani laughed. "In a real fight, I would treat you as a fish."

He threw his harpoon at a sapling. The tree shivered as the harpoon hit dead center.

"Well done, yourself." Nia pulled on the harpoon, then yanked harder before she finally freed it.

"I found food," Ludik announced.

Ahjin flinched and grabbed his head.

Ludik grimaced. Since Ahjin was fully visible, the most likely cause for the sudden headache was bad company of the divine variety.

Kani started toward Ahjin, but Nia held his arm.

"Leave him alone for a minute."

"I don't understand," Kani said.

"I know. Just wait." She patted his arm.

Ludik handed the squirrels to Izo and the bow to Zefra. He recognized the signs, and one way or another, Ahjin might need him.

"Thank you for the message," Ahjin said, "but—" His fingers tightened in his hair, and his face paled. "What—" He broke off, sweating, and leaned against the harpooned sapling. "Good flight." He rubbed his temples. "Ludik!"

Ludik strode to Ahjin's side. "My herbs were soaked, and I haven't found anything else. Let me ask Kani—"

"No, stop." Ahjin gritted his teeth. "Listen." He rubbed his forehead. "I'm sure you know who that was."

Ludik nodded. The signs of Irajahan's telepathic communication were too familiar. Ahjin paid a lot in personal coin to serve the gods.

"He gave me a message for you," Ahjin said.

Ludik bared his teeth in suspicion. "For me? But why?"

"Sheer pettiness, I'm sure." Ahjin reached up to clasp Ludik's shoulder. "I'm sorry. He says Nemerra is having more difficulties with her pregnancy. Okechuku has ordered her to stay in bed until the babies are born."

Ludik's heart sank into a wave of nausea. "Did he say what was wrong? Are they all right?"

He tugged on his marriage ring until his ear stung. What would they do if she lost the babies? What would he do if he lost them all? Lyell had never recovered from the deaths of his family, and a surge of empathy threatened to bury Ludik.

"Whether or not he knows the answer, Irajahan didn't say anything more." Ahjin's grip tightened. "Okechuku is the best. He knows what he's doing. They'll be fine. Irajahan just wants to make you miserable."

"Irajahan?" Kani leaned toward Nia and whispered, "He thinks a god talks to him?"

Nia nodded. "Hush, I want to listen."

Ludik ignored them and jerked free of Ahjin, pacing in a circle. He had to get home to Nemerra.

He whirled around. "Let's try the raft."

Ahjin rubbed his forehead. "Ludik, we talked about this."

Ludik growled at him. "I do not care."

Ahjin sighed. "Fine, let's talk about the raft again."

Ludik whirled to Zefra. "Pull out your patrol records."

18.MESSAGE

(DRAGON ISLES)

Advice most needed is least heeded.

Iojif Proverb

Ahjin watched Ludik, nothing more than a gold-capped shadow stalking in the moonlight.

He turned to Kani. "Your raft plan needs some revisions in order for us to make it home safely."

Kani nodded. With his blue-dyed skin, he was as invisible as Ludik, and his indigo hair disappeared entirely. "What do you want to do first?"

Ahjin looked at Zefra, who squinted at her slate.

"We should examine your materials first," she said. "If we cannot make an adequate raft for all of us, there is no point worrying about the pirate patrols."

"Certainly." Kani reached for his harpoon. "We can leave right now, if you want."

"Now is a great idea." Ludik tugged on his ear.

"Leave for where?" Ahjin peered into the distant blackness.

"It didn't make sense to store ship-building supplies this far from the coast," Kani said. "I left them in my lair by the shore."

Nia laughed. "How many lairs do you have?"

"Mmm, a few. Do you want to leave now?"

"How far is it?" Zefra asked.

"Several hours of walking," Kani said.

"I can fly back and forth each night," Ahjin said, "but the rest of you would take too long. We'll need to switch bases. Can it support all of us?"

"We'll take supplies with us," Kani said. "The bigger problem is that I don't think we will all fit to sleep during the day."

"Tell me about the terrain," Ahjin said.

If necessary, he could sit out in the open, invisibly, but he'd prefer a bit of shelter instead of the headache and sunburn.

"About like here," Kani said. "There's one small tree I plan to use for the mast if I can find a way to cut it down." He shrugged. "If not, we can float in the current."

"Until we cut it down," Ahjin said, "Ludik and I can sleep in the tree."

"I can hide in the water," Nia volunteered. "Does your lair have room for the Iskrins?"

"That should work," Kani said, "but are you sure the rest of you will be safe, especially in the tree?"

"We'll be fine," Ahjin assured him.

Nobody would see him, and nobody would tangle with Ludik. But they need not tell all their secrets before necessary.

Yet again, they gathered their belongings and set off to an unfamiliar location. After protesting, Kani let the others help carry his supplies, including his precious sail.

It took them most of the night to reach the coastal lair. Kani showed them various small dugouts and hollow logs to hide their supplies. The lair itself was an enlarged animal den in the ground between two large rocks. It would be tight indeed for the three who needed to use it. Ahjin thought of cramming his wings inside and winced. The headache from being invisible all day would still be worth it.

Before dawn, Ludik climbed into the lone tree, which was barely big enough to hold his weight. Nia waved and headed for the ocean, a few hundred feet away. After she disappeared under the waves and the other three wiggled into the den, Ahjin flew to a prominent branch and crept invisibly between limbs until he reached the trunk.

Ludik was a little below Ahjin, on a branch thick enough to support his jaguar weight. His tunic was draped on a nearby twig, ready to wear when he changed back in the morning. He already looked asleep, except for the twitching ear with the marriage ring. Poor Ludik. He wanted to be home with Nemerra so desperately. Ahjin didn't blame him. If he had a wife, he'd want to be with her, too.

Ahjin closed his eyes. He wasn't going to have a wife.

A twig stabbed him in the neck until he shifted. Then a knothole pressed into his spine. When he finally found a smoother place on the tree limb, his wings snagged in the next branch over.

Forget sleep. Ahjin looked toward the ocean, trying to spot Nia. From this distance, she was invisible. He expected her hair to disappear in the lavender ocean, but he was surprised her colorful Nokai suit didn't show. Perhaps she had found a deep place to dive, or a bed of kelp to hide her. He squinted. Was that school of colorful fish really her?

He always worried about her, but since he had discovered he loved her, it seemed his heart conspired with his brain to imagine every bad thing that could happen to her.

He couldn't turn off his worry any more than he could stop loving her, even at her request. And how could she ask that of him? His heart cramped again. He understood her not loving him. He'd get used to it. Eventually.

But how could he stop loving her? Ahjin had lived through Ludik telling him he'd never fly again and had learned to look for hope in other areas. He had survived the death of his dreams several times. Would he survive this, too? But this was Nia, his best friend and the heartbeat in his chest.

When he returned to Arupa and Nia to Nokailana, perhaps the distance would make things easier.

Ahjin pressed his hand to his chest. If he didn't sleep now, he'd be useless tonight. He draped an arm across his face to block the sunlight and forced himself to sleep.

At twilight, Ahjin woke from a fitful sleep. He flew up invisibly for a look around, but the sea was clear in all directions. "Come out, everyone," he called softly. "It's safe."

Ludik dressed, climbed down on two legs, and headed inland.

Ahjin flew to the ocean and dropped his invisibility before Kani caught him. He still didn't see Nia, but he threw a rock into the waves, then landed on the shore to wait for her.

After a few minutes, Nia swam up and shook her dripping braids from her face. "I assume we're ready to go?"

Ahjin looked behind him. Everyone had emerged from their hole. "You're the last one." He gave her a hand as she exited the water, dragging a two-foot fish behind her.

Kani was frowning when they reached him. "Where did Ludik go?"

"He's probably hunting. Who's hungry?" Nia held up the fish.

Ahjin reluctantly let go of her hand and pressed his hand to his empty belly. A chorus of growling stomachs echoed in the night, making the answer clear.

While Nia gutted and scaled the fish, Zefra set up a tiny fire between high rocks, turning her back to hide how she lit it without flint and steel. Kani collected more seaweed with Izo's help, and by the time Ludik returned with a rabbit, Zefra had the fish by the flames.

While they waited for the food to cook, they distracted themselves from hunger by examining Kani's collection of driftwood and flotsam. He had hidden the pieces all over the area, and it took all of them to bring it to one place before breakfast was ready. After that, they turned single-mindedly to their food.

Ahjin took a small bite of meat with every wad of seaweed he crammed into his mouth. The seaweed was no better than before, but it filled the spaces in his empty stomach around the scant-but-tasty rabbit and fish.

Kani gulped his meal as quickly as the younger crew. "You are handy to have around," he said. "If everyone is finished, are we ready to build a raft?"

Izo crammed the last of his food in his mouth and nodded. The others copied him.

"I suggest we begin by sorting the materials," Zefra said.

Of course she had a plan. Ahjin exchanged a carefully serious look with Ludik.

Nia rolled her eyes but marched to the pile and removed a broken plank. "Straight but short will go here." She set it down, then pulled out a twisted branch. "And crooked will go here. Is that what you meant, Zefra?"

"It will do." Zefra grabbed a plank and threw it into Nia's pile. "Make a pile for the longest pieces, for the framework."

"Kani, you mentioned tools," Izo said.

"Yes. I put the metal in this cache." Kani led him to yet another hole in the ground. "I kept everything from bent nails to broken swords."

"Perhaps I can straighten the nails now," Izo said, "but anything more elaborate will have to wait until I set up some sort of forge. Zefra can help me."

Kani gave him a dubious look but left him to sort the pile.

"Who knows how to sew?" Kani asked.

"I do," Ludik said.

"Really? I thought maybe Zefra," Kani said.

"She can, too," Ludik said, "but I know how, and I am sure Zefra will be busy with our supplies until she has every nail and splinter counted."

"Very well. You can help me finish the sail. Ahjin, I have rope here." Kani reached into a hollow log and pulled out coils of homemade rope of plant fibers. "Please measure it for us while we sew."

As Ahjin paced off the length of the rope, he watched Nia.

She and Zefra had sorted the wood, and while Zefra tallied the piles on her slate in probably excruciating detail, Nia went to help Izo. She was flirting again. The giggling was bad enough, but the fluttering eyelashes and compliments were enough to make Ahjin vomit. And the touching. Izo still hadn't found a shirt to fit him, and his white shoulders gleamed in the pale moonlight. Nia was supposedly helping him straighten the nails, but why did she have to touch Izo so much in the process?

Ahjin coiled the rope again and gave the measurements to Zefra. "Do we have enough of everything for the raft?"

Zefra tapped her chalk against her lips. "I think so, though it will be close."

Ahjin raised his voice enough for the others to hear. "Zefra thinks we can do it. Kani, come explain your construction plans to the others, then you can build while I spy for an escape route."

But first, he needed to talk to Nia. He pulled her aside while the others gathered around Kani.

"Nia," he whispered, "you still need to treat Izo with respect. Tell him the truth about your intentions and stop playing with his emotions. He's not used to Nokai ways. You'll hurt him, and he doesn't deserve that. Love is not a game."

Nia crossed her arms. "Love is the best game, and Izo wants to play with me. Besides, there's nobody here to love besides Izo."

Ahjin flinched. "I'm nobody? Or just nobody worthy of love?" He furled his wings so tightly they cramped.

Nia gasped and reached for him. "That wasn't what I meant."

He jerked away. "Never mind, it makes no difference."

He pulled his invisibility over him, without checking to see if Kani was watching, and flew away.

"Ahjin," Nia called softly. "Ahjin, get back here *now*!" Her voice rose with each word until someone muffled it.

Ahjin ignored her. He didn't even look back to see who had covered her foolish mouth. His heart couldn't take being stabbed one more time. He'd find an escape route for everyone, and he'd go home.

If he buried himself in work, he could forget Nia.

Her emerald eyes appeared in his mind and called him a liar. He would never forget her.

If he made himself available to the waiting rows of girls who thought courting the Mouth of the Gods was a good idea, he would find someone to replace Nia.

Her cheerful, laughing face mocked the idea. Who could replace the only girl for him?

Well, then, he might drown on the way home and not have to worry about it anymore.

Ahjin flew higher and higher to see as much of the island chain as possible. At least the lights on the pirate ships would stand out like wildfires in the dark.

"What are you doing now?" Irajahan asked in the back of Ahjin's head. "Are you still in the islands?"

The best part of Irajahan being angry at him had been his absence, other than his cruel message to Ludik.

"Never mind," Ahjin said. "I wouldn't want to bother you."

"You didn't mind bothering me before," Irajahan grumped.

Ahjin took a deep breath. "I'm sorry my mind wandered. It won't happen again, Almighty."

"Hmm."

Ahjin felt fingers scratching through his brain, picking his mental pockets.

"You're trying to escape," Irajahan blurted. "How enterprising."

"It is time I returned to serve you." Ahjin said solemnly.

True, more or less. He needed the work to keep his mind from other things.

"I approve of your priorities," Irajahan said. "Should I send a wind to blow your raft home when you finish it?"

"That... is kind of you. I thought the gods didn't believe in interfering." Ahjin hoped Irajahan didn't hear the rest of his thought, *even though you stranded us here in the first place.*

"Oh, perhaps I feel bad about the typhoon," Irajahan said. "Don't tell my siblings I helped you. Let them think you escaped by luck, then nobody will care about the stupid policy, and you won't get in trouble. Again."

"May I discuss this with my friends?" Ahjin asked.

"Let's not. If we're the only ones who know our little secret, no one can let it leak, can they? Let me know when you're ready for that wind."

That was unexpected. Ahjin didn't know if he should believe his good luck or not. Irajahan was a fickle wind, blowing hot and cold unexpectedly. When they were ready to leave, he'd decide if he'd call on Irajahan's favor or not.

Which reminded him, he was supposed to spy on the pirates and find an escape route. On the ocean, a small fishing ship appeared. Those pink-and-blue-striped sails were familiar. He swooped lower. Yes, it was Aolani's ship. The pirates had even fixed the major damage.

Irajahan chuckled. "Why are you building a measly raft when you can retake your own ship?"

"There are pirates on ours," Ahjin said.

"Not many."

It was true. There were only a few pirates aboard, and they seemed to struggle with the sails.

"You can do it," Irajahan whispered. "I'll help you. I can kill the wind as easily as I can raise it. With no wind, they can't sail away from you."

"I thought you wanted our escape to seem accidental." Ahjin swooped lower above the ship. Even the mast had been mended.

He got the impression of a shrug.

"Everyone knows winds rise and die all the time. If you don't tell, I won't. You know how to reach me." And then Irajahan was gone.

The offer was tempting. The ship was a much safer sailing vessel than a cobbled-together raft, and larger, as well.

Could they handle the ship with only six of them? They'd still had over a dozen crew after the Nokai women swam home. But they'd divided them into three shifts, as well, so the six of them could manage if they anchored at night.

Ludik wouldn't like that, but look at the advantages. More sails would be faster than one measly patchwork sail on a rickety raft.

Speed and safety meant getting home sooner.

Could they do it?

Ahjin counted pirates. There were only a handful. Most of them were young and obviously inexperienced sailors. If he had to guess, he'd say they were using Aolani's ship as a training vessel.

And if Irajahan kept his promise about the wind — did Ahjin dare believe he'd keep his promise? — the ship would be unable to sail. The pirates would have to fight.

If Ahjin told Ludik that only a few pirates stood between him and Nemerra, they wouldn't stand a chance.

Ahjin turned and flew toward the southern island. It was time to go home.

19.PLANS
(DRAGON ISLES)

Begin to weave and God will give the thread.
Iskrin Proverb

Nia laid the branches next to the new raft frame, in Zefra's latest configuration.

"No," Zefra mused. "Switch those. And these would be more efficient over there."

Nia groaned, but she and Izo moved the branches as directed, like they had been doing for the last hour in the moonlight. Ludik and Kani, lucky men, were too busy finishing the sail to be subject to Zefra's demands. Ahjin hadn't even returned to do his share of the work, which was completely unfair.

The older Nokai kept them entertained with funny or thrilling stories — an amazing number, considering he had been alone for who-knows-how-many years. They didn't distract her from her guilty conscience.

Nia glanced toward the ocean. Was Ahjin still scouting or merely avoiding her? She hadn't meant to sound so harsh or hurt his feelings. If he would give her a chance, she would explain better.

"Hmm," Zefra said, studying the layout.

Nia held her breath. If they were finished, she could look for Ahjin. She'd already lost Dad and couldn't bear to lose anyone else.

Zefra leaned to switch two branches and stood, hand on her chin. "Yes, I think that will do. We can assemble it now. Izo, move the branches to the frame. Nia, hold them in place while I tie them."

Nia's shoulders slumped. She would never get free.

Eventually, Ahjin walked in, moonlight shining on his white wings. He was frowning, shoulders hunched.

Her lips turned down in sympathy. She dumped her stick and rushed to him, eager to fix their misunderstanding. "I'm sorry," she blurted.

Ahjin held up his hand. "Not now, Nia. Everyone, I have a better idea than the raft. I just saw our ship, and it's lightly manned. Right now, it's the only ship out there. This is our chance to take it back. If there's an escape route for a raft, there's one for the ship, and the ship will be faster and safer." He eyed the unfinished raft with a raised eyebrow.

Nia didn't blame him. Not that they were doing a bad job, but they didn't have much to work with. Even after they finished the raft, Izo still had to forge the broken weapons into an ax or saw to cut down the tree and trim its branches for the mast. Both the tools and the mast would be a harder job than arranging sticks in a square.

But maybe they wouldn't have to worry about it.

"It would be nice to get Mom's ship back," Nia said.

"Fighting the pirates is riskier than a raft." Kani picked a branch from the edge of Zefra's square and laid it on the frame, turning it to find the most stable edge.

"There's only a handful of pirates on that ship," Ahjin said. "They barely outnumber us, and we've got Ludik on our side. We don't even have to kill them, if we shove them over the side."

Kani looked up and down Ludik's fathom-and-a-hand height but still didn't seem impressed.

Ludik tugged his earring and looked south. "Are you sure, Ahjin?"

Ahjin nodded. "I watched it for a while. It looks like it only has a training crew practicing maneuvers."

Nia shook her head. Sloppy pirates were good news for her, but shame on them.

"We have hours before dawn," Zefra said. "If we hurry, we can be out of sight by morning."

"What about weapons?" Izo asked. "We only have two swords, and they're both a bit rusty. We cannot swim with Zefra's bow."

"Ahjin can cover us from the air with his bow," Zefra said.

"I can take Ludik's knife," Nia said, "since he won't need it, right, Ludik?"

Her own serrated knife had been impervious to sea water, but Ludik's was steel and sharp enough for surgery. It would slice through pirates like mangoes.

Ludik showed his teeth in a wide grin. "Indeed. You are welcome to it."

"How will you fight with no weapon?" Kani asked.

"I will have weapons." Ludik clenched his fists. "Do not worry about me."

Kani gave him another dubious look.

"And Kani has a harpoon, so everyone is armed." Nia planned to ask for more harpoon lessons after they retook the ship. It would give her something to do on the way home.

"I won't help you in this foolishness," Kani said. "I have no desire to watch you die and even less to die myself. If you go, you go without me."

"Oh, but we need you!" Nia protested, but her words were nearly buried under Zefra's stream of logical arguments and Ludik's curses.

"Hush." Ahjin held up his hands and stared at them each in turn.

When the clamor died, Ahjin turned to Kani. "It's time we showed you our secrets. We have more advantages than you know."

Nia clapped her hands. "Yes, let's show him. It will be fun. You'll see, Kani, we have talents."

"Are you sure that is wise?" Ludik murmured, squeezing the walrus-tusk fragment around his neck.

Zefra looked up from her slate. "Kani has as much to lose in trusting us as we do in him. He shared his hideout and his own escape plan." She waved at the unfinished raft.

Ahjin waited, eyebrow raised.

Izo shrugged. "I vote yes."

Ludik stared at Kani with narrowed eyes. Kani returned the glare.

"How fast do you want to get home to Nemerra?" Ahjin asked.

Ludik kicked off his boots, and Nia clapped her hands. Yes, he was on board now.

"About this fast." Ludik pulled his tunic over his head and shifted into his giant kitty form in the same motion, fast enough to preserve his modesty. The leather tie with the walrus tusk remained around his neck, and the gold ring glinted in his ear. His black fur was nearly invisible in the darkness, but his eyes shone silver in the moonlight.

Kani screamed and fumbled for his harpoon, but Izo pulled it out of reach.

"Calm down," Ahjin said. "He's still the same person and still your ally."

"Who's next?" Nia petted Ludik's fur until he growled at her. It was a shame he was so grumpy, because his fur was silky and warm under her cold fingers.

Kani sat on the edge of the raft. "You all change like that?"

"Don't be silly," Nia said. "Only the Darrendrakar can shift. We're lucky Ludik is so formidable in his other shape."

"I knew the Darrendrakar could change somehow, though I didn't picture it quite like that." Kani glanced from one to the other with furrowed brows. "I don't understand about the rest of you. If you can't do that, what makes you think you can defeat the pirates?"

"Let me help you see." Ahjin's mouth twitched.

Nia giggled at the joke. At least Ahjin hadn't lost his sense of humor entirely.

Ahjin smiled and vanished.

Kani fell backward. "Where did he go? How fast can he fly? I thought I'd at least see him take off."

"I'm still here."

Kani stumbled to his feet and walked forward, hands in front of him, until he bumped into something invisible.

"Ow," Ahjin said mildly, reappearing under Kani's hands.

Kani flinched and stepped backward. "I've never heard a whisper of rumor that Iojif can do that."

"They can't," Ahjin said. "I'm afraid I'm unique."

"I'm beginning to understand how you escaped the pirates in the first place," Kani said.

"Not invisibly," Ahjin said. "I can't hide anyone else with me."

Kani smiled. "I meant you gave them heart palpitations."

Nia laughed. "And you haven't even seen Zefra's surprise yet."

Kani put a hand on his forehead. "Do I need to sit for this?"

"Maybe so," Nia said. "You aren't taking this well."

"Be nice." Izo led Kani back to the raft frame. "Sitting is a good idea. Go ahead, sister."

Zefra put her slate in her belt pouch. "Are you sure about this, Ahjin?"

Ahjin nodded.

Zefra picked up a twig. She showed Kani one empty hand, then snapped her fingers. A flame burst onto her hand.

Kani gasped. "That's a powerful illusion."

Zefra held the twig in the flame until it caught, then handed the burning twig to Kani.

Kani stuck a finger in the fire and yelped, dropping the twig. "It's real! How—" He leaned away from Izo. "Can you do that, too?"

"I'm quite ordinary," Izo said.

Kani gaped at them. "But how?"

"When we have more time," Nia said, "I'll tell you about our adventure with the gods. But right now, will you retake the ship with us? Someone must be waiting for you at home."

Kani looked sad. "It's been too long. No one is waiting for me anymore." He ran his long, blue braids through his fingers and examined the ends, then glared at Nia. "I don't want to talk about that, either."

"But you're welcome to come with us," Nia said. "Will you help?"

Kani stared at the raft for several minutes. "I can't. It's too risky. You will lose. I will wait until the pirates go home in the fall, and then I will take the raft."

Ludik growled and loped toward the ocean.

Nia kissed the blue Nokai on the cheek. "Pleasant journey, Kani."

"Good flight." Ahjin gathered pebbles from the shore and disappeared.

"Warmth to you," Izo and Zefra chorused.

"We'll be back," Nia said. "We'll pick up our things after we get the ship. If you want to come with us then, you can."

Nia pulled Ludik's knife from his discarded boot while the others gathered their weapons, abandoned their boots, and followed Ludik to the edge of the water.

"Which way, Ahjin?" Zefra asked.

"Almost straight east," Ahjin said. "You'll see it when you get closer. They had lanterns hanging at bow and stern."

"What's the plan, Zefra?" Nia teased.

"Only the obvious." Zefra spoke seriously. "We swim out and find a way on board, Ahjin shoots their leader and as many others as he can as a distraction. We board and kill or disable everyone left."

"It has the advantage of simplicity," Nia said. "Can you handle another swim?"

"I was getting used to it last time," Zefra said.

"You all take this very calmly," Izo said. "Are you so used to battle, then?"

Nia shrugged. "More than we'd like."

"Are we ready?" Ahjin's voice came from beside Nia, and she grabbed his invisible arm.

"The rest of you are slower than Ahjin and I are," she said. "Why don't you start swimming, and I'll catch up in a minute."

Zefra and Izo strapped their swords to logs borrowed from the raft.

Once Ludik led them out of earshot, Nia turned to Ahjin. "I still need to apologize for what I said. I don't think I was clear."

"You were perfectly clear." Ahjin's voice was cold. "I'm nobody and not worth your love."

"No, I — can you be visible for a minute so I can see your face?"

"No. Are you ready to go now?"

"No!" Nia tightened her grip on his arm. "I didn't mean you're nobody. Greasy walruses, you are the Mouth of the Gods! How can you be nobody?"

"So I'm only unlovable?"

Ahjin's arm yanked, and she held on with both hands.

"Ahjin! How can you say that? You're my best friend, and I do love you. It's just a different kind of love. Someday, someone will love you romantically, but I can't think of you that way. I can't flirt with you. Don't you understand?"

Ahjin sighed. "I understand. Can we go now?"

Nia squeezed his arm tighter. "The Nokai rarely make commitments, especially in love. You should be flattered. Friendship lasts longer than romance. Look how Mom has gone through three loves, and none of them lasted. I want you in my life longer than any flirt."

Ahjin jerked his arm away. "I'm leaving now. Are you coming?"

"But, Ahjin," Nia wailed, "we still need to talk."

"I doubt I'll ever want to hear this again."

Ahjin's wings beat, and dust puffed in Nia's face. The flapping sound rose in the air and disappeared.

Nia buried her face in her hands. He was so frustrating! Was it because he was Iojif, or just because he was a bird-brained boy? If Mom were here, she'd ask her. Zefra thought more about *plans* than about boys and had never been kissed. Nia certainly couldn't discuss this with Izo. But Ludik was married, and Nemerra put up with him. Maybe he could help her. Nia made a face. He'd lecture her about proper behavior. None of her friends were any fun.

She swam after the white patch of Izo's blinding Iskrin skin. Ludik's black fur and Zefra's violet shirt had disappeared in the dark water. Actually, it was *Ahjin's* fancy shirt from Makana that Zefra wore. If he weren't gloating about getting rid of the vivid color, Nia would eat her hair ribbons.

Ahjin was entirely out of sight. At the speed the Iskrins thrashed beside their logs, he'd have plenty of time to scout for targets on the ship.

What could she do about Ahjin? She felt bad about hurting his feelings, but he was overreacting. Ahjin had always enjoyed her company before. Why should she change to match his ridiculous ideas of romance? Friendship didn't mean you were the same as the other person, just that you liked being together.

Nia dove underwater and zigzagged through the long seaweed. Fish scattered as she blew bubbles at them. Moonlight glinted on the surface, but below was dark and cool and silent. And lonely.

Had she lost Ahjin's friendship? His temper flared when he was disappointed, but if she gave him time to cool off, he'd listen to reason. If she pressed him too hard now, he'd pull some prank for revenge. Yes, time was a good plan. Crusty crab shells, she sounded like Zefra, full of plans!

Speaking of Zefra, that red dot was probably her, technically swimming, but what a waste of energy. Izo was even worse, despite the log that kept his head above water. Nia sped up, cutting through the waves with ease, enjoying the flow of the cool water over her gills and around her limbs. This was her environment.

That was another reason not to let Ahjin romance her. Where would they even live? Nia shook her head and swam harder.

As she passed each of the others, she whispered, "Keep swimming. I'll see how far is left."

Only a minute later, she spotted the ship, sailing in crooked circles as the sails went up and down. It did look like a training voyage of some sort. Ahjin's plan could get them home.

Nia swam back to Ludik and reported. She left him paddling steadily in the correct direction and went for Zefra and Izo.

"We're almost there," she said. "You can do it."

"I'm tired," Izo admitted.

Zefra set her jaw and kept swimming, but her arms flailed more than usual.

"Oh, tangled seaweed," Nia said. "Both of you float on your backs. I'll tow you for a minute. Izo, link your hands over your head."

She grabbed Zefra's collar and Izo's hands and swam backwards with them for the last hundred fathoms. They paddled next to Ludik in the shadow of the wavering ship while Nia waved at the sky, hoping Ahjin was paying attention.

As soon as he started shooting arrows, they'd take back Mom's ship and go home. The voyage would give her time to smooth Ahjin's ruffled feathers.

20.BOARDING

(DRAGON ISLES)

Pray often, but beware of telling God what you want.
Iojif Proverb

As Ahjin flew invisibly over Aolani's ship, moonlight shimmered on the ocean from the two smaller moons. There were now a double-handful of pirates aboard, installing some kind of large, wooden machine along the bulwarks, but he couldn't get a good look at it from this angle. If he flew closer to investigate, they might hear his wingbeats. Curiosity ruffled his feathers, but it didn't matter. They'd be gone as soon as his friends retook the ship.

In a few minutes, it would be theirs, and they'd go home. It might be difficult for Ahjin to avoid Nia on the return journey, but he'd manage. They'd be too busy sailing a ship with too little crew to have time for awkward conversations. He wasn't interested in hearing her tell him yet again that she didn't love him, no matter what excuses she gave.

He searched the waves. If his friends didn't hurry, the pirates might sail away with Aolani's ship.

Until the others arrived, Ahjin could do nothing but watch the pirates and think about Nia. He rubbed his chest. Was Darravani sure she had fixed his heart? It burned as if the lightning still coursed through him.

It was Nia's fault. Her love was as out of reach as the moons in the sky. For the wind of his devotion, all she offered was friendship. It was what she had always offered, and once, he had thought it was enough. Now it was torture to look at his best friend and know he would never have anything more. Was her cheerful friendship worth the pain he felt with every glance? Yet, how could he give her up? Losing her entirely wouldn't ease the ache in his heart.

But which was worse, staying away or having her nearby and untouchable? Love was an unwelcome storm that tore his life to shreds, deadening the current that should carry his wings. He'd be better without that curse. When he got home, he'd bury himself in paperwork and forget her, somehow. He wouldn't watch her flirting; he wouldn't ask how many kisses she gave to how many other men. He would learn not to care.

Somehow, he would learn to ignore his heart.

In the meantime, he had pirates to kick off a ship so he could go home.

And there was Nia, waving next to Izo, only a few yards from the ship. Everyone had made it, though Ludik and Zefra were nearly invisible in the dark water.

How could they board the ship? Perhaps they should have planned more. Ahjin scanned the ship and found a fishing net dangling half over the side. That would do. He pointed to it, then realized his friends couldn't see him any more than the pirates could.

He swooped low over Nia and tapped her head with his foot as he passed.

She raised her arm high, and he flew low again, moving her arm to point the right direction.

Nia squinted at the ship, then nodded. She leaned toward the others, pointing again, and they swam toward the net.

Ahjin pulled out his bow. "Oh, Irajahan, My Lord Omnipotent, if you'd be so kind as to let the wind die over here?"

He held his breath and waited to see if the fickle God of Air would keep his promise. If not, they'd continue the attack even with a smaller chance of success. Was Irajahan's word to his Mouth worth anything, or would his grudge last forever?

Silence echoed in Ahjin's mind, but the wind gradually faded to nothing. The sails flapped listlessly and then hung empty. The pirate ship stopped moving, and the sailors cursed loudly.

Irajahan had come through. Ahjin would have to thank him later, when the danger was over and he had time for the elaborate praise the god preferred.

Nia and the others waited under the net. Ahjin swooped through the air, hooked the net on a belaying pin, and threw the end overboard to dangle in the ocean waves. He set an arrow to the string and aimed at the oldest pirate on board, the one who bellowed orders.

Ahjin's conscience twinged. He had never killed anyone on purpose, though when they'd been escaping their execution at Orrik's jail, he hadn't bothered to pick his targets carefully. He might have killed someone then, accidentally, in self-defense.

Though these men were pirates, did they deserve to die without even a chance to defend themselves? They'd be willing to kill Ahjin if they saw him. More importantly, they would kill his friends as they boarded the ship.

Ahjin had no choice. It was his fault his friends had died once, and that was more than enough for a lifetime. He would not let them be destroyed again.

As soon as Ludik put a paw on the net, Ahjin fired. His arrow became visible as it left his bow, streaking through the air to thud into the pirate captain's chest.

The captain toppled to the deck and clutched the arrow. Ahjin swallowed the bile in his throat and turned away from the dark stain spreading across the wooden deck. No matter how necessary, he would never be used to this. His hands would never be clean again.

The pirates ducked below the railing. "What? Where are they coming from?" They reached for weapons and searched the ocean.

Ahjin shot at another pirate and missed.

Ludik streaked up the net like black lightning. He jumped on the closest sailor and clawed across his neck. The pirate fell in a shower of blood. Ludik turned to the next, who dodged and grabbed his sword, stabbing at Ludik. The jaguar ducked and clawed the pirate's arm. As they continued their deadly dance, Ahjin turned to guard the arrival of his other friends.

Ahjin fumbled for an arrow while Izo climbed the net with Zefra and Nia close behind him.

Ludik chased his pirate around the mast, and Ahjin lost sight of him behind the limp sail.

"Find the archer and kill him," a pirate shouted. "Wake the other shift."

Ahjin fired again and hit the would-be leader in the shoulder. The pirate staggered back and slumped against the cabin.

Izo fell over the bulwark and stumbled to his feet, drawing his sword to protect the girls while they finished their climb up the net and into the ship.

"Kill them all," another pirate shouted. They waved their weapons and ran toward the boarding party.

Izo slashed awkwardly at the closest pirate, who parried and hacked in return. Izo ducked the blow. Zefra dashed behind Izo and slashed at the pirate's arm, and he turned to face her instead. She raised her sword in one hand and her knife in the other and moved away from her brother.

Nia climbed over the side and landed at the feet of a hulking pirate.

The ugly Nokai raised a nasty, serrated blade above his head.

Ahjin saw red. He forgot about his bow and plummeted, slamming into the pirate and pushing him away from Nia.

The pirate smashed to the deck, and his blade flew out of reach.

"What trickery is this?" The pirate searched frantically, even as he felt around and grabbed Ahjin. "What are you?"

Ahjin struggled to get free, but the pirate held on, wrapping his fingers in Ahjin's coat and bow string. No matter how hard Ahjin pulled, he was stuck.

"Ahjin!" Nia screamed. "Stop being stupid. Get out of here." She grabbed an oar and smacked the pirate's back.

"You get out of here." Ahjin kicked the pirate's knee. "I can handle this."

The pirate ignored their blows as if they were butterflies. "I don't know who you are," he said to Ahjin, "but you'll die just the same." He wrapped one arm around Ahjin's invisible neck and squeezed.

No matter how Ahjin pulled, he couldn't free himself. He was dizzy from lack of air and couldn't focus. A weapon, something sharp, anything...

His arrows. He scrabbled at his quiver, groping blindly. Swirling dark encroached on his vision.

The pirate stretched toward his own weapon and almost had his fingers on it when Ahjin finally found an arrow. With the last of his energy, he stabbed the bully in his overgrown gut.

The pirate screamed and jerked backwards.

Ahjin yanked himself free, gasping for breath, but his bow stayed with the pirate.

"I have a sharp tooth, too," Nia panted, waving Ludik's knife in one hand and her tiny hairpin dagger in the other.

"Nia, move!" Ahjin shouted as he launched himself into the air.

The pirate staggered to his feet and reached for his blade again.

Ahjin searched for his bow. There it was, broken in half. He landed and grabbed another arrow.

Nia raised the knife and balanced on her bare feet. She did not look intimidating despite her experienced stance.

The pirate ran toward her, blade raised. He was only a step away when the giant black panther jumped on his back and drove him to the deck.

The pirate died face down, without a chance to see his attacker.

Ludik growled and bounded after his next victim.

Ahjin leaped in the air again, triumph lending him strength. They were winning! Half the pirates were already down. Their defeat was in the wind, and Nia would have her mother's ship again. They could go home.

Nia grabbed the oar again and jumped on the rowboat to survey the top of the battle.

Since Nia was fine, and Ludik was a terror, Ahjin searched for the siblings.

Zefra stood over Izo, red braids unraveling around her face. She still fought the pirate with her sword and knife, sleeve flapping in strips. "Stay away from my brother!"

Izo pressed one hand to his shoulder. Blood poured from a slash across his arm and back, painting the deck red. He thrashed his bare feet at the pirate whenever he came in range, but he wavered with every kick.

"Load the catapult!" The pirate Ahjin had wounded pulled himself to his feet. "Take them down, or Crow will have your heads!"

Ahjin grabbed his slingshot and flung a rock at the pirate fighting Zefra, grazing his head.

Zefra took advantage of the momentary stun and slashed the pirate's neck. As soon as he collapsed, Zefra yanked her torn sleeve from her shirt and pressed it to Izo's back.

More pirates poured up from the hold. What had they been doing down there the whole time Ahjin had spied on the ship? Now his friends were badly outnumbered, and their new opponents were fresh and bristling with weapons.

Ahjin put another pebble in his slingshot. Ludik was a whirlwind of black fur across the ship, and everywhere he landed, a pirate bled. Nia followed him, stabbing the downed pirates with Ludik's razor-sharp knife or whacking them with her oar. Ahjin slung rocks as fast as he loaded them.

The pirates rallied together. Half of them fought back to back, warding off Ludik with harpoons and spears, while the others ran for the machine by the cabin. They dragged it out and anchored it to new hooks in the wooden planks. Before Ahjin could tell what they were doing, the battle shifted and hid them from sight.

A few pirates headed across the ship for Zefra and Izo.

A pirate grabbed the oar from Nia and swung it at her. She jumped toward the railing, too slowly. The oar hit her side and knocked her over the bulwark into the ocean.

Ahjin reached uselessly for her.

Another splash followed, as Zefra shoved Izo over the side without his sword. "Ludik," she screamed, "Ahjin, retreat!" She sheathed her knife and jumped after her brother, leaving her own sword on the deck.

Ludik dodged one pirate and bit another, who screamed as his arm crunched. Ludik lunged for the next pirate between him and the side of the ship.

Ahjin grabbed more stones to distract the pirates long enough to cover Ludik's escape.

The panther was surrounded, but he leaped closer to the side of the ship with every pirate he downed. If Ahjin held back the pirates for a few minutes longer, Ludik could escape. Then they'd be safe, with the pirates stranded and Ahjin undetectable.

Ahjin slung one rock after another until he reached and came up empty. He shoved his slingshot back into his belt and threw an arrow with his bare hands. It scratched a pirate's face but didn't slow him.

Ludik sprang overboard, and Ahjin flew higher, speeding toward the island.

They had failed, but they could still escape as long as the doldrums left the ship helpless. He really would have to thank Irajahan later.

"Ahjin," Nia shouted.

He looked down. His friends were together in the ocean. Nia towed Izo toward the approaching island, but she gaped at Ahjin and pointed frantically toward him. "Look!"

Ahjin looked behind him, but nothing was there.

"I see you," Nia called again. "Fly!"

"Fire," the pirates shouted. A rock hurtled toward Ahjin's head.

He dove sideways, his arm flung in front of him.

His arm. He could see his arm. What had happened to his invisibility? Ahjin grabbed at the magic that had always worked before and pulled. Nothing. He could still see his hands.

The ship's sails billowed in a sudden wind.

"Irajahan," Ahjin called inside his head. "Help! We are in danger. Hold the wind a while longer."

"Turn about," someone called from the deck. The ship tacked and chased after the swimmers.

Ahjin's friends swam for their lives.

"Fire!" a pirate shouted.

Ahjin soared upward to avoid the missile. "My Lord Omnipotent," he called again.

"Fair winds," Irajahan said. "Oh, that's right. You didn't want wind right now. I'm sorry."

"What?" Ahjin gasped as he flew toward the island again.

He'd make better progress if he didn't have to dodge stones. Whose idea had it been to install a catapult, anyway?

Another rock hurtled through the air, and Ahjin dove under it. The pirates' aim was improving. Ahjin didn't approve, under the circumstances.

"Irajahan, what happened?"

"Your magic," Irajahan said, "was a gift from me. And now I've taken it back."

"Why, Almighty?" Ahjin darted toward the island.

Ludik was almost there, with the others not far behind. If the pirates stopped flinging stones for a minute, Ahjin could catch up.

Irajahan snickered. "You're a disrespectful nuisance. I told you not to come here. You don't deserve favors from me. Good flight."

Another rock flew. Ahjin let himself drop, but it was too late. The stone glanced along his head, and his world dissolved into pain and blackness.

He plummeted toward the dark ocean, trying to move his unresponsive limbs. As he splashed into the waves, air bubbled from his lungs.

He sank, and the water dragged at his wings.

21.FALLEN
(DRAGON ISLES)

We know the worth of something when we lose it.
Iskrin Proverb

Nia heard a loud splash as she towed Izo. Maybe Ahjin had pushed a pirate overboard. He got all the fun.

"Nia," Izo gasped. "Ahjin suddenly became visible, and the pirates catapulted a rock into him."

"What?" Nia turned her head and saw the tips of Ahjin's wings reflecting the moonlight as they slid under the dark waves.

"Ahjin, no!" Nia wailed.

Ahjin didn't rise to the surface, but if she let go of Izo, he'd drown with his wounds. How could she save both of them?

Ludik was ahead of her, and the cat crawled on land and bounded for his tunic.

"Come on, Ahjin, swim," Nia begged as she stroked harder for the island. Her side hurt from the oar strike, but she must keep swimming.

Nia's feet touched sand, and she sobbed. "Almost there, Izo." She cast another glance behind her. Still no Ahjin.

Izo pulled away from her, splashing through the water with one arm cradled and blood streaming from his back. "Go," he choked.

Zefra struggled out behind Nia and slung Izo's good arm over her shoulder. "I have him."

Nia leaped back into the ocean. Ahjin wasn't that far away, but it had already been too long for someone without gills. She scanned the waves. Nothing, nothing. Even in the dark, Ahjin's white feathers should catch the moonlight.

In the distance, Mom's ship sailed north. With Izo wounded and Ahjin down, the pirates surely assumed they were drowned or bled to death.

It might be true.

It couldn't be true. Nia dove underwater, searching the darkness for white feathers.

Still nothing. Had the tide pulled him away? Had he fallen to the bottom of the ocean?

Why had he dropped his invisibility in front of the pirates? It didn't make sense. Ahjin *didn't* make sense lately. First, he declared his love for her, and then he tackled that pirate instead of turning him into a hedgehog of arrows, and now this. Nia would never understand him.

If he died, she wouldn't get the chance.

Something moved at the edge of Nia's vision, and she whirled.

Ahjin's wings quavered in the ocean currents. He floated underwater, limbs relaxed and eyes closed. A cloud of red streamed from his head, and fish already nibbled at his curls.

Nia grabbed Ahjin's collar and kicked upward, but his wings dragged against the current. Her side complained as she yanked again, but he finally moved. As soon as she surfaced, she pulled Ahjin's head above the water.

He didn't gasp for air. Blood still flowed across his face, but he sagged as if dead.

Until she got him out of the water, she couldn't help him. It might already be too late.

Nia swam for the island, sobbing with every jerk against Ahjin's collar. Her struggle felt like forever and a week, though he had been nearly to the island before he was hit.

When she reached the shore, she was alone. Didn't anyone care?

Nia wrapped one arm around her aching side and pulled Ahjin across the waves. If she had to save him by herself, she would. When his feet hit the sand, she let the water flip him over, then dragged him the last steps.

Once on dry land, she pushed on his back, ignoring the blood. He had to breathe. She pushed again. He had to live. Water gushed from his mouth, but he still didn't inhale. Push. *Breathe, Ahjin.* Push. *Live.* With the next push, more water spewed out.

"Rotten dragon eggs," Nia swore between sobs. "Breathe, you stupid man."

Ludik pushed her shoulder. "Move."

Nia scrambled out of his way. "Where were you?"

Ludik tipped Ahjin to his side and listened to his chest. "His heart is beating."

He rolled Ahjin back to his stomach and levered a knee under him until Ahjin dangled head down, then pounded on his back again.

Ahjin gasped and coughed out more water. He took a breath and then another and settled into a jagged rhythm of gasps.

Nia burst into tears.

"Where is he bleeding?" Ludik lowered Ahjin to the ground.

Zefra ran over with the pitiful remnants of his healing kit, shoving bandages and salve at Nia.

"His head," Nia sobbed. "He'll bleed to death."

Zefra pressed a wadded cloth to Ahjin's head wound. "Stop that wailing. It helps nothing."

"You're heartless," Nia said.

Zefra didn't look at her. "My brother still bleeds, but Ludik is here, and so am I. Be quiet and make yourself useful."

"Head wounds bleed a lot." Ludik put a hand over Zefra's and closed his eyes. "Nia, any other wounds?"

Nia patted Ahjin's arms and chest with shaking hands. No wounds there. She reached into the water to feel his stomach and legs. Still nothing, though it was hard to tell. Except for the lack of burns and broken wings, this was too much like the first time Ahjin died, rescuing the gods. She blinked hard to clear her vision of tears and checked again for injuries.

"I've stopped most of the bleeding. Wash and bandage his head," Ludik said. "I'll be back."

"Where are you going?" Nia asked. "You can't leave him like this."

"Ahjin is breathing, but Izo still bleeds," Ludik stepped away.

"What about Ahjin?" Nia jumped to her feet and hung on Ludik's arm.

Zefra touched her knife. "Let Ludik help my brother."

Nia gaped at Zefra. "You wouldn't dare!" She let go, to be safe.

Ludik ran off in the dark, as silent on two bare feet as he was on four.

Zefra put pressure on Ahjin's head again. "See, the bleeding has almost stopped, like Ludik told you. Ahjin, does anything else hurt?"

Ahjin turned his face toward her voice but didn't speak or open his eyes.

"Hold still." Zefra put one hand on his shoulder, and Ahjin froze. "Nia, check his wings." She kept her other hand on Ahjin's head.

Nia carefully spread his free wing and patted along it, then rolled him a little to pull the other from under him. Both seemed undamaged, though his feathers were soaked to a spiky mess.

"Unless he's wounded on his back, I think his head is the only injury." The struggle to roll him made her own side ache worse, and she flinched as she pressed fingers against it.

"Hand me the bandages," Zefra ordered.

Nia's cheeks heated. "I dropped them," she whispered. She patted the sand until she found the roll and held it up, dripping salt water.

Zefra frowned at her. "Hold this." She pressed Nia's hand to the cloth on Ahjin's head.

The bone under Nia's fingers dipped. She swallowed hard and pressed a little more softly, shifting the pressure to the sides where the bone was still solid. Disgusting. And dangerous. Why hadn't Zefra told Ludik that Ahjin's head was broken?

Nia squeezed his hand. "It will be fine, Ahjin. We'll fix you. You'll see."

Ahjin's fingers twitched, but he didn't squeeze.

Zefra yanked one of Nia's ribbons from her hair and wound it around Ahjin's head to hold the cloth in place.

Ludik reappeared suddenly. "Izo is stabilized, and I made a place for Ahjin. Are we ready?"

Zefra pulled the last knot tighter. "Be careful. I think his skull is broken."

"Plague fleas," Ludik said. "You should have told me earlier."

"We only have one of you," Zefra said, "and too many who need help." She rubbed her arms.

"Only one," Ludik said like a curse.

Nia narrowed her eyes and looked closer. In Zefra's one-sleeved shirt, red cuts showed on her white arm and across her knuckles. Her violet shirt showed lines of white where skin peeked through slashes. Some of them were rimmed in dark splotches. Ahjin wasn't the only one who had suffered to save Izo's life.

"Is there anything else I should know?" Ludik asked. "Can I pick him up?"

"I didn't find any other injuries," Nia said, "but I couldn't see his back."

Ludik crouched and hoisted Ahjin over his shoulder. Before standing, he said, "Check it now."

Zefra snapped a flame into her hand and moved it down Ahjin's back. "Only scratches."

Ludik struggled to his feet. "Let's go."

Zefra blew out her light and grabbed Nia's elbow. "Come, Nia."

Nia grabbed the dripping bandages and the ointment and followed Ludik through the dark with Zefra. Fatigue crept over Nia, and her side hurt more as they walked. She leaned more and more on Zefra with every step.

The unfinished frame of the raft had been leaned against a large rock and buried under the pile of branches meant to make its floor. Fresh-cut foliage stuck out between the logs, disguising it as a large, sloppy bush.

Kani held another leafy branch. Ludik slid under the raft with Ahjin, and the girls followed. Kani covered the open end of the hideout with his leafy camouflage, then his limping footsteps trailed into the distance.

Izo scooted to the far corner and leaned sideways against the rock. Reddened bandages wrapped his torso and left arm.

Ludik laid Ahjin in the short end of the slanted space and crouched next to him. Nia sat out of the way by the entrance and wrapped her arm around her belly.

Zefra wiggled past Ludik to sit by her brother. "Are you well?" Her fingers hovered above his bandaged shoulder.

"For now," Izo said. "The bleeding has stopped, and Ludik patched the deeper injuries."

"I'll help him more later," Ludik promised. "Now, hush, so I can concentrate."

He put his hands over Ahjin's bleeding left temple and closed his eyes, moving his lips in inaudible curses.

Zefra laid her head on Izo's good arm. They both closed their eyes, and soon their heavy breathing echoed in the small space.

Nia leaned against the rock and kept watch, one eye on the leaf-covered opening and one on Ludik and Ahjin.

For a long time, nothing happened, and neither of her friends moved before Nia fell asleep.

〰〰〰〰

B ird song woke Nia. Sunlight filtered green through their leafy hideout. She blinked and sat up, and her side protested the abuse.

"Ow." She lifted the hem of her shirt. Black and blue crawled across her torso, and her side was swollen and hot. She tugged her shirt down.

Izo still slept against the rock, but Zefra was reading her slate. Ludik slept on the ground next to Ahjin. Ahjin wasn't moving, though Nia couldn't tell if he was unconscious or asleep. She refused to consider the third alternative.

"Zefra," Nia whispered.

"Hmm?"

"What time is it?"

"Daylight."

Nia inhaled. "Yes, I know. Can you be more specific?"

"It was light when I woke two hours ago."

"Should we wake the others?" Nia asked.

"No."

"Should we look outside?" Nia leaned toward the entrance.

"No."

"Well, then, what should we do?"

"Be quiet so nobody hears us."

Nia crossed her arms and dropped them on her stomach, then hissed. *Ow.* She dropped her head against the rock and watched flies buzz. She counted caterpillars in the branches of their tent. She watched Zefra's eyes move as she read. She mentally sorted leaves by shade of green. She mouthed the words to every song she knew.

When Ahjin twitched and opened his eyes, hours later, Nia crawled between him and Ludik.

"How do you feel?"

Ahjin blinked. He opened his mouth and closed it again, then frowned. He raised his left hand and patted his bandaged head. He tried talking again, and again failed. His eyes widened, and he punched the ground, frowning.

Nia grabbed his hand and reached behind her to shake Ludik. "Wake up, wake up. Something's wrong with Ahjin."

Ludik jerked to a sitting position, almost hitting his head on the raft. He rubbed his eyes, then leaned around Nia to look at Ahjin.

"This would be easier if you moved," he told Nia.

She crawled toward Ahjin's knees and held his hand while Ludik examined him. Zefra woke Izo, and they watched in silence.

Ludik asked Ahjin questions about pain and vision while he unwound the bandage and examined the wound. Ahjin nodded or shook his head gingerly but said nothing. His head was swollen and covered in bruises spreading from his left temple. Under Ludik's fingers, the swelling went down and the bruises faded a little.

After a while, Ludik sat back and sighed. "That's all I can do for now. You have seriously messed yourself up, my friend, worse than a concussion. I can't do more for the internal swelling until your body absorbs the blood leakage. I don't know how much you will recover in the long hunt, but can you see any better now?"

Ahjin nodded.

Ludik rubbed more ointment on Ahjin's head but left off the bandage. "Would you like to sit?"

Ahjin nodded again, and Ludik rolled him carefully into the center of the tent. Ahjin tried to push himself up with only his left hand but flopped back again.

Ludik and Nia grabbed him on either side and pulled him up to rest against the rock between Zefra and Nia. Ahjin folded his left wing behind him, but the right one sagged against Nia.

Nia brushed her fingers across his head. The bone was solid again. Ahjin smiled at her with half his mouth.

"Who's next?" Ludik rubbed his face wearily and looked at Izo.

Zefra whispered in her brother's ear.

Izo stared at Nia. "I think Nia has an injury you have not treated yet."

Ludik frowned at Nia.

"I'm fine," she insisted. "I just have bruises from that oar."

"Show me." Ludik stared until she gave up and raised her shirt halfway.

Izo blushed and turned his face away, but Ahjin squinted at her bare stomach and then frowned. He stretched across his lap to hold her hand with his left while Ludik poked at her.

"Just bruises?" Ludik said. "You cracked your lowest rib. You're lucky it didn't break entirely and puncture something. But I can fix this. Hold still." He spread one hand across her stomach.

Warmth snaked under her skin, and the pain dropped to a murmur. Nia sighed, and Ahjin squeezed her hand.

"The bruises can heal on their own. They might keep you out of trouble." Ludik handed her his salve and crawled to the Iskrins.

Nia rubbed the ointment into her bruises while Izo turned his back and Zefra unwrapped his bandages. A thick gash cut from Izo's left arm, across his back to his lower right side.

Nia covered her mouth and blinked away tears. No wonder Zefra had been so upset last night.

As Ludik rubbed ointment into each cut, the edges of the skin pulled together into a thin red line. "This should be re-bandaged, but not with this filthy thing." He nudged the old bandage.

"I will be fine," Izo said. "It already feels improved." He flexed his arm and winced.

Zefra drew her hairpin knife and hacked off her other sleeve. She sliced it into strips and tied them together, then wrapped it around Izo's torso. The violet silk was striking against his pale skin, but less alarming than the red had been.

"I do not have enough for his arm," she fretted.

Ludik nodded. "Better than nothing. Your turn."

Zefra turned bright red.

Izo turned his back. Ahjin faced the entrance, and Nia rested her head on his shoulder, eyes closed.

After a few minutes, Ludik sighed. "Nia, will you help me, please?"

She turned her head to look at Zefra, who had her shirt unbuttoned but held it closed. Ointment gleamed on the cuts on her arms.

Ludik held out his jar of salve. "Please put this on her other cuts. Zefra, if I don't touch you, can you stop cringing enough for me to at least see your wounds?"

Zefra's blush spread from her hair to the hint of bare stomach below her buttons, but she nodded.

Nia crawled over Ahjin to reach Zefra. She dipped her fingers in the salve and moved the bottom half of one shirt panel. This side had three cuts, none deep. She pointed subtly to the longest one as she spread the ointment. Ludik narrowed his eyes, then shook his head.

Nia finished that side and moved to the other. This time, one of the cuts was deeper, though not wide. Blood oozed, one slow drop at a time.

"I need to heal that one," Ludik said. "I'll be as fast as I can. May I?"

"Zefra," Izo warned, without turning. "Let him help."

Zefra turned so crimson it hurt Nia's eyes. "Yes."

Ludik touched one finger to Zefra's belly, covering the puncture. When he moved back, the hole was nothing but a red line.

"Is that all of them?" Nia asked.

Zefra shook her head but didn't expose whatever wounds were still left. Her red face turned nearly purple. Ludik looked at Nia, then turned his back.

Zefra opened her shirt and showed a gash in the beautiful silk scarf wrapped around her chest.

Nia peeked at the scratch across the top of one of Zefra's breasts, then held out the salve for Zefra to anoint herself. "Is that all now?"

"Yes," Zefra whispered.

As soon as Zefra re-buttoned her shirt, Nia said, "Everyone can turn around now."

She nodded to Ludik when she handed him the ointment. The scratch wasn't bad enough to embarrass Zefra further. It would scar without Ludik's help, but that was Zefra's problem.

Nia reclaimed her seat by Ahjin's side and stared between the leaves of their makeshift door. They still had hours of daylight left, stuck in a tiny space with nothing to do.

"Is now a good time to plan?" Zefra asked.

Nia sighed. Ahjin patted her hand.

"Today is Nemerra's birthday," Ludik said. "I need to get back to her. What do you suggest?"

"We lost most of our weapons." Zefra tapped her slate. "And we have too many injured to consider fighting again."

Ludik grimaced, but when he said nothing, Zefra continued. "Since this plan failed, it makes the most sense to return to our last one. We can slip through unseen on the raft."

Nia tried to swallow the lump in her throat. She shouldn't have been so eager to reclaim Mom's ship. This was her fault. She bit her lip and blinked hard. Why had she been so stupid?

"We could ask the gods for help," Izo said.

Ahjin choked, and the sounds that emerged bore no resemblance to words. He pressed his hand to his head and tried again, still unsuccessfully. Finally, he dropped his hand and shook his head, scowling.

Nia patted his arm. "Don't worry, Ahjin, you'll get better. Do you mean we can't ask the gods, or we shouldn't?"

Ahjin shook his head, nodded, then shrugged, still frowning.

Nia patted his arm again. He would improve. He must.

Ludik tugged on his earring. "Then we're on our own. I shouldn't have let Okechuku bully me into leaving Nemerra. If he needs that herb so badly, he can come find it himself."

Zefra tapped her slate again. "When night falls, we can find Kani and finish the raft. Agreed?"

Nia tightened her grip on Ahjin's hand. "Will we have enough able bodies to sail?"

"I'll continue healing everyone," Ludik said, "but it will take time."

"It will also take time to finish the raft." Zefra slipped her slate in her belt pouch. "Since we cannot work until dark, rest while you can." She leaned against Izo and closed her eyes.

Ludik lay under the low part of the roof and stared up at the raft's frame. Ahjin closed his eyes and sagged sideways. Nia tugged his shirt until he slumped against her shoulder.

She closed her eyes, but she couldn't sleep while images of Ahjin falling through the air flashed behind her eyelids.

22. TEST

(DRAGON ISLES)

If there is no wind, row.
Nokai Proverb

When the sun set, Zefra was already awake in their makeshift tent. Ahjin and Izo slept all day, healing, and Ludik waited patiently, but Nia twitched like an anthill. It was probably only Ahjin's head on her shoulder that kept her seated.

Zefra held a tiny flame next to her slate to look at the list again.

Drag the supplies to the beach. Build the frame of the raft.
Cut down the tree for the mast. Trim the branches. Fasten it to
    the frame.
Connect the sail to the lines and the mast.
Take a test sail.
Load their belongings. Sneak past the pirates. Go home.

Yes, an excellent plan. She tucked her slate in her pouch and shook Izo. "Time to wake."

Her brother stretched and winced. Zefra searched, but no blood spotted the violet silk around his back, thank Resef.

Ahjin rolled his head upright against the rock.

Freed, Nia crawled for the entrance and dashed out as if every ant in the desert were after her.

Ludik chuckled. "I thought she would explode hours ago."

He peeked under Izo's bandage and glanced at Zefra's arms, but only nodded. "Why don't both of you unbury us? We need the tent for the raft, anyway."

Izo pushed over the "door" on his end. Zefra followed, and they removed the leafy camouflage. It was a dim night, with only one small moon gleaming, and they could finish much of the raft floor in the masking dark.

Nia reappeared and threw the logs from the tent into a crazy pile.

"Now we will have to sort them again," Zefra scolded. "If you only take a little care, you could save us work."

Nia ignored her and kept tossing branches until only the plank frame was left. Zefra took one side, and Izo reached for the other.

Nia bumped him with her hip. "I'll do this. Why don't you go find Kani?"

Izo grinned and bowed. "As you wish, my lady." He ambled into the darkness, his injured arm tucked against his side.

Zefra smiled at Nia as they set the frame on the ground, grateful for the kind heart under her butterfly nature.

Ludik hauled Ahjin to his feet, but as soon as he let go, the younger man would have fallen if Ludik had not eased him back to the ground. His right limbs still hung limp, and the right side of his mouth did not smile with the left.

Could Zefra count on his help to sail, or must she count him as a liability? She looked at Nia to ask her opinion, but the Nokai was staring at Ahjin, mouth quivering.

When Nia saw Zefra watching, she rubbed her nose and reached for a log. "Where is your plan for the raft?"

Zefra pulled out her slate, but they were still sorting branches when Izo came back with Kani and coils of rope.

Kani looked at Ahjin and the other wounded. "I see your plan didn't work as you hoped. I told you it was too dangerous."

"Ooohhh," Nia squealed. "You pompous, lazy, backstabbing sea sponge! You didn't help, you coward." She lunged toward the older Nokai.

Izo grabbed her with his good arm. "Bright stars, beautiful. Ignore him."

Though Nia smiled, her eyes remained cold. "Never mind, we're trying your plan next, Kani. If it works, you can gloat all you like." She tossed the next branch to Kani.

Zefra put Ludik to work sorting with Nia, while Kani fit the logs in place. The frame had used all the nails, so Izo lashed each branch with the homemade rope.

Kani yet again entertained them with stories while they worked. It took them half the night to finish the floor, and the rest to cut down the tree with the pitiful tools Izo had sharpened from Kani's collected remnants.

Nia dropped her hatchet as dawn's first rays peeked over the horizon. "Now what do we do?"

Zefra shrugged. "We hide until night, then finish the raft. Pray the pirates do not come close enough to tell the raft is not a bush."

"I can hide myself." Ludik tipped the raft over Ahjin with leafy branches to disguise one end. "It won't be as crowded with only four of you."

Nia looked toward the ocean, then at the raft. She tapped her finger on her lip, then sighed and crawled under the raft by Ahjin.

Zefra considered sharing Kani's shelter, but it was too cramped to be proper and would leave the two men at Nia's mercy. Besides, if the pirates did find them, who would protect the wounded? She picked up the leafy branch for the remaining entrance and backed under the raft. She took her time adjusting the door, and when she swivelled around, Ahjin was already asleep against the rock. Izo was nearly asleep at the other end, lying on his uninjured side. Nia leaned against Ahjin. Her eyes were closed, but her fingers and toes twitched, her head bobbed, and she mouthed something to herself.

Zefra rolled under the low part of the raft and closed her eyes. If she feigned sleep, she could plan without interruption.

All was quiet for a few minutes, and Zefra planned a route for the sailing test. Then Izo snored, and Nia hummed, and Ahjin twitched his wing against the rock in irregular flutters. Zefra opened her eyes and stared at the sunlight filtering through the raft. This would be a long day.

At noon, Ludik traded places with Zefra. She crawled through the grass to the closest remaining tree with branches low enough to reach, climbing as high as possible in its meager branches. At least pants did not snag on every twig the way her robe would have. After tucking herself into a sturdy fork, she closed her eyes and drifted to sleep.

<p style="text-align:center">~~~~</p>

At dusk, Zefra climbed down. Ludik had obviously been healing again, since Izo's gash had closed to a pink line, and he could use his arm with partial strength. Ahjin still was not talking, and his right limbs were clumsy, but he stood without support and smiled almost evenly.

After a scanty meal, they carried the raft to the shoreline to make the mast. Kani and Ludik cut the biggest limbs on the trunk with a saw made from a notched sword. Nia, Izo, and Zefra used the makeshift hatchets to hack off the smaller branches.

"Why didn't we use these branches for the raft?" Nia complained.

Zefra held up a crooked branch that bristled with twigs and needles. "We don't have enough time to trim them, especially when they aren't even straight. We're lucky to get a mast out of this tree."

Nia grumbled but kept hacking at the trunk. By the time the mast was lashed to the raft, morning was only three hours away.

Zefra and Kani inspected the raft from one end to the other and found no errors. Their plan had worked flawlessly so far. For the sake of harmony, she refrained from mentioning it to Nia.

"We're ready for a test run," Kani said.

Zefra nodded. "An excellent idea. Ludik, please help Ahjin board."

Nia gasped. "Ahjin can wait for us here."

"We need to test it with the full weight," Zefra explained.

Nia folded her arms and glared. "Five of us will be close enough."

"We're already leaving the supplies behind. Leaving a person will make the test inaccurate."

"What if it isn't safe?" Nia asked.

Zefra raised her chin. "Are you suggesting my plan is inadequate? Or you doubt your efforts?"

"Ladies," Ludik said.

Nia swatted at him. "Be quiet. You listen to me, Zefra."

Ahjin stumbled to his feet and patted Nia on the shoulder. He half-fell onto the raft and looped his good arm around the mast. He raised an eyebrow and motioned to the deck.

With Ludik's help, Kani pushed the raft into the water and climbed aboard.

The crippled blue Nokai reached for the lines. "Who's steering?"

Ludik and Izo swung themselves aboard. Zefra stared at Nia straight-faced.

Nia threw her hands in the air and swam to the raft, boarding by the tiller. "Coming, Zefra?"

Zefra shook her head and made her way onto the raft beside Ludik.

Kani let the sail fly behind them. The salty breeze blew Zefra's hair into her eyes, and the waves rocked the raft. Water splashed up between the branches, but they stayed afloat.

Nia swung the tiller, and the raft left the island. They sailed south for about half an hour, and all went well until a wave rocked them again and a branch slipped from its lashings.

Izo grabbed the log and fit it back into position. "What happened? Did the knot come untied?" He fumbled with the rope, then held up a frayed end. "It broke."

"I did my best," Kani said, "but the materials aren't top quality, and I wasn't trained in rope-making. We can make new rope for next time."

"'Tis not your fault." Izo pounded the log into its hole and put a foot over it.

That would not work for long. What had gone wrong with Zefra's plan?

"Nia, head for the beach." Zefra scanned the raft, looking for the next spot of weak rope.

Everywhere she looked, the rope was fraying. Strand after strand pulled and snapped. Nia's new course dragged across the current, loosening logs and pulling them free of the raft. The bottom sprouted large holes. Once the edges parted ways, the raft disintegrated in seconds. Every log of the base went a different direction, and the mast toppled from the frame.

Ludik draped Ahjin over a log and held on to both. Izo grabbed his own branch, while Kani and Nia swam free of the wreck.

Zefra dangled from the edge of the frame and lunged for the mast. If she saved it and the sail, perhaps they could try again with another batch of logs. It would take time, but they could trim the newly cut branches.

A gust of wind caught the sail and swept the mast farther from the shore. She held on tightly, but when the mast settled, it was in a farther current, running swiftly northward.

She wrapped an arm in the lines and twisted to look behind her. Heads bobbed toward the island, but she could not count how many before the mast jerked her around again.

Were the others still alive? If she let the sail go, could she swim for land?

A wave pulled her off the sea-slick wood into the ocean. Saltwater filled her mouth and nose, and she choked. Where was air? She flailed toward the surface she dimly saw through salt-stung eyes. Finally, she pulled her head above water and coughed, grabbing for the dubious safety of the mast. Her fingers caught the edge of a line, and she hauled herself hand over hand until she crawled on top of the mast and clutched desperately to the sail.

She coughed out water and sucked in another breath. The soggy fabric twitched under her trembling fingers. The current had swept her farther from shore, and the waves were choppy. If she did nothing, the sail would drag her down, too far from land to swim.

After wrapping a line around her arm, she drew her knife. She cut the mast free of the first line and scooted forward on the mast. It rolled, dunking her again. Desperately, she held her breath and prayed, and her safety line pulled her back to the air. Somehow, she had not dropped the knife, and she cut the next two lines before the mast bucked her off.

She could not tell up from down in the churning water. The rope jerked her around until her mouthful of air was nearly gone. She reached her knife toward her safety line, desperate to cut herself free, but she could not find the rope. The line jerked again, and she rose to the surface, trailing the mast like a caught fish.

She coughed out water and reeled herself forward. Her hands slipped from the wet log until she stabbed it with her knife for a handhold. After two tries, she climbed aboard again, shivering for long minutes with her arms wrapped around the log.

The sail caught in the waves and jerked the log again. If she did not cut it free, it would surely drown her. She forced herself to inch forward and grab the end of the sail. She dragged it toward the mast and sat on it, then scooted forward again. One inch at a time. Legs wrapped around the mast, and thank Resef for Ahjin's pants. One frozen hand on the lines. Hold the knife, slash the line, stab the mast. Roll the sail, sit on it, scoot. Flat on the mast when the current bucked, praying to stay afloat.

When she reached the end of the mast an eternity later, she tied the rolled sail to the mast and collapsed. She coughed and closed her eyes, letting the current sweep her away. Wherever she landed, she could walk back to the others.

They must have survived, with two Nokai to help them. But Izo and Nia were injured, and Kani crippled, while Ahjin could barely stand by himself. What if Izo's wound reopened? How would they all get back alive?

This was her fault. She had pushed the others into a test run and had not inspected the raft well enough. She should have known better.

Ship lights appeared in front of her. She dropped off the mast and into the water, as low as possible to still breathe, and watched. The ship sailed closer, revealing armed pirates on the deck. She held her breath and let the current sweep her farther into the ocean. Land would have to wait. She could not afford to be discovered now.

The ship traveled in a straight line, sails billowing in the night breeze. In only a few minutes, it was out of sight behind her, though it seemed like hours.

The pirates were heading for her friends. Zefra took a shivering breath and kicked for shore. She had to get back before the pirates found them.

But it was dark, and the others were smart. They would hide.

Without the raft-tent, where would all of them hide? The tree was gone, and Ahjin's wings would not fit in Kani's tiny lair.

The pirates would find them all. Zefra sucked in another breath and kicked harder.

Forcing her way across the strong current took much too long. The cold water seeped into her bones until she could barely move. Yesterday's injuries burned until they froze. Zefra was swept farther and farther north, edging closer to the islands she saw as dark masses against the sea under the lightening sky.

Her attempts settled into a dreary pattern. Kick, kick, angle the mast toward land. Think what she should have done better. Kick, kick, angle. Should have tested the rope. Kick, kick, angle. Should have tethered the raft during the test. Kick, kick, kick. Should have run the first test without the stress of the sail. Kick, kick, angle. Should have let Ahjin stay behind.

She was no kind of leader. Her incompetence had endangered her friends. She was inadequate and foolish. The broken raft was her fault. The loss of her friends was her fault. Everything was her fault. Except the pirates. The pirates were their own stupid fault.

She was almost to land. The sun rose above the horizon. Zefra raised her face to soak in the rays. Silhouetted in front of her was a strange forest of branchless trees. She kicked until one end of the mast hit ground. Zefra cut the sail free and staggered to the beach.

The forest shifted, rocking from side to side in the early sunlight. Zefra slumped to the ground and blinked. How could trees move?

They rocked again, and Zefra gasped. The trees were masts. A forest of masts docked at the island. Masts on pirate ships.

Her heart pounded louder than the hooves of her father's horses at the annual races. The pirates had a base here, with many more than two ships. There were too many ships to even anchor at the dock, and the bay was lined with the rest of them.

Her borrowed violet shirt, camouflage in the night sea, stood out like an explosion of flowers on land. Zefra crawled to the nearest bush and hid behind it, shivering. She prayed none of the pirates on the shore had seen her before she took cover.

She hid all day, cowering behind her pitiful shelter and gathering energy from the sun. While reconstructing the map on her washed-clean slate, she prayed to Resef. How could she rescue herself, much less anyone else? Even if her friends were still alive, they could not escape so many pirates. When Kaito returned, he could not save everyone before the pirates killed them all.

And then she overheard some of the pirates talking on their way back from hunting, and what they said was terrible.

She had to escape and tell the others, or all was lost.

23.LOST
(DRAGON ISLES)

Venture all, see what fate brings.

Iojif Proverb

Nia swam underwater to avoid the broken raft pieces. Their test sail was ruined, and only the pirates could make it worse. Unless someone drowned.

In front of her, Kani was almost to shore, though he swam awkwardly with his crippled leg and ruined gills. Nia squinted in the dark ocean behind her until she spotted flashes of white behind the chaos of flotsam. There! Izo and Ahjin hung over logs with Ludik paddling between them.

Nia swam toward them. "Where's Zefra?"

Izo coughed out the wave that splashed his face. "I hoped you had her."

"I haven't seen her yet." Nia searched uselessly.

Nothing but wood showed above the surface, and nothing was under the waves. Whichever log Zefra was using to float must be hiding her.

Izo flailed his legs, and Ahjin slipped and choked on the water. Nia shoved him back onto the log. Zefra would have to wait.

"Who am I taking in first?" she asked.

"What about my sister?" Izo asked.

"She'd be the first to be practical." Nia searched the water once more, anyway.

Ludik shoved Ahjin's log toward land. "I'll keep looking with Izo. Take Ahjin."

Nia kicked hard to keep him moving in the right direction despite his wings dragging in the water. He hung limply over the log, kicking one leg more or less in time with her.

"Ahjin, can you tuck your wings?"

He shuddered, and one wing mostly folded. The other only curved until Nia pressed it gently against his back.

When they reached land, Kani was waiting in the shallows. "I'll help him."

Ahjin stretched one hand in front of him and dragged the other through the mud. He moved one knee, and Kani shoved the other. On hands and knees, they crawled for higher ground.

Nia swam back out, looking for Zefra as she went. She had to be somewhere. Ludik's paddling was weaker, and Izo shivered hard enough to clack his teeth together.

"We can't find Zefra," Ludik said.

"If we haven't found her yet, there's nothing we can do," Nia said. "Pray to Makana she was merely swept away. Ludik, swim in. I'll bring Izo."

"But Zefra—" Izo coughed.

Ludik shook his head and swam for the beach.

"Pray." Nia pulled Izo from the log. "Float on your back, please."

She hooked an arm around him and stroked with her other. This was easier than pushing a log against the current, but she was so tired.

As she swam, she searched both the surface and underwater for Zefra but saw nothing amid the logs in the dim moonlight. Where *was* she? Had she been sucked under the waves to her death?

This was her fault. It was her idea to come here in the first place, and her idea to keep going after the first pirates. She had insisted on trying Kani's plan. And now Zefra was missing, probably dead. Izo would never forgive her, and she couldn't blame him. If Zefra died, Nia would never forgive herself. After seventeen years, she should have accepted Dad's death without looking for him.

They were almost to the sand where Ludik waited, chest-deep in water, and still no sign of Zefra.

Nia staggered out. "What about Zefra?"

"None of us can swim any longer." Ludik half-carried Izo past the tide. "Kani is working on a fire over here."

"We can't." Nia sighed, exhaustion turning her bones to water. "There's still a couple of hours before dawn. The pirates will see."

"He's hiding it."

Nia dragged her feet after the men. Ludik's dark skin nearly vanished in the night, but his gold hair gleamed almost as brightly as Izo's skin. From here, they looked like opposites: one dark skin and bright hair, one white skin and black hair. She squinted at a dark line trickling across Izo's pale back. Blood?

Ludik followed some invisible path, maybe scenting Kani, and before long, they arrived at a thicket of bushes. Nia caught up as Ludik hissed a greeting to the leaves. The bushes rustled, and Kani swung open a leafy door. The three wiggled through the narrow entry, and Kani shut the door.

A tiny fire burned in the middle of the covered hedge. Ahjin lay between the fire and the bushes, eyes closed but chest rising and falling. Nia threw herself into a heap next to him and closed her eyes. Quiet thumps announced the others sitting.

"Where's Zefra?" Kani asked.

"Do not give up hope." Izo coughed. "Zefra is tough. Unless we find her body, I will assume she is alive."

"We will look for her later," Ludik said. "Turn, Izo. Let me see what you did to yourself."

Izo hissed.

"If you wouldn't tear open your wound, I wouldn't have to mend it twice," Ludik scolded.

The heat from the tiny fire spread through the enclosed space until Nia's tired muscles relaxed into puddles.

"What is this place?" she murmured without opening her eyes.

"I made lairs all over this island," Kani whispered, "in case the pirates came while I was away from home. I don't have food stored here, but we can rest a bit before we leave."

"Hmm." In the morning, they would search for Zefra again. Nia stretched her hand to touch one of Ahjin's feathers, then drifted into sleep.

~~~~

S omeone tapped Nia. "Wake up," Ludik rumbled.

Nia groaned and rolled over. It wasn't even light yet.

The tap became a shove. "Wake up. We have to get back before dawn."

Nia stuck her fingers in her ears. Feathers tickled her face until she opened her eyes.

Ahjin grinned at her, only a little lopsidedly, and motioned toward the door.

Ludik moved his foot away from Nia and took Ahjin's arm. "Come on, Nia."

Nia blinked and yawned. It was too early to move. She shuffled her feet outside and closed her eyes while Kani shut the door.

"Wait here while I check the coast one more time," Kani said.

Too soon, someone led her into the night with a hand on her elbow. After a while, the darkness thinned and faint rays of sunlight flickered on the horizon.

When she finally opened her eyes, Izo let go of her elbow. "Bright day, Nia."

Kani led the way through the twilight with his harpoon-staff. The blue Nokai moved rapidly enough to turn his limp into a jerk with every other step.

Behind him, Ahjin stumbled along with Ludik's hand keeping him upright. Nia squinted. Ahjin seemed to move a little better this morning, and his wings folded almost evenly.

She tilted her head toward Izo and whispered, "How long did Ludik stay up?"

Izo frowned. "We only slept an hour. He listened for Zefra while he healed everybody."

Nia leaned backward and examined Izo's back. The blood had dried in a nasty streak, but the resealed gash was thinner than before. "You look better."

"I feel better." He swung his arm in several directions, wincing.

"Stop that," Nia ordered.

They arrived back at their launch site just as the sun rose. Ludik boosted Ahjin into a spindly tree and climbed another. Nia and Izo crawled into Kani's den and squeezed beside the Nokai. She waited until Izo arranged his back as comfortably as possible against the dirt wall, then laid her head on his shoulder.

"The sail is gone, the raft is gone, and the rope didn't even work," Nia said. "What now?"

Izo's voice was sad. "Zefra would have an idea."

"Hush," Kani whispered. "Sleep if you can; plot silently if you must." He closed his eyes and tapped his fingers silently in a dancing rhythm.

Nia snuggled closer to Izo's warmth and slept.

～～～～

It was still light when something growled outside the den. Nia shot upright and smothered her gasp.

Kani peered outside. "It's the panther."

"Let me talk to him." Nia crawled to the exit. "What's wrong, Ludik?"

Ludik growled at her in the Felid dialect. "I'm going after Zefra."

"No, it's still daylight," Nia protested. "Wait."

Ludik growled again and disappeared.

Nia threw herself backward, and Izo grunted. "Sorry, Izo." She shifted position. "He's looking for Zefra, the idiot."

Izo made a sound halfway between a grunt and a sigh.

"Sorry, Izo. I didn't mean it that way." She patted his arm. "I mean, we don't know where to look, and the pirates might see him."

"I don't think the pirates are looking for a big black cat," Kani said. "He can hide in the shadows, and I pity any pirates who tangle with him."

"Some pirates have bows," Nia grouched.

Izo ran his fingers over her braids. "He can keep himself safe. I'm grateful to him."

Nia grinned. "He told me to take care of the rest of you."

"I think we can take care of ourselves," Izo said.

"I'll believe that when you can move your arm all the way."

Kani chuckled.

"You're no better," Nia retorted.

"Don't nag me," Kani said. "I know better than to argue with a pretty lady with her mind set on something." His smile faded into a sigh.

Nia smelled a story. "What pretty lady did you know?"

"It doesn't matter anymore," Kani said. "I've been gone too long."

"Oh." Nia sighed. "That's sad."

What would *she* do if she couldn't get home? How long would she be stranded here? She bit her lip. It might be years, like Kani, unless she abandoned her friends. She could spend decades in a hole, sitting in one place all day, every day, until she went insane. Or she could be as brave as Ludik.

"Kani, how many times have pirates almost found you here?" Nia asked.

"Four." Kani didn't open his eyes.

"In how many years?"

"Too many."

Nia sat up. "I'll take the risk."

"No, Nia." Izo tried to grab her, but she dove out the exit.

Nia dashed away, watching the beach. No ship was in sight, but she ducked behind bushes and tall grasses, anyway. After coming out only at night for so long, the sunlight on her face felt wonderful.

She held herself sideways behind Ahjin's skinny, crooked tree and whispered upward. "Ahjin, are you awake?"

A twig bounced off her head.

"Come talk to me," Nia demanded.

Another twig hit her.

"Fine, come sit with me."

Leaves rustled as Ahjin struggled down, one limb at a time, slow enough that he was still descending when Izo and Kani joined them.

When he dangled a leg toward the ground, three people helped him down.

Izo hung onto Ahjin until he was steady on his feet. "Nia, this was your idea. What is your plan?"

Nia's stomach growled. "Food and group planning."

Izo looked toward the ocean. "We can search for Zefra."

"Give Ludik a chance to find her," Nia said. "How would she feel if we get caught by pirates looking for her? If he isn't back by the time we eat something, we'll help."

"Zefra left out snares." Izo cleared his throat several times. "I will see if they caught anything." He was almost out of sight before he rubbed his eyes.

Nia rubbed her own eyes. They had better find Zefra, or Izo wouldn't be the only one crying.

"Ahjin and I can light a fire," Kani said. "We'll keep it small enough to be undetected."

"I'll go fishing." Nia ran for the water.

Rather than fish from the shore with Kani's homemade net, she dove into the water and chased fish with her bare hands.

After catching two fish, she found the others behind the biggest shrub in the area, hovering around a tiny fire. Izo skinned small rodents while Ahjin carefully skewered them, then gave them to Kani to settle over the flames.

"We cannot fit everything at once," Izo said.

"No worry," Nia said. "Kani and I will eat the fish raw."

Ahjin's lips puckered, but Izo's face smoothed to the same diplomatic mask Zefra used.

Nia squeezed her eyes closed. Where was Zefra? Why wasn't Ludik back yet?

Ahjin tugged on Nia's ankle until she sat.

"So," Izo said, "what should we do after Ludik returns with my sister?"

"We're back to my original plan," Kani said, "only harder. We wait until the pirates go home for winter, and then we build a raft and sail home."

"The raft plan failed spectacularly," Nia complained. "Besides, that's months away."

"It will take that long to sew a new sail and gather enough wood," Kani said. "Even with five — six — of us working."

"We can wait for Kaito," Nia said. "Ludik won't be happy, but it's faster than winter."

"We can gather wood *and* wait for Kaito," Izo said. "A backup plan never hurts." He blinked rapidly. "Ludik is not back. We should split up. Ahjin can take the closer route."

Ahjin stood and spread his wings, then bent his knees and jumped into the air. His flight was wobbly, without his usual grace, but he stayed up.

Nia swallowed hard and blinked away tears. He could fly again.

Ahjin landed almost immediately and sank to the ground, panting.

"That was wonderful," Nia said, "but why didn't you go invisible? The pirates might see you."

Ahjin shook his head and shrugged.

This no-talking thing was as frustrating as fishing with a broken net.

Nia handed him a stick. "Write what happened."

Ahjin pursed his lips and shrugged again.

"Write in the dirt," Nia said slowly.

Ahjin raised an eyebrow. He scratched the dirt with the stick, but the results were gibberish.

Nia tilted her head sideways. Still gibberish.

Izo frowned. "I cannot read Iojif. What does it say?"

"That says nothing," Nia said. "Is this some kind of prank?"

Ahjin shook his head, then tapped the dent at his temple.

"You obviously understand us," Nia protested. "Why can't you write?"

Ahjin shrugged and struggled to his feet.

"We can't send you visible and wounded," Nia said.

Ahjin nodded.

"Don't you dare," Nia said.

Ahjin shrugged and smiled.

"Listen, you feather-brain," Nia said.

Izo elbowed her. "He has the right to choose his own risks."

Nia glared at both of them.

"Breakfast is ready." Kani shoved a skewer of hot rat at Ahjin and another at Izo, then picked up one of the fish he had gutted while the others argued.

Nia's stomach rumbled again, and she bit into the juicy fish without a second thought.

No one spoke while they ate, and the pile of rodents and fish vanished. Even Ahjin choked down his first rat, though he waved away the second.

Nia's belly still ached, but the hunger was easier to ignore now. "Anyone want more fish?" she asked. "I can hunt again."

"We should search now," Izo said.

"Ludik went north," Nia said. "We should go south and east. We don't know which current she was caught in."

She didn't mention the undertow that might have pulled Zefra below the waves. If they hadn't thought of it, there was no need to make everyone worry with her.

Ahjin flapped his wings.

Nia ignored him. She couldn't stop him, but she wouldn't encourage him, either.

"I'll go west," Kani said.

"Why inland?" Nia asked. "The current can't sweep her that way."

"You never know. I need to check some things, anyway."

"I will go with you," Nia said.

"No! Stay out of my private affairs. You go with Izo."

Nia folded her arms. For such a nice guy, he was so distrustful. "Fine. Izo, may I accompany you east? If Zefra made it back to our starting point, that's where she would be, anyway."

She glanced at Ahjin, who looked sad but waved his hand at the two of them.

"I would be pleased, my dear." Izo bowed and helped her to her feet.

"Everyone be careful," Nia said, "and be back here by tonight."

She watched Ahjin take off again and wobble south through the air before she left with Izo.

Under the stark sunshine, every scrawny blade of grass cast a shadow. They walked in silence for hours, dodging behind bushes as they watched for pirates, but all was quiet. Izo found a few ripe berries for their still-empty stomachs.

At every rest break, Nia tried to distract them from their worries by kissing Izo. He returned her affection, but as soon as they walked again, his frown returned. She didn't blame him. As delightful as his kisses were, she continued to worry. Zefra didn't swim well enough to survive in the water for long.

They reached the ocean and paced each direction, finding nothing. Even the raft debris had swept out of sight.

"'Tis good news," Izo said. "As long as there is no body, I am convinced my sister still lives." He rubbed his hands on his arms and turned for the long walk back.

Nia patted Izo's shoulder, though without hope. Zefra had been adrift for a day. How could she still live?

The walk back took longer without hope. Even her kissing sessions with Izo distracted her less. As night approached, they walked more freely in the increasing dimness, but Nia's feet hurt, and her stomach ached almost as much as her heart.

As they neared their hideout, she could barely see Ahjin in the twilight sky. His wingbeats were a little smoother now, but slow and tired.

Izo put an arm around Nia's shoulder. "Nia, I — You — Will you marry me?" He stopped and took her hands in his. "I know this is poor timing, but I have lost enough. I do not want to wait longer to know." His warm brown eyes searched hers.

Nia glanced at Ahjin. He had been right. Izo did want something permanent and exclusive. Her heart cramped. Why wasn't flirting enough?

"I — You're a wonderful man," she said. "You'll make a wonderful husband."

A smile crept across his face, and he leaned in for a kiss.

She took a step backward. "But I'm not ready for marriage."

Izo's smile faded. "We can wait a few months. I'm not in a hurry."

Nia turned away from the sorrow in Izo's face. It wasn't fair. They had been doing so well.

This was Ahjin's fault. Without his annoying lectures, she would have laughed off Izo's question and redirected him with a kiss. But now, all she could think about was whether or not she would break his heart.

She stomped toward Ahjin's shadow, shaking her fist. "Why do you have to ruin everything?" she yelled.

Kani popped out of his den and stared at her wide-eyed, holding a finger to his lips. She glared at him and turned back to the sky.

Ahjin bent his head to stare at her, one eyebrow raised, and circled to land. No, he had already said enough. Nia turned her back to him and folded her arms.

But that brought Izo back to her view, head bowed and shoulders slumped. Nia threw her arms into the air. She could ignore Ahjin, but it wasn't fair to ignore Izo when she was the reason for his unhappiness. She trudged back to him.

Before she figured out what to say, he spoke. "Do you love Ahjin?"

"What? Don't be ridiculous. He's my best friend."

"Then you just do not love me?" His Iskrin-polite face hid his feelings.

"No, Izo, that isn't it. You're great, but..."

How could she explain their relationship was perfect the way it was? Marriage was a lousy idea. Nia sighed.

Izo raised his head and ran past her.

She hadn't said anything. Where was he going?

Above her, Ahjin swung toward shore. Nia turned. Someone was coming from the water, followed by a long, dark figure. She took a defensive position.

No, it wasn't pirates; it was a black panther. And Zefra!

24.WARNING

(DRAGON ISLES)

**Makana, optimist of the gods, hides Her intellect under Her
love of parties and entertainment.**

*Everything You Ever Wanted to Know about the Nokailana Islands but Were
Too Lazy to Ask*

Nia squealed happily. The last rays of the sun sank, shining like hope
across the ocean.

Ludik had found Zefra alive.

Nia ran for her, arriving just after Ahjin and Izo. She waited until Izo
finally let go of Zefra, then flung her arms around her friend.

"Where have you been?" Nia let go so Ahjin could hug Zefra.

The panther bounded past them and disappeared.

Zefra swayed when Ahjin released her, and Izo ducked under her arm
for support.

"I swam back," Zefra whispered. "It took me a long time to find a
southern current."

"What happened to your legs?" Izo asked.

Nia gasped. Zefra's trousers were shredded at the knees, and her skin
was bloody and crusted with dirt.

"I had to crawl until I reached the ocean," Zefra said. "It does not matter. I still have to tell you..." She swayed again, and Izo bent to pick her up.

"Don't you dare reopen your wounds," Ludik said, running up on two legs.

Izo stepped back to let him scoop Zefra in his arms. He headed inland with everyone trailing after him. Kani was already pouring water into a bowl and moistening rags.

"Listen," Zefra said. "I found the pirates. They're swarming the next island like ants."

Ludik set her on the ground and reached for the rags.

"They have an entire fleet." Zefra drank the water Izo handed her. "They plan to conquer..." The water jug wobbled as she passed it back. Without warning, she fainted.

"Zefra!" Izo gathered her into his arms.

Ludik checked the pulse at her neck and started cleaning her knees. "She is exhausted. Let her sleep. She wouldn't enjoy this part, anyway."

Nia watched the water in the bowl turn red. Eww. Ludik could deal with the injuries without her help. She pulled Kani to the side. "She'll be hungry. What do we have?"

The blue Nokai rubbed his chin. "Not much. I'll go fishing. Relight the fire." He gave her his flint and steel and limped toward the water.

"Ahjin, come help me," Nia ordered.

They gathered twigs and lit a new fire in the same place as the old, keeping it as tiny as before.

Ahjin tapped Nia on the shoulder and pointed at Izo, then back at Nia. He raised an eyebrow and waited.

"Oh." Nia shrugged. "We'll be fine." And she didn't want to talk about it. She busied herself making sure the twigs fit in a needlessly precise circle. "Is Kani back yet with those fish?"

Ahjin tapped her again.

"Yes, isn't it terrible what happened to Zefra? Do you think she's right about the fleet?"

Ahjin frowned and pointed at Izo.

"I'm sure he's very worried about his sister," Nia said. "Let's see how she's doing."

She walked away, steadfastly refusing to think about what Ahjin actually meant. If she ignored the problem long enough, it might disappear.

Ahjin flared his wings and followed her, still scowling.

Ludik held one hand on each of Zefra's cleaned knees, eyes closed in concentration.

Nia carried the bowl of disgusting water away from their camp before dumping it. When she returned, Kani was back with a half-ell-long fish, which he chopped into large chunks before arranging them over the fire.

Zefra shuddered and bolted to her feet, fists raised.

Izo grabbed her shoulders. "Zefra, you're safe."

She took a deep breath and lowered her fists, then sniffed again. "I smell fish."

"It isn't cooked yet." Nia reached for a chunk. "Did you want it raw?"

Though Zefra's stomach growled, she wrinkled her nose the tiniest bit. "I can wait. It will give us time to talk." She sat beside the fire and stared at the fish. "What can we do about the pirates?"

Nia shrugged and put the fish back on the fire. If Zefra was as squeamish as Ahjin, they could suffer while it cooked.

Ahjin pointed to Zefra and then his eyes, raising an eyebrow.

"What did I see?" Zefra said. "I was swept into a north current and landed halfway up the next island. The pirates have so many ships in a port there, they do not even fit by the docks. I could not count the forest of masts."

"What did you do?" Nia asked.

"I landed in early morning. Too many pirates ran around the beach, so I hid under a large bush, waiting for a good time to escape. While I rested, I heard them talking about conquering other lands. They did not mention any details but complained about their captains wasting time and about 'the black menace.' They used to be here only in the summer, but they settled in permanently last fall and have no intention of leaving until they are ready to fight the other lands."

Zefra took a breath and clenched her fists. "They patrol the waters constantly. We have no chance of sneaking past them, and if Kaito returns, he will be killed along with everyone on his ship."

"Oh, no." Nia looked north and then south. Maybe it was good their raft failed while they were still close enough to swim back, rather than be caught by the pirates.

"How did you escape?" Izo asked.

Zefra poked the fish. "I waited until most of the pirates left for patrol or fishing. I knew I had to find a different current, so I crawled out of sight, then walked southwest until I reached the tip of the island. Then I swam across the strait. Oh, Ludik, what did you do with the sail?"

"The sail? You saved the sail?" Kani reached toward her with shaking hands.

"I gave it to Ludik."

Nia clapped her hands and looked at Ludik. They had a chance!

"I dropped it on the beach. We can get it after you eat and I finish healing your knees." Ludik held out his hand until she stretched out her legs and let him touch her wounds again.

"What can we do about the pirates?" Nia asked.

"If we escaped, can we tell someone?" Izo asked.

"We cannot escape," Zefra said.

"There is no one to tell," Nia said. "The ocean is considered neutral territory, and everyone protects themselves."

Ahjin drew a ship in the dirt, then pulled a burning twig from the fire and scratched it across the picture. When the paltry grass caught fire, he pounded on it until the fire was out and his drawing was smashed.

"I already told you I cannot burn a whole ship," Zefra said, "let alone an entire fleet."

"How *can* we fight a whole pirate fleet?" Nia asked.

"What choice do we have?" Izo asked. "If we cannot escape, we must fight or hide for the rest of our lives."

"Can't we retrieve our ship somehow?" Ludik asked.

"A forest of masts," Zefra repeated. "And when I snuck away, there were still a few anchored at port. We must plan how to destroy the pirates before Kaito returns."

"I vote for hiding," Kani said. "It has worked so far."

"What sort of life is this?" Nia shoved her fists on her hips. "Is it enough for you, building new lairs to hide from pirates? What of the fair lady you still miss? If you could have escaped before, it might not have been too late for you."

Kani flinched. "But Zefra saved the sail. We can still rebuild the raft."

"The pirates no longer leave in winter," Zefra said. "You will not slip past them."

Nia touched Kani's arm. "If you want to go home, you need to help us."

"We lost most of our weapons," Izo said. "And we already turned Kani's stash into tools. I'm not sure I can change them back again."

"I still have my bow," Zefra said, "though few arrows. Ahjin can carry it across the ocean for me again."

Kani squared his shoulders. "I collected broken weapons for years. I only gave you a few for tools. If you can build a forge, I can give you plenty of material."

Izo nudged Zefra. "What do you say, sister? My hammer and your fire?"

Zefra sighed. "I told you I'm not a stove."

Izo grinned and nudged her again. Nia hid a grin.

Zefra glared at him. "Yes, we can do it." She pulled her slate from her pouch and frowned at it. "I must make a new list and redraw my map."

Ahjin pulled out his slingshot and fired a pebble across the grass.

"I don't think that will help much," Nia said. "Kani's idea is better."

Ahjin shook his head and stretched his arms wide, then pointed to a boulder.

"Yes, can we build a catapult to smash holes in the pirate ships?" Nia asked.

"I do not think we can build one that big," Zefra said, "but 'tis an interesting idea."

Ludik winced. "I can't believe I'm suggesting it, but what about some of your pranks, Ahjin? If we distract the pirates and use flammable grasses and leaves as fuel, maybe Zefra can make the ships burn fast enough."

Ahjin grinned and rubbed his hands together. He pointed to himself and nodded. He pointed to Ludik, crumbled an imaginary something into an imaginary cup, drank it, and fell on the ground with his tongue sticking out crookedly.

Nia didn't like the picture. Besides being savage, she was tired of Ahjin looking dead.

"I'd rather not poison them," Ludik said, "but maybe Kani can help me find something to make them ill or sleepy."

"If you can concoct something stickier," Kani said, "I have a stash of blow darts. Then we can send your drug right to the pirates."

Nia cheered. "These are wonderful ideas. Those pirates don't stand a chance."

Everyone stared at her. Ahjin put a hand over his face.

"A forest of masts," Zefra said.

Nia crossed her arms. "I was trying to be encouraging."

Zefra rubbed her sore knees. "Nia, you're the only one who might be able to make it home alone. If we fail, you need to escape and warn someone."

The men all nodded.

"I won't leave you." Nia folded her arms and tightened her quivering lip. Why did Zefra have to dwell on unhappy possibilities? What was wrong with hope? The pirates had already killed Dad, and she refused to consider anyone else's death.

"You might have to." Zefra poked the fish again, then grabbed a chunk and bit into it. She savored the first mouthful, then devoured the rest as if it might swim away.

Ludik blew on a chunk. "It must be nice to have a fireproof mouth." He blew again and crammed half the piece into his mouth.

"Are we ready now?" Nia asked. "Let's get as much done tonight as possible."

Never mind Zefra's pessimism. The sooner they escaped, the better. And if they were busy working on the raft, she could avoid talking to Izo until she decided what to tell him.

Zefra rubbed the new skin on her knees. "We should divide into teams again. Izo and I forging, once Kani gives us the broken weapons. Ludik and Kani searching for herbs. And Ahjin and Nia, you can look for ingredients for Ahjin's pranks. Are we agreed?"

Zefra stuck her hand into the fire, ignoring Kani's squawk, and absorbed the flame.

"How did you do that?" Kani grabbed Zefra's hand and examined it for burns. "And why did you put it out? Won't you need a fire to remake the weapons?"

Zefra narrowed her eyes, and her finger burst into flame.

Kani dropped her hand with another yelp. "What if I don't ask how you run your forge? Ludik, we can look for herbs and flammable plants on the way to my cache, and you can help me carry back the broken weapons I've collected."

"Come on, Ahjin," Nia said. "Let's go look for pranks. Where do you want to start?"

Ahjin moved his arm up and down in a wave.

Nia climbed to her feet. "I see how it is. You'll throw me in the ocean and make me do the work."

Ahjin chuckled and rubbed her head.

Nia swatted his hand. "Stop that. Why can't you treat me with as much respect as Izo does?"

Ahjin turned his head and walked toward the ocean.

Nia followed, cursing herself for bringing up Izo. She wanted Ahjin to forget about that mess. She certainly couldn't ask his advice, because he'd only gloat that he was right about Izo's feelings.

Actually, since Zefra's return had interrupted them, she didn't know how much of a mess she had with Izo. Maybe she could explain things.

Yes, that would work. Assuming they survived, she'd convince Izo that marriage was an unnecessary complication. He was such a nice man, he'd surely see it her way. She'd understand his feelings being hurt if she didn't want to keep seeing him, but that wasn't the case at all.

She hummed "Where Are the Ladies" under her breath. It would be fine. Ahjin was wrong; men were mangoes, not oranges. She finished the chorus with a flourish and moved on to the next verse.

Ahjin hummed a line of the song with her and then snorted.

"Enough, Ahjin!" Nia exploded. "You made your opinion perfectly clear. I don't want to hear any more about it. Let's find your pranks and get back to the others."

Ahjin was neither a mango nor an orange. He was a spiky pineapple with sour juice. She should stop talking to the annoying magpie.

Ahjin put his arm around her shoulders.

Nia sighed. No, she couldn't give up the magpie. Even annoying best friends were still worth keeping. "Fine, Ahjin, I forgive you."

They reached the water, and Nia's romantic woes were forgotten in the struggle to interpret Ahjin's signs as they hunted for ways to trouble the pirates.

Nia and Ahjin returned to the others near sunrise, loaded with small nets and Kani's sun-dried jars full of surprises for the pirates.

"If only I had perfume with me," Nia said, "I could make another explosive."

Ahjin patted her on the shoulder.

"Never mind," she said. "We'll make do. Izo, how did your task go?"

"These are primitive, ugly weapons," Izo complained. "I would be ashamed to show these to my customers." He spread out a collection of knives, spears, and hatchets with bamboo or wooden handles.

Nia selected a short spear. "Considering you had a rock for an anvil, broken trash to repair, and your sister's hands for fire, I think you did marvelously well."

Ludik swung a long-handled hatchet. Everyone picked a weapon or two, sliding knives into pockets or waistbands and laying longer weapons at their sides.

"Your turn, Ludik, Kani," Zefra said. "How did your hunt go?"

"I mixed a few herbs," Ludik said. "It *should* be a fairly quick sedative, but it has more possible side effects than I like."

"They are pirates," Zefra said. "Save your qualms for your patients."

"Kani and I already have a set of darts drying," Ludik continued. "Don't touch the tips, please."

Kani handed everyone a bamboo tube. "You drop the dart in here and then blow hard. I saved some untreated darts so we can practice."

Nia yawned. "We can try that later today, if there are no pirates around."

"Day is almost here," Zefra said. "Get some sleep. We will practice with the darts later, if we can, and leave after midday."

"Don't fall asleep before I heal you again." Ludik eyed each of them. "Nia first."

Nia let him heal her bruises again, but the biggest relief came from the final healing of her ribs. "We're so lucky to have you, Ludik."

Ludik frowned in Ahjin's direction and grunted.

"Can we finish talking now?" Izo asked her.

Nia patted the handsome blacksmith on his shoulder. "Later. I'm too tired, and we have other worries."

"You're next." Ludik pulled Izo down for healing.

Nia walked away, glad for the excuse, and yet it was true.

One more day of rest before battling an entire fleet of pirates. What were they thinking?

25.DISCOVERIES

(DRAGON ISLES)

Resef's rare fire-touched are powerful, and their influence may stray outside His purposes for their flame-calling.
Iskrin Culture and History, vol. 3

Zefra glanced at the sun. It felt odd to be out in daylight again. The pirates had only appeared in the far distance today, so she and the others were taking the risk to get to their next base in time.

They had already practiced with the blow darts until everyone could at least avoid shooting themselves in the foot. Zefra was reasonably good with the darts, but Kani remained the master, able to put a dart within a thumb-length of where he wanted.

Zefra had sketched a map of her travels in the dirt, and then the two Nokai had argued about currents and the best way to land where they wished. Once they chose a route, Zefra added it to her map, only to wipe out the whole thing before they left.

And now 'twas time to go. She strapped the weapons and supplies to a miniature raft of a few branches lashed together.

"G-go," Ahjin stammered. Since Ludik's last healing session with him, he had been speaking halting single words. As the others pushed off from shore, he flew with Zefra's bow.

Nia giggled like a child as she waded into the water.

Zefra envied her glee. She would not admit it to the others, but the ocean now terrified her. 'Twas powerful and heartless and could kill her in minutes. After hours of battling it earlier, she wished they had another way to reach the other island. Even a rickety raft gave more illusion of safety, at least for as long as it held together. And after the ocean, the pirates waited.

She held onto the branches between Izo and Ludik and kicked to the rhythm of Kani's chant. Only Nia swam free in front of the raft to watch for danger and navigate, and Zefra hoped the flighty young woman had memorized the path.

The water was cold, and if she died in the salty waves, the pirates would win. She kicked harder.

"Zefra, ease off," Izo whispered. "Stay even with the rest of us."

Zefra kicked more gently.

Izo and Ludik whispered the chant along with Kani. Ahjin still said nothing as his wings rustled above them.

A wave hit Zefra in the face, and she coughed at the salty cold. It would be a long afternoon.

Over an hour later, they staggered onto land and fell into a tired heap.

Zefra forced herself to her feet. "Get up. We still have land to cross before dark."

She loaded herself with several water jugs, a miserable sword, and a slightly less terrible knife.

Nia kept her eyes closed. "In a minute."

Kani groaned and stood. He unloaded the raft and took his weapons and a share of the supplies. "She's right. We have to keep moving."

Izo dragged Nia to her feet. "Walking will make us warmer," he coaxed over her moan.

"If we do not walk now, we will have to crawl when the pirates return," Zefra warned.

"You're a cruel taskmaster," Nia said, but she picked up her weapons and half of Ahjin's pranks and walked.

Ahjin took a non-breakable selection of supplies and staggered after Nia.

Izo rubbed his arms briskly, then carried half the branches.

Ludik picked up the other branches and waved his arm forward. "You know the way, Zefra. Lead, and I'll cover the rear."

Zefra wrung the hem of her shirt and shivered. Walking *would* keep them warmer. She strode past the others and fell into step with Nia. Walking was also faster than crawling. The wind blew through the rips in her pants and chilled her knees.

Several hours later, they found dry spots out of sight of the pirate dock. Kani kept guard while the others took a desperately needed nap in the warm sunlight.

～～～～

Z efra woke when the sun hung low in the evening sky, and Izo stirred not long after. Everyone else seemed asleep, even Kani.

"How long should we let them sleep?" Izo asked.

"As long as they want," Ludik mumbled without opening his eyes.

Zefra assumed he was using his excellent senses of smell and hearing to guard them.

"There is no hurry." She did not want to disturb their last sleep. "Rest is more important. Izo, will you take the next watch?"

Izo nodded and walked northeast with some of the catapult branches. Before he reached the top of the small hill that hid them from the pirates, he dropped to his hands and knees, dragging the wood.

"I scouted while you slept," Ludik murmured. "I found fuel." He motioned to a large pile of grasses and herbs and scented leaves. "I also found a marsh." He yawned wide enough to show all his teeth.

"I do not understand the significance."

Ludik smiled. "We had two original objectives here: discover the fate of Nia's father, which we did, and look for the petika. I just found it."

"That will be nice after we defeat the pirates," Zefra said, "but it is not important now."

"I plan to test it on Ahjin." Ludik stretched his long limbs in every direction and sat. "He might like saying an entire sentence."

Zefra glanced at Ahjin. "Do you think it will help?"

"It's supposed to be an excellent anti-inflammatory, among other things. The brain is difficult to treat. If I can reduce the inflammation with the petika, he might function a lot better." Ludik rubbed his hands over his face. "Or he might have damaged his brain beyond repair."

Zefra bit her lip. If he never recovered, that would be terrible for him and worse for everyone who needed the Mouth of the Gods. "Should we wake him?"

"No. Sleep will also help him, and I need to decide what to do with these." He unwrapped a rag to show a small pile of five-petaled, yellow flowers with ragged teardrop leaves.

"I can heat water for a tea," Zefra offered.

"Under other circumstances, I would try a topical application first."

Zefra blinked. "No, I do not recommend that for Ahjin's brain."

Ludik grinned. "I should tell him that, though. Then when I tell him he only has to drink a tea, he won't fuss so much."

Zefra laughed. Ahjin's irrational hatred of medicine was legendary.

Kani rolled over. "What's so funny?"

Ludik chuckled. "Never mind."

Ahjin stretched into an upright position. "What?"

"I have a new medicine for you to try." Ludik dumped the yellow flowers in Zefra's hands. "Zefra will make a tea, and I want you to drink it all."

Ahjin made a face. "Smell?"

"No, I don't know how it will taste," Ludik said, "and I don't care."

Zefra stuffed the flowers into a water jug and fed heat through the sides while Ahjin shook Nia until she grumbled into wakefulness.

"We need to discuss what I found while scouting," Ludik said.

Zefra wrinkled her forehead. "Do we need to discuss more about the herb?"

Nia scrubbed her face with her hands. "What herb?"

Zefra handed the steaming jug to Ahjin. "Ludik found the petika and thinks it will help Ahjin."

"The pakai? That's wonderful. Okechuku will be so happy with Ludik."

Kani flinched. "You found pakai?"

Ahjin gulped from the jug, then held his hand over his mouth and scrunched his eyes shut.

"Swallow," Ludik commanded. "I also found an inland building we need to include in our plans, or we'll end up fighting pirates from two directions at once."

"We are already fighting too many pirates," Kani said, "and now you want to add more?"

Ahjin held up his hand and whistled a bird song.

In response to the signal, Izo rejoined them. "Is it time to plan, then?"

Ludik tipped the jug toward Ahjin's mouth and put his other hand over the head injury. "Hold still, Ahjin. I was thinking about your exploding perfume, Nia. The pirates probably have some kind of alcohol stored. If we burn the building, it will make an excellent distraction before we destroy the ships."

"That's a great idea," Nia said.

"Is anyone in the building?" Izo asked.

"I didn't smell anyone," Ludik said.

"How far away is it?" Zefra asked. "Can we get back in time to attack the ships?"

Ludik shrugged. "A few minutes for a jaguar. Not too far even on two legs."

"I will go," Zefra said.

"I will go with you," Izo volunteered.

"Ahjin needs you to build his catapult," Zefra said. "I can take care of myself."

Izo folded his arms and glowered. "I will not let my little sister go into danger alone."

"I'll go with her," Ludik said, "when I finish with Ahjin." He put down the jug but kept one hand on Ahjin's head no matter how the Iojif squirmed.

"I need to check on the port before I leave," Zefra said. "Is anyone going with me?"

"All of you," Ludik said. "I'm busy now, and I don't need to see. Kani can tell Ahjin what he needs to know. Hold still, Ahjin."

"That hurts," Ahjin said without a hint of a stammer.

"Two words," Nia cheered. "How wonderful."

Ahjin rolled his eyes.

"We will return soon." Zefra pulled Nia away, and they crawled with

Izo and Kani to the top of the hill to spy on the pirates, dragging more catapult branches behind them.

One by one, ships pulled into the harbor from all directions and tied up at the dock for the night. The sailors strung hammocks and dimmed lanterns on board.

Zefra squinted at the crowded bay. There were not as many ships as she remembered. Several dozen, probably, with hundreds of men instead of thousands.

"I do not think they are all here. They must have sent more on patrol."

Kani rubbed his neck. "We can't do anything about that. If we take care of these, we can escape and worry about the others later." He shrugged. "It makes our job easier."

"There's Mom's ship," Nia said. "It looks like they're fixing it."

"Everyone has nets hanging over the side to catch fish," Kani said.

"They must be hungry," Nia said, "without enough ships to be raided."

Zefra's stomach growled. "They could have found an honorable profession to put food on the table. Does it look like our plan will work?"

"I think the ships are close enough together," Nia said. "Or will be."

Zefra glanced at the sun. "It will be dark soon. Ludik and I must go. Does everyone understand the plan?"

"Yes, Zefra." Nia sighed. "You drilled us for hours. We understand."

Zefra left Nia at the top of the hill, crawling down until she was out of sight and could walk to Ahjin.

"Nia is on watch, and Izo is ready to build your catapult." Zefra glanced over her shoulder. Izo was already connecting the branches in the pattern he designed, just below the top of the hill. "You can super-vise, if you like." She handed her bow and few remaining arrows to him.

Ahjin grinned, both sides of his mouth turning up evenly. "Yes, Zef-ra." He saluted and worked his way up the hill.

"Ludik, are you ready?" Zefra asked.

Ludik nodded and led her north and inland. The building was not far from the port, but the low structure was hard to see in the tall grass until Zefra was nearly upon it.

Ludik pulled Zefra to the ground, and they crawled silently around to the back.

Pirates were terrible builders. The large hut was a hodgepodge of styles and materials, shoved together in a haphazard manner. It leaned sideways on its foundation, if widely spaced rocks made a foundation.

Zefra saw no windows at all, nor any back door. How were they to get in?

Ludik stopped by a particularly large gap in the foundation and pointed down. "They have a cellar. I can smell alcohol. Do you think you can get through and burn it from the bottom?"

Zefra measured the gap between the stones and the crooked boards in the wall. "Perhaps. It will be tight." She eyed Ludik. "You will never fit."

"I'll wait here for you."

Zefra nodded, tightening her scarf around her head. She should remember to thank Ahjin for the loan of his clothes, since her robe would be too awkward. She lay on the ground and slid her feet through the hole. All well so far. She wiggled backward until her legs dangled in mid-air. Her shoulders nearly got stuck, but she pressed herself to the earth and pushed, scraping through and dropping into the cellar. Fortunately, 'twas not far down. The pirates had excavated only a shallow pit, and Zefra had to duck to avoid bumping her head on the ceiling.

Blue sunset trickled through the floorboards. Ludik passed his hatchet through the foundation gap. Zefra held her breath, pressing against the wall while she waited for her eyes to adjust to the dim light in the rough-cut room.

Rows of barrels lined the dirt walls between the support pillars. Some were open, revealing fruits and vegetables. Some smelled of fish. Her stomach grumbled, and she pressed her hand against it. 'Twas no time to eat now, but she filled a basket with produce and passed it through the hole. Ludik whistled under his breath when she passed it to him. He bit into a mango and motioned for her to hurry.

She bit her tongue to keep from retorting and turned back to her mission. Some carefully sealed barrels had spouts. Just what she needed. And on shelves above those casks, empty clay jugs sat in tipsy lines. Perhaps she could add alcohol to Ludik's flammable plants and make the ships burn even faster. Two successes for the risk of one.

Zefra grabbed a jug and filled it from one of the sealed casks. The alcohol fumes made her eyes water. Perfect. She passed it to Ludik and worked her way through the entire shelf of jugs. When all were outside, she pried apart the almost empty barrel with the hatchet, as quietly as possible, and stacked the rum-soaked boards at the base of the support columns.

No one came to investigate, so she unwound her scarf and held it under the next spout until it dripped rum. That also went outside. After securing her hairpins in her crown of braids, she opened the spigot on each barrel, jumping back from the gush of rum. Now 'twas time to get out.

She gave Ludik the hatchet, then grabbed his hands. He pulled until her elbows passed the wall, then she braced herself to wiggle through.

Ludik picked up jugs while she dropped one end of her rum-soaked scarf through the hole until it dangled in the rising puddle of alcohol.

She picked up three jugs with one hand and held the other hand near the upper end of her scarf.

If she got this wrong, the pirates would catch them. Or the fire might kill them, too. She inhaled and looked at Ludik. When he nodded, she called flame and dropped the fire on the scarf, which promptly ignited.

Now to escape before the flame reached the pooled rum at the bottom. Zefra and Ludik ran in the darkness, jugs clinking and her heart thudding almost as loudly as their boots. The noise worried her, but speed was more important, and as soon as the rum caught, their racket would not matter.

They were not much more than a stone's throw away before flames shot to the sky. Pirates ran from the hut, screaming and slapping at their burning clothing.

A wall of heat flooded them, and Zefra's heart sped faster. Could they outrun the fire? They ran a little farther and threw themselves into a dip in the ground to watch the building burn. Within minutes, more pirates poured in from the east. Handfuls and then a stream of pirates ran to the blaze.

The grass burst into flames in all directions. Surrounding trees caught fire. Flames ran up the trunks and flowered across the branches. Ludik and Zefra scrambled to their feet and backed farther from the inferno.

"You were right, Ludik," Zefra said. "This is a wonderful distraction."

26. BURNED

(DRAGON ISLES)

In case of doubt, it is best to lean to the side of mercy.

Darrendran Proverb

Ludik stared at the flames engulfing the entire building. They lit the night almost as brightly as day.

Pirates frantically threw dirt on it, but the fire still grew. Those caught in the original blaze now lay motionless. Some moaned, but others were ominously silent. Some of the pirates who came later had been caught by the spreading flames, and their screams echoed into the night sky.

Ludik clutched the burned walrus tusk around his neck. This had been his idea. Their injuries were on his head, and if they died, that would be his fault, too. He had thought the building was empty, but apparently the smell of the rum had covered the pirates' scents.

"Time to go, Ludik," Zefra said. "Hurry; the others will need us."

His friends did need him. Even with so many pirates drawn here, they still faced an army against the six of them. Five, because his feet didn't move back toward the ocean.

Ludik tightened his grip on the tusk until the point dug into his palm. He had fought enemies before, hand to hand, or teeth and claws. What had changed?

A pirate crawled away from the fire, sobbing in pain.

"Ludik," Zefra called.

He looked away from the pirate and blinked. It was time to help his friends escape. He adjusted his grip on the jugs and took a step toward Zefra.

"Help me," a pirate moaned behind him.

Ludik froze mid-step. The pirate wasn't talking to him, didn't even know he was there, but the plea went straight to his heart. He was a healer. How could he ignore the suffering behind him?

He touched the walrus tusk again, remembering the hard lessons of last autumn. Hate was poison, and he had already sworn to abandon it. It didn't matter how inadequate his healing was if he was the only one here.

Ludik lowered his rum jugs to the ground. "Zefra, go without me. I need to help the injured."

Zefra blinked. "They are pirates."

"And I'm a healer."

"You cannot help the enemy. They are fighting against us. Would you heal them so they can murder your friends?"

Ludik touched the walrus tusk again. "Healers don't recognize enemies, only patients."

Zefra dropped her jugs and stared at him. "They tried to kill us!"

"They did not even know we were here. It is one thing to fight pirates when they are attacking us but another to set a trap." Ludik felt for his knife and water jug. His half-empty jar of salve was still in his pocket. It was too bad he didn't have his medical kit, but it was nearly empty, anyway. The rest of his medicines and bandages were ruined.

"Their allies tried to kill us," Zefra said. "They would have been our enemies as soon as they discovered us. 'Tis too dangerous to help them. Not all of them are injured. They will kill you."

Ludik shrugged. "I hope to convince them not to. If I can, I will pretend to be one of them."

"We need your help."

"You will have to do without me." He took a step away.

"What about Nemerra?" Zefra blurted. "What will I tell her about your foolishness?"

Ludik stopped. His chest ached. What could he tell Nemerra? If he died from this folly, she would be left with half-orphaned children. He tugged on his wedding ring until his ear burned.

But how could he live with himself if he betrayed his conscience? Nemerra would understand. Ludik swallowed. The bite marks on her neck were proof. He tucked the walrus tusk into his tunic and turned to Zefra.

"Do you still have your slate?"

Zefra pulled it from her pouch along with her chalk. "The battle plans washed off in the swim. I redrew the map to the best of my memory."

Ludik found a mostly empty corner of the slate and scribbled a message for Nemerra, using the compact Darrendran runes for privacy. *I love you. I'm sorry. I find I'm a healer, after all.* He snorted. She probably already knew. Whenever he complained about healing, she only smiled.

Zefra put away her slate, and Ludik piled the jugs and fruit basket in her arms. "Try to survive," she whispered.

She walked away, and Ludik ran back toward the fiery building, stopping only to hack off the plump arms of a spiky, succulent plant.

Here he was, abandoning his friends while they still had a battle in front of them. Ahjin had just started walking straight again, and they were outnumbered ten to one, or worse. If Ludik healed the pirates, would they join the fight against his friends? Would his absence tip the battle against them? And he might be cut down before he healed a single pirate. What good would that do anyone? He reached for his earring again, but his feet still carried him toward the blaze.

It took only a few minutes to retrace his steps. The pirates had abandoned the building and were stomping on the grass to keep the fire from spreading. The pleasant smell of burning wood and grass was horribly laced with the smell of burnt meat and coppery blood. Screams and moans echoed over the crackle of the flames and the snaps of falling branches and breaking wood.

He heard Zefra's voice in his head. *They are the enemy.* If they were not here at the burning building, they would be at the ships to face his friends, who could not fight such a large group. The distraction was a necessary strategy, and yet, how horrible for so many to be caught in the fire he helped light.

He looked at his hands. Though brown, they seemed red, soaked in blood. It was time to finally become the healer he was training to be. If that meant he died, he would accept that.

Ludik dropped to his knees by the first victim he found, laying the succulent leaves at his side.

The Nokai man was silent, and his skin bubbled through the scorched holes in his clothes. Half his face had melted, and his shriveled hands clutched a blackened hole in his belly.

Ludik choked as the acrid reek of melted skin and scorched hair filled his nose with a mix of charcoal, sulfur, and the tang of branded leather. He leaned closer and sniffed the pirate's belly wound. Burnt liver fought with a sweet, musky perfume.

Ludik spat, but the odor stuck to his tongue. Though the pirate still breathed, he was beyond help and would die in minutes. Ludik climbed to his feet.

The next victim, a pale Iskrin, moaned face-down on the ground. His hands and back were blistered, but Ludik didn't smell burnt internal organs, and the man had no gaping wounds.

Ludik poured water over the burns, then sliced open one of the succulent leaves. He cut out as much of the thick pulp as possible, spreading it on the worst burns, then laid the skin, juice-side-down, over the last of the wounds. He sliced the dead Nokai's shirt into strips and wrapped it around the Iskrin, checking for more burns as he rolled the man from side to side. Nothing was visible. It seemed likely the man had been hurt running from the fire.

"Do you hurt anywhere else?" Ludik asked in trade tongue.

The Iskrin stared at him blankly, then closed his eyes and passed out.

Ludik glanced at the fire, which spread ravenously farther inland but not in his direction, thanks to the efforts of the pirates. The next victim was another Nokai, unconscious but with treatable burns.

Ludik washed the injuries and reached for his knife and the next succulent leaf. He didn't get a chance to apply it before someone pressed a sword to his back. The pirate barked something in another language.

Ludik glanced over his shoulder and glimpsed a webbed hand. Nokai, then. Ludik spoke a little Iskrit after six months as an apprentice, but only a word or two of Noki.

"I'm a healer," he said in trade tongue, holding his knife away from his patient.

"I not recognize you." The pirate switched to halting trade tongue. "That man can live. No need death mercy."

"I am a healer, new to Captain Crow's fleet," Ludik said. "I want to help."

Crow's name seemed to calm the pirate a little. "Where you from?"

"Darrendra, as you can tell." Ludik lowered his knife to the plant, then flinched as the sword poked through his tunic.

"Knife up," the pirate said.

Ludik raised his knife again and waved the succulent. "Shall we waste time talking, or do you want me to help his burns?"

The wounded Nokai on the ground moaned, then opened his eyes and screamed. The Nokai behind Ludik flinched, and the point of his blade dug into Ludik's back. Ludik leaned forward a little but otherwise didn't move. The wounded Nokai clutched at Ludik and wept. The sword at Ludik's back finally moved away.

"You help," the pirate demanded, coming around where Ludik could see him. Under the dirt, his matted hair was a browner gold than his skin, like scorched sugar. "You heal with magic?"

Ludik shook his head in a lie. Healing all these pirates with his gift would kill him. The pirates might not care, but he still cherished a faint hope of returning to Nemerra.

"I can treat more of our comrades if you help me," Ludik said.

"What you need?" the pirate asked. He didn't sheathe his sword, but he kept it pointed away from Ludik.

Ludik handed him a leaf. "More of this plant, and water. Bandages. More people to help. If we can get the injured onto beds, that would be good. If you have more healers, even better."

The pirate shook his head. "No healers."

He bellowed something in Noki, and pirates came running from all directions. The golden pirate barked orders, pointing at each pirate surrounding him. They scattered, half returning to fighting the fire. Two with lanterns took samples of the succulent with them.

A Darrendrakar with a bristly chin knelt by Ludik and held a lamp above the wounded man. His nose ring marked him as a married member of the Pig kindred. He said something in a Darrendran dialect Ludik didn't recognize, then switched to Canid, which Ludik recognized but didn't speak.

"Do you speak Felid?" Ludik asked.

The Pig nodded and changed to the Felid dialect. "Captain Aukai did not understand everything you said. I will translate for you. What do we do first?"

"Have them collect the wounded and bring them here." Ludik checked to be sure the fire was still headed the opposite direction. "He sent people for water and that plant, did he not?"

The Pig chattered at the golden Nokai. "He did, but he did not understand what you said about beds. Are you injured?"

"Beds to get the wounded off the ground, if we can." Ludik cut the pulp from the leaf he held and spread it on the burns. "Even mats or grass would be better than dirt in their burns."

While translating, the Pig held the man's hands out of the way and ignored his screams.

Captain Aukai headed for the trees, sword still drawn. Each time he passed a walking pirate, he stopped to give orders.

"How long have you been here?" the Pig asked. "I have seen few Darrendrakar in my years aboard."

"Oh, not long," Ludik said. "Do we have any bandages yet?"

The Pig glanced down and turned green. He turned his head and yelled something in Noki, then repeated it in Iskrit. "Where are the bandages?"

Ludik decided not to mention he understood the Iskrit. The more advantages he kept secret, the more chance he had of surviving.

"I am finished with this patient." Ludik sheathed his knife and stood, careful not to startle the Pig. "Who is next? Do we have anyone who can sort them by severity?"

The Pig scratched his bristles. "I will try, if you teach me what to do."

Pirates came back with more succulent, buckets of water, and filthy shirts dangling in the dirt.

Ludik pinched the bridge of his nose. "We need clean cloth for bandages. Dirt creates infection."

The Pig bellowed, and the pirates with dirty clothing turned at a run. Captain Aukai reappeared with his arms full of palm fronds, and men followed him with more.

Ludik inhaled with relief. More pirates helping him not only gave the injured more chances to live, but it also kept them away from the fight with his friends.

"They will bring mats," the Pig said. "Tell me how to sort the injuries."

"If someone has only a mild burn, they can wait," Ludik explained. "The more severe the damage, or in a more vital place, the sooner I need to see them. With one exception. If they are too badly burned to live, there is no point in taking my time from someone I can help." He pointed behind him. "I already found one too injured to save."

The Pig nodded. "I understand." He grabbed a pirate by the arm and motioned toward the Nokai Ludik had been unable to help.

The pirate drew his sword and walked away.

Ludik squeezed his eyes shut. "I meant we should leave them alone."

The Pig widened his eyes. "And let them suffer?"

"If I had painkillers—" Ludik started.

The pirate came back, sword still clean, and dragged one of the wounded to a new pile of palm leaves.

"No worries," the Pig told Ludik. "He was already dead. Start with this one."

The Pig led Ludik to a shivering Iskrin whose robe had been half-burned off his torso, then moved to look at the next man carried to the line of palm mats.

While Ludik worked, an Iskrin pirate joined him with a bucket of water and a relatively clean robe in his hands. Ludik pointed to the robe and mimed ripping it. The Iskrin nodded and sliced the robe into strips.

Ludik turned his attention to the wounded man. As pirates reported for duty, he gave them orders in trade tongue or gestures, or rarely in Darrendran. Most of the pirates were Nokai or Iskrin, with only a few from Darrendra or Ioj. The Iojif were all damaged in ways that preceded the fire; poorly healed wings were common.

In less time than he expected, all the injured had someone helping them. Other pirates carried water, cut apart succulent leaves, ripped bandages, or did laundry for future bandages.

Ludik treated most of the wounded with the succulent juice, but for a few, he snuck a dab of his enhanced ointment on the worst burns. If he had a bucket of the salve, it would not be enough to treat them all.

After prioritizing the injured in a ring of lamplight, the Pig rejoined

Ludik. Once only minor injuries were left, their conversation drifted from medical instructions.

"Why did you join the pirates?" Ludik asked him, grateful for the Darrendran that allowed them a private conversation.

"Why did *you*?" the Pig retorted. "None of us had many options. Some are running from the law, some from something else. There is nowhere else for us to go, though Crow will change that."

"I have not heard the plan. What does he have in mind?"

The Pig looked away. "I am not in the council. I should not say what I overheard."

Ludik bandaged the last injured pirate and sat back on his heels. "If none of you want to be here, why go along with Crow's plan?"

"When you have been here longer, you will see we have no choice, nowhere else to go. We are lucky you joined our crew. You saved many good crewmen today."

"Lucky." Ludik tugged the wedding ring in his ear and thought hard.

"Yes, we can never repay you. Now, we must return to the ships."

"What if you could repay me?" Ludik ran his hand over his cropped hair. His next questions were risky but might save his friends.

"What if I gave you the chance to save yourselves and leave this life? Would you take it?"

27.BATTLE
(DRAGON ISLES)

In Kassian's long absence was the world divided without Him, leaving Him no land for His possession.
A Comprehensive History of the Gods, vol. 5

Nia peered over the top of the hill at the fleet of pirate ships, careful to keep her head down. The docking spots were full, and the last ships had to anchor in the water. Most of the pirates must be in by now. Zefra was right; it did look like a forest of masts against the starry sky. At least they were merchant ships and fishing craft, not troop carriers.

But the cramped harbor meant their plan would work. It had to, if they were ever to go home. She'd risked so much to find out what happened to Dad, and the only part left was telling Mom.

Nia crawled back to the others. Izo had nearly finished assembling the simple catapult below the crest of the hill, and Ahjin lined his jars of trouble in neat rows according to a system he hadn't explained. He grinned as he tapped each jug.

"Are you ready, Kani?" Nia asked. "We have a lot to do before Zefra and Ludik return."

Kani leaned on his harpoon and nodded. "I'll take the anchors if you take the rudders."

Nia rubbed her hands together. "Fine with me. I have ideas."

Both of them scrambled down the dark hill and dove into the water toward the first ship. She harvested seaweed from the bottom of the cove and stuffed it around the rudders of each ship, starting with her mom's. If the pirates tried to sail, they wouldn't get far without the steering.

Nia waved as she passed Kani. Though the blue man had to go up for air as if he weren't Nokai, he was nearly invisible in the night-darkened water. After cutting the anchor to Aolani's ship, he swam silently from pirate ship to pirate ship. He raised every other anchor, knotting their ropes and chains around each other until they were all connected but still held in place. Her mom's ship, however, rocked gently in the ebbing tide, slowly pulling out to sea as the waves retreated.

Nia finished blocking the rudders and swam for land. Kani was not far behind her, and they crawled up the hill together and joined the others.

Ahjin pulled her down next to Izo and patted her shoulder. "Now wait," he said.

While she was gone, he had added piles of rocks and thistles to his rows of ammunition and tied the flammable plants into loose bundles of tinder.

Izo watched Nia with red eyes and a quavery smile.

Nia fidgeted. They had time to talk, but no privacy. She couldn't talk to either of the boys without the other hearing, and Kani, too. What would she say, anyway? *So, Ahjin, you were right about hurting Izo's feelings, and I feel bad about it, but Izo, can we kiss even if I don't want to marry you?* Even if that weren't an entirely embarrassing prospect, she didn't think either of them would like it.

"Ahjin, how do you feel?" she asked instead.

Ahjin shrugged. "Words remember me better."

Nia tried not to laugh. "That's wonderful, Ahjin. You're doing so well."

Ahjin snorted.

Izo twisted his mouth into something between a smile and a grimace and patted Ahjin's shoulder. "I'm sure it will continue to improve."

Kani sharpened his harpoon on a rock and didn't comment.

The inland sky lit up like dawn. The four of them jerked to attention.

"Hurricane and halcyon," Nia said. "What did they do?"

They watched the flickering light on the horizon until another sound caught their attention. Pirates jumped from their ships and stampeded off the dock and toward the spreading fire.

Nia watched open-mouthed for a long time. There were a lot of pirates.

"Oh, well done, Zefra and Ludik," she whispered. "Look at them go. This might actually work."

"Now all we need is for our friends to return," Izo murmured, adjusting something on the awkward catapult.

Ahjin silently pointed at each of his jars and squinted at the ships. He moved his finger down the row, as if counting, then started over with wider spaces between his gestures.

Only the barest of crews were left on the ships.

Nia waited with her friends, and waited some more, until the grass rustled. Zefra crept up the hill, burdened by jugs and a woven basket. Her uncovered hair flamed in the light of the distant fire. She walked quietly, but the careful placement of her feet somehow gave the impression of stomping.

"Where is Ludik?" Izo asked.

Zefra pressed her lips into a tight line. "He stayed behind because some pirates were wounded. I brought ammunition for Ahjin and food for everyone. Are you ready?"

"Ludik did what?" Nia exclaimed.

Zefra dropped the jugs on the ground and hacked off her torn trousers at the knee. "I told him 'twas foolish." Her white legs shone until she rubbed dirt on them.

"He's helping the enemy?" Kani asked. "Why would he do that?"

"'Tis what I asked." Zefra clipped off her words.

Ahjin grabbed one of the small jugs, wiggled out the cork, and smelled it. A grin crept across his face.

Izo grabbed a fruit. "Who can understand a healer? They must have something different in their heads to do what they do."

"But we're already outnumbered," Nia complained. "How can he abandon us like this?"

Ahjin frowned at her and shoved food into her hand.

The first taste made her mouth water, and she crammed in the rest as fast as she could chew.

"Quiet," Zefra said, "and help me with the wicks. We must do without him." She cut her trouser legs into strips and stuffed one into the neck of each jug. "Are the ships ready?"

"Yes," Nia mumbled through another mouthful.

"I have watched the patrol rhythms," Izo said, "and we are unlikely to get a better chance."

Zefra looked intently at Ahjin. "Can you turn invisible again?"

Ahjin shook his head. "But fly." He flapped his wings and grinned. "Izo, jar well." He leaned close to Nia. "Choose wisely. Be happy." He kissed her on the cheek and took the first two jars and bundles of tinder from Zefra.

"Ahjin," Nia called, but he was gone.

Zefra lit the wicks, and Ahjin shot into the air with them burning ever closer to his hands. The two dots of light flew swiftly and almost smoothly to the first ship. By the time the pirates shouted and waved weapons, it was too late. Ahjin dropped tinder into the crow's nest and smashed the jug on top. The flame caught in the rum-splashed wicker basket and spread to the lines. The sail burst into flames a moment later. By then, Ahjin had already dropped the second jar, two ships away, and was on his way back for more.

While he burned the ships, Nia, Izo, and Zefra dragged the catapult the last few ells to its firing position on top of the hill.

The crews on the burning ships shouted and tried to cut the sails free, but it was too late. The fire spread to the masts, and the constant splashing of sailors jumping overboard provided a rhythmic counterpoint to the crackle of the fires and the screams of the pirates. Not all the pirates made it to shore.

Now that the pirates knew he was coming, Ahjin smashed the burning jugs of rum at the base of the masts of every third ship so the sail and deck would both catch fire. His skipping pattern ensured every ship was either set on fire or had a burning ship next to it.

The unaffected ships tried to pull out from between the flaming ones, but their rudders didn't respond. Nia cackled as they jerked to a halt at the ends of their tangled anchors and swung to crash into the burning ships.

The fire spread from ship to ship and to the dock, illuminating the whole area with a flickering light. At the free end, the sailors tried to sail, but they also couldn't steer clear. Only Aolani's ship was far enough from the blazing fleet to stay safe.

Once Ahjin was past the first ships, Izo aimed the catapult, lobbing Ahjin's prank jars at the pirates on Aolani's ship. It was fortunate they had a downhill shot, since the catapult wasn't very powerful.

His first missiles landed only on the deck, but Ahjin had chosen the ammunition order wisely. The first jar shattered, spewing tiny scorpions in all directions. Bellowing sailors danced away. The second jar was full of spiny sea urchins, unable to chase the men and seemingly harmless until barefooted pirates stepped on them in their zeal to avoid the furious scorpions and discovered the urchins were sharper and just as venomous.

Izo's aim improved with every shot, and soon the pirates got stinging sea nettles and showers of rocks directly in their faces. The captain, judging by the orders he bellowed, was hit by a small octopus that clung to his face despite all attempts to remove him. As soon as he and the octopus fell overboard, his men also abandoned ship.

Ahjin made more trips to drop burning jugs, and the blazing ships cast enough light to make it obvious Zefra's plan was working. After the battle, Nia could retake her mom's ship and sail home.

Nia cheered until she realized most of the pirates who had jumped overboard had made their way to land despite the flaming deck and were now storming the hill where her group was exposed by the necessary position of the catapult.

"Get them!" the pirates shouted. Some had weapons and some only the rocks and sticks they grabbed along the way, but there were many of them and only five to oppose them with weapons created from broken junk on a boulder-anvil. Fortunately, none seemed to have bows.

Nia cursed and picked up her makeshift spear. Izo shot the last of Ahjin's jars at the oncoming army and grabbed his own spear. They stepped in front of Zefra and lowered their weapons toward the enemy. Ahjin needed more time to deliver all the jars, and Zefra was their only flame for the wicks.

Kani threw himself flat on the hilltop and blew darts at the sailors

with every breath. The pirates he hit ran a moment longer, then staggered to their knees before falling under the feet of their crew mates.

Zefra calmly lit wicks as fast as Ahjin came for the jugs, her weapons
ready at her feet. Nia clenched her shaking hands around her spear,
envying Zefra's calm.

Ahjin continued to ferry the explosives at top speed until he finished
his pattern.

Now that the rum was gone, Zefra raised her bow and stepped to her
brother's back. Ahjin flew circles above them, using a bamboo tube to
blow darts at the enemy.

The pirates were almost at the top of the hill, howling and waving
their weapons. Zefra loosed her arrows, hitting most of her targets. Kani
scrambled backward and grabbed his harpoon. He stood back-to-back
with Nia, mirroring the Iskrins. The advancing pirates slowed, encouraging each other to go first. Between their cowardice and the men gone
to deal with Zefra's distraction, maybe there was a chance.

And then Zefra's arrows were gone, and the pirates ran again.

Nia stabbed and swung and stabbed again, glad of her prior experience against monsters. Kani fought like a madman, and his growls
rumbled in her ears. Izo dueled with one sword, but Zefra now battled
with sword and knife, using the back of the shorter blade to parry.

Any pirate who circled around their group got a pebble from Ahjin's
slingshot buried in his head. None of the sailors got past the defense at
the top, though it was only a matter of time before Nia or her friends
tired enough to make a fatal mistake.

Another pirate fell to Ahjin's darts, and the rest slowed their charge.
Their battle cries dwindled to disheartened grunts as they lingered
halfway up the hill, and some of the laggards deserted the battle.

At the bottom of the hill, a new voice rose. Someone bellowed orders
and shoved the pirates forward when they faltered.

Ahjin's voice came from above Nia's head. "Crow here."

"What a nuisance," Nia said. "Can anyone hit him with a dart?"

"Keep fighting, you cowards," the captain screeched from the bottom
of the hill. "You have them outnumbered. Take them down!"

That was disappointing. Crow was too far away for the darts, and Nia
preferred winning. Zefra motioned toward the ocean, but Nia ignored

the suggestion to flee and smacked the butt of her spear into the next pirate's face.

"Lapwing!" Crow yelled again. "Where are you, you moth-eaten craven?"

A tan-winged Iojif fluttered from the dock. "Here I am, Crow," he screamed in a high-pitched voice. "What do you want? How can I serve you, Crow?"

"Get up there and take out that winged boy," Crow demanded, waving his arms toward the top of the hill.

Nia panted for breath. "I wish we could eliminate the creepy captain."

"Oh, no, I couldn't do that, Crow," Lapwing whined. "I'm no fighter." The tan wings flapped in an awkward circle at the bottom of the hill. "No, no, I couldn't, Crow. Did you see what he did to those sailors?"

If he came up the hill, Nia would be happy to show him at close range. She ducked a pirate's blow and kicked him down the hill.

Crow shrieked and waved his sword at Lapwing. "Why do I keep you around? You're worthless!" His bellows carried easily up the hill.

"Oh, don't say that, Crow."

Crow said something about getting the other men, but Nia couldn't hear the details while she lunged at the next pirate. She ducked behind Kani long enough to take a breath.

"Yes, Crow. I won't let you down, Crow." Tan wings headed inland in a jerky swoop, and Ahjin chased after him.

Good for him. Ruining Zefra's lovely distraction was the last thing they needed.

Blood ran down Izo's bare skin again, but he kept moving. Zefra's sword flashed in the firelight, cutting down another pirate.

Nia stabbed the next pirate in the belly and yanked back her spear for the next attacker. A pirate with a long sword swung for her head. She ducked, and Kani knocked away the sword and buried his harpoon in the man's chest. Nia panted for breath and looked for her next opponent.

Above them, Lapwing turned and flew over the ocean, calling for Crow to help him. Ahjin chased him out of sight.

"You worthless coward!" Crow shook his fist at Lapwing, then bellowed at his men. The pirates rallied for another push up the hill.

Nia sagged, then raised her spear again. When would this end? How many more could they fight? Why wouldn't the pirates give up?

A flash of white swept overhead, and Ahjin landed in front of Crow.

Nia gasped. What was that idiot doing? Weren't they in enough danger without him volunteering to be chopped to bits?

This was her fault for suggesting someone go after Crow. An unexpectedly strong pang cramped her chest. If Ahjin got himself killed, what would she do without him?

28. WRECKED

(DRAGON ISLES)

Win the battle, lose the war.

Darrendran Proverb

Ahjin landed in front of the wingless Iojif known as Crow. This battle had gone on long enough. His friends were fighting well but couldn't hold out forever. He was already broken and unloved. If he died saving them, it would be worth it. It would also solve the problem of his broken heart.

"Stop," he yelled, loading another stone in his slingshot. "Can't win. Building gone, ships burned."

"I will win," Crow shouted, waving his sword and storming toward Ahjin. "You are outnumbered and out-armed."

He swung at Ahjin, who leaped into the air.

"We will chop you into little pieces," Crow said. "I personally will cut off your pretty wings."

This time, Ahjin circled, landing behind the pirate. "No kill and steal," he tried.

"It is no crime to be strong." Crow whirled and swung again.

Ahjin jumped and flew circles around Crow's head. Now it would be handy for the fires to be less bright.

"Whatever I conquer," Crow said, "I deserve to hold. I was exiled from my own land, with no way to support myself. The evil magistrates even stripped me unfairly of my wings."

He shrugged his shoulders, and as Ahjin looped around, he saw the black stumps of Crow's wings pressing against his shirt.

"Fair," Ahjin said. "Flew to murder."

Crow ignored his comment. "It is only through my genius and good management that I have built my dominion into such prosperity."

He continued to swing his sword at Ahjin, who stayed out of reach above him.

Crow kept screaming. "My wealth and leadership have attracted good warriors and intelligent men who do not believe the foolish customs of their leaders." He slashed at Ahjin's feet. "They were oppressed in their own lands, kept in bondage to the system that gave the profit of their labors to the very men that beat them down." He jumped and swung and still missed. "I gave them the freedom to enjoy their natural rights. I gave them opportunities beyond their dreams. I saved them all."

"Not now." Ahjin raised his voice to the bellow he had learned from Irajahan. "Isles claimed by god. Kassian comes. He stop you."

Crow screamed and swung his sword even harder. When he missed, he spun uselessly in a circle.

"Stop in name of god," Ahjin shouted.

"Kill them all," Crow yelled.

The pirates looked at Crow, frothing and swinging wildly at Ahjin, and kept fighting. More fell to the makeshift weapons that faced them. A few of them edged away from the battle.

From the direction of the burning sky, men trotted in, some with blisters or scorched clothing. They surrounded the hill and kept the fighting crew from escaping, but they did not march against Ahjin's friends. The newcomers spoke in urgent whispers, and more of the pirates stopped fighting and stood at the bottom of the hill. But some still fought at the top, and a few turned viciously against the new arrivals.

"Men forsake," Ahjin said. "Not fight god."

"These islands are already claimed by a god," Crow lowered his voice, as if telling a secret.

Ahjin furrowed his brows. He had asked all the gods, and they denied any knowledge or control of the Dragon Isles.

Crow whispered fiercely, "The one true god, who will restore my wings after I give him the world. He told me to reclaim his people, and I have served him well. I will conquer in his name, and—"

A harpoon thudded into his chest. Crow staggered. Blood bubbled from his mouth. He dropped his sword and fell to his knees.

Ahjin landed beside him and reached for the harpoon. "Need healer."

If Ludik were here, he could keep the pirate captain alive long enough to answer questions. Crow gurgled an awful laugh and collapsed. He shuddered once and lay still next to his sword. The dragon on his hilt twinkled in the firelight.

The leaderless pirates gasped and scattered. Most of the Nokai threw themselves into the ocean. The other men ran inland and vanished in all directions, dragging their wounded with them.

Ahjin nudged the captain with his boot. Nothing. He was dead, and whatever he knew was lost. What god did he think had claimed the islands? Was he right or merely insane?

"Good throw, Kani," Nia cheered, running down the hill. She threw her arms around Ahjin. "*You're* an idiot, though. What were you thinking, confronting a vicious pirate like that?"

"Stop pirates," Ahjin said.

The others joined them, and Ahjin turned to the crippled Nokai, whose dyed skin was finally fading to a lighter blue. "Why kill? Need talk."

"Who cares about his threats?" Nia said. "He's gone now."

Kani rubbed the scarf covering his ruined gills. "That evil man crippled me and left me to die. You would never convince him to surrender."

"Said god claim isles," Ahjin tried to explain.

"*You* said that," Zefra said.

"Said wings and conquer and—" Ahjin fumbled for the right words.

"We heard what he said about cutting off your wings," Izo said. "Do not worry; he is dead now and cannot hurt you."

"His men have scattered," Kani said. "The world is better without the Crow. The curse of the Dragon Isles is over."

Ahjin's wings flared. They weren't listening, and he couldn't explain the problem. He missed the ease of language on his tongue.

"We won!" Nia swung around him in a happy circle and stretched up to kiss him.

Her lips were chapped, but it was the sweetest kiss he'd ever experienced. He closed his eyes and memorized the feel of it.

She let go and turned to Izo for another kiss.

Ahjin jerked. The kiss had meant nothing. She would never love him.

He took a deep breath. Love couldn't be forced. No, her happiness was more important. His earlier decision was still true. If he truly loved her, the best way to show it was to let her go without a fuss.

"Nia." He reached for her arm, but she pulled away and ran past him.

"Ludik! Where have you been, you idiot?"

Ahjin turned to see his friend returning, soot-streaked and red-eyed.

Ludik hugged Nia. "They needed my help. You had everyone else to help you."

She slugged his arm. "That's a lousy excuse. What if the pirates killed you?"

Ludik tugged his earring. "Zefra had a note for Nemerra. And it worked out well enough. I healed the injured and persuaded some of the others to help you. Didn't you find their arrival useful?"

Nia slugged him again. "I'll tell Nemerra what you did." She kissed his cheek. "All of it. Are we ready to leave now?"

"We need to collect the petika I found," Ludik reminded her.

"I suppose I should swim out and bring back Mom's ship," Nia said.

Ahjin shook his head and pointed to himself.

"Can you handle it by yourself?"

Ahjin raised an eyebrow and pretended to measure the short distance between the ship and the dock. He frowned at Nia.

"Fine, I'm sorry for insulting your prowess," she teased. "I'll help Ludik with the pakai."

Kani flinched. He bent and pulled his harpoon from the Crow's chest, inspecting the blood. "I'll help you gather your herb."

Zefra surveyed the battlefield. "I think our plan worked well."

Ahjin glanced at Crow's dead body. They had stopped the pirates here, but had they stopped the conquest of the world? Was there really a god behind this, and would he find others to fulfill his plan?

Izo looked at the two columns of smoke, inland and at sea, and the bodies that littered the ground. "Remind me not to anger you, sister."

Zefra dropped her ugly sword on the ground. "I still expect you to make me new weapons."

Izo threw his arm around her shoulders. "I will. Lead the way, Ludik."

"That way." Ludik pointed southwest, and the others followed.

When Ludik passed the hill, he crouched by one of the bodies and rolled it over. He took something from the body, then stood with a sigh and walked away.

Ahjin flew to Aolani's ship and used the smallest sail to bring it around the burning ships and close to shore. The dock was too close to the flames to be safe, but they could use the dinghy to get everyone aboard.

Now, what to do about the dead pirates? Ahjin squinted at the burning ships. Those would do.

He flew to the first body, shoved the pirate over his shoulder, and walked to the end of the dock. When he was close enough to feel the scorching heat from the ships, he jumped up and out and dropped the pirate onto a burning deck. The boards broke, and the dead pirate tumbled into the hold.

Sailor after sailor, he dropped them into the funeral pyre. By the time he worked his way to the body Ludik had examined, he quivered with exhaustion and knelt to rest. This was one of the pirates that had come from the inland building, a brown Darrendrakar with a stubbly chin and a hole in his nostril. His sword was sheathed, but a long gash opened his belly.

Pirates had no loyalty, even to their own.

Ahjin stood and stretched his aching back. There were only a few pirates left, so he could clear them before Nia returned.

The trek to the funeral pyre got longer with every trip. When Ahjin dumped the last of the dead, he sat on the beach and closed his eyes in the first light of dawn. His wings shook when he extended them. Time for a nap.

He glanced at Aolani's ship to make sure he'd anchored it well enough, and a flash of color caught his gaze. Ships sailed toward the island.

Ahjin shot to his feet. If the pirates were already returning from patrol, their chance to escape was gone. Two, four, six ships. Some flew colorful Nokai sails, and the rest were plain Iskrin white. He had to warn his friends. Ahjin leaped into the air but fell back when his shaking wings couldn't hold him.

Shouts echoed across the water from the lead ship. All the ships turned toward Ahjin. He tried again to take off and failed.

The smallest ship at the rear ran up a flag, which billowed in the early morning breeze and opened to reveal the banner of Arupa.

Ahjin sat and covered his head with his wings. Rescue had arrived, and the pirates had been defeated just in time. He stayed on the sand while the ships anchored and small boats were lowered over the side.

Kaito arrived in the first boat and knelt by Ahjin's side to poke at every cut and bruise.

Ahjin swatted at him. "How find?" he asked.

Kaito widened his eyes and indicated the plumes of smoke and fire rising through the sky.

"Not me?" Ahjin suggested.

Kaito raised an eyebrow.

Ahjin waved at the new fleet. "So many?"

Kaito shrugged. He pointed to the gods' emblems on the banner and jabbed Ahjin's shoulder.

Ahjin grunted. They had handled the pirates themselves. One ship to carry them home was sufficient.

Kaito handed him a scroll sealed with a waxen wolf's head.

Ahjin wearily read the long scolding from Lyell. *When you return from playing, there is still much work to do. Shame... Behave...* Blathering drivel. Ahjin crumpled the scroll.

Lyell worked for *him*. When Ahjin got back, things would change.

A sailor cleared his throat.

Ahjin sat straighter. "Yes?"

"Lyell sent us to retrieve you." The sailor yanked off his hat and bobbed his head. "At Nokailana, Captain Inna told us about the pirates, and we found Kaito on our way here." The sailor twisted his cap. "Are there other survivors?"

Ahjin pointed inland.

The sailor turned and pumped his hands above his head. Cheers rose from the ships. He turned back to Ahjin. "Can we get you aboard or do you prefer to wait for your friends?"

Ahjin rolled his head to stretch his aching neck. "More pirates." He waved at the ocean. "Find."

"Yes, Your Holiness. We will return for you."

Ahjin shook his head and waved at Aolani's ship.

Kaito nodded firmly and waved the crumpled scroll toward the protective fleet.

Ahjin growled. Why couldn't he travel with his friends? After a minute, he nodded at Kaito. Duty won again.

The sailor looked from one to the other, then hopped back in the boat and returned to the ship. Within minutes, the fleet spread out to hunt patrolling pirates.

Ahjin lay on the sand and closed his eyes.

<p style="text-align:center">~~~~</p>

"Wake up, Ahjin." Nia shook him. "It's time to go."

Ahjin opened his eyes and took the jug of water Kaito held ready.

Nia danced impatiently. "We're going back to Kani's lair to get our stuff, then to a *different* lair to get whatever 'treasures' he's been hiding. I guess he still didn't trust us. Are you ready?"

Kaito shook his head and waved Lyell's message.

"Other ship," Ahjin said.

"I'll bring your stuff back with me, then." Nia pulled him to his feet.

Everyone was ready and waiting, and Ahjin worked his way around, saying farewells.

Ludik shoved the last of the pakai tea at him and clasped his arm long enough to send more healing rushing up it. Kani and the Iskrins merely bowed or kissed his cheeks.

When Ahjin kissed Nia on the cheek, she flinched. He turned away from her disdain and boarded the fastest ship without looking behind. The faster half of the fleet sailed with Ahjin, while the other half stayed to escort everyone else.

As soon as he stepped on board, people were waiting with things for him to do. Some were pleasant, like a warm bath and hot food, but when he was clean and fed, he sat to talk to the gods. He still couldn't hear Ira-jahan, and he didn't have seeds for Darravani. Words fought against his mental grip, either verbally or in writing, despite drinking the last of the nasty tea. That left Resef, perhaps.

Ahjin sent Kaito to ask every Iskrin sailor aboard for a set of runes, then set himself in the corner and tried to remember what each one meant. It took a while, but each time he puzzled out one that might help, he laid it aside. When he had it narrowed to pertinent runes, he hunted again for the meanings in his damaged brain to put them in order for Resef.

By the time he had the message prepared, it was several hours later, and his tired mind turned gray while he waited for a reply.

At some point, something touched his mind. No words, just a warm touch that tingled under his skin. Gradually, words swarmed him, floating around his brain until they settled in.

The touch vanished, and a note appeared in Ahjin's hand. "No one knows what Crow was talking about. Makana doesn't really want the Dragon Isles, so I accept them. We will discuss international waters when you return. Kassian."

"Oh, there you are," Irajahan said in Ahjin's head. "Where did you go?"

"You know where I was," Ahjin said. "You stripped my invisibility and left me to die by the pirates."

"I did not. You must have lost concentration. And then the damage to your poor head meant you couldn't talk to me or turn invisible. Without contact, I lost track of you, or I would have rescued you sooner. It is so sad. With your brains scrambled, you can't even remember properly what happened. I have proof: now that your brain is healed, your invisibility works."

Ahjin slammed his mental doors shut. That didn't seem to match his memories, but what if Irajahan was right? What if he didn't remember what the god had actually said? And none of his friends had heard.

His friends were on their way home, anyway. He didn't know how long it would be before he saw them again. Before he saw Nia again. If Darravani could heal wounded emotions, he'd beg her to wipe Nia from his aching heart.

Tears burned his eyes. He would move forward without Nia. Who knew what the future would bring? He certainly had enough work to do for the gods.

But his traitor heart sang, "I went a-sailing, across the wide sea. Alas, I found no one to be loved by me."

29.HOME

(DRAGON ISLES AND NOKAILANA)

Love rules without rules.

Nokai Proverb

The ships were waiting to take Nia home, but she wasn't sure she was ready to face her messy life. At least Ahjin could talk a little now, but he and Kaito held whole conversations with gestures and facial expressions. It was amusing, in a way.

It was not amusing that the poor boy had to go directly back to Arupa. He'd worn his stiff diplomatic mask all day, but every time Nia tried to ask him what was wrong, he walked away. She was too busy getting ready to go home to deal with it now, but if her best friend thought he could ignore her like this forever, he would be sorely disappointed.

"Time to go," the captain of Ahjin's ship said, and Kaito walked on board.

Nia squeezed Ahjin's hands. "Pleasant journey."

"Good flight." Ahjin leaned down to kiss her on the cheek.

His lips were so chapped they scratched Nia's equally dry skin. She flinched, and he sighed. Before she could kiss him in return, he boarded his ship. She waved, but he never turned.

A pang of loneliness washed over her. Nia would have to wait until she got back to pry into Ahjin's mysterious brain. Maybe by then, he could have a real conversation. If not, they'd figure it out. And if he never recovered completely? She blinked away tears and ignored the terrible prospect. One way or another, she would get her friend back. She *had* to get him back, or her life would be incomplete.

"Are you ready, Nia?" Ludik frowned and tugged the wedding ring in his ear.

He had already carried armloads of pakai on board, and Zefra had copied the map of its location to a sheet of parchment begged from a ship captain.

"Let's go." The pirates were gone, and she knew what happened to Dad, but one big problem remained. Nia glanced at Izo in the crow's nest. Slimy wiggling squids, she had to tell him *something* by the time she got home.

They boarded with a few Nokai from each ship left to escort them. Nia was captain, since it was Mom's ship.

"South," Nia bellowed into the wind, swinging the tiller.

The remaining ships from the protective fleet surrounded them. First on their route was Kani's lair to retrieve everyone's belongings. Nia would deliver Ahjin's after they took Ludik to Iskra and his darling wife.

The wind smelled of salt and seaweed and safety. It was good to head home. Mostly good. Mom hoped for pleasant news, and Nia didn't have any. How would Nia tell Mom that her secret hope had shipwrecked? At least she could tell her they had buried Dad properly and marked Alaneo's grave on the map.

Maybe someday Nia's heart would be at peace knowing what happened to Dad and where he was buried, but for now, the pain drowned her heart. Her dad had been murdered by pirates, and so had his brothers and cousins and everyone on his ship. He was never coming home.

All her friends had good dads. Ludik was possibly days from *being* a good dad. Nia had nobody. She rubbed the sting in her eyes. That wasn't exactly true, but almost. Her fathers weren't her *Dad*. Their other children had a better claim on them than she did.

The stupid pirates had ruined everything. Blowing up their shack and burning their ships didn't feel like enough punishment. She wanted to chase them all down and feed them to sharks. No, sharks ate too quickly.

Sea nettles would be a better choice, slowly dissolving them into paralyzed goo.

Nia steered toward the island next to her dad's bones. Somewhere ahead was the crooked stick that marked the grave, topped with the worn bracelet Mom had made for Alaneo. Nia touched the matching bracelet under her sleeve. Ludik had found his herb and was on his way home to Nemerra. Zefra had found a home for Kassian. Nia didn't know why Ahjin had come, so she had no idea if he considered the trip a success. Later, she would ask if he got what he wanted.

As for her, she had discovered what happened to her dad but had lost the real prize. Dad was long dead, and it seemed she couldn't keep a nice flirtation, either. No matter how much she offered, Izo would not accept less than marriage, and she couldn't commit to that. Both of her missions were failures. She could do nothing about Dad, but if there was a way to salvage love, she needed to find it.

Nia glanced south again. Ahjin had been right about Izo, and despite his stubbornness and crazy ideas, he was still her best friend. Maybe she would have to face his disapproval and talk to him about mending the shipwreck of her love life.

She sighed. He'd be so smug, but who else understood the cultural differences and cared enough about her to help her figure out love?

~~~~

With the favorable wind, it only took a few hours to reach the large southern island and grab their pitiful belongings.

"It's time, Kani," Nia said. "Which way to your hidden loot?"

Kani pointed. "It will be faster if we sail around the coast to the west side. If we land across from the little island, that's the closest we can get by sea."

Across from the little island. Nia glanced at Zefra, who nodded. Close by Dad's grave, then. She could visit before going home.

She cleared her throat. "That will be fine. May the sailors help you carry your goods?"

Kani narrowed his eyes. "I'll need a few private minutes to pack."

So suspicious. Nia rolled her eyes. "Whatever you like." She bellowed orders and turned the tiller.

It was afternoon when they reached the little strait between the two islands. Nia's ship anchored inside while the protective fleet blocked the passage. Kani led Zefra, Izo, Ludik, and most of the sailors inland.

Nia bathed in the ocean, clothes and all, then combed her hair and visited Dad's grave. The post still held the bracelet at the top, the beads and faded threads marking Nia's childhood sorrow. It had been foolish to ever let her hopes rise in a tide of wishful dreams. Sometimes, life was nothing but a nightmare.

She stood knee-deep in the waves and tried to think like practical Zefra. Nia had always thought Dad was dead, anyway. If nothing had changed, there was no need for her heart to ache, no point to mourn as if she had just lost her beloved dad, no matter how much she longed for what she never had. In fact, since she had never known him, he couldn't be beloved, either. Yes, that was the practical way to think about it.

Nia wiped a single tear and boarded the ship. The pink and pale blue sail flapped as if to mourn with her.

With the help of the remaining crew, she made a feast from the provisions they had brought.

Kani and the others trickled back, sniffing the air. Kani bossed them through careful loading of his mysteriously wrapped packages before he let them devour the spiced rice and fish.

Nia held her stuffed belly and groaned in delighted misery. "I love food."

"Now are we going home?" Ludik pleaded.

"Almost. You all stink." Nia pointed toward the low tide. "Bathe, clothes and all, before your stench kills the seagulls."

Her friends and Kani dove overboard. When the noise settled, Nia ordered the sailors to throw down a rope. Ludik, Izo, and Zefra came up quickly, but Kani didn't.

Nia handed around towels and peered over the bulwark. "Where did Kani go?"

Izo shook water from his hair. "He wanted to look at something."

Ludik stalked across the deck, leaning south as if a wind blew him. "When can we leave?"

"Does he think he can make the ship sail through sheer force of will?" a short, slight sailor asked Nia, leaning casually against the railing. His straight, brown hair was cut just above his ears, and his skin was tan instead of Nokai golden.

Nia shrugged, then gasped. Though his plain green shirt and blue trousers made him look like a common workman, he had such sharp visual edges that it hurt to look at him.

"Kassian! When did you get here?" She blushed. "Well met, and how can we serve you?"

Kassian's black eyes twinkled. "I came to talk about the Dragon Isles."

"Zefra," Nia bellowed. "I need you, and put a fire under it."

Zefra rushed over and bowed wide-eyed to Kassian. "Bright day, My Lord Celestial."

"Sit, Zefra, and talk to me." Kassian waved off Nia and settled on the deck.

After a brief discussion that Nia couldn't overhear, he stood and bowed. "And now, if anyone with a strong stomach would like to get home faster, I can carry one." He raised an eyebrow at Ludik.

Ludik dashed off, returning in under a minute with the sad remains of his pack. "Keep well, Nia."

Kassian grabbed his arm, and they both disappeared. High above them, Ludik's terrified screams echoed as he and Kassian reappeared, a tiny dark spot falling in the sky. They vanished, then reappeared farther away, again and again until they were too far to see.

"Nemerra will be so happy to see him," Nia said to Zefra. At least *his* children would get their dad back. She sighed and watched the fish swim in the bay.

Before long, Kani paddled back in sight, much too awkwardly for a Nokai. Considering his injuries, he was lucky to be alive. Kani grabbed the rope and hauled himself aboard.

Years of dirt had finally soaked away, and even his blue skin was fading more. He wrapped a towel around his dripping hair, and his ragged sleeve slipped up, exposing a faded, beaded bracelet.

Nia gasped. Kani had stolen Alaneo's bracelet!

"How dare you!" she howled, grabbing at his wrist but catching only the towel. She snatched again and missed as Kani sidestepped.

"What is wrong with you?" Kani said.

"You thief!"

"Nia?" Izo approached with Zefra.

Kani ducked Nia's next lunge. "I haven't stolen anything."

Nia snagged his shirt and clawed her way up to his wrist. She yanked on the bracelet until the worn threads snapped, scattering beads across the deck.

She shook the bracelet in his face. "You're a grave robber!"

Izo and Zefra felt for their missing weapons.

Kani held up his empty hands. "You're crazy. It's my bracelet. I found it on the beach."

"How dare you!" Nia clutched the broken bracelet to her chest. As if it weren't bad enough her dad was dead, now his grave was desecrated.

Kani took a step backward. "You don't understand."

"No, I don't," Nia sobbed. "I don't understand how you could do this to me. I liked you."

"But it's mine," Kani said.

"Be quiet." Zefra's voice was harsh as she waved an oar. "Sit while we decide what to do with you."

Izo flanked them with a frying pan. Kani sank to the deck and bowed his head.

Nia picked up beads from the deck. She didn't know how to mend the bracelet. If she took it home for Mom to fix, Alaneo's grave would stay unmarked. She whirled on Kani, too furious to speak. How dare he touch her dad's grave! How dare he ruin the only bit of him she had left.

He still sat with bowed head, but one eye watched her through his dripping hair. A thin line of hibiscus pink showed at the roots of his blue braids.

If she explained about the bracelet, would he give up his claim, or would his demonstrated greed for loot make it a useless attempt?

"This belongs to my—" Nia stopped, mouth hanging open.

Hibiscus pink hair?

She shoved the bracelet at Zefra and turned Kani's head so the late afternoon sun shone on the stripe of pink.

"Ouch," Kani protested. "What are you doing?"

"Look." Nia twisted his head toward her friends. "Pink."

"So what?" Kani mumbled into his shoulder. "Yours is lavender. What does this have to do with my bracelet?"

Nia fell to her knees. "*Your* bracelet. You keep saying that." She sucked in a breath. "You're Alaneokawakani."

Izo whistled, and Zefra narrowed her eyes.

Kani stared at Nia. "How do you know that?"

Nia pressed her hands flat against the deck and gasped for breath. "Aolanikalia told me."

Kani clutched his chest. "You know Lani?"

Nia shoved up her sleeve to show the matching bracelet below her elbow. "She sent me to find what happened to you."

Kani — no, Alaneo, reached for her bracelet, then pulled back. "I tried to return." He touched his damaged gills, then rubbed the back of his leg. "But Crow—" His voice choked off.

"We thought you were dead," Nia whispered. "And you said your name was KANI!"

She covered her face with her hands. All this time without her dad, and he had been right here.

"We were looking for Alaneo," Zefra added.

"After Crow maimed me," Alaneo said, "another pirate stole my bracelet and kicked me overboard to drown. I lived but couldn't swim home. Lani's interest in name meanings wore off on me, so I changed my short name from 'Unclouded' to 'Strong One' to give myself hope."

Nia dropped her hands. Alaneo's smiling face was blurry through her tears.

"Why did Lani wait so long to send for me?" Alaneo asked.

"Everyone was afraid of the curse," Nia said. "She had to wait for me to grow up."

"Why you?" Alaneo asked.

"Lani is my mom." Nia choked to a stop.

Alaneo wrinkled his forehead, then his mouth dropped open. "Your mom! How old are you?" When Nia couldn't answer, he turned to the others. "How old is she?"

"Six thousand..." Izo said.

"And twenty-four days." Zefra nodded once.

"Six..." Alaneo turned pale.

Zefra handed her oar to Izo and knelt beside Alaneo. "Deep breaths. In, out." She dragged Nia next to Alaneo and put her hand in his. "Here."

Nia's dad squeezed her hand, and she burst into tears. Alaneo wrapped both arms around her, while she threw her arms around his neck and sobbed into his ruined gills.

Zefra dragged everyone else away. Voices called, and the sails flapped in the wind. The ship rocked as the fleet sailed south for Nokailana.

Nia stayed with her arms around her dad until night fell, and then they shifted only enough to lean against the hull and sleep with her head on his shoulder.

In the morning, Nia let go of Alaneo, though they kept each other in view.

Zefra wrapped the broken bracelet in a scrap of violet silk, which Alaneo tucked next to his heart. Nia pulled her bracelet to the outside of her sleeve as a badge of triumph.

All during the week they traveled home, Nia's cheeks hurt from grinning. She spent every day with her dad, filling the empty spot in her heart.

Izo didn't repeat his marriage proposal, but he spent each day with her and Alaneo. Though he was giving her time to think, the way he watched her told her he hadn't given up.

What should she do? Izo was a wonderful man and could make her happy, if she went along with marriage. Did she want him enough for such a change in her beliefs? What *did* she want?

This was all Ahjin's fault. Before he spun her into a typhoon of confusion and speculation, she had been perfectly happy sailing through life with the usual Nokai expectations.

Then they reached East Coral Island, and Nia had no more time to ponder love and marriage and confusing boys.

Within minutes, the beach filled with babbling, grinning Nokai. Mom's pale blue hair wound through the crowd until she stood on the deck, fingers twisted together.

The gang plank dropped to the dock, and Nia ran into Mom's arms. "I love you, Mom."

"I love you, too." Mom buried her face in Nia's hair. "When the women arrived here without you or the ship, I worried. Then the men came, and I couldn't find another ship to go after you. I'm so glad you're home safe. I shouldn't have sent you on my fool's quest."

Sailors poured from the ship and curved around them to their own families. Izo and Zefra patted Nia's shoulders as they passed.

Finally, only one man was left aboard, and his harpoon thumped with every other step as he limped down the dock. He paused behind Nia and cleared his throat.

"Mom." Nia pulled away. "Look."

Alaneokawakani stepped forward. "Lani." He choked and pressed his lips together.

Nia's mom stiffened and closed her eyes. "I'm dreaming," she said in a quaking voice.

He took her hand and placed the broken bracelet in her shaking fingers. "I'm back."

Nia hugged herself as Mom opened her eyes, tears flowing down her cheeks.

Alaneo cleared his throat and rubbed his hands on his tattered shirt. "I brought back riches for you. Will you marry me?"

Mom laughed and held her hand to her mouth. "You were always bold, Alaneo."

He shook his head. "That was foolish after my long absence. Never mind."

"Who cares about riches?" Mom asked. "I'll marry you." She touched Alaneo's face, and he leaned his forehead against hers.

Nia squealed with joy.

Izo pulled Nia aside. "Give them time alone."

"I said your mother still loved your father," Zefra said. "Your siblings' names, their fathers' hair, the sail. I knew it."

Nia crammed her fists on her hips. "Hush and enjoy their reunion, then."

When her brother and sister got tired of waiting, Nia made the adults stop kissing long enough to introduce the children to her dad. He cheerfully greeted them without a word to Mom about their dads, and asked them many questions until they both grinned.

Izo groaned. "Here we go again."

Zefra folded her arms. "Hmph."

"What?" Nia tore her gaze from her reunited family and discovered a line of young men in front of her. Most of them held gifts.

Nia looked at her suitors. They were charming and handsome and willing to share kisses with no commitments. Wasn't that what she wanted?

Her parents planned to marry after seventeen years apart. A Nokai marriage was forever. How could they promise to be only with each other for the rest of their lives? What if they got bored or fell in love with someone else?

And yet, ever-changing suitors seemed shallow. The Nokai she used to consider light-hearted now seemed merely uncommitted.

Nia inhaled. Forever had a certain appeal. She waved away the boys. "I'll see you later."

Izo's eyebrows rose, but he smiled at Nia.

Nia smiled back. Izo would be forever if she said yes. He'd be a faithful husband for the rest of her life.

Was that the forever she wanted?

"When will we go see Ludik's new babies?" Zefra asked.

"What babies?" Olina tugged on her elbow. "Can I come, too?"

Nia blinked and transferred her gaze from Izo to her little sister. Oh, yes, the babies. Their trip wasn't quite over yet.

She flopped on the sand and patted beside her. "You can't come, but I'll tell you what Ludik's nieces and nephews were like, and you can imagine his children."

Izo could wait one more day.

30. ORANGES

(EAST CORAL ISLAND AND ISKRA)

What the heart thinks, the tongue speaks.
Iojif Proverb

Nia watched Mom and Alaneo talk to her siblings. When they weren't holding hands, they touched shoulders or feet. They discussed everything from how to sell Alaneo's hoarded loot to which fish had the prettiest scales.

Dad answered most questions, but when asked about his brother and cousins, he only rubbed his ruined gills and murmured, "They're gone."

Mom changed the subject, and the conversation continued late into the night. All these years, Nia hadn't realized the soft undercurrent in Mom's voice was sorrow. Now, every time Mom replied to Dad's murmur, joy bubbled under the surface.

In the morning, Zefra, clothed in Kamea's second-best dress, dragged Nia from bed much too early. It would take days to reach Iskra, so what difference did another hour make? She made faces at Zefra's colorful back all the way on board and curled in a hammock on deck.

But sleep eluded her. Mom and Alaneo were going with them to sell his pakai and rare shells. Nia was thrilled to have Dad back, but how could Mom be so sure Dad was right for marriage?

How could Nia know if someone was right for *her*?

She rolled from the hammock and leaned over the bulwark to watch the waves caress the ship.

Izo strolled over. "Bright day, Nia."

Nia forced a smile. "The waves are fair, and we visit a good friend. What more can I ask of a journey?"

"I know what I could ask." Izo leaned against the railing. "We never did finish our discussion."

Nia turned her face toward the ocean and sighed. "No, we didn't."

Izo rested his hand over hers on the railing. "I'm glad you visit Iskra. My home is different, but you will learn to love it as I do."

Nia grinned. "Silly, I've been to Iskra before."

Izo blinked, then laughed. "Certainly; 'tis where we met. After seeing you in your own land, I forgot. You fit so well in the Islands, it seems you could be nowhere else." He bit his lip. "But our customs are not so hard, and you are brave and smart. You will soon blend in among my people."

Nia tried to smile at him. "I'm not sure I want to blend in."

Izo touched one long, lavender braid. "Your beauty will always stand out." He took half a step forward. "You will be the brightest color in the desert," he whispered. "Please say yes."

The closest sailors turned toward her and stared.

Nia looked into Izo's dark brown eyes and lowered her voice. "You know it isn't our way."

Izo shrugged. "It is if you want it to be." He leaned in until she felt the warmth of his breath. "If you say yes, we can wait to marry until you are ready." He kissed her hands and walked away.

Half the people on the ship watched him go, then looked at Nia.

She turned her back. What would she do now? Did she love Izo, or was he merely a flirtation?

What was love, anyway? Was Zefra right about compatibility and stability? Nia wrinkled her nose. Please, let romance be more than boring stability.

She hummed "Where are the Ladies?" to herself. Were the Nokai right to merely seek excitement and affection? But what about dedication and commitment? She made another face. Since when was commitment a Nokai trait?

What about Ahjin's ideas of a perfect fit, a complement to her uniqueness? That didn't speak of passion, either, but at least it left room for it. It left room for whatever her "uniqueness" desired. She leaned over the railing and watched the waves splash against the ship. If she told Ahjin he was right, his head would swell so fat he'd turn upside-down when he flew.

Obviously, she first had to decide on the meaning of love, and then she could tell if Izo would fit it. Yes, that was a good plan. Nia groaned. Who *planned* romance? Her friends were making her entirely un-Nokai. She sighed and returned to pondering love.

～～～

N ia bounced on her toes and watched the Iskrin coast approach. The dock was only a small, wooden platform with a single mooring post on each side. One was occupied by Ahjin's yacht, so he'd apparently finished his most urgent duties already and come to see the babies.

There were no buildings, no trees, and only a faint green on the horizon. A dozen dull Iskrin tents clustered where the sand turned to hard-packed dirt. Most flew small flags with a brown-and-saffron bee, but two flew a lavender crescent moon, and one had a rough sketch of a black cat.

When the gangplank dropped, Nia ran for the tent with the cat banner. Was Nemerra well? Had Ludik made it back in time? Where were the babies?

The cat tent was laced closed.

"Ahh!" Nia threw her hands in the air. Where was everyone?

"Hush." Ahjin leaned around the tent, holding his finger to his lips. "Sit," he whispered.

He wore an old shirt, dusty and sweaty, and his trousers had holes in the knees. His bare feet were dirty, and his white curls stuck out wildly.

Nia flopped on the dirt, knees nearly touching his. "Well met, Ahjin. How do you feel?"

His lap was full of Tala and a basket of black, white, and yellow fuzz, maybe balls of yarn or wool to be carded. The wolf pup yipped at Nia and put a foot in the basket.

"Hush, Tala," Ahjin whispered, moving her foot. "Darravani healed me, Nia. How's your mother?"

He looked and sounded like his old self, with an even smile and easy movements.

"Mom and Dad are wonderful," Nia said. "They're at the market selling the pakai."

"Dad?" Ahjin said. "I thought we buried your father."

"Oh, you haven't heard!" Nia bounced on the dry earth. "Kani is my Dad. The skeleton we found was probably the pirate who stole his bracelet."

"Shh," Ahjin said. "That's wonderful! So your quest was a complete success. And how is Izo?"

Nia fidgeted. She hadn't even decided what to tell Izo, and now Ahjin was flapping his wings into everything. "He's fine. Where is everyone?"

"Ludik and Nemerra are napping while the babies sleep. Lyell is at the market. You can see the babies now, if you don't wake them."

One of the fuzzballs stuck a tiny paw across another fuzz.

"Oh," Nia gasped. "They're kitties."

Ahjin shook his head. "Did you expect bears?"

"I expected two-legged babies." Nia hovered one finger over the basket, barely touching the dandelion-soft fur. Black, yellow, black-spotted-white, and black-spotted-yellow.

"Sometimes they are," Ahjin said. "But Nemerra spent so much time as a leopard during her pregnancy, they will mostly be kittens for a few months."

"Can I hold one?" Nia asked.

"When they wake."

"Are they girls or boys?" Nia picked up Tala to keep from touching the kittens.

"The black jaguar and the leopard are girls. The snow leopard and the lion are boys."

"They're so tiny," Nia cooed. "What are their names?"

"They were born a little early," Ahjin whispered. "We waited for you for their naming ceremony."

"Who's doing the ceremony?"

Ahjin's ears turned red.

"You?" Nia said. "Then you can tell me the names now."

Ahjin shook his head. "It's considered bad luck. Oh, look, there's Zefra and Izo." He stood with the basket under one arm.

Nia scrambled after him, tapping Tala's nose to quiet her baby barks. "Friends, Tala."

Izo reached for Nia's hand, and she shoved the wolf pup at him. "Here, Tala, get reacquainted with Izo." She ignored Izo's disappointed look.

The tent flap opened, and Ludik ducked out. "Good to see you, everyone."

Ahjin handed him the basket of kittens, and Ludik touched all four fuzzy lumps with one long-fingered hand. Despite dark circles under his eyes, a grin stretched across his face.

Izo peered into the basket. "Congratulations."

Zefra bowed. "Congratulations, Ludik."

"They're adorable," Nia said. "Can I hold one?"

Nemerra ducked through the tent door. "Let them sleep, Nia." She yawned. "It's hard to get them all asleep at the same time." Her russet hair shone like silk in the sunlight, but her dress had tiny snags all over the front.

"Lyell will return soon," Ludik said. "Ahjin, you should get ready."

"Just Darravani's gear, right?"

Ludik's mouth twitched. "Yes. We don't need you looking like a butterfly."

Ahjin snorted and headed for one of the tents.

The fluff in the basket stirred and meeped. All four kittens rolled blindly into each other until their parents handed one to each avid observer. Izo put Tala on the ground and held the yellow lion, Zefra had the white leopard in her just-as-white hands, and Nia got the teeny black kitty. Nemerra cuddled the yellow leopard, and Ludik watched everyone else like a vulture.

"Such a cute little fuzzy black kitty," Nia cooed over the double-handful of warm, needle-tipped fluff. "Just like your dad." She ignored Ludik's grunt.

Tala yipped and ran inland, waving her tail frantically.

"Don't get under my feet," Lyell's low voice said beyond the tents. "I can't see you over this lot."

He appeared a minute later, arms piled high with packages and Tala frisking in a wide circle around him.

Ludik took half of Lyell's cargo and led him into the tent. They emerged shortly, and Lyell gathered Tala while Ludik went straight to Nemerra.

"It's time," Nemerra said. "I need my children, please."

She collected all four in the basket, then leaned for a kiss. Ludik wrapped his arms around her and the basket.

Ahjin exited his tent, and Ludik stopped kissing his wife, separating just enough to face their visitors.

"If you will all sit, please." Nemerra cradled the basket in both arms and beamed at everyone. "We're so glad you came."

Nia sat between Zefra and Lyell and tried to tempt Tala to her lap.

Ahjin stood between Nemerra and Ludik. Somehow, he'd gotten the dust off his skin and hair, and his curls were tied at the back of his neck. He wore his official green Darrendran-shaman boots below clean black trousers and a silk shirt in a softer green than the boots. The harsh desert sunlight outlined the branching scars on his face and hands, and every feather in his outstretched wings glowed white. His outfit was similar enough to the one he'd worn to her party that, for a moment, it felt like time went backwards to that carefree day. Then he turned his head, and she saw the new dimple at his temple.

Nia's chest cramped. Everything was different now. Her best friend's injuries could have killed him. His reckless confrontation with Crow had been suicidal. Her Nokai attitude toward romance had almost cost her his friendship, but a thousand flirts wouldn't be worth losing him in her life.

"We are here today to name these Darrendrakar," Ahjin said, "children of Ludik and Nemerra Moriko."

Ludik plucked the mewling white fuzzball from the basket. The tiny snow leopard batted his blind head against his dad's hand.

Ahjin reached into his pocket and sprinkled a handful of petals over the kitten. From the pleased smiles of Ludik and Nemerra, Nia was sure the flowers meant something nice in the Darrendran code.

"This male child shall be known as Rurru," Ahjin said.

Nia smirked. It was even more of a growly name than Ludik's brother, Gurryon.

Ludik tucked Rurru back in the basket and grabbed the spotted leopard, who rolled over and waved tiny paws.

Ahjin repeated the flower-sprinkle. "This female child shall be known as Kamakana."

Nia gaped at Ludik. That was a Nokai name. And if she remembered correctly... She whispered "gift" in Zefra's ear. What about traditional Darrendran names?

Ludik winked at her as he returned Kamakana to the basket and picked up the miniature lion.

"This male child shall be known as Terru." Ahjin dumped more petals on the lion cub, who was too busy gnawing on Ludik's thumb to notice.

Zefra and Izo looked at each other with wide eyes. Was it an Iskrin name, then, instead of Darrendran?

Nia leaned her ear toward Zefra, who whispered, "Brilliant."

As Ludik swapped Terru for the fuzzy panther, Nia kept her eyes on Ahjin.

"This female child shall be known as Zurrahava." Ahjin sprinkled the petals with a straight face, but his wings twitched.

The name sounded Darrendran, but the twitch was a giveaway. Maybe they altered the pronunciation, but Nia was sure it originated as Iojif.

Ludik pried his daughter's claws from his skin and returned her to the basket.

"Thank you all for coming," Nemerra said.

Zefra hopped to her feet. "What do the Darrendran and Iojif names mean?"

"Rurru means owl," Nemerra said, "And Zurrahava is divine feeling." She leaned her head on Ludik's shoulder. "I like having a baby that resembles her father, and it honors Ahjin, too."

Ahjin raised an eyebrow. "I don't need honor, but I do need to get back to work." He clasped Ludik's left arm and hugged Nemerra. "I'll visit again later. Nia, may I talk to you, please?"

He pulled her behind the cat-bannered tent.

If he asked about Izo, what would she tell him? "But Ahjin," she started.

"I don't want to argue," Ahjin said. "I have a peace offering." He picked up a small clay pot with a tiny seedling and pressed it into her hands. "I found a merchant with orange trees. I know your clan grows them, but this one celebrates you finding your other half."

He kissed her forehead. A stripe of lavender showed inside his green collar, but he straightened before she could identify it. "Enjoy the babies. Bring Izo to visit. Good flight, Nia."

Ahjin flapped his wings and took off before she thought of a reply. What a rotten birdbrain. Next time she visited, he'd get an earful.

Nia headed back to hold the fuzzballs again. As she set down the miniature tree and petted the whisper-soft fur, her thoughts whirled around oranges. Her Mom and Dad were two halves of the same orange. Ludik and Nemerra were, too. Nia had thought a fruit basket of variety was more fun, but their steadfast loyalty and joy were compelling.

She rubbed the lion cub against her face, then winced when a prickly paw batted her nose. Izo smiled at her. The kitten patted again, and his tiny claws caught in her hair. In the process of untangling the squalling lion, Nia's fingers brushed against the lock pick hairpins Izo had made.

She'd never noticed before, but Izo and Ahjin were the only men to give her gifts chosen specifically for her. Her island suitors gave her the same tokens they gave their other ladies. It was the way things were done. She cuddled the fuzzy kitten closer and pressed a hand across her suddenly burning stomach. Had the breakfast fish been bad?

The sailor's ditty echoed in her head. *Oh, I love the ladies, and ladies love me.* Ladies, plural. Always more than one.

Her stomach churned again. If Nia took lovers among the Nokai, she would be one among many. A month ago, that didn't matter, but now... It wasn't the fish; she was jealous! How could a Nokai be jealous?

Ludik kissed Nemerra, and Nia's stomach clenched.

Would she prefer a basketful of bitter oranges or one perfectly sweet and juicy one?

Her mouth puckered at the imagined sour orange. Quality was better than quantity.

Izo smiled at her. The handsome blacksmith was certainly quality. He was kind and brave and faithful. He thought she was beautiful and loved her.

But he expected her to comply with Iskrin customs and give up Nokai ways. She could, if she loved him enough. What was enough?

Nia stroked the lion cub's flat ear. Her Mom and Dad had been devastated without the other's company. Would she be devastated without Izo in her life?

She'd be disappointed, even sad. She *liked* the sweet blacksmith. He was a good friend and fun to kiss. But devastated? No.

Beached and becalmed, that answered that question. Nia sighed. She couldn't marry Izo, since the only boy's absence that would devastate her was her best friend's. She should tell Izo now, to end his waiting.

Nia kissed the fuzzy yellow cub sadly. Now that she'd decided one perfect orange was better, she didn't even have a perfect orange. Would she have to settle for a fruit basket? Where did one find a love like her parents had, or Ludik and Nemerra?

The only boy's absence that would devastate her was her best friend's.

Nia gasped and almost dropped the kitten. She didn't love Izo because she already loved Ahjin.

When had that happened? Ahjin never called her beautiful. He didn't even notice.

Nia spun to stare at the orange seedling. Ahjin didn't care about her beauty, only about her happiness. He was the only one brave enough to face her anger when they found the skeleton in the cave. He loved her the way she was and didn't ask her to change except to be a better person. He fit against all her peculiarities.

Ahjin loved her, and she had thrown his love back in his face.

Was it too late?

Nia shoved the lion cub at Ludik, grabbed the seedling, and took three steps toward the dock. Then she turned back and pulled Izo down for a kiss on the cheek.

"The answer is no, but when you find the right girl, invite me to your wedding." Nia turned and ran, screaming, "Ahjin."

She ignored the cheer behind her and raced faster, her bare feet pounding the dirt into clouds of dust. Ahjin's small yacht was gone from the dock. When she reached the damp sand, it slid under her toes, slowing her headlong pace until she reached the wooden dock.

She skidded to a stop at the end of the pier as the ship sailed away. And there was Ahjin, looping in the air above the sails.

Nia shouted and waved her arms.

He somersaulted to face her and waved, then flew to the ship.

Nia's heart sank. He thought she was saying pleasant journey.

Briny sea cucumbers. It couldn't be too late. She put the sapling on the dock and tightened her hair ribbons. She'd swum to his island before and could do it again.

Before she could dive off the pier, the ship furled its sails and drifted to a stop. White wings sprang toward Iskra. Nia clasped her hands in front of her and waited.

It took forever — at least a minute — for Ahjin to return, and she backed up to let him land on the dock.

"Is something wrong?" Ahjin asked.

"I love you," Nia blurted. "You are the other half of my orange."

Ahjin stayed at arm's-length and folded his wings tightly enough to make Nia wince. He wore his new diplomatic face that Nia hated more than ever. "But you want children and variety. And what about Izo?"

"Izo wants someone stable. He wouldn't be happy with an adventurous scamp like me." Nia took a step closer and smiled. "You and I can adopt children later."

Ahjin said nothing.

Nia's smile faded, and her shoulders sagged.

"What did you tell Izo?" Ahjin asked.

"I told him to invite me to his wedding to the right lady," Nia said.

Ahjin touched something under his collar. "What if I'm not satisfied with a temporary relationship?"

Nia stepped forward until she felt every breath Ahjin took. "I only want you, forever and ever."

Ahjin raised an eyebrow. "Forever?" But the corners of his mouth twitched upward.

The flash of lavender caught her attention again. Nia ran a hand around Ahjin's neck and pulled him closer. She hooked one finger in the lavender stripe and dragged it free. Kassian's silver star dangled from one of Nia's frayed hair ribbons.

"Why do you have my ribbon?" Nia whispered against Ahjin's cheek.

"It's a reminder." Ahjin cleared his throat. "Here is the lady. One lady for me." His voice wavered in the vicinity of the correct notes.

Nia had never heard anything better.

She turned her head until their lips almost touched. "Will you kiss me now?"

Ahjin closed his eyes. "You didn't like it last time."

"Are your lips still chapped?" Nia dropped the amulet and slid both arms around his neck.

Ahjin opened his eyes and grinned. His arms pulled her close, and his wings wrapped around her. "No."

She leaned up to check, and his lips were smooth and sweet and perfect.

Yes, indeed, his kisses were the only ones she wanted.

~~~~

YAY! NOW OUR HEROES WILL LIVE
HAPPILY EVER AFTER!

Will they, dear reader?

DEAR AUTHOR, YOU ARE MAKING ME
NERVOUS. EVERYONE WILL BE HAPPY,
RIGHT? RIGHT??

Well... Maybe not.

More surprises await our poor heroes. Turn the page for info about **Spark of Intrigue**, wherein Zefra is not having luck finding a job. Starving is a real possibility, but then the problems... get worse.

SPARK OF INTRIGUE

Assassins, kidnappers, and conspiracies.

In the last two years, Zefra helped defeat a band of pirates, avert a war, and even rescue the gods. What *can't the fire mage do?

Get her dream job as a guide and explorer.

Though her deeds are famous, no one believes the legends are about a scrawny, sixteen-year-old girl. With no prospects for work, Zefra is on the edge of starvation.

After someone tries to kidnap her, and assassins and poison menace her friends, they leave to try their luck in another city, safe from threats.

But danger follows them...

*Spark of Intrigue is full of conspiracies, gods, and shapeshifting spies, intertwining elemental magic, faith, and friendship. It is the fourth book in the **Unexpected Heroes** series of clean YA secondary world fantasy and is best read in order for the most enjoyment.*

Check my website MCLeeBooks.com for links to buy the next story or get the entire series at once.

Still want more? Get free stories by joining my newsletter. Every two weeks, I chat about my current writing or my life & offer book news and deals. And did I mention free stories?

Sign up at MCLeeBooks.com

Free Story: The Cat's Fortune

On another world, so long ago that truth faded into legend, a cat and a boy seek their fortune together.

Orphaned and homeless, young Aktar travels to the city of Rapata for a better life.

But it seems the rumors of gold-paved streets are false. Can he find a home and a job before he starves? Maybe with the help of a foundling kitten.

*A retelling of Puss in Boots and Dick Whittington, with timeless themes of belonging, courage, and self-discovery, set on the fantasy world of Kaiatan, home of the **Unexpected Heroes**.*

Please leave an honest review on any retailer or reader site. Seriously, it would really help me. :)

If you found a typo, you're welcome to report it at mcleebooks.com/report-a-typo/

CHARACTER LIST AND PRONUNCIATION GUIDE

IF YOU ARE INTERESTED IN THE MEANINGS OF THE NAMES, PLEASE SEE MCLEEBOOKS.COM

Name (Pronunciation) Identity

<u>People</u>

Ahjin Machol (AH-jzin MACK-ole) Iojif, 16 years old, skydancer

Alaneo(kawakani) (Alaneo) (AH-la-NAY-oh-KAH-wah-KAH-nee) Nokai, Nia's missing dad

Aolani(kalia) (Aolani) (AY-oh-LAHN-ee-kah-LEE-uh) Nokai, Nia's mom

Aukai (AWK-eye) Nokai pirate captain

Crow (CROE) Nickname of Iojif serial killer/pirate captain

Darravani the Omnifarious (DAR-uh-VAHN-ee) Darrendrakar Goddess of Earth

Enaki (Eh-NACK-ee) Nokai, Nia's "uncle," closest father-figure

Gurryon Moriko (GURR-yon) Darrendrakar, Ludik's brother

Inna (IN-nuh) Nokai, fisherwoman, temporary captain

Irajahan the Omnipotent (Ear-AH-jzuh-han) Iojif God of Air

Izo Ashvakosha (EE-zoe) Iskrin, Zefra's older brother

Kaito (KAY-toe) Darrendrakar, seal

Kala(lamoanani) (Kah-LA-la-moe-uh-NAHN-ee or KAH-la) Nokai, Nia's older near-sister

Kaliya(kaomoana) (kuh-LEE-yuh-KAY-oh-moe-ANN-uh or kuh-LEE-yuh) Nokai, Nia's younger brother

Kama (KAH-mah) Nokai, healer apprentice boy

Kamea(keikilani) (Kuh-MAY-ah-KAY-kee-lah-nee) Nokai, Nia's younger far-sister

Kani (KAH-nee) Nokai, shipwrecked on Dragon Isles

Kassian (KASS-ee-an) Fifth god, oldest brother

Lapwing (Lap-wing) Nickname of Crow's first mate

Lelei (Leh-LAY) Nokai, old healer woman

Ludik Moriko (LUD-ick) Darrendrakar, 18 years old, healer

Lyell Ulriksin (LIE-el UL-rick-sin) Darrendrakar wolf, Ahjin's chief of staff

Makana(vailea) the Omniscient (Mah-KAHN-uh-vie-LEE-uh) Nokai Goddess of Water

Malu (MAH-loo) Nokai fisherman, temporary first mate

Manuai (MAHN-oo-aye) Nokai, one of Nia's fathers

Nemerra (Neh-MERR-uh) Darrendrakar, Ludik's wife

Nia(molenulanami) (NEE-ah-moe-LEN-noo-la-NAHM-ee) Nokai, 16 years old, singer

Olinamalulani (Oh-LEEN-uh-MAH-loo-LAH-nee) Nokai, Nia's younger sister

Resef the Omnificent (RES-eff) Iskrin God of Fire

Risa Ashvakosha (REE-suh) Iskrin, Zefra's younger sister

Shri Okechuku (SHREE OH-keh-CHOO-koo) Iskrin, Tukiko healer

Tala Lyelldin (TALL-uh LIE-ul-din) Darrendrakar, Lyell's second-born child

Ya'eel (YAH-eel, with click between syllables and a squeal-whistle) Nokai dolphin, Nia's friend

Zefra Ashvakosha Kezhkori (ZEF-rah ASH-vah-KOASH-uh KEZ-eh-KORE-ee) Iskrin, 15 years old, Hotaru guide

Zeva (ZEE-vuh) Nokai, one of Nia's fathers

Groups, Locations, Languages

Arupa (Uh-RUPE-uh) Island

Darrendra (Duh-RREND-druh) Northern country

Darrendrakar (Duh-RREND-druh-car) People of Darrendra, shapeshifters

Darrendran (Duh-RREND-drun) Darrendrakar language

Dragon Isles, Islands between Nokailana and Darrendra

East Coral Island, Farthest occupied island in Nokailana

Hotaru (Hoe-TARE-oo) Iskrin clan, specialty: maps

Ioj (EYE-ojze) Eastern country
Iojif (Eye-OH-jziff) People of Ioj, avians
Iojo (Eye-OH-jzo) Iojif language
Iskra (ISK-ruh) Southern country
Iskrin (ISK-ree)People of Iskra, desert-dwellers
Iskrit (ISK-rit) Iskrin language
Kairri (KERR-ree) Village in Canid tribe, Darrendra
Nokai (NO-kie) People of Nokailana, aquastrians
Nokailana (NO-kie-LAHN-uh) Western islands
Noki (NO-kee) Nokai language
Rikatsu (Rick-AT-soo) Iskrin clan, speciality: ships
Tukiko (Too-KEE-koe) Iskrin clan, speciality: healing

ACKNOWLEDGMENTS

Thanks to my Day Group: Cheree Myatt, Donna Gonzales, and Gail Porter, for their excellent advice,
Joanne Morris, for a medical critique,
Rebecca Zeines, for fixing the first chapter,
and to my extraordinary alpha and beta readers, Chris Cornetto, Emma Shelford, Laura Drake, Maria Farb, Matt Peel, Michelle Henrie, Rachel Perez, Robin Cranney, Rosalie Howe, Sarah Gardner, Sarah Jensen, and Virginia Cummings

Special thanks to Skylie Cheney and Laura Dotson for musical help, and to my editor, Carol Malone, for romantic magic.

ABOUT THE AUTHOR

Marty C. Lee told stories for most of her life, but never took them seriously until her daughter asked her to write this one. Between writing and spending time with her family, she reads, embroiders, paints-by-number, and gardens.

She has lived in five states, seven cities, and ten houses so far. She currently lives in the West, but not in a tropical paradise. She doesn't like flying, even in an airplane. She wishes she could produce her own fire to warm her hands. She's glad she didn't have to wait a year to marry her sweetheart, who also wishes she could warm her hands.

You can find her at
  MCLeeBooks.com and on Facebook and book sites

www.ingramcontent.com/pod-product-compliance
Lightning Source LLC
Chambersburg PA
CBHW031214020726
47499CB00002B/581